THE VEILED TRUTHS TRILOGY

HALF-TRUTHS

The closer she gets to the truth, the harder it is to keep her own.

BRIANA SULLIVAN

Half-Truths
© 2025 Briana Sullivan
All rights reserved.

Published by Briana Sullivan
Cover design by Dami Shawn

To find out more about Briana and what she is working on, please visit authorbrianasullivan.com

ISBN: PB: 979-8-9924658-1-5 eBook: 979-8-9924658-0-8
Print locations vary by retailer and fulfillment partner.

For my husband,

You have always seen me, rough edges and all.

Thank you for being the boat to both my anchor and my parasail. Whether in the ocean's depths or somewhere in the clouds, I know you'll always be there to pull me back in when I'm ready.

There's no greater honor in this life than being loved by you.

I love you more.

Also for my dad,

My first champion as a writer and the person who demanded I chase my dreams, no matter how big or small.

You've been asking for years when I'd write a book. It might be a decade late, but we did it! I hope this makes you as proud of me as I am to call you my father.

But for the love of everything, please skip over the sex scenes.

CHAPTER 1

I've never wanted to use the small knife sewn into the inside of my handbag more than I do right now.

"So, how does a woman like you end up working in cybersecurity?" Charles Goodfield, a banker with an inflated ego, asks me. An oily smile clings to the wrinkles around his mouth as he sips his whiskey, eyes fixed on me over the edge of his glass.

Charles had planted himself beside me a few minutes ago, cutting off my view of the ballroom from my corner perch at the bar. At first, I tolerated his polite small talk, but within six questions, he'd steered our conversation from friendly to flirty. This man, old enough to be my father, has nothing to offer me other than a headache.

I sigh, tracing the rim of my cocktail glass with my finger. For the better part of a month, I've been enduring these pretentious fundraisers, and all I've gained are the unrelenting attention of wealthy, near-geriatric men like Charles. I think back to the message Peter sent me before walking into this event:

Peter: What use are you if you can't get me what I need?

Clenching my teeth, I summon the last of my patience and signal the bartender with a polite smile. He approaches with a shaker in hand and leans in to take my order. As he moves away to prepare my drink, I smooth the front of my black velvet dress, forcing myself to look back at Charles.

1

"Protecting people from unwanted intrusions comes naturally to me," I reply, my smile all teeth.

He's either too confident or too stupid—likely both—because his eyes light up as though I've presented him with a challenge. He runs a hand through his full head of white hair.

"I bet it does." His voice drops an octave, and it makes my skin crawl.

Using the knife in my handbag is feeling more likely by the second.

"It pays the bills," I respond, my tone deliberately flat as my gaze wanders over the ballroom. Guests mingle around us in tuxedos and designer gowns, champagne flutes sparkling in their hands. A jazz band plays in the corner, their perfectly timed notes carrying through the space like a gentle caress.

The tables, adorned with black-and-white elegance, sit before towering windows that frame Chicago's Magnificent Mile. Even under the cover of night, the city's lights illuminate snow-dusted rooftops and bustling streets below.

"Speaking of who pays the bills," Charles says, his tone turning smug, "I don't see a ring on any of those pretty fingers."

Ah, there it is.

Before I can unleash a retort sharp enough to give the old man a heart attack, a woman in a navy satin dress strides to the bar behind him. Her dress clings in all the right places, and her hazel eyes meet mine with a question only women ask each other in such situations: *Are you okay?*

I press my lips together, silently counting to three.

Breathe. I'm Scarlett Page, and Scarlett doesn't stab pompous men with handbag knives.

Exhaling slowly, I focus on Charles again. "I'm not married. Maybe you know someone who might be a good match for me? Perhaps a friend of the son you were telling me about?" I ask, tightening my grip on my glass.

Charles, oblivious to the woman behind him, waves my comment away. She orders a drink, her weight shifting subtly in our direction as she listens.

2

"You'd eat those young boys alive," Charles says, his grin widening. "You need someone with more experience."

The bartender returns with my drink, and I exchange my empty glass for the fresh one with a nod of thanks. Turning back to Charles, I feign confusion, pulling my chestnut, wavy hair over one shoulder.

"Do you have a friend, then? Or maybe a friend of your wife?"

I want him to flinch, to squirm, to show even a glimmer of guilt. But there's nothing. Not a shred of shame behind his calculating brown eyes. He doesn't even hesitate to brush off the woman he'd so proudly claimed to have just celebrated forty-two years of marriage with.

Heat thrums in my chest, but I keep my expression neutral.

He slinks closer, his movements clunky and forced. "Not quite. I was thinking—" he starts, but the woman behind him interrupts, stepping forward with a practiced air of nonchalance.

"Charles," she exclaims, her voice dripping with exaggerated warmth. The man stiffens, his complexion paling as he turns to face her. "Lovely to see you. I was just talking to Nora. She was telling me how wonderful your holiday in Greece was."

"Natalie," Charles replies, his voice gruff as he sets his whiskey on the counter. He ignores her remark about Greece entirely. "You look well."

"I am. Nora's looking for you, by the way. You'll find her in the hallway with Felicity and the others." She places a manicured hand on his shoulder, leaning in conspiratorially. "You know how she hates it when you wander too far." Her tone sharpens subtly, hazel eyes turning cold as they lock onto his.

I take a long sip of my drink, suppressing a smirk.

Charles glances between us, his strained smile faltering. "Of course. I hope you ladies enjoy the evening." He pivots stiffly and retreats toward the hallway, shoulders sagging with every step. As soon as he's out of earshot, Natalie scoffs.

"The nerve of these men," she mutters, her eyes flicking to mine. "Are you okay? Unfortunately, this isn't the first time I've seen Charles try his luck."

I don't need to research Natalie Sinclair to know who she is, but I have. Extensively. The thirty-one-year-old middle child of William Wells, one of three heirs to a billion-dollar pharmaceutical empire. She bears the family's hallmarks: sharp features, olive skin, and a smattering of freckles across her nose. But there's a softness in her expression that sets her apart from her brothers.

"It seems married men around here share Charles's mindset," I reply, frowning. "But you're the first woman to step in, so thank you."

She nods, her jaw tightening. A brilliant yellow diamond glints on her ring finger as she raises her glass. "Most of these wives prefer to blame anyone but their husbands for their wanderings eyes," she whispers before clearing her throat. "Not that you looked like you needed help, but I can't seem to keep my opinions to myself."

"Sounds like we're two sides of the same coin." I smile, extending my hand. "Scarlett Page." The fake name slides off my tongue almost too easily.

Her grip is firm, but not unkind. "Natalie Sinclair. It's a pleasure."

"I knew you looked familiar," I lie smoothly. "Kimberly Glines pointed you out to me at her luncheon last month. She spoke very highly of you."

Natalie's cheeks flush. "Kimberly is too kind," she says dismissively. "Are you new to the area?"

"Just moved here from Philadelphia."

"How are you finding it?"

"The city's wonderful. I thought these events would help me network, but it's been... a mixed bag."

She chuckles. "Tell me about it. I've spent half the night dodging questions about when I'll have children."

Over her shoulder, a tall, auburn-haired man in a sharp tux watches us from several yards away. His eyes are sharp and calculating, a stark contrast to Natalie's warmth. I've studied his dossier as carefully as hers: Davey Sinclair, her husband and Wells Corporation's Director of Security.

4

Natalie, for her part, has distanced herself from the family business, preferring charity work and art initiatives over the corporate empire. Davey's fierce protectiveness over her, combined with her lack of involvement, made Natalie seem like a dead-end for my goals. But after weeks of making little progress, her unexpected approach feels like a potential opening I can't afford to ignore.

I turn my attention back to the Wells daughter. "Kimberly mentioned you're hosting an art exhibit soon?"

Her face brightens. "Yes! It's to raise tuition funds for local art students."

Reaching into my handbag, I pull out a business card. My fingers brush the hidden knife's hilt—a stark reminder of the evening's frustrations. "I'd love to attend. Supporting the arts is close to my heart."

Natalie's eyes widen slightly, her expression softening. "That's very kind of you. I'll have my assistant send you the details."

"Thank you." I smile, glancing at the clock above the bar. Two minutes until dinner begins. "I won't keep you any longer. Thank you again for stepping in."

"Of course. You'll hear from me soon."

As she moves toward Davey, I weave through the crowd to my assigned table. The place settings are lavish, and the dinner menu is written in elaborate calligraphy. Settling into my seat, I pull out my phone and type a message to Peter.

Me: Contact established.

CHAPTER 2

"**L**ook what the cat dragged in." Harrison's voice cuts through the hum of the coffee shop, sharp and unwelcome. My grip around the mug I've been holding tightens.

The last man I wanted to see slaps a manila envelope onto the table as he drops into the seat across from me, throwing one arm lazily over the back of his chair. "Haven't seen your pretty face in a while. What name are you going by now? Scarlett, right?"

"Where's Peter?" I ask, ignoring his question. Harrison looks exactly as he always does: unkempt and careless. His winter coat is creased, his dress shirt untucked, and the hems of his jeans are frayed. Dark blond hair falls messily over his forehead, his cheeks flushed pink—like he's just sprinted through the icy streets of Chicago.

Harrison is Peter's errand boy, though he likes to think of himself as second-in-command. In my head, I call him Peter's bitch.

"Clarissa's causing trouble in New York," he says, peering suspiciously into the coffee cup in before him. "Peter's dealing with it. This black?"

I nod, gesturing to the sugar and cream at the edge of the table. "What kind of trouble?"

He pauses, lifting his eyes to meet mine, and his usual smirk fades. Something darker, sharper, flickers there. "The kind you're familiar with."

My stomach lurches. I glance at the scratched, laminated menu beneath my coffee cup, focusing on the small imperfections in the plastic. The memories from five years ago come in bursts, but I shove them aside.

Peter Lynch has been my handler for over a decade, though it's just a polite term for what he really is: a puppet master for the ultrarich. He calls what he does "investigative services," but that's a crock of shit. What he offers is a menu of both legal and illegal solutions for the top one percent. Anything from digging up dirt to outright sabotage.

When I first joined Peter's team, I thought I was doing something noble, even if it skirted the edges of legality. As a cyber investigator, I believed I was helping people; tracking down predators, exposing criminals, and delivering a twisted kind of justice for those who couldn't get it through official channels. The first year felt rewarding. Corrupt businessmen were taken down, stolen assets recovered, and abusive partners exposed. I told myself the moral gray area was worth it because the ends justified the means.

But then things changed.

Maybe Peter saw that I was skilled, I didn't ask many questions, or he was waiting for me to get comfortable. Regardless of the reason, the information he began asking me to uncover never made it to a courtroom or a victim's hands. Instead, it became leverage. Blackmail. A way to silence people or bend them into submission. Most of the time, these people deserved it, so I was able to write it off in my mind, but the jobs only seemed to get progressive worse. Everything I dug up was slowly weaponized to make Peter's clients more powerful. With every successful contract, Peter's network grew stronger and his connections more entrenched.

Now? Peter isn't just untouchable; he's terrifying. He's the guy billionaires go to when they need a scandal buried or an enemy ruined. And he doesn't just control his clients; he controls everyone around him. Step out of line, and he'll turn the same methods we use against you. He's always watching, always calculating, and always one move ahead. If anything, Peter is more dangerous than his clients because once you're in, there's seldom a way out.

I just hope he doesn't kill Clarissa. She's young, and I like her.

"Anyway," Harrison says, the edge in his voice disappearing as quickly as it came. He smacks three sugar packets against his palm, tearing them open all at once. "Peter had those extra IDs made." He slides the oversized envelope towards me.

I don't touch it. Instead, I glance around the coffee shop. It's quaint with lime-green walls faded to a muted hue, mismatched mugs on every table, and black-and-white checkered floors that have seen better days. It's the kind of place people like the Wells family would never step foot in, which is precisely why I chose it. Still, I'm careful.

"When's Peter back?" I ask, turning back to Harrison.

"Cops are involved, so not anytime soon. I'll be your point guy for now," he says, too loudly for my comfort. I blink at him, irritated by his lack of subtlety.

"Natalie Sinclair invited me to an art exhibit next week. I think I can use it to secure an invitation to the Wells' silent auction," I say, lowering my voice.

The silent auction is the Wells family's annual charity event, a cornerstone of their public image, held in either the late winter or early spring. Invitations are notoriously exclusive, as the event is hosted at one of the Wells family's private estates. This year, the auction is set to take place at the home of the eldest son and Wells Corporation President, Silas Wells.

Silas is something of a mystery. When I first arrived in Chicago, I assumed it would be easy to approach him. The media loves to paint him as a playboy—a perpetual bachelor at the ripe age of thirty-five and always seen with a different woman on his arm. I thought I could charm my way into his orbit, but I couldn't have been more wrong. Silas rarely attends social events, and when he does, there's an unspoken rule: no one approaches him unless explicitly invited. He's as guarded and discerning as his brother-in-law, and his aloofness only heightens his allure.

If I can secure a spot at the auction, I might finally have the chance to strike up a conversation with him. Building rapport with Silas could be the key to gaining access to the Wells family's inner circle and a crucial step toward completing what Peter sent me here to do.

Harrison snorts. "This is taking too long. You've been at it for weeks and have nothing to show for it."

My jaw tightens. Men like Harrison never think beyond the immediate. And now he's here out of the blue, trying to throw his weight around. If he interferes, he'll destroy everything I've been building and every bit of progress I've made with Peter over the past five years will be gone. I will *not* start over.

"I'd also love to be done with this," I agree through clenched teeth, my voice barely audible.

Wells Corporation's cloud had been my first target on this contract, and it took me over three weeks to breach it, which turned out to be the least of my worries. I expected a Fortune 500 pharmaceutical company to have phenomenal security, but this system is an absolute fortress. The data is fragmented across unrelated directories with vague names, and every file is locked behind encryption so strong it's useless without the decryption keys. On top of that, the system limited my access to mimic a low-clearance employee, keeping anything truly sensitive unreachable.

Their automated monitors tracked every move I made. Accessing files at odd hours or opening too many at once risks tripping an alarm, so I had to erase my tracks constantly. Peter's vague instructions to look for "financial discrepancies" or "patient data" only led to dead ends. I sent him fragments, off-the-books payments, encrypted logs, but nothing felt like what he's really after.

After ten days of searching, all I had to show for my efforts were bloodshot eyes, a pounding headache that felt like a drill to the base of my skull, and Peter breathing down my neck harder than ever. Thousands of files were still unexamined, and Peter didn't care. He wanted results. When I finally admitted that the company's cloud wasn't going to yield whatever he was looking for in the next century, I thought that was the end of it. I'd done my part. I'd gone above and beyond.

I should've known better.

Peter loves to dole out any type of punishment, and his favorite for me is yanking me out from behind my keyboard and throwing me into the field, knowing it's the last place I want to be. So, when I didn't deliver him the impossible results he asked for, I was on a plane to Chicago. He's convinced himself that if I get close enough to one of the Wells family members, I'll be able to gain access to someone's office that might have the answers.

This sloppy idea isn't usually Peter's MO, which tells me he's pretty desperate for whatever he's looking for. Normally, he thrives on precision and control, but this? This feels rushed, reckless. More like a Hail Mary than a calculated plan. I don't have a choice, though. Peter told me to figure it out, and this is me figuring it out, whether I like it or not.

"Then get me results," Harrison snaps, sinking back into his chair.

I grip my coffee tighter, hunching forward. "Do you think I'm not doing everything I can? Peter won't let me bring anyone else in to help with the cloud. Getting close to their personal devices is the fastest way."

Harrison's shakes his head in disbelief. "He must have lost his mind listening to you."

Heat rushes through me, white-hot and consuming. For a fleeting moment, I imagine reaching across the table, grabbing him by the back of the head and—

I exhale sharply, forcing the thought away. Harrison isn't worth it.

"I guess you don't realize how charming I can be," I say, baring my teeth in a smile. "I'll get you answers when I actually *have* them."

My meeting with Harrison didn't last much longer. I discreetly reviewed the additional paperwork Peter procured for my fake identity, and after I made sure that all the information matched, I left. I took public transportation to a popular shopping area just a few miles from my apartment and paid in cash, then switched to a ride-share the remainder of the way.

The apartment I stay in at Bucktown is one Peter arranged for me. He handed me the keys and address a month ago, stating that this would be my home for the foreseeable future. The place is meticulously staged, furnished just enough to create the illusion of a well-lived-in space. A facade designed to help me blend into the image of a relatively affluent woman.

It's a two-bedroom unit in a sleek, high-rise building with a cookie-cutter layout and sterile gray finishes. The design feels cold and almost clinical in its precision. But it's mine. For the first time in what feels like forever, I have a place to myself. A sliver of autonomy in a life so tightly controlled. Peter may have given it to me for his own reasons, but I intend to savor every moment of the solitude it offers.

I toss my keys onto the entry table and lock the door behind me. Shrugging off my coat and slipping off my shoes, I stow them neatly in the closet before sweeping a quick glance across the living room.

Peter may have given me the illusion of freedom by providing this apartment, but it's just that: an illusion. In the month since I've been here, he's bugged the place three separate times. It took me only a few hours to locate and disable each device: audio transmitters hidden in the vents, a pinhole camera tucked into the smoke detector, and even a wireless keystroke logger discreetly attached to my workstation.

I wiped all traces clean, rendering the devices useless but leaving them physically intact. I know Peter too well to think this was simply about spying. This was a test—a way to gauge my awareness, my reactions, and whether I'd confront him or handle it quietly. I chose the latter. It seems he's stopped trying.

For now.

After being out all morning, I'd normally perform a thorough sweep of the apartment but with Peter leaving town in such a rush, I doubt he had time to set up anything new. For now, I head to the bedroom to retrieve my personal phone; the one tied to the real me.

I wipe it regularly and the numbers I truly need are committed to memory. Still, I can't help but check it. There are no new messages.

With a sigh, I wander to the kitchen and pull open the refrigerator door. As expected, last week's groceries are nearly gone. I peel back the lid on a container of strawberries, relieved to find they haven't spoiled yet. After chopping them, I toss them into a bowl and grab a fork before sinking into the couch, phone still in hand.

The television stares back at me from across the room, but I don't bother turning it on. The news, streaming shows—none of it can silence the ever-present quiet that fills this space. If anything, it only amplifies it, dragging my thoughts back to a time when my old apartment's TV was always on, playing something inconsequential in the background. Back then, the noise was comforting. Now, it feels foreign.

I open a new message and start typing.

Me: I miss you.

The words linger on the screen, taunting me. My thumb hovers over the send button, but I can't do it. The number is etched into my memory, deeper than any other, but the futility of the gesture stings. With a sharp exhale, I press backspace until the screen is blank again.

The phone lands on the cushion beside me with a dull *thud* as a whooshing sound fills my ears, the rhythm of it matching the pounding of my pulse.

Even if I sent the message, it's not like it'd even reach Drew, anyway.

CHAPTER 3

I can't breathe.

Stars explode in the corners of my vision. No matter how hard I try to work my way free, the vice around my neck only tightens. There's endless pressure on the top of my chest, and the burning across my skin only intensifies with each passing second.

Just as the white stars begin to dim into the dreaded black of unconsciousness, a grunt vibrates against my cheek, shaking me awake enough to stop the darkness from consuming me.

"Come on, Scarlett. Quit being a sore loser and just tap out." The voice sounds frustrated and muffled, as if I'm being held just under the surface of water.

With a groan, I tap twice on one of the legs wrapped around my head. The pressure releases and I gulp down a breath that scorches my throat, falling back onto the mat. The black-painted ceiling's fluorescent lights spin and double like a kaleidoscope.

"Sometimes I'm convinced you have a death wish," Jeff, the gym owner, mutters through his mouth guard as he untangles his body from mine. I'm too focused on the ringing in my ears and tingling fingertips to notice much else.

"I would have gotten out of it," I wheeze out, and Jeff snorts in response as he stands and moves to the edge of the mat.

"There's a fine line between bravery and stupidity, and you're toeing it," he starts from several feet away and reappears in my line of vision to extend a water bottle to me, the rubber mouth protector hanging from his lip. "You can't just muscle your way through everything. Sometimes the smarter move is to step back, assess the situation, and find the opening you're missing."

I reach for the water and sit up at the same time, curling my legs inward. Using the front of my shirt, I wipe the sweat off my forehead, splotches of white appearing behind my eyelids. After a few moments, my vision stops spinning, and I drop my rash guard from my face to meet his icy blue eyes.

With my free hand, I pop out my own guard. "Kind of difficult to do when I'm having the literal life choked out of me." My tone is flat and Jeff grins as he flops onto the mat next to me on his back. His chest rises and falls heavily, and though he'd never admit it out loud, I just gave him a run for his money.

"And yet, you keep coming back."

I can't argue with him there. Jeff's gym is one of the few places I feel myself anymore, even if he doesn't know my real name.

Four years ago, combat sports were a big part of who I was. It started as an outlet for the anger buried so deep inside me that I felt it in my bones. It seeped into every crevice of me, and I had nowhere to put it all before it bled into more than just my mind. Therapy wasn't an option; there was no way I could tell a stranger about the things I did or the day that changed me. What could they offer me besides condolences and a few breathing exercises, anyway? Not to mention, I couldn't risk anyone else finding out what happened to make me act that way.

So, for a while, I allowed myself to become everything I hated. That vile version of me led all of my thoughts and decisions, and it destroyed the few meaningful relationships I had left. I threw myself into the jobs Peter would give me, looking for a distraction from reality and having no other options. It wasn't long before I was a machine, oiling the cogs with water, alcohol, and food occasionally. And that's how I chose to exist for the better part of six months. I allowed it to swallow me whole.

Then, on a blistering summer afternoon when I went to a coffee shop just to get out of the apartment I'd been staying in after a bender in between jobs, I spotted an ad for discounted boxing lessons at a local gym and everything just *clicked*. There was a soft voice in the back of my brain, the one that used to belong to me, urging me to take a picture of the ad and contact the gym. The feeling seemed so silly at the time, but now I know it saved my life.

Boxing introduced me to other contact sports that made me feel something again, like Jiu Jitsu and Muay Thai. I even made a few friends, though they were fleeting. With literal blood, sweat, and tears, I dug myself out of that place and molded the version of me that exists now. I promised myself I'd never feel helpless again, mentally or physically. It's still hard for me to recognize that something as small as an ad on a bulletin board gave me something to work towards. A purpose.

Then, I was on the move again. Peter had me trekking from city to city, taking on contracts and staying temporarily in places while I worked. It prevented me from establishing a routine at any of the nearby gyms. I started to weight train in chain gyms instead, knowing that it would give me an outlet, but it's just never been the same. So, when I knew that I'd be staying in Chicago for a while, I went looking for somewhere to pick up where I left off and walking into this gym felt like returning home.

I partially chose this location because it was just far enough outside of downtown that I wasn't likely to run into any of the new acquaintances I've made. The other reason I chose it was because it was the first time I met Jeff.

When I stopped by to ask for a tour on a quiet Tuesday morning, there was a man in his late thirties, tattooed neck to toe, head shaved to the skin, mopping the floor in front of the reception desk.

He talked to me as one might an old friend, asking questions about the types of training I was looking for. The facility tour quickly dissolved into an on-mat assessment where he handed my ass to me over and over again. I was half convinced he thought he was wasting his time, but he didn't outwardly show it.

After breaking the chokehold he had me in and catching our breath, he told me the classes they currently offered would be too basic for my skill level. Instead, he mentioned he provided private instruction for those serious about Jiu-Jitsu, grappling, and other combat sports. A month later, I'm still getting tossed around like a rag doll four times a week during their slower hours, grinding through sessions that push me harder than I've ever trained. Though we usually opt for no-gi BJJ for the sake of time, he's taught me everything. Sparring, drilling techniques. It's relentless, but exactly what I signed up for.

"Can we run that back?" I ask him, squeezing some water into my mouth and swishing it once before swallowing. My esophagus burns and I welcome it.

"You've had enough grappling for today. I don't need you passing out on me." Jeff's tone is firm, leaving no room for argument. I already know better than to push back when it comes to training. "We can work on strikes or call it a day."

"Striking it is." I exhale sharply, shaking out my arms. The corner of his mouth twitches into a smirk as he stands and extends his hand. I clasp his rough, calloused grip, hauling myself to my feet and blinking away the lingering haze from the last round. Without another word, Jeff walks to the edge of the mat, grabbing the punch mitts and kick shield from the pile. I roll my neck from side to side while he straps the mitts on, slipping my mouth guard back in place.

"You're solid on offense, but your defense still needs work," he says as he tightens the straps. Jeff's critiques are rarely sugar-coated, and his tone always carries that expectation of more. "It's not about power. It's technique. You need to focus on defensive maneuvers and how to get out of holds *safely*."

I bite down on my guard, holding back the urge to roll my eyes at the way he emphasizes the word.

"Maybe I don't find myself on the defense often, so I don't use it," I quip, though muffled from the plastic protecting my teeth.

The joke doesn't land when Jeff turns back to me, his face unreadable as always. The mitts are up, his wrists exposed, showing off the ink coiled around them; one arm marked with the belly of a snake, the other a sprawling map of constellations. He steps into range, planting his feet as I square up, settling into my stance. And just like that, we fall into the rhythm of mitt drills, the kind of silent, focused exchange that feels almost meditative.

Jab, double jab, block. Body shot, head jab, double jab, block.

The flow is steady at first, my punches precise and controlled. I stay light on my feet, bouncing between combinations, until I throw a hook that lands solidly against the mitt. In the blink of an eye, Jeff counters with a jab aimed straight at my face. I manage to block it just in time, my forearm absorbing the impact.

"If you don't work on it, the next time you end up in a bad position, you might not walk away from it." The warning in his words lands as heavy as any punch.

One thing I've come to appreciate about Jeff: he doesn't pry. He doesn't ask questions about the reasons behind my drive. That silent understanding is rare, and I don't take it for granted.

Our breathing grows heavier as the drill picks up intensity, my punches landing harder with each combination. My eyes stay locked on Jeff's hands, tracking every movement as we circle each other.

"Why do you think I let you wail on me four days a week?" I ask. Jeff barks out a laugh, eyes sharp and focused like a predator stalking its prey.

I press forward, the pace increasing. It's a deadly dance. Controlled chaos. *Jab, hook, cross, block.* We circle each other, feet shuffling across the mat in perfect sync. The rhythm builds into a crescendo until I throw a jab that snaps the mitt back into Jeff's face.

I freeze for a moment, my chest heaving as Jeff lowers his hands and pulls off one glove to shake out his palm. He glances at it briefly, flexing his fingers, before looking up at me with a mischievous grin through his guard.

"I'll say this," he pants, a glimmer of pride in his eyes. "I feel sorry for any poor bastard who ends up on the other side of your offense."

CHAPTER 4

Swiveling on my bar stool, I tap my manicured index finger against the smooth, black marble countertop. The sleek, circular bar is a centerpiece of the minimalist art gallery, its black shelving system lined with some of the finest liquors and wines in the world. Soft lighting glows beneath the bottles, casting a subtle warmth that contrasts with the starkness of the venue.

Moments later, the bartender slides a tequila, lime, and soda water toward me. I flash him a smile as he winks, placing a few bills on the counter as a tip.

When I first arrived in Chicago, I never imagined I'd end up at so many of these fundraisers. But they seem to be the only places Silas Wells makes public appearances, especially if it involves his sister. Still, I can't help but roll my eyes at the extravagance. The money spent hosting these events could do far more good by directly supporting the community. Then again, what do I know?

Across the bar, I spot the man of the hour. Silas stands with his forearms braced against the counter, leaning slightly forward as he waits for his drink. The movement shifts his impeccably tailored dark suit, revealing a hint of ink peeking out from under the sleeve of his black-faced watch, wrapping around his left wrist and disappearing beneath the fabric.

Silas is the eldest of the Wells siblings, the heir apparent to Wells Corporation whenever their father decides to retire. And as if his future power and wealth weren't enough, he's devastatingly handsome. His dark curls are slightly longer than what's typical for men of his social caliber, but they suit him. The black-framed glasses perched on his sharp, angular face somehow enhance the air of mystery he carries.

It's a fact that the Wells family is undeniably lucky—or unlucky, depending on your perspective—that they're so attractive. If they weren't, I might have found a reason to abandon this job weeks ago. At least following them around has some perks.

Setting my glass down on the counter, I reach into my small handbag for my phone. The screen lights up with a text message waiting for me. It's from Peter.

Peter: Don't make me regret agreeing to your plan.

I set my jaw and count to ten before replying.

Me: Noted.

To say Peter is unimpressed with my suggested timeline for this job would be the understatement of the year. He practically spat nails when I laid out my multi-month plan. But even he can see there's no way to infiltrate a family of this status overnight without raising suspicion. That doesn't mean he'll stop reminding me he doesn't like it. Subtlety and patience aren't his strong suits, and he seems determined to let me know at every opportunity.

By the time I clear the messages and put my phone away, Silas has moved from the bar to his usual group of companions. They're stationed in their typical half-circle formation, quietly surveying the room while exchanging clipped comments out of the corners of their mouths. Two are members of his security team. Discreet, but always present. Another is Natalie's husband, Davey, who seems as much a fixture of Silas's orbit as the others. The remaining three are business associates. Boarding school friends, from what I've pieced together, their families nearly as wealthy as his.

They're all dressed in the kind of tailored suits and understated luxury brands that signal old money. Unlike others in the room, who flaunt loud designer logos plastered across every item they wear, this group doesn't need to advertise their wealth. It's evident in their presence.

I've made brief attempts to crack into Silas's inner circle at other events, but none of them have been particularly fruitful. The group shares Silas's skepticism and preference for keeping outsiders at arm's length. Originally, I thought Davey would be my best entry point. With his background in tech, I figured we'd connect over our shared professional interests. But I've since realized that approach is a mistake. Someone like Davey sees our mutual interest in technology as more than a coincidence; it's a giant red flag.

For now, I watch them from a distance, assessing the group dynamic. Cracking this circle will take finesse, but I've already decided it's worth the effort. Silas may be a recluse, but he's also the linchpin. If I can find the right way in, the rest will follow, and maybe I can be out of this city before I originally told Peter. Under promise, overdeliver.

I slide out of my seat, holding my glass in one hand while tucking my handbag securely under the other arm. Behind me, a beautiful oil painting of Washington Park catches my eye; a vibrant perspective of the park as if viewed from one of its many benches. After a brief pause to admire it, I let my feet carry me toward the next piece of art, each step inching me closer to where Silas and his entourage linger.

The next canvas stops me in my tracks; a striking black-and-white drawing of a woman caught in a rainstorm. The detail is so hyperrealistic that, for a moment, I'm convinced it's a photograph.

"This student is one of my favorites," a soft voice murmurs close to my side. I glance over my shoulder as Natalie steps beside me. She's dressed in a sleek black business dress, her hair pulled neatly into a bun, and her hands clasped in front of her. Her polished elegance doesn't overshadow the kindness in her hazel eyes. "Hana Yoo. She's incredibly talented."

I turn back to the artwork and smile. "It took me a second to realize it wasn't a photo. I can't imagine what it must feel like to create something this lifelike."

"She's meticulous to a fault," Natalie says thoughtfully, her gaze fixed on the piece. "But it works in her favor."

I nod, letting the silence linger for a moment before Natalie turns to me, her expression shifting slightly. "I wanted to check in and see if things have been... more pleasant for you since last week."

Her words bring me back to the banker who had practically glued himself to my side. A few nights later, while doing recon at a popular lounge, I noticed something remarkable—no one approached me. Not a single unwanted advance. It hadn't been my body language that kept them away, after all. It had been this stranger watching my back.

The warmth in my chest grows, a mix of gratitude and an ache I can't quite name.

"They have been," I admit, raising an eyebrow at her. "Do I have you to thank for that?"

A playful glint lights up her eyes as she tilts her head slightly. "Potentially."

I laugh softly. "Well, whatever you did, thank you."

"No need to thank me," she replies, shaking her head in exasperation. "There's no winning with these people sometimes."

"I couldn't agree more," I say with a dramatic roll of my eyes. "This is a beautiful event. Did you choose the pieces displayed, or did you collaborate with the students?"

Her polite, practiced smile melts into something more genuine. Her hands clasp tighter for a brief moment before she begins explaining, her voice brimming with excitement. She walks me through the process she undertook with the students to create the gallery, pointing animatedly from one canvas to another as she dives into every meticulous detail.

But as Natalie speaks, jealousy stirs in the pit of my stomach. It's uninvited, sharp-edged, and bitter. For some people, their life path is rigid, predetermined by their family's legacy. But for many like Natalie, endless resources and wealth offer something even more valuable: freedom. Freedom to explore, to be picky, to discard a career like an ill-fitting pair of pants and try another. Money doesn't buy happiness, sure. But it does buy options, time, and the chance to find happiness on your own terms. And Natalie is one of the lucky ones who is doing something she cares about.

For me, survival has always been the goal. There's never been room for luxuries or exploration. From a young age, I knew I needed a career that could buy me a sliver of freedom, even if it would never be the kind Natalie has. That has been the plan since day one, and I've spent nearly a decade chasing it. Yet, as I stand here, I can't help but feel like I'm no closer to that dream than when I started.

Natalie barely pauses to take a breath, her passion bubbling over until she finally reins it in. Her cheeks flush a delicate pink as she finishes speaking.

"I've talked your ear off," she says with a self-conscious laugh, gesturing for us to move to the next gallery piece. "Tell me, what do you do for work?"

"I asked because I wanted to hear about it," I reply, brushing off her insecurity with a wave of my hand. "And cybersecurity," I add—a carefully chosen half-truth. Half-truths are easier for me to say than the full-out lies I've become so accustomed to telling. They ease my conscious just enough to keep me from drowning in the guilt I'll face when the contract is over.

We stop in front of a wildly abstract painting, its canvas drenched in shades of deep, chaotic red. I move my head side-to-side, trying to decipher what it's supposed to represent, but I come up empty.

"Oh, you're in a much different line of work than me," Natalie says with a chuckle. "That's what my husband does."

"What do I do?" a low, measured voice asks from behind us. Natalie's eyes soften instantly, a clear giveaway before I even turn around. I don't need to look to know it's Davey Sinclair; the man behind the security system that's had me running in circles.

"My new friend Scarlett was just telling me she works in cybersecurity," Natalie explains, nodding in my direction with a smile. "Scarlett, this is my husband, Davey Sinclair. Davey, Scarlett Page."

"Nice to meet you," I say, inclining my head with practiced politeness. My pulse quickens slightly as our eyes meet, and I catch a flicker of his silent assessment.

"Likewise," Davey says, his tone even as he places a protective hand on the small of Natalie's back. His posture is relaxed, but there's an air of calculation in the way he carries himself, like he's always one step ahead of the conversation. "Do you work for yourself?"

"I do," I answer smoothly. "I prefer the lifestyle it offers."

His sharp green eyes narrow slightly, studying me with quiet precision. His head tilts ever so slightly to the side as he asks, "And what kind of lifestyle is that?"

Jesus. Two sentences in, and he's already searching for any cracks in my response.

"One where I make my own hours and travel as I please," I reply, raising my glass for another sip.

"I can't argue with that," Davey says with a refined smile before his attention shifts to Natalie. "Silas has a question about the catering."

She glances over her shoulder, presumably toward Silas's location. "Care to join us, Scarlett? Most of my duties are done for the evening. I can introduce you to some friends."

Davey's gaze narrows just a hair as he looks at his wife. It's clear he wishes she hadn't extended the invitation. She either doesn't notice or, more likely, chooses to ignore him entirely. That bodes well for me. If this is how he usually reacts to strangers, then his discomfort likely isn't personal, it's just his default state. Unfortunately for him, catering to his paranoia isn't exactly high on my priority list. Still, I can't afford to appear too eager.

"I wouldn't want to intrude," I say, adding a touch of embarrassment to my tone.

"It's not an intrusion if you're invited," Natalie replies with a wink, looping her arm through Davey's. "Come. I'm sure forcing my brother to socialize with someone other than Davey at one of these events will do him good."

I catch the way Davey's jaw tenses beneath the light stubble on his face. His muscles flex subtly, his displeasure barely masked. He's been described as the most paranoid member of Silas's inner circle, and moments like this confirm the reputation. But I force a meek smile in his direction as he turns with Natalie, careful not to give him more of a reason to be suspicious.

Trailing a step or two behind the couple, I watch as they lean close to whisper something to each other. It doesn't take much imagination to guess that Davey is quietly urging his wife to be more cautious. But Natalie, with a teasing grin on her lips, lightly elbows him in response, brushing off his concern.

Davey's stern expression softens slightly as he leans in and presses a brief kiss to the side of her temple. The protective way he carries himself doesn't falter, though. He glides through the small crowd of guests with an effortless control, as if Natalie is the most precious cargo in the room.

A waiter carrying a silver tray of hors d'oeuvres steps aside to make room for us, but Davey subtly motions with two fingers, signaling the server to follow before adjusting our course and leading us away from the bar and the main throng of fundraiser attendees. I follow a few paces behind, matching their unhurried stride but careful to maintain a respectful distance.

The dynamic between them is fascinating: her lightness, his seriousness, the way they balance each other out. It's something to catalog for later, but for now, I stay focused on the path ahead. Every move I make here needs to count.

Silas has relocated from the bar to an impromptu sitting area on the outskirts of the gallery, where oversized leather chairs surround a low coffee table designed for casual conversation. He's sprawled in the center chair, his long legs splayed in a posture that manages to strike the perfect balance between casual and commanding. His impeccably tailored jacket is unbuttoned, revealing a crisp white collared shirt and a dark tie that sits perfectly in place. One arm rests lazily along the back of the chair, while the other is propped on the armrest, hand braced under his chin as if he's lost in thought.

Everything about him exudes an effortless kind of power—the sort that draws attention like a gravitational pull. My skin warms as my eyes linger on him longer than I should. There's an undeniable magnetism to his presence: sharp, self-assured, captivating. I can't help but admire the way he wears these traits so naturally, as though power and confidence are stitched into the fabric of his suit.

As we approach, the hum of voices and the soft background music fade into a distant murmur. Natalie walks straight to her brother, the waiter trailing obediently behind her, and leans over his chair to speak. Silas shifts subtly, moving the hand under his chin to partially cover his mouth as he speaks, ensuring his words are hidden from prying eyes and ears. Natalie's brows knit together, and she waves the waiter closer.

If there's one thing I've learned about earning trust, it's knowing when to give people space. Especially in moments when you might want to do the opposite.

I pivot on my heel and head toward a nearby cluster of artwork just beyond the sitting area. On the way, I place my empty cocktail glass on an abandoned table, taking a moment to reposition my clutch, so I'm holding it neatly with both hands at my waist. I let my gaze flick over the art in front of me, though my attention stays partially trained on Silas and Natalie from the corner of my eye. There's no rush to insert myself.

Timing, as always, is everything.

Though the paintings in front of me are stunning, my mind is elsewhere. Figuring out how to deal with Davey will be a challenge. I've spent years perfecting the art of seamlessly integrating myself into groups like this one. It's a skill I've honed to near perfection. Sometimes, I slip into a role so effortlessly that I lose track of where my real self ends and the persona begins. And yet, here I am, over a month into this assignment, and Davey has already subconsciously clocked me before I've even truly started.

It's likely just his overprotectiveness of Natalie and her safety, but that doesn't make him any less dangerous. Peter's IDs are always bulletproof, though I'm sure Scarlett's online presence could probably use more refinement. Davey has already come close to besting me without even knowing it. I can't afford to let it happen again.

"Scarlett," Natalie calls, snapping me out of my thoughts. I take a breath and count to five before turning away from the paintings to face her. All eyes are on me now, including her brother's, whose dark gaze seems nearly black from across the room. I paste on a polite smile as I approach.

"Figure everything out?" I ask lightly. Natalie rolls her eyes in a way only a younger sibling can and jerks her head toward Silas.

"Yes. Someone is just being particular about the seafood options," she says, clearly exasperated.

I open my mouth to respond, but another voice cuts me off.

"You'd think, with my own sister running this event, I could make a request."

My eyes lock onto Silas, who now stands shoulder-to-shoulder with Davey. He glances past his brother-in-law, fixing his teasing gaze on Natalie, a glimmer of amusement dancing in his eyes.

His voice is unexpected—deep and earthy, like the low rumble of a crackling fire as it cools. The men of his stature who I've dealt with don't usually sound like this. They're usually nasally or sharp. Grating. But Silas's voice is warm and smoky, and it settles somewhere deep in my stomach, unbidden and stubborn.

"Maybe you should have thought of that last week when I confirmed the menu," Natalie fires back. Then, she gestures toward me with a small smile. "Please behave yourself in front of my new friend. Scarlett, this is my brother, Silas. Silas, Scarlett Page."

I'm not prepared for the wave of heat that slides down my spine when our eyes meet. His gaze is sharp and mischievous, framed by dark glasses that do nothing to hide the devilish glint in his expression. A faint dimple cuts into his left cheek, barely visible beneath his scruff, adding a touch of rugged charm to his otherwise polished exterior. Beneath the tailored suit and carefully cultivated demeanor, there's nothing corporate about this man. He looks like every reckless decision I wanted to make as a teenager, wrapped into more than six feet of devastatingly handsome, self-assured billionaire.

For a moment, I let myself revel in the full-body tingle that Silas Wells evokes, before I lock it away.

"It's not every day Nat brings a new friend around," he says, his voice rich and teasing as he extends a hand across the circle.

I match the firmness of his grip, surprised by the rough texture of his palm. It's not what I expected from a man who could easily spend all day behind a desk. There's something disarming about the contrast.

"I'm not sure if that's a compliment or a dig at your sister," I reply, raising an eyebrow as I release his hand.

His smile widens, revealing a perfect row of teeth that could grace the cover of any magazine. "I guess the answer will be one of life's great mysteries."

If I were a weaker woman, that smile might have reduced me to a puddle right then and there. But something about Silas unsettles me in a way I can't quite name. He's too perfect, too put together, too aware of his own charm. Unfortunately for him, I have a hard time resisting the urge to humble people like him, no matter who I'm pretending to be.

I mull over his words. "That might be pushing it."

It takes a moment for my quiet insult to settle before his eyebrow arches slightly, surprise crossing his features. To his right, one of his friends snorts, unable to hold back their amusement.

I introduce myself to the rest of the circle, breaking eye contact with Silas as I shift my focus to the others. But I can feel him tracking my every move with unrelenting intensity. When I glance back at him, it's just in time to catch him running a hand along the sharp line of his jaw, those endlessly dark eyes pinned on me in a way that sends a chill skating over my skin.

Silas Wells may be the picture of control, but his curiosity tells me one thing: I've got his attention.

Good.

"So, you're new to Chicago?" Gordon, the man seated to my right, asks. His voice is as warm and inviting as his dark skin, a soothing contrast to the simmering tension I feel from elsewhere in the circle.

"I am," I reply with a nod. "I've been here about a month now."

"Scarlett is in my line of work," Davey interjects, nursing his whiskey.

My eyes flick to Davey, surprised by his unprompted contribution, before returning to Gordon. It seems whatever Natalie whispered during our walk here struck a chord; Davey's willingness to keep me in the conversation is unexpected.

"Some healthy competition, then," Gordon muses, his grin widening as he looks between the two of us. There's an incredulous look on Davey's face, as if the idea of competition is beneath him.

Well, that lasted all of two seconds.

"I'm happy with my existing clientele," I say, offering a small, closed-mouth smile to defuse the moment.

"Smart," Silas remarks, his smirk barely concealed as he brings his whiskey glass to his lips. The subtle barb in his tone reignites the temper I usually keep tightly leashed.

Fighting every impulse to wipe that smirk off his face with the truth—that I've been digging around in his company's multi-million-dollar cloud, the very system his beloved Davey built—I turn toward him instead, waiting for him to lower his glass.

"If I wanted Davey's job," I say, my voice sharp yet sweetened by the angelic smile I wear like armor, "I'd have taken it already."

Silas's smirk deepens into a full grin, and he tilts his head to the side, watching me like a predator sizing up its prey. My heart stutters, but I force my expression to remain neutral. Bored, even. Looking away first or showing even a flicker of emotion would be submission, and there's no way in hell this man will get that satisfaction from me.

Unblinking, I hold his gaze, ignoring the subtle flame flickering behind his dark, chocolate-colored eyes. A small voice in the back of my mind warns that if I keep pushing, I might just stoke it into a full-blown inferno.

The silence stretches—seconds, maybe a full minute—before Natalie breaks it with a stifled laugh, effectively extinguishing the tension between us. Both Silas and I glance her way, her smile a welcome reprieve.

"I love you, Silas, but my money's on her," Natalie quips, sliding her hand down Davey's arm and interlocking their fingers.

"I knew I was going to like you," I say to her, offering a genuine smile. Natalie returns it with a sly grin while the others exchange wary glances.

One of the other men, Brian, thankfully redirects the conversation, asking where I'm from. I exhale slowly, releasing my frustration along with the breath. Though I respond and keep my expression friendly, my thoughts are elsewhere.

It's unnerving how quickly Silas managed to get under my skin just now. Maybe it's the stark contrast between Natalie's warm kindness and his sharp-edged demeanor that caught me off guard. Or maybe it's the fact that I had to skip my gym session this morning to hunt down a dress for this event. Whatever it is, I need to get my shit together.

The last thing I can afford is for Silas and Davey to dislike me. If they do, I can kiss any chance of getting near their devices goodbye.

Just as I turn to answer Gordon's next question about my time in Philadelphia, I catch Silas's eyes from across the circle. His stare is hard, a mix of frustration and something else I can't quite place. It burns hot, sinking into my gut and setting my teeth on edge.

Game on, Silas Wells. Game on.

CHAPTER 5

"**A**bout damn time," Harrison's voice booms through the phone, loud enough to make me wince. I pull my hand from my face to shield my ear from the assault. "I need an update."

Tucking my jacket more securely under my opposite arm, I continue browsing the rack in front of me, lined with tweed pants and ridiculously expensive wool sweaters.

The boutique is small, as are most of the high-end stores in Chicago. They're curated for exclusivity, designed with quality over quantity in mind, both in their inventory and in the clientele they attract. Black metal clothing racks stand sparsely across the space, rustic tables stacked neatly with folded garments occupy the center, and dark wood shelves line the cream-colored walls. The style isn't really mine, but that hardly matters. It can be Scarlett's if I decide it suits her.

"I'm working right now," I say, my fingers gliding over the fabrics. Pressing the volume button on my phone until Harrison's voice is a manageable whisper. "I'll call you back with that information in a bit."

"Working? I can hear music. You're shopping."

"They aren't mutually exclusive," I reply breezily, moving to the next rack, this one filled with neatly hung jeans. Without caring about the style or cut, I grab a dark wash pair in my size and hold them against my waist for reference.

An older associate approaches me as I glance up, her sleek dark bob framing her face. She bows her head in a polite, silent greeting. I offer a small smile in return, and she mouths, *"Dressing room?"* while pointing across the store. I nod and hand her the jeans, watching as she tilts her head for me to follow.

"Find somewhere we can speak. Now," Harrison growls.

Trailing the associate, I pluck two sweaters from a nearby table. One is a dark green casual knit, the other thinner and tailored-looking, perfect for layering over a collared shirt.

"I'm afraid that's not possible," I respond lightly. "I'm about to start an important business meeting that can't be postponed."

Harrison goes silent, the kind of pause meant to intimidate. It might work on someone else, but not on me, especially through a phone. A pair of block-heeled boots catches my eye from a display to my right, and I pause just long enough to check the size before adding them to the growing pile in my arms.

"Call me back when you're done," Harrison finally seethes.

"Will do," I say cheerfully, though my thumb is already hovering over the end call button. I hang up without so much as a goodbye, smiling to myself as I do. There's something so satisfying about getting under his skin with so little effort.

As I slide my phone into my back pocket, the associate leads me out of the main shopping area and through an elegant archway at the back of the store. Along the far wall, several dark wood doors are evenly spaced, each fitting room blending seamlessly into the boutique's sophisticated aesthetic. Chic wall sconces and ornate chandeliers cast a warm, inviting glow.

On the far left, another associate stands outside the only occupied fitting room, leaning slightly toward the door as she speaks to the customer inside. Her voice is low, a gentle murmur in the otherwise quiet space.

"Sorry about that," I say, forcing my gaze away from the far door and back to the associate assisting me.

"No need to apologize. It happens all the time," she replies warmly, gesturing toward a slightly ajar fitting room door. With practiced ease, she takes the pile of clothes from my arms. "Do you need anything else to start your try-on? Maybe something in a particular style or size?"

"You know," I begin, glancing briefly toward the other fitting room again, where the second associate now stands quietly with her hands clasped in front of her. "I've been thinking about adding more variety to my wardrobe. Something beyond just slacks and jeans. Do you have any recommendations?"

She opens her mouth to respond, but the soft squeak of the other dressing room door draws both of our attention. The other associate steps forward, reaching out to collect the items from the customer inside.

I keep my expression carefully neutral, then feign surprise as Natalie steps into view, buttoning up her tailored peacoat while saying something to the associate beside her. Her dark hair falls across her face until she tucks it neatly behind one ear.

"Natalie!" I exclaim, my voice tinged with just the right amount of delight. Her eyes flick upward, her posture stiffening for a split second before relaxing as she recognizes me.

"Scarlett," she says with a small smile. "What a nice surprise."

"Surprise" is one way to describe it. Convenient, perhaps. Staged, definitely. In reality, I've been trailing her and her driver for the past two hours running errands. Ever since her art exhibit, where we exchanged numbers at the end of the night, I hadn't heard from her. The charity events have worked so far, but I need more—another reason to be around her without forcing it. This was the most natural way I could think of.

I watched her from the coffee shop across the street, patiently waiting for the perfect moment to follow her in. I'd barely had time to ditch my untouched espresso in the trash can outside before I saw her heading toward the dressing rooms. But, of course, none of that is information she needs to know.

"The best kind of surprise," I say, keeping my tone light. "I hope you've been well?"

"I have. And you?"

"The same. Just enjoying the weather and thought a little shopping might be nice," I reply with a kind smile. The weather is unusually mild for Chicago at the end of February, hovering in the mid forties. A rare reprieve from the biting cold this time of year.

"I had the same thought," she says with a soft laugh, glancing at the associate holding her clothes. Her eyes widen in realization. "Oh, I don't want you to carry those any longer. Let's get them to the register."

Her voice is sincere, apologetic even, as she turns toward the doorway with the associate following closely behind. The contrast between her warm demeanor and her brother's arrogance is already striking. Where Silas had exuded an almost predatory self-assurance during our first meeting, Natalie is all softness and thoughtful consideration.

As she steps toward the register, offering parting words to me, I hesitate for only a moment before speaking.

"I'm not sure what you have planned for the rest of the afternoon," I say, interrupting her goodbye. Natalie pauses mid-step and turns back to me, her expression curious as she waits for me to continue. "But I was planning on grabbing lunch just around the corner. If you're not busy, I'd love your company."

Her face softens further, the thoughtful kindness I've come to associate with her now tinged with a hint of surprise. Just as she did the night I first handed her my business card, she looks at me with a rawness in her golden eyes that's disarming. It's a kind of vulnerability that makes holding her gaze difficult.

"That sounds... nice," she says, her voice carrying a quiet sincerity. "Would you like me to wait out here for you?"

I blink, momentarily caught off guard. My gaze shifts to the associate still holding my pile of clothes, and heat rises to my cheeks as I silently curse myself for not asking her to set them down sooner.

"If you wouldn't mind," I say, my grin tinged with embarrassment. "I shouldn't be long."

I made short work of the items I brought into the dressing room, settling on a pair of flared pants and a skirt the associate suggested. Both are neutral pieces and practical enough to wear in the future.

If I'm being honest, the clothing is the least of my concerns. But walking into the dressing room with an armful of clothes only to leave empty-handed would have raised eyebrows. Better to maintain appearances, even for something as inconsequential as this.

This orchestrated run-in with Natalie worked out better than I could have anticipated. I didn't expect her to agree to lunch so readily. I assumed she'd tell me she was busy, forcing me to maneuver my way into scheduling something for another day.

But the look on her face when I asked sticks with me. Genuine surprise, almost as though she'd been waiting for the catch. I'll have to play the long game with her. Natalie's warmth and kindness may be disarming, but she's no fool. If I bring up her family—or her brother—too quickly, she'll shut me out for good.

Now, as we settle into our seats at a nearby restaurant, I steal a glance at her from across the table. There were plenty of dining options nearby the boutique, but this spot felt the most casual. We're seated by the floor-to-ceiling windows, the natural light spilling over our table. Natalie sits with her back to an antiqued brick wall, her posture relaxed but poised.

It's prime lunch hour, and the restaurant is buzzing with professionals in suits and pencil skirts, their conversations blending into a low hum of background noise. Fortunately, Natalie's driver, James, is parked somewhere nearby, so we were able to leave our shopping bags with him instead of awkwardly cramming them under the table.

I clasp my hands in my lap, reminding myself to keep the conversation easy and unassuming. For now, this is about building rapport, nothing more.

"Thanks for joining me," I say, picking up the menu. The options are mostly elevated pub food, and my stomach growls at the thought. "It's been a while since I've had someone to have lunch with."

Natalie offers me a small smile, mirroring my actions as she opens her menu.

"Do you miss your friends back home?" she asks, her voice soft, just as the waiter approaches to place two glasses of water in front of us. He tells us he'll be back shortly to take our drink orders, and Natalie gives him a polite nod before turning her attention back to me.

Her question makes my chest tightens and I swallow hard, forcing unwelcome memories back into the dark recesses of my mind. No matter how much I try to bury them, some resurface in flashes of fleeting moments of a life that once felt whole. But the images never stop there. They always lead to the same haunting memory: cold, green eyes staring lifelessly at the ceiling.

I shake my head once, focusing on the menu in front of me as I steady my voice. "The few I had, yes," I say, clearing my throat. "I came to Chicago to try something new and severely underestimated how hard it is to make friends."

Natalie nods passionately, the sadness behind her gaze revealing an unexpected vulnerability. It's clear she understands. Her reaction surprises me. Could she really be someone who struggles to connect? She's well-mannered, poised, and kind—everything I imagined her to be, yet more approachable than anyone I've met in this city so far. She's witty and thoughtful, and I have a feeling she'd have a sharp tongue like mine if she weren't a Wells child bound by the weight of public expectations.

"Finding genuine friends in these circles is challenging," she clarifies after a pause, her eyes dropping back to the menu. Redness creeps up the sides of her neck, as though she's revealed too much.

Her phrasing is telling. She's been burned before—used by people she thought were friends. Just like I'm about to do.

A knot tightens in my throat, and I reach for my water, taking a sip in an attempt to dissolve it. "I'm sorry that's been your experience," I murmur, my lips brushing the edge of the glass.

She waves off my comment with a quick flick of her hand. "I'm used to it. I still have my childhood best friend, but she lives in California. It's hard to see her as often as I'd like."

"Long-distance friendships are tough," I say quietly. "But worth it."

"They are," she agrees, her words laced with a quiet melancholy.

For a brief moment, the silence between us feels heavier than I intended, and I sip my water again, hoping the conversation will shift to lighter ground.

The waiter returns to take our drink orders. I opt for an iced tea, while Natalie requests sparkling water with lemon. He nods before disappearing again, leaving behind a quiet that lingers between us, just the kind that comes when a conversation pauses between two people still figuring out where they stand.

The pause starts to weigh on me, thickening with every second that passes. I take a slow breath and sip my water, hoping she'll say something to fill the quiet, but Natalie remains thoughtful, her gaze drifting to the window. She seems like the type of woman who values directness. Someone who appreciates cutting through the pretense and getting to the heart of the matter.

There's no reason to delay the inevitable.

"Okay, so," I begin, leaning slightly toward her.

Natalie lifts an eyebrow, intrigued but not entirely surprised. She mimics my posture, bending slightly at the waist to meet me halfway, her hazel eyes locking onto mine.

"This is probably going to sound very forward, and maybe even a little weird, but... you're the only person I've met in this entire city who I actually like, and I think we'd get along really well. Since it seems like we're both in need of new friends, I propose we skip the awkward back-and-forth of trying to figure out if the other person is interested and just be friends. What do you say?"

For a moment, she stares at me, her expression unreadable. Then, she leans back in her chair and bursts into laughter, a warm, hearty sound that takes me completely off guard. Her hand lands on her stomach as she tips her head back, catching the attention of a few nearby diners, who glance over before returning to their conversations.

Well, that's not the reaction I was expecting. Did I come on too strong? Did she see right through me?

Natalie wipes under her eyes, still chuckling. "I thought you were about to pitch me some kind of investment opportunity."

I exhale the breath I didn't realize I was holding and sink back into my chair, laughing along with her. "And I thought you were about to laugh me out the door," I admit, placing a hand over my chest. "I know it's an odd question, but I really think we'd make great friends."

Running a hand through her dark hair, Natalie gives me a smile so bright and genuine that it momentarily takes me off guard. Just then, the waiter returns with our drinks. We ask for a few more minutes to decide on our orders, and he obliges with another polite nod before moving on to another table.

"That's honestly the most flattering thing anyone's asked me in a long time," Natalie says, lifting her glass and holding it over the table toward me.

Grinning, I pick up my iced tea and gently tap it against hers. The satisfying ring of glass meeting glass cuts through the hum of the restaurant.

"Let's skip the awkward stage," she says, her tone playful, "and just be friends."

"Friends it is," I agree, both of us taking a long sip of our drinks.

She sets her glass down and props her chin on her hand, a teasing glint in her eyes as her smile widens. "Alright, let's cover the basics. Siblings? Parents? Boyfriend? I'm ready."

And so, I give her all the half-truths I've rehearsed. The carefully curated pieces of the life I'm willing to share. But as we talk, my chest tightens with a pang of guilt. Because despite my ulterior motives, I can't deny what's staring me in the face: Natalie and the real me might actually have made great friends.

CHAPTER 6

Natalie and I slide into her driver's car after a lunch that feels disarmingly normal. Though she'd seemed kind in our limited interactions before today, she still isn't what I expected. She's warmer, more genuine, easy to talk to in a way that feels effortless. It only makes this situation harder to stomach. I've done this before—used connections, played the part until I got what I needed—but Natalie already proving to be different than most of the others. She's maybe a little too trusting and shockingly open about how often people in her world try to use her. And now, I'm one of them.

As James, the soft-spoken man in the driver's seat, navigates the busy downtown streets, Natalie chats effortlessly about her favorite lunch spots. I nod and laugh in all the right places, forcing myself to stay engaged instead. of allowing my mind to wander . This job was already delicate, but now there's a growing pit in my stomach that makes it harder to focus.

"You've got to let me take you to the little café on Elm next time," Natalie says, her tone bright, pulling me back to the moment. "Their lavender lattes are amazing, and the owner is the sweetest woman."

"That sounds great," I reply, meaning it more than I should. From the corner of my eye, I catch Natalie glancing at me with a thoughtful expression.

"I'm glad we ran into each other today," she says softly.

Her sincerity lands like a punch. She has no idea that I'm cataloging every detail of her life for my own agenda, no idea that I'm here to use her. I smile instead, slipping the guilt behind a mask I've perfected after years in this line of work.

"Me too," I respond, and for a fleeting moment, I almost believe it.

Natalie perks up suddenly, as if remembering something. "Oh, before I forget. I need to make a quick stop at the office. Silas's assistant wants to finalize the plans for the summer employee golf tournament fundraiser I'm helping organize. Would you mind coming along? It shouldn't take long, and then we can drop you wherever you need to go."

The mention of the Wells Corporate office sends a jolt of adrenaline through me. Peter would lose his mind if he knew I was about to walk through the front doors of their headquarters.

"Not at all," I reply smoothly, keeping my voice casual despite the quickening pace of my thoughts. "It'll be cool to see the Wells empire."

Natalie laughs. "Well, it's definitely something. Just wait until you see the lobby."

Minutes later, the car pulls up in front of a sleek, glass-fronted building in the heart of downtown. James steps out to open her door, and she exits with the practiced grace of someone who's done this a thousand times. I follow, my heart pounding as I take in the modern façade, discreet security cameras, and the building's imposing presence.

Inside, the lobby is just as polished as I imagined. Gleaming marble floors reflect the soft, strategically placed lighting, while a massive abstract sculpture commands attention in the center of the space. Natalie waves to the receptionists, who greet her with warm smiles, and we make our way toward a set of elevators. She pulls a keycard from her bag and swipes it against the scanner before pressing a button for an upper floor.

I've spent as much time studying this company as I have the family itself. Wells Corporation isn't just another pharmaceutical giant; it's a legacy, one that began nearly a century ago when Silas and Natalie's great-grandfather, a medical scientist, developed a revolutionary antibiotic that changed the trajectory of modern medicine. What started as a small research firm exploded into an empire under William Wells's control, expanding beyond prescription drugs into consumer health products, medical devices, and even biotech.

That's what makes them untouchable. Their name is printed on everything from high-stakes cancer treatments to the bandages in every household first-aid kit. Hospitals, insurance companies, government health programs—everyone depends on Wells Corporation for something. It's not just about profits; it's about influence.

And companies like this? They always have secrets. Whatever Peter has been hired to find has to be something only the Wells family had access to.

"Leslie's desk is just outside Silas's office," Natalie explains as the elevator begins to ascend. "I've already texted her and there's a meeting room where you can wait while I go over the fundraiser details. It won't take long, I promise."

I nod, though my thoughts are already racing. I know exactly who Leslie is. Silas's assistant has been on my radar for weeks. I've combed through her background and work history, but I've yet to put a face to the name.

"Take your time," I answer, my tone easy. The more time I spend here, the better my chances of learning something useful.

When the elevator doors open, we step into a sleek and bustling floor where polished glass walls and modern furnishings dominate the design. Natalie exchanges a quick greeting with Leslie, a sharp-looking woman who barely glances at me as she ushers Natalie toward her desk.

"Why don't you wait in here?" Natalie gestures to a small, glass-walled meeting room whose door is around the corner. "It'll be more comfortable."

"Sure," I reply, settling into one of the chairs. From this vantage point, I can see most of the common area, including the corner of Leslie's desk and the steady flow of employees moving in and out.

Natalie flashes me a quick smile before turning to join Leslie. As I watch her walk away, I can't help but marvel at how effortlessly she navigates this world after just seeing how she struggles with the confidence to make friends. Meanwhile, I sit quietly, waiting, all too aware that every moment here is a delicate balance between opportunity and risk.

For the first few minutes, I sit still, trying to appear relaxed while mentally cataloging everything around me. Employees come and go, swiping keycards at doors and chatting in low tones. There's a rhythm to the place; a well-oiled billion-dollar machine running seamlessly. The weight of opportunity presses against my chest, but it's not alone. Shame lurks just beneath the surface, unwelcome and persistent.

Just as I'm about to stand and wander—casually to find the bathroom, of course—the door to the meeting room swings open. None other than Silas strides in, followed by a man I don't recognize. Both are carrying laptops, deep in conversation.

"Oh," Silas says, stopping short when he sees me. His deep brown eyes narrow before shifting to one of guarded curiosity. "Ms. Page, what are you doing here?"

I rise smoothly, keeping my demeanor respectful but not overly apologetic. "Natalie asked me to wait here while she spoke with Leslie. I can go—"

The other man, mid-forties with the no-nonsense look of a lifetime spent in IT, mutters something under his breath about "guests getting comfortable." His dismissive tone grates on me immediately.

Silas glances at him, then back at me. "There are a few seats just outside my office near Leslie's desk if you'd prefer to wait there."

His words are polite, surprisingly so, and I nod in agreement, moving toward the door. Just as I'm about to leave, I hear the man mention phishing attempts and email security. He's explaining his solution: stricter spam filters and refresher training for employees. My steps falter.

Before I can stop myself, I turn back. "There might be a more effective way to handle that."

The man's head snaps toward me, his expression a mix of irritation and condescension as he sets his laptop down on the conference table. "I'm sure there might be, but this is a technical matter. No offense."

Silas raises an eyebrow at him, his tone cutting and cool. "Warren, Ms. Page is a successful cybersecurity consultant. She might *rightfully* take offense." Then, his sharp gaze shifts to me. "What would you suggest?"

A flicker of appreciation runs through me. Not many people in his position would defend someone they barely know so decisively. Steeling myself, I straighten my back. "Spam filters and training are helpful, but phishing has evolved. AI-powered email security tools can analyze patterns in email traffic and block threats before they even reach inboxes. Pairing that with real-time phishing simulations would give employees practical experience and significantly reduce the risk."

Warren crosses his arms, his irritation barely masked. "Those tools are expensive and overkill for an internal issue. People just need to be more careful."

"They are expensive," I admit, my tone measured. "But a data breach would cost far more. Even careful employees make mistakes. AI tools reduce the risk by catching threats before they land. And with phishing simulations, you reinforce good habits without waiting for someone to slip up." I turn my attention back to Silas, a faint, knowing smile tugging at the corner of my mouth. "Can Wells front the bill?"

Silas watches me intently, his expression unreadable but far from indifferent. The way his eyes hold mine makes me feel like I'm being evaluated, and it's equal parts unnerving and flattering. Finally, he speaks. "Warren, is there a reason we can't explore these tools?"

Warren's jaw tightens. "No, they're viable options. But we'd need to evaluate costs and implementation."

"Perfect," Silas says, setting his laptop down before turning back to me. "Do you have a few minutes to walk us through how that would work?"

The question jolts me. His tone is neutral, professional, but there's an undercurrent of curiosity, maybe even respect. He gestures toward the wall-mounted TV, where his laptop is already connected. My response catches in my throat for a second, the weight of conflicting priorities pressing down. Offering advice like this goes against my self-interest. The stronger Wells Corp's security gets, the harder my job becomes. But trust is currency, and if I show Silas I know what I'm talking about, it could help me later.

Besides, the way he's watching me makes me want to prove myself.

"Sure," I say finally, letting a faint smile creep into my tone. "But only because I'm feeling generous today." I move toward the table, sitting in front of Silas's laptop and angling it toward me. "Normally, I'd charge for this kind of consulting, but let's call this a... complimentary demonstration."

My fingers move purposefully across the trackpad, navigating to an internet browser to pull up the tools and programs I know are among the best for combating phishing threats. I keep my focus on the screen, trying to ignore the heat of Silas's presence as he takes the seat beside me.

Soon, I'm diving into the details of the three companies I'd recommend, carefully outlining the pros and cons of each. Warren interjects occasionally, his tone more combative than curious. But I counter every objection with precise answers. The longer I talk, the more I feel Silas's gaze. It's steady, unwavering, and when I glance at him briefly, I catch the faintest tilt of his head, like he's impressed.

Despite myself, a quiet sense of validation stirs within me. It's a reminder that being acknowledged for my expertise, no matter the situation, still carries weight. It's infuriating how much that matters to me, and I shove the thought aside, forcing my focus back to the task at hand.

By the time I finish, I realize I've completely lost myself in the conversation. Leaning back, I look toward Silas again, who is watching me with an intensity that sends tingles down to my fingertips. His dark eyes are focused, but there's something softer beneath them now, something that feels almost personal rather than professional. I don't know what to make of it, and I'm not sure that I want to.

"Let's move forward with this." Silas turns to Warren. "I want a full evaluation of the tools she mentioned."

Warren nods stiffly, his frustration thinly veiled as he collects his things and exits the room without another word. The door clicks shut behind him, punctuating his departure, and for a brief moment, the room falls silent. Silas's attention shifts fully to me as we both stand.

"That was impressive," he says after a beat as he extends a hand toward me. "Thank you for stepping in."

His grip firm and warm, his thumb brushing lightly against my knuckles. The gesture is subtle but enough to send a ripple of warmth through me as the faintest tug of a smile at the corner of his mouth.

"Is Davey too important to take these meetings, or does the future CEO always handle phishing scams?" I ask, my tone playful. I pull my hand back, watching him closely for a reaction. Amusement flickering across his face.

"Davey's tied up with a few high-priority projects for my father," he says with a casual shrug. "I jump in where I can."

My eyebrows raise. "I didn't think someone like you would take on something so... minor."

His posture shifts subtly, annoyance crossing his face for only a moment before he smooths it away. "There's no unimportant job. If it's worth doing, it's worth doing well."

The conviction in his voice surprises me. It's not the kind of canned response I'd expect from someone born into privilege. There's a weight to his words that resonates more than I'd like to admit.

"That's a refreshing perspective," I say, stepping back to put a little more space between us. "It's not something you often hear." I pause, offering him a small, polite smile. "I should get back to Natalie before she starts wondering if I've run off with her brother."

A flicker of heat ignites behind his stare and his tongue runs over his teeth, as if he's biting back a smirk.

"We can't have that now, can we?" Silas replies smoothly, though his eyes linger on me for a moment longer. "Where can I send the consulting bill?"

"Like I said earlier," I reply, waving him off lightly, "this one's on the house."

As I turn to leave, his voice stops me. "Careful, Scarlett. Giving things away for free could ruin your reputation."

I pause, glancing back over my shoulder. My smile doesn't quite reach my eyes. "Don't mistake generosity for habit, Mr. Wells. I know exactly what my time is worth."

His brows lift slightly, entertained but not surprised. Instead of pressing further, his smirk deepens, as if he's just uncovered something about me that he finds intriguing. It's maddening, and before he can say anything else, I turn on my heel and shut the door firmly behind me, the sound echoing through the quiet hallway.

I approach Natalie and Leslie, who both don't notice me until I'm almost in front of them. Natalie looks up from the paperwork she's sifting through, her eyes darting between me and the glass meeting room where she can see Silas packing up his things. Her expression is a mix of curiosity and something close to concern.

"Please tell me my brother didn't hold a meeting while you were in there," she says, her brows pulling together.

I smile, a polished, practiced thing that masks the whirlwind of thoughts swirling inside me. "I ended up giving him some advice on a program," I reply, clasping my hands in front of me. It's not exactly a lie, though it's far from the full story. "Do you need more time? I can find somewhere else to wait."

Natalie shakes her head quickly and glances at Leslie, who barely looks up from her screen as she nods in agreement. "No, we're done," Natalie says, her voice bright, though her gaze flicks back toward the meeting room. "Ready?"

"Yup," I say, adding a playful pop to the "p." It's a small, casual attempt to lighten the mood, but it feels hollow against the knot of tension sitting in my chest. I follow her to the elevators as I try to make sense of the jumble of thoughts fighting for my attention.

Natalie chats as we descend. She talks about the fundraiser's potential themes, sponsors, and logistics. She even mentions setting up more lunches together. I nod when appropriate, offer a few noncommittal responses, but my mind is elsewhere.

Because part of me is still in that room. With her brother.

Something about the way Silas's lips curved ever so slightly when I made that flippant comment about running off with him stays with me. It felt too deliberate, too calculated, like he wanted me to notice. I tell myself it doesn't matter, that it's meaningless in the grand scheme of things. But the tightening in my chest won't let me believe it.

I lean against the elevator wall, doing my best to look at ease while my thoughts churn. Natalie, oblivious, continues her stream of conversation, her voice filled with a kind of openness that only makes the guilt settle deeper.

And yet, here I am, playing the part like I always do.

By the time we're back in the car, I'm staring out the window, watching the city smear into a blur of gray and glass. Natalie fills the silence with new lunch spots we should try, and I do my best to stay present with her.

But in the back of my mind, a voice reminds me of something I'm not ready to admit: Silas Wells, for all his charm and striking looks, is a pompous ass I can't afford to get tangled up with. And yet, the thought of staying away feels like its own kind of challenge. One that will be difficult to resist.

Chapter 7

"**J**esus Christ, I'm coming," I grumble toward the front door from my bedroom, yanking a sweatshirt over my head. The pounding hasn't let up for the three minutes it's taken me to wake up and throw on something remotely acceptable to answer the door, which is a dead giveaway for who's on the other side.

The clock next to the entrance reads 7:53 AM, and I wince, already bracing for the noise complaint emails I'll inevitably get from the leasing office.

I kick out the door security bar and set it aside, then unlock the deadbolt and pull open the door. Sure enough, my brown eyes meet Harrison's blue ones. His blond hair is dark with rain, and his long coat drips water onto the hallway rug.

"You look like a wet rat," I say flatly, opening the door wider before turning away. He slips in, not even bothering to catch the door as it slams against the frame, rattling the entire room. I whip my head back toward him, my voice sharp. "I have neighbors, Harrison. I'd like to avoid getting evicted because you stomp around like an asshole every time you come by."

He ignores me entirely, peeling off his soaked trench coat and giving it a shake that sprays water onto the shoes I neatly arranged by the closet. With an infuriating grin, he flings the coat onto the catch-all table next to him, drenching everything underneath it. My fists clench inside the front pocket of my sweatshirt.

If I kill him, how long would it take for Peter to notice? I could make it look like an accident. Hell, I'd even shed a few fake tears if needed.

Harrison strides toward me with his usual overconfidence, standing so close that we're nearly nose-to-nose. It's always bothered him that I'm on the taller side and harder to intimidate.

The air around him reeks of stale coffee and cigarettes. Instantly, his hand shoots out, gripping my throat with just enough pressure to make breathing difficult. My body doesn't even have time to panic. I inhale through my nose, forcing his acrid scent further into my memory, and it takes everything in me not to gag.

"Shut the fuck up," he growls before shoving me to the side by my neck as he continues down the hall and into my living room. My shoulder takes the brunt of the impact as I collide with the wall, a sharp jolt of pain shooting down my arm.

"Aren't you in a pleasant mood this morning," I bite out, rolling my shoulder as it quickly turns into a warm, dull ache. Trailing behind him, I watch his black boots, still caked in mud and whatever filth he's picked up from the streets, leave a trail on my floors. "What do you want?"

He drops onto my couch like he owns the place, arms sprawling across the backrest. Today, he's wearing a worn blue flannel and jeans, and the bags under his eyes tell me he hasn't slept.

No wonder he's acting like such a peach.

On the down low, I've been trying to figure out why Harrison's still here. Peter never keeps two of us in the same city unless our jobs overlap, and even then, it's rare. He's obsessive about keeping his contractors siloed. Says it's to avoid complications, but we all know it's so we don't compare notes or accidentally screw up each other's work. Usually, we're left in the dark about who's working on what unless collaboration is absolutely necessary.

From what I've pieced together, Harrison's not working on anything to do with the Wells contract, which only raises more questions. Is he here to babysit me, or is there something bigger going on that Peter hasn't bothered to share? I can't tell, and it's making me itch to push him for answers, but with Harrison, that's like poking a bear just to see if it'll bite.

Still ignoring me, Harrison lifts his hips off the couch to reach into his back pocket. He pulls out his phone and, without a second thought, throws it in my direction. I snatch it out of the air just before it can hit the same shoulder he shoved into the wall.

"I need you to encrypt the email in my drafts and send it to Peter," he says casually, as if I'm his personal IT department.

I glare at him, gripping the phone tightly. "I taught you how to send encrypted emails years ago."

"Well, I forgot," he responds in a slow, condescending cadence, the kind you'd use with a particularly dense toddler. Fire ignites in the pit of my stomach, and it takes every ounce of willpower not to hurl the phone back at his face.

"Please tell me this is a recent problem, and you've been encrypting your other emails?" I bite out, the venom clear in my tone.

"Sure," he replies with a lazy wave of his hand, dismissing me and the concern like it's nothing.

This idiot will be the death of me—if not directly, then indirectly when Peter comes down on me for his incompetence. For reasons I'll never understand, Harrison is Peter's golden boy. If something goes wrong, Peter will blame me and my encryption methods long before he finds fault with his precious Harrison.

"You need to encrypt your emails, Harrison," I say, my voice sharp. "I'll do it for you this time, but I'm showing you how to do it again before you leave."

"Whatever you say, sweetheart," he sighs dramatically, inspecting his fingernails as if they're far more interesting than anything I could possibly have to say.

I drop into the chair across from him, already gritting my teeth. Unlocking his phone takes no effort. It doesn't even have a passcode. *Typical.* I clench the device in my hand, resisting the urge to throw it against the wall. Leaving our phones unsecured is criminally reckless. If he ever loses it, even the world's least competent hacker could access everything on it.

Pulling up his email app, I navigate to the draft he mentioned. It takes me all of thirty seconds to encrypt the message using a secure relay I've configured to reroute through encrypted servers. At least I can rest easy knowing *my* work won't be the weak link in this mess.

Still, my fingers twitch as I skim the message and the vaguely labeled attachments. As much as I'd love to open them and see what Harrison's been working on, I don't have the time or the tools to dig through them without raising suspicion. If I were feeling particularly bold, I could install spyware on his phone without him ever noticing. Harrison's so oblivious when it comes to tech that I could send him a fake system update, and he'd click the link without a second thought.

But that's a dangerous game. The bigger question is whether I even want to know what he's up to. And is it worth the risk of Peter finding out?

Before Harrison has a chance to ask why I'm still holding his phone, I toss it onto the empty seat next to him. "There," I say flatly. "It's sent."

Harrison smirks, lounging back on the couch like a man who doesn't have a care in the world. "Knew I could count on you."

For a brief, satisfying moment, I imagine Peter finding out exactly how reckless Harrison is. But just as quickly, I push the thought aside. Harrison screws up, and I'm the one who gets burned—that's the way it's always been.

Leaning back, I rub my eyes, trying to push back the exhaustion that's etched so deeply into my bones it feels permanent.

I've barely slept this week. Between combing through the Wells cloud during the day and expanding Scarlett Page's online footprint by night, my head feels like it's been shoved into a never-ending spin cycle. I was holding out hope for a breakthrough with the Wells data, and, in a way, I found one; a cluster of heavily encrypted files buried deep within their storage.

But these files are locked down tight. They're restricted to top-level executives, meaning only a handful of people even know they exist, let alone have access. On top of that, their system is fortified with every safeguard imaginable.

Trying to break into this remotely isn't just risky, it's borderline impossible. One mistake, and I could trip their alarms, get locked out, or worse, leave a trail that points directly to me. Davey Sinclair clearly knows his stuff. The files are protected by every trick he can throw at them, and without full access, I'm stuck playing a very dangerous waiting game on the outside.

"If that's all..." I trail off, dragging my fingers down my face, willing Harrison to finally leave and take his chaos with him.

"While I'm here," Harrison continues, blatantly ignoring my hint as he props his muddy boots on my coffee table. The sight of them scuffing my green-and-blue patterned rug makes my blood simmer, but I bite my tongue. "Did you get an invitation to that silent auction?"

The past three weeks have been filled with carefully placed social outings with Natalie woven between my other work—casual coffee runs when I conveniently "happened to be in her neighborhood," a last-minute yoga class, even an impromptu stop at a boutique opening where she needed a familiar face by her side. And it worked. Just two days ago, after a brisk winter walk through Lincoln Park, she handed me an invitation with a meek smile, which, of course, I accepted.

It didn't even feel like a chore. Not with Natalie. She's easy to be around, the kind of effortless company that makes blending in feel natural instead of calculated. And that's dangerous in its own way.

I exhale sharply, bracing myself for whatever ridiculous request he's about to make. "Yes. It's next Thursday."

"It's about time you do something useful for us," he says with a smile that makes my skin crawl. "While you're there, I want you to find the Wells kid's office. See if he's got any files stored there. Maybe a laptop you can access."

I lean forward, clasping my hands together as my palms start to sweat. Peter tried to push this idea on me earlier this week, and I had to remind him what kind of event this is. With so many of Chicago's elite in attendance, the security will be airtight, both literally and figuratively. Sneaking around a 12,000-square-foot mansion without being caught isn't just risky; it's suicidal.

"I'll do my best," I reply carefully, choosing my words with precision. "But I've already told Peter my concerns. I'm not going to risk everything on this one event."

Harrison rolls his eyes, standing as he tucks his phone back into his pocket. He's clearly not sticking around for me to give him another tutorial on encrypting emails. Leaning over me, his expression hardens. "I don't give a shit what you think. I want results."

The "or else" lingers heavily in the air as he stalks toward the door, not bothering to wait for a response. As he picks up his jacket, he knocks several items off the table. He slams the door shut behind him, the sound reverberating through the apartment. Only when the echo fades into silence do I sink back into the couch, my chest heavy.

The silence isn't comforting. My ears thrum with static, a constant noise that fills the void whenever I'm left alone with my thoughts. Pressing my fingers to my temples, I rub small circles, waiting for it to dull and for the familiar numbness to take its place. It's the only way I'll be able to focus on what comes next.

CHAPTER 8

J ust as the server sets a glass of sparkling water with lime in front of me, Silas walks into the upscale Indian restaurant two blocks from his office. He doesn't notice me as the hostess leads him to a table a few yards away. I straighten in my seat, forcing my attention back to my laptop screen.

While Davey might have Silas's corporate calendars locked down tight, he probably doesn't realize Leslie, Silas's assistant, has a glaring blind spot. Like a lot of support staff, Leslie takes shortcuts. Instead of relying solely on Silas's secured company calendar, she mirrors most of his daily events onto her personal one. My guess is that the multifactor authentication slows her down when she's juggling meetings or making last-minute changes. So, her "solution" is to update her personal calendar first and sync it to the company system later.

It took me less than ten minutes to breach her account. Once inside, I installed a persistent malware payload for ongoing access that's virtually undetectable.

Unfortunately for Silas, Leslie's shortcuts make her the weakest link in his meticulously guarded world. And fortunately for me, her lapse in judgment has given me a constant stream of updates about his work schedule, including today's one o'clock lunch with his Director of Production.

Silas's calendar events aren't what I'd expect. His lunch meetings are always booked with reservations set for thirty minutes before the actual meeting time, presumably so he can prepare. He's obsessively punctual, which is surprising for someone who's been handed everything on a platinum platter since day one.

After securing Leslie's account, I dug deeper, scanning her connected cloud storage and synced email accounts. It's mostly mundane: personal photos, irrelevant emails, and a handful of company documents that definitely shouldn't have been saved in her private files. Nothing earth-shattering, but I didn't stop there. I set up a crawler to comb her accounts for flagged keywords and tags Peter specifically instructed me to search for in Wells Corporation's cloud. The program runs weekly, silently monitoring any new uploads or updates.

So far, nothing substantial has surfaced. For now, the crawler hums along in the background, minimized in the corner of my laptop screen. It tracks and processes files with clinical precision, flagging anything remotely relevant.

While the program does its work, I shift focus back to my other tasks. By the time I'm done here, it'll have cycled through her entire account.

My gaze drifts back to the future CEO as he smiles politely at the hostess, his expression professional but approachable. He chooses a seat with a clear view of the front door, which also puts my table directly in his line of sight.

Perfect.

He places his briefcase neatly against the leg of his chair. I reach for the naan bread in the basket beside me, tearing off a piece and dipping it into the green chutney.

While he's sufficiently distracted, I allow myself to study him. He unbuttons his tailored suit jacket with practiced ease, smoothing a hand down the crisp fabric of his shirt and adjusting his tie. I'd half convinced myself that maybe I'd exaggerated his looks in my memory, but seeing him now only solidifies the fact that Silas Wells is unfairly attractive. The bastard even looks good under the overexposed restaurant lights.

Beneath his neatly trimmed stubble is a jawline that could have been carved from stone. His thick-framed glasses add a level of sophistication that almost feels criminal, and there's nothing awkward about his height.

While some men his size come off lanky or uncoordinated, Silas exudes power and control. Broad shoulders and lean muscle fill out his perfectly tailored shirt, and every movement is infused with the kind of confidence that only comes from knowing you're at the top of the food chain.

As breathtaking as he is, the thought of trailing this asshole around more than I already have irritates me. But it's necessary. I'm trying to piece together his routines, understand the rhythm of his life. I can't waltz into his office for a second time, so I have to watch him from the outside. Observe where he goes and whether it leads me closer to the information I need. Until now, I've done this unnoticed, keeping myself safely out of his awareness. But not today. Today, I want him to see me.

"Ma'am? Are you ready to order?"

I jolt, startled, and look up to find a waiter standing at my side, his notepad poised. My pulse quickens as I scramble to cover my slip, forcing a smile. I nod and point to my favorite vegetarian dish, rattling off the order. He acknowledges me with a polite nod and heads toward the back of the restaurant.

As I exhale, trying to steady my nerves, a strange sensation prickles at the back of my neck and the hairs on my arm rise in warning. Slowly, I glance up and find Silas's dark, penetrating eyes lock onto mine from across the room, holding me in place.

The corners of his mouth twitch upward, hinting at a smirk equal parts infuriating and dangerously charming. My breath catches for a fraction of a second and with all the nonchalance I can muster, I nod in his direction before returning to my laptop screen. My skin burns where his gaze lingers.

Exactly as I hoped.

The gesture seems to be invitation enough. Silas approaches my table with long, self-assured strides, his polished leather shoes barely making a sound on the restaurant's tiled floor. As he stops across from me, I discreetly dim my computer's brightness with a few quick keystrokes, pretending to focus on the page in front of me.

"Ms. Page," he begins in that vexing gravelly voice, one hand resting on the back of the chair in front of him, long fingers curling over its edge. "Twice in one week? If I didn't know any better, I'd think you were following me."

Gone is the more subtle, professional man I encountered in his office last week. The Silas standing in front of me now is sharper, bolder and, somehow, more exasperating.

"Careful," I reply, my voice dripping with saccharine sweetness. "Your neck might snap carrying the weight of your giant head." I rest my chin in my palm, elbow propped on the table, and flash him a practiced smile. My pulse flutters faintly beneath the finger pressed near my jaw, but I keep my tone even. "Have you ever had the Malai Kofta here? It's my favorite."

His smile widens, unapologetically amused. "Client meeting?" he asks, pointedly ignoring my question.

"No," I reply with ease, leaning back slightly. "Sometimes I like a change of scenery."

Without asking, he pulls the chair out and sinks into it, resting his elbows on the table and steepling his fingers in front of him. His espresso eyes gleam with something almost predatory, and he tilts his head just enough to give me the distinct impression I'm being sized up. "How's the view?" he asks, his voice low and teasing.

I huff out a laugh, rolling my eyes. "Getting worse by the second," I say dryly, opening a new browser tab in an attempt to look busy. There's something about this man who makes my brain short-circuit and my filter vanish. My usual charm has always been my greatest strength, but with him, my snarky attitude continues to slip through. A trait that most men have never found particularly appealing.

The worst part? He isn't the least bit deterred by it. His shoulders shake as he chuckles, his glasses sliding slightly down the bridge of his nose. He pushes them back up with one finger before fixing his gaze on me again.

"What types of clients do you work with?" he asks, his tone deceptively casual.

"That's confidential," I respond, meeting his eyes without hesitation.

"A woman of honor," he muses, his lips twitching into a small smirk.

"Spare me the fake flattery," I counter, though my voice is light.

"How long have you been in security?" he presses.

"A decade," I answer. The truth is a small reprieve from the web of lies I've been spinning.

"Ten years, huh? That makes you, what? Thirty-two?"

I arch an eyebrow, refusing to let him bait me. "Let's not pretend like Davey hasn't already looked into me. I'm thirty."

He leans back in his chair, fingers splayed across the table. "And scooped up by a Fortune 1000 company before you even finished school. That's really impressive," he says, repeating the fabricated story Davey undoubtedly unearthed in my carefully crafted background.

"What's *really* impressive is how you can make a compliment sound condescending," I shoot back, my voice sharp despite the smile I wear.

His posture shifts slightly, his playful expression giving way to something more sincere. "Do I sound condescending?" he asks, his tone almost thoughtful. "I'm being genuine. You're clearly very talented."

His words catch me off guard, and for the briefest of moments, I don't know how to respond. The sharp edges in his voice have softened, leaving behind a tone that almost sounds like respect. It's unnerving.

I pause, studying him for a moment before giving a brief nod in thanks. I may not be Scarlett Page, but her strengths and mine are one and the same. It's one of the few things I'm genuinely proud of, even if the circumstances of my life have twisted that pride into something bitter and sharp.

"So," Silas continues, his tongue brushing along the edge of his teeth in a way that feels frustratingly calculated. "Your turn to give me the third degree." His eyes lift to meet mine, but I'm a fraction too late to look away from his mouth. His grin deepens, smug and knowing, as if he's caught me in the act of something I shouldn't have been doing. My breath falters, but I quickly recover, raising an unimpressed brow.

"I already know everything I need to know about you," I say deadpan, crossing one leg over the other.

"Ah, so you've looked into me," he says, feigning surprise, though the slight smile betrays his amusement.

"I didn't say that," I reply, my own smirk tugging at the corners of my lips. A sharp, precise expression meant to bait him. "I've gathered plenty from the few times we've met. Enough, at least."

He clutches a hand to his chest like I've wounded him. "Ouch."

I roll my eyes and shift my focus back to the laptop, tapping a few keys to pull up the minimized browser tab running Leslie's account scan. Once again, nothing. Clean. Empty. The same result I've gotten for weeks.

Frustration churns beneath the surface as I stare at the results. Aside from a cluster of encrypted files on Wells server—an anomaly but not unusual for a company of this size—there's nothing. No signs of illegal activity, no breadcrumbs leading to whatever Peter is so eager to uncover. Silas is arrogant and insufferable, but he doesn't fit the mold of the targets I've gone after in the past. If anything, he's too polished and calculated.

Unable to stop myself, I decide to tug the tiger's tail. "Did you get stood up on a date?"

Silas doesn't miss a beat. He glances at his watch, revealing a sliver of the tattoo on his wrist beneath his tailored cuff. "My lunch meeting doesn't start for another seventeen minutes," he says casually.

"Anything interesting to discuss?" I press, dipping a piece of naan into the chutney and popping it into my mouth. He drums his fingers against the table, each tap as deliberate as his words.

"It's confidential," he says, his voice layered with mockery.

"Touché," I reply with a laugh, breaking off another piece of naan. Silas watches the movement, his gaze lingering on my lips with an intensity that heats my cheeks, betraying me despite my best efforts to stay composed.

Silas's expression shifts, his features relaxing while he looks at me with an air of quiet curiosity. It's not malicious or calculating, just...studying, as though he's trying to piece something together.

"Natalie seems to really like you," he says suddenly, his voice softer, yet still probing.

The statement lodges somewhere deep in my chest. For someone who's been burned more times than she can count, Natalie's willingness to let me in feels undeserved, and the realization stings. I clear my throat and reach for my drink to buy time.

"Good," I say finally, my voice steadier than I feel. At least this isn't a lie. "I really like her too."

Silas opens his mouth as though to respond, but the waiter arrives with my food, carefully setting the plate on the already crowded table. I thank him and move to shut down my laptop, sliding it into the leather slot of my bag near my feet. When I look up, I freeze.

My fork is in Silas's mouth, and half of one of the fried potato balls from my dish is gone.

For a moment, I can only stare. My mind trips over itself, the simmering guilt from earlier evaporating under the molten heat of outrage that spreads through me like wildfire. He doesn't flinch under my glare; if anything, he looks pleased with himself and my reaction, licking the fork with an exaggerated slowness that makes my blood boil.

"You're right," he says, his voice dropping low and rough, like we're sharing a secret. "The Malai Kofta *is* delicious."

Before I can form a coherent thought, he sets the fork down with deliberate care on the napkin next to the dish, winks, and rises from his seat with the ease of someone who knows exactly how much he's riled me up.

"Enjoy your meal," he tosses over his shoulder as he walks back to his table.

My fingers curl into fists at my sides as I watch him sit down, adjust his glasses, and pull a stack of files from his briefcase like nothing happened.

The upward tilt of his mouth makes me want to throw my drink at him, but I resist, though just barely.

I know exactly what this is. Silas is testing me, pressing at my edges to see if I'll crack, pushing just far enough to watch me bend but not break. Maybe he enjoys pushing boundaries, seeing how far people will go before they snap.

But that's not it, not entirely.

Women fall at his feet. I don't. And that bothers him. This isn't about my food—it's about control. About the fact that I refuse to give him the reactions he's used to.

I take a deep breath, counting to ten as I stare at my meal. But the anger refuses to dissipate. Even as I force myself to focus on eating after purposefully asking for a new fork, I can feel the air between us crackling with unspoken challenge.

When the bill comes, I reach for my wallet, only for the waiter to shake his head. "It's already been taken care of," he says, tilting his chin toward Silas's table.

I don't react. Not a thank you, not a protest—nothing. I simply gather my things, push my chair in, and walk out the door. I don't look in his direction. Not when I'm told, not when I stand, not even as I leave.

But I feel him watching me the entire way out.

Chapter 9

Peter: Learn something useful for once tonight, will you?

I glance up from Peter's text and out the window of the SUV I rented for the evening. The buildings around us transform as we turn onto a more residential stretch of North Side, each townhome more luxurious and meticulously maintained than the last. My tulle skirt shifts against the leather seat as the driver navigates the curved streets, and I grip the edge of the seat to steady myself.

Though I wasn't lying to Harrison when I told him Peter understood why I couldn't just strut into Silas Wells's mansion and start snooping, that understanding didn't last long. Less than two hours after Harrison's visit, Peter called. His temper burned through the phone, demanding results, insisting I *something* at the party. I still don't understand how Harrison holds sway over a man like Peter, but the pressure is suffocating.

Chewing on the inside of my lip, I text back.

Me: I'll do my best.

After sending it, I delete the messages and slip my phone into the handbag tucked neatly in my lap. Inside is the bare minimum: lipstick, my apartment keys, a wallet, and, disappointingly, no concealed blade. I know better than to try sneaking anything sharp into a party that will undoubtedly have security scouring every pocket and lining.

As the SUV slows to a crawl, the traffic ahead grows heavier. Through the windshield, I catch glimpses of luxury cars lining the street, their blinkers flashing as they wait to approach the grand estate. Staff dressed in sleek black uniforms move in synchronized motions, opening car doors for guests draped in designer gowns and tailored suits.

Straightening my back, I take a deep breath, running through the finer details of Scarlett Page's life in my mind. The fake name and identity feel like a second skin now, but even second skins can slip when the stakes are high. Tonight, I can't afford that.

"Ma'am," Keith, the driver I hired for the evening, speaks up, looking at me through the rearview mirror. "I have it on the calendar that you'd like to be picked up at ten o'clock. Does that still work?"

"Yes, ten's perfect. Thank you," I reply, offering him a small smile. He nods and turns his attention back to the road.

After a few minutes, the SUV glides up to the front of the mansion. Resisting the instinct to let myself out, I wait as one of the uniformed staff opens my door and extends a hand. I take it gracefully, stepping onto the sidewalk and feeling the sharp winter air bite through my coat. Wrapping it tighter around myself, I glance up at the estate.

Though several skyscrapers tower around it, this three-story detached home feels like a relic of a bygone era, stubbornly refusing to yield to the modern city. Every carved detail of the stone facade has been painstakingly preserved, a testament to the wealth required to maintain such beauty. Its presence alone commands respect, and I can't help but marvel for a moment.

The wind cuts through my thoughts, and I force my legs to move. As I approach the entrance, a woman bundled in a thick coat and scarf greets me with a clipboard. Her nose is red, and she shuffles from foot to foot in order to keep warm. I hand her my ID, which she studies twice, her brows knitting briefly before she nods.

"Enjoy the auction," she says, motioning toward the door with her chin.

"Thank you," I reply, climbing the stone stairs. A soft hum of voices grows louder as I near the entrance, the warmth of the party beckoning me inside. My eyes catch on the couple ahead of me; a woman in an elegant gown with a glittering neckline turns slightly, glancing at me. Faith Desmont. Her husband, Gary, stands tall beside her, his hand resting protectively on her back. They're the power couple behind one of Chicago's largest real estate investment firms.

I school my features into polite neutrality, ensuring my expression matches the carefully curated refinement of my surroundings. Faith offers me a tight smile, and I respond with one of my own, knowing full well that every interaction tonight, no matter how small, is part of the game.

"Ms. Page," Faith greets me, her voice clipped. She's as stunning as ever, a middle-aged woman with sleek light-brown hair and flawless fair skin. Faith tolerates me out of necessity, though her solidarity with her less fortunate friends, whose husbands have a tendency to flirt with me, keeps her demeanor frosty. "It's nice to see you."

"Good to see you again, Faith," I reply, adding just a hint of sincerity. My gaze shifts to her husband as he turns toward me. "Gary."

"Scarlett, lovely to see you," Gary says, his tone noticeably friendlier. The edges of my smile soften ever so slightly in response. In a room full of people who've made a sport of writing me off for months, Gary's affable nature is oddly comforting.

The line moves steadily, and over the heads of a few guests in front of us, I see the security station; a guard with a handheld metal detector scanning each attendee before they hand off their coats at the nearby check. It's efficient, but the slow pace gives Faith plenty of time to size me up.

"I didn't realize you'd be here tonight," she remarks, her tone carefully indifferent. "How do you know the Wells family?"

"I've recently become friends with Natalie," I answer, maintaining eye contact. "She insisted I come."

"Ah, yes. Natalie is a sweet girl," Gary interjects, nodding earnestly. "I'm glad to see you making friends. I was starting to worry all the husbands would scare you off before you could."

Faith's gaze snaps to her husband, eyes narrowing as though he's just said something he shouldn't have. It's a futile attempt to disguise what I already know all too well: my presence in this circle comes with a reputation I didn't ask for and certainly don't deserve. I've ignored the men's inappropriate remarks in the past, thinking it would discourage them without casting myself. Instead, it only fueled their boldness, and now it's become part of my identity here. One I despise.

I lift my chin and square my shoulders, refusing to let the moment linger. "Yes," I say evenly, my voice cool but firm. "I'm glad to have made a friend, too."

Thankfully, the conversation cuts off as we step over the threshold of the open front door. Faith's fur-lined coat slips off her shoulders to reveal an emerald gown that complements her features, while Gary looks every bit the dashing partner in his perfectly tailored dark suit.

When it's my turn, I hand over my coat and bag before stepping up to the security station. I hold my arms out as the guard sweeps the wand over my body, the steady hum of chatter from other guests filling the grand entryway. Despite the distraction, I take a moment to absorb the scene. White marble floors stretch across the expansive space, blending seamlessly into pristine white walls adorned with subtle yet intricate wood details. A curved staircase behind the temporary coat check draws the eye, its wrought-iron railing an elegant masterpiece. This home is every bit as spectacular as I imagined, a testament to the Wells family's wealth and influence.

Searching through this mansion—three stories, possibly four if I can manage to get to the basement—will be next to impossible. My frustration simmers as I recall the hours I spent hunting for blueprints online. Davey Sinclair's meticulous efforts to scrub any updated specs from public records have paid off, leaving me with only a decade-old floor plan that's largely irrelevant after Silas's extensive renovations a few summers back. The remodel was splashed across every local newspaper at the time, celebrated as a reflection of his "timeless" taste. Conveniently, none of those articles included details about the new layout.

The Desmonts move past me, nodding a polite farewell as they make their way into the adjacent room where most of the guests are gathering. After handing off my coat and tucking the ticket into my handbag, I follow suit, stepping into what appears to be a large reception area. Like magic, a server materializes at my side, balancing a silver tray laden with full champagne flutes. His timing is impeccable, as is his silent offering.

With a smile and a quiet thank-you, I pluck a flute from the tray with practiced grace. As I continue into the room, the sparkling drink in hand, I let my gaze sweep over the guests. Conversation swirls around me, mingling with the soft clinking of glasses and the faint strains of a live quartet tucked into a corner. This is a world of carefully curated opulence, where every glance, every word, and every move is a calculated performance.

I'm standing in what, I assume, is typically a formal dining room, now transformed for the evening's event. The chandelier has been pinned closer to the ceiling, and the grand dining table has been replaced by small cocktail tables, each draped in crisp white linens. There's more than enough room for a sleek bar, its robust marble countertop blending seamlessly with the home's elegant design, though it doesn't seem to be a permanent fixture. The dark, wood-paneled walls, adorned with perfectly centered sconces, lend the massive room an unexpected sense of warmth and intimacy.

Straight ahead, a cased opening leads into a formal living room where guests perch delicately on leather sofas, their conversations weaving into the soft hum of the party. To my right, through another wide doorway, lies a lavish charcuterie display spanning multiple tables draped in pristine white linens, an impressive spread that commands the attention of anyone passing by.

In the heart of the dining room, a set of French doors opens onto a fully enclosed courtyard. The small outdoor space is framed by three walls, each adorned with matching French doors leading to the other adjoining rooms. The fourth wall is a backdrop of aged stone draped in browned vines that likely bloom with vibrant colors in the summer months. Even amidst Silas's extensive renovations, it's clear he preserved the home's original European-inspired charm, a testament to his appreciation for classic elegance.

As I make my first sweep of the room, there isn't a Wells family member to be found. Not a single sibling, nor their enigmatic father, is in sight, which strikes me as odd. This annual auction is one of their most publicized and important family events, always a united front to raise money for a handpicked local nonprofit. This year, the beneficiary is an organization dedicated to helping lower-income families secure affordable housing. A cause they will no doubt broadcast as proof of their benevolence.

With none of the Wells family present, I straighten my posture and begin my rounds. For the next forty minutes, I engage in polite small talk with a handful of women who seem to tolerate my presence, fend off two advances from men who clearly haven't gotten the memo from Natalie to steer clear of me, and flag down a staff member for a second drink after draining my first a little quicker than I intended.

On my second pass through the interconnected spaces surrounding the courtyard, something new catches my attention: a small sign, neatly propped on an easel positioned deeper within the room with the charcuterie tables, standing beside a doorway that seems to lead further into the house.

SILENT AUCTION
BIDDING CLOSES AT 9:00 PM

Following the arrow on the sign, I find myself in a slightly quieter room—still massive, but smaller in comparison to the grand spaces I've just passed through. It offers a momentary reprieve from the noise of the main event. A handful of guests wander between the tables, examining the displayed auction items. Each table is carefully arranged, with every item accompanied by a small card featuring a QR code for mobile bidding. The prizes are as extravagant as expected: five-star resort stays in tropical destinations, exclusive dining experiences, private yacht charters, and stunning artwork curated by local artists.

I stop in front of a package for an all-inclusive spa experience at one of the city's most beloved luxury hotels. After a moment of consideration, I place a moderate bid, one I know will easily be outdone before the night is over. I do the same for a few more items, feigning interest but ensuring my bids are just high enough to appear engaged without actually winning anything. My goal isn't to leave with a prize, it's to be seen participating, another layer to the carefully crafted persona I've been building since I arrived in Chicago.

On a separate table, set apart from the auction items, is a QR code for direct donations. Without hesitation, I scan it and make a contribution. I could never ignore organizations focused on low-income housing. At one point, a program like this could have changed everything for me and my best friend, Drew, when we were struggling to get through school.

The sharp ache in my chest flares as her name crosses my mind, the familiar burn filling my lungs. I wish she were here with me now. She'd laugh at the absurdity of it all and tell me that this world I've stepped into is straight out of one of her beloved romance novels. But this isn't a romance novel. No hero is coming to save me. In this reality, the only person who can fix anything—who can save me—*is* me, and most days, I'm not even sure I know what the hell I'm doing.

I inhale deeply, the breath trembling as it fills my chest. With effort, I exhale, forcing the memories and guilt back into the dark corners of my mind where they belong. It's a routine I've perfected, though it never gets easier.

On the same table, I spot a stack of reading material about the nonprofit, New Beginnings Housing Project. The organization's mission is outlined on a glossy pamphlet, and I carefully fold one to tuck into my handbag. It's a small token to remind myself of the cause, one I genuinely support, even if my presence here tonight has little to do with charity. Abandoning my empty champagne flute on a collapsible serving tray in the corner, I glance around the auction room. It's eerily quiet now, the lull of early evening leaving the space deserted. With the frenzy of last-minute bids still hours away, the solitude offers a moment to reassess.

I take in my surroundings again. The room, with its dimmed lighting and soft instrumental music humming through speakers, feels refined yet intimate. A baby grand piano is tucked into one corner, its black lacquered surface gleaming softly in the low light. Judging by the setup, this must be some type of music room.

My gaze shifts to the left, where an open doorway reveals a dark hallway. Likely a staff corridor used to discreetly clear away empty glasses and plates. At the opposite end of the hallway, I spot a wood-paneled staircase, faintly illuminated by a light I can't see from here.

With one final glance around the auction room, ensuring no one is watching, I slip through the doorway and into the hallway, my heels whispering against the polished floor. I stay light on the balls of my feet, hyperaware of the sound of every movement as the noise of the party fades behind me.

I don't bother peeking into the few doors I pass along the corridor. Silas Wells isn't careless enough to leave anything important or incriminating in the main living areas of his home. If there's something to find, it won't be here. My focus narrows on the staircase ahead.

At the base of the stairs, I pause briefly, gripping the smooth wood railing with one hand and lifting the hem of my dress with the other. Moving with intention is critical. If I'm caught, confidence will be my armor. The trick to convincing people you belong somewhere is to act like you do, like it's obvious you're undoubtedly where you're supposed to be.

I bound up the stairs quickly but carefully, my grip tightening on the railing. The polished wood feels cool beneath my fingers, and the staircase turns midway at a landing before continuing in the opposite direction.

When I reach the top, I find myself in a tucked-away corner. It's quiet. On one side, there are two closed doorways, and on the other, the hallway veers sharply to the left, disappearing from view. I take a moment to collect myself, heart pounding in my chest, before deciding where to start.

I peek into the two darkened rooms. One turns out to be an immaculately decorated bathroom, its marble countertops and gold fixtures gleaming under soft recessed lighting. The other is a comically oversized laundry room, complete with multiple industrial-grade washers and dryers, folding tables, and cabinets that likely hold everything from linens to uniforms. It doesn't surprise me that a billionaire like Silas Wells would have an entire house staff, but who on earth needs this many washers and dryers? I shake my head, quietly marveling at the excess.

The silence on this floor is unsettling, but I've already come this far. If there's anything worth finding in this maze of a house, it won't be on the first floor with the guests. I straighten my back, lift my chin, and round the corner of the hallway. Confidence is my best weapon, but before I complete the turn, I collide headfirst into what feels like a brick wall.

With a startled gasp, I stumble back, my hand shooting out to steady myself. Before I can regain my footing, a firm hand clamps onto my elbow, keeping me upright. My heart leaps into my throat as the world rights itself, and I lift my eyes to meet warm, honey-colored ones set in a familiar face.

Cillian. The head of Silas's personal security team.

Well, shit.

The towering man dressed in black radiates authority. His dark blond hair is neatly combed, and the veins in his neck flex as his sharp gaze locks onto mine. He keeps a firm hold on my elbow—not painful, though the tension in his jaw suggests he's moments away from hauling me back down the stairs and out the front door.

"What are you doing up here?" His eyebrows draw together, his expression tight with suspicion. "This floor is off-limits to guests."

My heartbeat pounds in my ears, and I silently pray the heat creeping up my neck isn't visible. His clean-shaven face only emphasizes the muscle working in his jaw as he scrutinizes me.

"I'm sorry," I breathe out, channeling every ounce of startled innocence I can muster. I widen my eyes slightly, as if caught off guard by the accusation. "I'm Natalie's guest, and Faith Desmont mentioned she might be upstairs, so I came to look for her."

Cillian's gaze narrows, scanning me from head to toe with a practiced, critical eye. His posture doesn't relax, and neither does his grip on my arm. I shift my weight from one leg to the other under his examination, feeling the walls of this brilliant plan closing in on me.

This was a terrible idea. I should've trusted my instincts and stuck to my original plan of ingratiating myself into their inner circle, slow and steady. But no. Peter and Harrison had to push, and now I'm caught red-fucking-handed by Silas's most loyal guard dog.

"You're right," I continue quickly, breaking the tense silence. His eyebrows lift slightly in surprise at my admission. "I shouldn't have wandered so far. I'll head back downstairs and see if I missed her."

I begin to pull my arm back, but Cillian doesn't let go immediately. Just as he opens his mouth to respond, another voice—low, smooth, and unmistakably familiar—filters through the hallway behind him.

"Sneaking around my home, Ms. Page?"

My blood runs cold.

The bodyguard steps aside, revealing Silas in all his irritating glory. Hands stuffed casually into the pockets of his tailored dark gray slacks, he looks as though he's just stepped off the cover of a luxury lifestyle magazine. Despite this being the Wells family's most high-profile event of the year, he's traded a suit for a fitted, ribbed black sweater with a slight V-neck that reveals the curve of his collarbone. The sleeves are pushed back to the middle of his forearms, exposing part of that elusive tattoo I've been wanting a closer look at.

The dim light of the hallway plays tricks with the sharp lines of his face, making the faint smirk tugging at the corner of his mouth appear both amused and dangerous. His dark eyes, framed by those perpetually slipping glasses, glint with a curiosity that feels far too intrusive. One look at him, and I know the excuse I fed Cillian won't hold water here. Silas isn't buying it for a second.

This was an *absolutely* terrible idea.

"Now, what could you be doing up here?" His voice is laced with mock curiosity, though the slight tilt of his head betrays his sharp edge. The weight of his stare sends a shiver down my spine, and I swallow hard, forcing down the panic clawing at the edges of my composure.

"Hi, Silas," I start, my voice a shade too bright, ignoring the questions entirely. "Do you know where Natalie is? I was told she might be up here."

He lets the silence hang for a beat too long, his brows drawing together ever so slightly, as if he's trying to decide just how much of my nonsense he's willing to entertain. When he speaks, his tone is softer but no less cutting. "The blocked-off main stairwell wasn't enough of a hint that I didn't want guests up here?"

My jaw tightens as his glasses slide down the bridge of his nose, a movement that adds to my growing frustration. "After you helped yourself to my lunch, I figured I might be more than just another guest," I snap before I can stop myself. The words hang between us, bold and reckless, and I immediately regret them. My chest tightens as I rush to reel it back in. "The door to the back stairwell in the auction area was open. I hadn't seen her, but you're right. I shouldn't have come up here. I just wanted to make sure she was okay."

Silas watches me for a moment longer than I'd like, his gaze flicking over my face, searching for cracks in my story. Then, with an almost imperceptible sigh, he adjusts his glasses with one hand, the muscles in his jaw flexing as if he's holding back whatever sharp comment sits on the tip of his tongue.

"How... thoughtful of you," he says finally, though his tone is unreadable. Breaking eye contact, he shifts his attention to Cillian, who remains uncomfortably close, his chest brushing against my shoulder every time he exhales.

"She's fine, Cil. I'll bring her to Natalie," Silas says, his tone firm and dismissive.

The words hit me like a bucket of cold water. *She's fine.* I release a breath I hadn't realized I was holding. Silas doesn't see me as a threat—not right now, anyway. In any other situation, I might be offended that he thinks so little of me, but I'll take whatever small mercies I can get. I certainly didn't have a plan for what I'd do if I were caught snooping through his private rooms.

"I'm going to shut the door to the music room to keep other guests from getting ideas," Cillian says, his tone deliberately casual, though the insult lands with precision.

I whip my head toward him, catching his sarcastic smile as he turns to leave. "Charming," I mutter under my breath, glaring at his retreating form.

"He's not wrong," Silas chimes in, drawing my attention back to him. He's leaning lazily against the wall now, one shoulder propped against it and ankles crossed like he owns the place—which, of course, he does. The taut fabric of his sweater stretches over his arms, hinting at the strength beneath his lean frame. His gaze sweeps over me, lingering for a moment too long on the bodice of my muted green dress that flares out to a tulle skirt with subtle volume. His previously guarded expression softens into something warmer, though no less intense. "That color suits you."

Heat rushes through me, sparking at my fingertips and spreading across my skin. My hand instinctively smooths the fabric over my stomach as I try to ground myself. The silence between us thickens, the dim lighting and muted green walls amplifying the sudden intimacy of the moment.

"Complimenting me doesn't make up for the insults," I retort, narrowing my eyes. The corner of his mouth twitches into a devilish smirk that has no business looking as good as it does.

He straightens, pushing off the wall with an easy grace, and gestures for me to follow him. "We usually join the party an hour or so after it starts, but I'll make an exception and bring you to my study."

An exception? Like he's being generous?

My teeth clench as I place a hand dramatically over my heart. "How will I ever repay you?" I say, batting my eyelashes in mock gratitude.

He glances back at me, one brow arching in amusement. "You just can't help yourself, can you?"

"I'm not sure what you're talking about," I reply with a sugary smile that does nothing to hide my sarcasm. He shakes his head once, muttering something under his breath that sounds suspiciously like, "That mouth," before turning away.

And despite myself, my pulse quickens, unsure whether I want to laugh or throttle him. Or maybe both.

We pass several doors as we move through the dimly lit hallway, each one open just enough to reveal shadows of neatly made beds and elegant furniture. The soft glow filtering in from the hall lights highlights the polished wood and understated luxury of Silas's home. The muted hum of the party grows louder as we near the main staircase. My fingers trail along the banister. With the curved design of the stairs, there's no direct view of the festivities, but the faint laughter and clinking glasses carry enough ambiance to remind me of the high-stakes event happening just a floor beneath us.

A small sense of victory simmers in my chest. Not only am I in Silas Wells's home—an accomplishment in itself—but I'm about to step into a private setting with his family. It's a small win, one step closer to completing this job and, with any luck, convincing Peter to finally walk away from all of this.

I keep a measured distance behind Silas, studying him in his element. He moves with a kind of effortless confidence that feels innate, not learned. His posture is relaxed but purposeful, his steps unhurried yet methodical. It's the kind of presence that commands attention without trying, as if the world instinctively rearranges itself to accommodate him.

We round a second corner, and Silas approaches a closed door on the right. His fingers curl around the handle, and he pushes it open with ease. Turning slightly, he motions for me to go first, a subtle curl of his fingers accompanying the gesture. I lift an eyebrow, surprised by the act of courtesy. Maybe, just maybe, there's a sliver of decency buried deep in there.

The room is dimmer than the hallway, and I blink a few times to adjust to the change in lighting. Just as my eyes start to focus, Silas's voice cuts through the silence, smooth and amused. "Nat, you'll never guess who I caught snooping near the back staircase."

My head snaps toward him as he walks past me, my fists clenching at his audacity. His smirk deepens when our eyes meet, and the infuriating glint in his gaze makes my blood simmer.

God, he's unbearable.

"And I'm the one who can't help myself?" I shoot back, my voice low and biting. He brushes past me to lean casually against the dark mahogany desk in the center, the picture of unbothered arrogance. His laptop sits closed behind him, partially obscured by his frame. One hand grips the edge of the desk while the other picks up what must be his abandoned drink. He takes a slow sip, eyes never leaving mine, as if daring me to continue.

For someone who's supposed to be a professional, I find myself dangerously close to memorizing every detail about him. His strong arms stretching against the fabric of his sweater, the way his dark stubble accentuates the sharp lines of his jaw, and how damn good he looks with the backdrop of floor-to-ceiling bookshelves framing him.

Before I can spiral further into frustration, Natalie's voice breaks through the tension. "Silas, do you always have to be an ass?"

She's perched on the arm of a leather sofa against the wall, her nose scrunching in a way that somehow makes her look both annoyed and endearing. An intricate crystal glass dangles delicately from her fingers, its clear liquor catching the low light. Beside her, Davey lounges on the cushion, his arm resting protectively on her lower back. His eyes are locked on me, scrutinizing my every move as though I might bite if spooked.

Natalie uncrosses her legs and stands, her luxurious French blue velvet dress hugging her curves like it was made just for her. "Scarlett," she says warmly, closing the distance between us with a radiant smile. Before I can react, she pulls me into a hug.

My body stiffens, unprepared for the physical contact. Her embrace is soft, genuine, and uncomplicated—the kind of hug you give someone you're genuinely happy to see. My arms hover awkwardly for a moment before I force myself to loosely return the gesture.

Natalie's kindness, her effortless warmth, feels like a blade against my ribs. I don't deserve it. She's offering me something I haven't earned, and the weight of that realization settles like lead in my chest. It's been years since I've hugged someone I care about, and the loneliness of that truth presses against my lungs, making it difficult to breathe.

"Hi, Natalie," I manage, my voice hoarse. I blink rapidly, pushing back the sting of tears before she pulls away, her hand lingering briefly on my arm. "Sorry to interrupt. I didn't see you downstairs, so I wanted to make sure everything was okay."

She glances toward Silas as she answers, though I keep my gaze firmly on her. "What a perfectly reasonable and nice thing for a friend to do for me." Her tone carries a subtle dig at her brother, but her sincerity is still clear. She pats my arm lightly, a reassuring gesture. "I should've told you we have a little tradition of being fashionably late to our own party."

"We do like to make a dramatic entrance," a new voice chimes in from my left.

I don't have to turn to know who it is. The final Wells sibling steps into view, standing shoulder-to-shoulder with his sister. She drops her hand from my arm and takes half a step back, making space for him. Jeremy Wells, the youngest of the three siblings.

Compared to his older brother, Jeremy is shorter and more solidly built. While Silas is all sharp angles and lean strength, Jeremy's frame carries a sturdiness that sets him apart. The similarities among the Wells siblings, however, are unmistakable: upturned eyes, olive skin, and the kind of dark hair that always looks freshly styled. But where Natalie and Silas have strikingly defined cheekbones and chiseled jawlines, Jeremy's features are softer like their father's. He lacks the almost predatory elegance his siblings exude, yet there's no denying the Wells genes run strong. Jeremy is attractive in his own way, though his corporate appearance—short hair, clean-shaven face, and rigid posture—suggests someone trying to compensate for something.

And that "something" is well-documented.

Jeremy might have the longest dossier of all his family. When he was just eighteen, he was expelled from the same elite boarding school Silas graduated from. The reason? A freshman football hazing incident so brutal it made national headlines. Though the specifics were carefully obscured, no doubt thanks to the Wells patriarch's influence, what little leaked to the press was damning. A younger student had been beaten so severely that he was placed in a medically induced coma. Unsurprisingly, the hospital records were curiously incomplete, and the family must have paid a hefty price to ensure they stayed that way.

He and three other seniors, all legal adults, pled guilty to several charges, including second-degree assault. Their wealth and influence spared them prison, but it didn't spare Jeremy's reputation. He was sentenced to community service and mandatory therapy, a slap on the wrist considering the damage done. The victim, meanwhile, took months to recover and had to repeat a grade. The Wells family footed the bill for his boarding school and college education, likely an attempt at reparations. Or damage control.

The scandal followed Jeremy, making him radioactive in the world of prep schools. He bounced from one to the next, expelled for smaller infractions that the schools refused to overlook given his record. By the time he scraped together a diploma from a third-rate institution, it was clear most people were eager to wash their hands of him.

Adulthood didn't go much better. Jeremy became a walking stereotype: a rich kid with unlimited access to drugs and alcohol. His college career barely lasted two years before he dropped out. By his twenty-one, he was addicted to opioids, spiraling deeper until even his family's vast fortune couldn't hide the cracks. His father cut him off, hoping it would scare him into sobriety. Instead, Jeremy burned bridges and his inheritance in equal measure.

When it became clear he wouldn't stop on his own, Silas and their father intervened. They convinced him to check into a live-in rehab facility, footing the bill for his long and expensive recovery. Jeremy eventually got clean, and the family's PR machine spun his redemption story into gold. Now, he's the poster child for overcoming adversity. Magazines praise him for turning his life around, he's been the face of several national sobriety campaigns, and the public sees him as proof that anyone—with enough resources and money—can change.

"Scarlett, this is my brother, Jeremy," Natalie introduces him with a strained politeness that doesn't quite mask her discomfort. I tuck the observation into the growing folder of mental notes I've compiled on this family.

I extend my hand toward Jeremy, watching him carefully. His smile is practiced, all teeth and surface-level charm, as he takes my hand. But instead of shaking it, he brings my fingers to his lips, letting them linger a beat too long. The gesture would be chivalrous if it didn't feel so robotic.

Up close, I notice his eyes. They're the same deep brown as Silas's, but that's where the similarities end. Silas's gaze is sharp, teasing, and occasionally disarming.

But Jeremy's? I can't detect any true emotion behind them at all.

CHAPTER 10

The alarm bells in my brain ring louder, reverberating through every corner of my mind. Jeremy Wells is calculated. His demeanor, his tone, the way he carries himself. It's all by design. To the casual observer, he's the very embodiment of the success story the magazines claim. But it's his eyes that betray him. They're too empty, too hollow.

Something's just *off*.

"A pleasure, Scarlett," Jeremy says, his voice oozing charm. "Where has my sister been hiding you?"

I pull my hand back with careful precision, schooling my features into a courteous smile. My instincts tell me that Jeremy's the kind of man who doesn't take rejection lightly. I shift my handbag in front of me, holding it with both hands to make a subtle barrier between us. If he notices the move, he doesn't show it.

"We're new friends," I reply, keeping my tone cordial but distant. "It's nice to meet you, too."

Natalie takes a step closer, quietly positioning herself between her brother and me. Jeremy glances at her from the corner of his eye, his lips twitching as if he's just won some unspoken game. The tension between them is sharp. Hoping to diffuse the subtle hostility strung taut between the two of them, I offer a hello to Davey over Natalie's shoulder. His response is a curt nod, his eyes lingering on me like I'm a puzzle he's still deciding if he wants to solve.

The silence stretches uncomfortably before Natalie clears her throat, forcing a smile. "My father had to take a call in one of the guest rooms, so we'll meet him at the top of the stairs. Do you want to have a quick drink before we head down? It'll only be a few minutes."

Before I can respond, a glass of clear liquid appears between us, and Silas's presence pulses beside me like a live current. His chest brushes my shoulder lightly, the faint scent of cedarwood and something warm surrounding him. Both Natalie and I glance up as he offers the drink, his mischievous brown eyes darting between us.

"If you're going to walk down with us, you'll need it." He shrugs.

My pulse skips. The implications of entering the party alongside the Wells family hit me like a wave. This would set a precedent I'm not sure if I can afford to establish, and my mind scrambles to calculate the potential fallout. My voice comes out an octave too high, betraying my unease. "I'll go down ahead of you all. Or maybe I'll take the back staircase again."

Silas raises an eyebrow. "And draw attention to the hallway no one is supposed to be using?" His lips twitch with suppressed amusement. "Guests are expecting us any minute. You wouldn't want them thinking you were sneaking around my house. Or worse, sneaking off for a little rendezvous with one of us. Would you?"

My mind stumbles over the images they conjure, soliciting two opposite reactions I don't want to think too much about.

"A rendezvous? What are we, in a Shakespearean play?" I fire back, narrowing my eyes. My quick retort is a desperate attempt to deflect, but Silas doesn't miss a beat.

"It's French," he counters, his smirk widening. "16th century, if we're being precise."

I roll my eyes, annoyed by his impeccable timing and his ability to make even etymology sound arrogant. "Does Merriam-Webster pay you commission?"

The sparks between us flare brighter as his smirk deepens. Before he can retract his offer, I reach for the glass. His fingers brush mine as I take it, and the feel of his skin sends a cascade of heat rippling through me. He doesn't let go immediately, lingering just long enough to feel purposeful. When he finally does, his fingers slide against mine in a way that makes my skin erupt with goosebumps.

I keep my eyes fixed on the drink, refusing to meet his gaze. Natalie raises her own nearly empty glass in a silent toast, and I follow suit, needing the liquid courage more than I care to admit.

"Down the hatch," I mutter, draining the drink in one long swallow. The burn ignites at the back of my throat, spreading like fire to my stomach. It's smoother than most, but vodka has never been my drink of choice, and I grimace slightly as I force it down.

When the stinging subsides, I suck on one of the ice cubes to dull the aftertaste, holding it between my lips. Once the sting begins to soothe, and I open my eyes, I immediately notice that Silas hasn't moved an inch. If anything, he might be leaning in closer; his chest pressing more firmly against my shoulder when I shift.

His jaw is tight, but it's his eyes that freeze me in place. They're darker than before, molten and intense as they lock onto my lips. For a brief, dizzying moment, I can't move, can't think, can't do anything but feel the slow, deliberate path of his attention.

And then, just as suddenly as it started, the moment snaps. Natalie's voice cuts through the air as she speaks to Davey, and I tear my eyes away from Silas, blinking rapidly to clear the haze. But the heat he's left in his wake lingers, pooling low in my stomach and making it impossible to forget just how close he remains.

"You know what? I'll escort you downstairs," Silas announces, his tone equal parts confident and casual, like he's doing me a favor I never asked for. I roll my lips between my teeth, feeling the last remnants of the ice cube melt completely on my tongue, and hold back the sharp retort that rises.

Letting people think there's something more between us could be socially isolating in these circles. It would paint a target on my back, making me a topic of whispered conversations and envious glances. I need to get closer to the Wells family, but not like *that*. And it doesn't help knowing he's only saying it to get a rise out of me.

"That would give the impression that I'm your date," I say carefully, my voice even.

"It would," Silas agrees, his tongue grazing his bottom lip in that infuriatingly deliberate way. His dark eyes flick up to meet mine, glinting with amusement as he begins to straighten the sleeves he had rolled up. "I'm not in the business of caring what anyone down there thinks, but I suppose you're right."

"Good." I nod, relieved that, for once, we're on the same page. His fingers pause mid-roll on his sleeve, and his lips curl into that signature smirk that makes my pulse tick faster than I'd like.

"So," he drawls, "would you prefer to walk on my left or my right?"

My head snaps up, neck going ramrod straight. "Come again?"

His smirk widens as he runs a hand over his stubble, clearly enjoying himself. "I don't have a date, and as the host of this event, I probably should. Plus, it'll look odd if you walk down with our family without someone by your side."

"Leave her alone, Si," Natalie interjects, waving him off with a hand as if dismissing his antics entirely. "She can do whatever she'd like."

Davey, who's been silent this whole time, stands and adjusts his suit jacket. His bored expression doesn't waver as he leans toward his wife and murmurs something I can't quite catch.

The instinct to agree with Natalie dies on my tongue. Refusing Silas outright could backfire in more ways than one. He might tell me to leave, or worse, hand me over to Jeremy. And, admittedly, there's a strategic advantage to this arrangement. Spending the rest of the evening by Silas's side could grant me access to conversations and insights I'd never get otherwise.

Exhaling sharply, I grit out, "It'd be an honor."

Silas chuckles, the sound low and rich, vibrating through my chest like a drumbeat. His presence seems to radiate through the room as he plucks the empty glass from my hand and carries it back to the bar cart in the corner. While his back is turned, I seize the opportunity to scan the room again, letting my eyes rake over every detail, searching for something useful.

The bookshelves lining the walls are immaculate, filled with leather-bound volumes and glossy spines that gleam under the warm light. Nothing is out of place. The desk itself is devoid of clutter, save for his laptop and a minimalist desk lamp. Still, I mentally catalog the desk. Those drawers could hold something valuable. I file the thought away for later.

"If I didn't know any better, I'd think you were unhappy with this proposal," Silas's voice is laced with mock offense as he returns to my side. That damn errant curl has fallen over his glasses again, and in this lighting, with the bookshelves framing him like a portrait, he looks like the kind of handsome that could ruin lives. My palms start to sweat, despite my best efforts to stay composed.

"Whatever would give you that impression?" I reply, tilting my head just enough to match his energy.

"Just a hunch." He steps closer and extends his arm, gesturing for me to take it. I hesitate for a moment before lightly grasping the crook of his elbow with my free hand, my fingers barely brushing the taut muscle of his arm. His bicep flexes slightly under my touch, a subtle reminder of the strength coiled beneath his polished exterior.

"You can always keep me company instead, Scarlett," Jeremy interjects from the corner, his vacant smile fixed in place.

I force a polite, almost thankful look in his direction. "I appreciate the offer, but now I need to prove I can survive being tortured."

Natalie snorts from behind us, clearly enjoying the exchange. "God, I love when a woman wants nothing to do with you," she says, her gaze locked on her older brother. There's an undeniable satisfaction in her voice. "Someone needs to keep you humble."

"I have a feeling Ms. Page won't have any issues doing that." Silas's smirk turns sharper as he glances down at me. "This might be my most entertaining auction yet."

"I'm so glad I can be a source of entertainment for you," I mutter, my tone dripping with sarcasm as I shift my hair over one shoulder awkwardly with my small handbag still between my fingers. "Maybe next time you can hire a circus monkey instead."

Leaning in closer, Silas lowers his voice to a near whisper, his breath tickling the sensitive spot just below my jaw. "I'm partial to the fire-breathing woman, so this arrangement works."

The space between us feels off-kilter, like he's tilted the balance in his favor without me noticing. "Be careful," I whisper back, meeting his gaze with a sharpness of my own. "If you get too close, you'll burn."

His lips part slightly as his eyes trace the slope of my neck. "And what if I'm into fireplay?" The words are barely audible, meant only for me. My heart stutters, but by some miracle, I manage to keep my expression neutral.

"Save the fake charm for the next poor woman who stumbles into your path," I retort with a sigh, brushing off his comment as I straighten my spine. "I've already agreed to be your date."

Silas chuckles before opening the door with me still on his arm. His proximity is a constant, almost oppressive force, but I can't deny that it's effective. He knows exactly how to command a room, even one as private as this.

"Is he still harassing you?" Natalie asks, her tone a mix of humor and exasperation.

"Ms. Page can handle herself," Davey interjects, his voice dry as he exhales heavily. It's clear he's eager to leave the room, and I don't blame him.

As we step into the hallway, I can't shake the feeling that the real tension in the room wasn't between Silas and me, but between Jeremy and his siblings. Jeremy's hollow demeanor is unsettling, and the way his gaze lingered on me still makes my skin crawl.

We file out in a line, and Silas pauses behind to wait for Jeremy, who exits last, allowing his older brother to lock the door behind us. I hear the faint beep of a fingerprint scanner, and my stomach drops as I spot the sleek mechanism I missed on my way in. Of course, Silas would have one of the best on the market.

The door is solid wood, and the frame and hinges scream of custom reinforcement, designed to withstand brute force. Even with the highest-rated tools, breaking into this room would take time no intruder would have before the scanner's secondary security measures kicked in. The system is state-of-the-art, durable, and encrypted to a point that would challenge even the most seasoned hacker.

It's impressive, but not impenetrable. Not if someone came prepared.

"Like what you see?" Silas's voice snaps me out of my analysis, the low taunt in his tone unmistakable. His eyes flick between me and the now-locked door, his grin forming in slow, deliberate degrees. If I were the kind of woman who let her hormones get the better of her, I might've flushed at the innuendo laced in his words.

"I shouldn't be surprised that Davey would outfit your office like that," I reply, keeping my expression unimpressed.

Silas hums, his thumb still pressed to the scanner as he seems to savor the moment. "I trust Davey's judgment."

"That's a surprisingly kind acknowledgment," I admit, studying the angle of his jaw as the lock clicks into place. He steps away from the door, falling into stride beside me as we make our way toward the stairs.

"Davey has improved our existing protocols. He's an asset to my team," Silas says, the appreciation in his tone subtle but genuine.

As much as I'd love to write him off as an entitled brat, his intelligence is glaringly obvious. Davey might be the architect of their security, but Silas knows how it works, and likely how to wield it. These two men are mirrors of each other: calculated, paranoid, and annoyingly competent.

"As he should be. Successful people turn to experts for advice and actually use it." The compliment tastes bitter on my tongue, knowing full well that one day soon, I'll be the one working to dismantle all those safeguards.

"Spoken like a true business owner," he replies, his tone appreciative, as though recognizing a kindred spirit. The intention in his words makes something in my chest tighten, a feeling I quickly suppress.

We are not the same, and I need to remember that.

My thoughts come to an abrupt halt as we round the corner and I spot the Wells patriarch waiting at the top of the staircase. William Wells's dark suit is perfectly tailored, his posture impossibly straight, and his eyes, sharp and assessing, land on me with the precision of a scalpel.

I've read countless articles about William Wells, his ruthlessness in business, and his ability to outmaneuver competitors with terrifying ease. But being the focus of his gaze is something else entirely. There's no preparing for it. No magazine article can replicate the weight of his authority.

To no one's surprise, the Wells genes dominate across all generations. Though William's features are softer, he shares the same wavy hair and brown eyes as his sons while his daughter's hazel color comes from his late wife. The lines around his eyes and salt-and-pepper hair are the only signs of age, and even they seem like afterthoughts. The striking difference lies in his demeanor. Unlike Silas's playful glint or Natalie's warmth, William is all sharp edges and certainty.

Peter originally wanted me to go after William directly, but that would have been an instant red flag—a thirty-year-old woman cozying up to a sixty-year-old powerhouse? I wouldn't last more than two interactions before Davey or someone else called me out. William is too powerful, too private, and far too calculating to let someone like me slip through the cracks. Silas may be just as guarded, but at least with him, my attention feels natural.

"Natalie mentioned a friend would be joining us," William begins, though he doesn't address me directly. His mouth tightens into a line as he shifts his attention to Silas. "Does it seem wise to find a date an hour *into* the event?"

"Ms. Page is about as pleased with this arrangement as you are," Silas responds, his mirth barely concealed. William doesn't take his son's word for it and glances at Davey, who offers a single nod.

"Scarlett and Natalie are new friends. She checks out," Davey says, his tone skeptical despite the confirmation. Even though he doesn't trust his own research, at least the time I spent refining Scarlett's online presence wasn't wasted.

"I'd hope so, considering she's standing here," William retorts. Natalie's face flushes with embarrassment, her gaze darting between her father and me. It takes everything in me not to bristle at William's comments.

I force a smile and decide to tread lightly. "I did try to excuse myself, but Silas... convinced me to join him."

"Don't you mean I charmed you?" Silas interjects, flexing his arm slightly under my hold. I glance up at him, catching the faintest hint of warmth in his expression. It's subtle, but enough to send an unwelcome tingle down my spine.

"Coerced, strong-armed, annoyed incessantly... those are also acceptable answers," I reply, squeezing the crease of his elbow for emphasis.

William lets out a breath, the smallest trace of a smirk breaking through his stoicism. "At least she'll give you a run for your money." He steps forward and extends his hand toward me. "It's nice to meet you, Ms. Page."

A man like William doesn't need to introduce himself. His reputation precedes him, and the power dynamics are clear. Still, I let go of Silas to take his hand with a firm grip, meeting his gaze head-on. "Likewise. I'll be on my best behavior in front of your guests."

"You'll be a reflection of my son, not me. So if you want to raise hell, by all means," he responds, his charisma shifting gears seamlessly. He winks, a calculated move that's both disarming and unnerving.

"Tempting," I say with a coy smile as I place my hands back on Silas's bicep. "Depending on how the night goes, it could be a possibility."

William chuckles, turning toward the staircase where a staff member waits halfway down. With a nod from William, the music downstairs cuts off abruptly. There's no announcement. The absence of sound and the weight of the family's presence are enough to command the room's attention.

"Showtime," Jeremy mutters, clapping his father on the shoulder. William exhales and begins his descent, his children following in order of birth. Silas guides me with measured steps, the strength of his muscles under my hand grounding me.

As we reach the top of the stairs, my grip tightens on Silas's arm and my pulse races. Not from fear, but from the sudden realization of what I've just committed to. In this moment, under the scrutiny of Chicago's elite, I've tethered myself to Silas Wells. And there's no turning back now.

Chapter 11

We reach the turning point of the staircase where the guests can see us from the entryway, but I keep my eyes trained on the steps in front of me. The last thing I need is to trip and send myself sprawling onto the marble floor.

As we near the bottom, Silas and I pause a few steps behind William, who stops to address the room. I finally lift my gaze, nerves twisting in my stomach as I take in the scene below.

It's a sea of faces—over a hundred guests gathered in the expansive entryway, every pair of eyes fixed on the family at the center of their attention. The coat check table has been relocated to another corner, clearing the space to make room for the crowd. The air is heavy with anticipation, the kind of silence that feels amplified by the weight of collective scrutiny.

In that split second, the realization hits the room like a ripple across water: one of these people is not like the others. Whispers begin to spread as guests register the unfamiliar woman not just standing with the Wells family, but attached to one of the most eligible and powerful men in the city.

The reactions are instant and varied, each one hitting me like a distinct note in a discordant symphony. Older women purse their lips, dissecting me from head to toe. Men of all ages exchange nods of approval, as though Silas's choice has somehow validated their own tastes. Younger women roll their eyes, some barely concealing their irritation, before redirecting their attention to Silas with laser focus. Their longing is so palpable, I'm almost shocked their gazes don't physically burn holes through him.

But above all, the crowd is united by one common reaction: confusion. A healthy dose of it. And frankly, I can't blame them. This wasn't on my bingo card for the evening, either.

The sudden flashes of cameras nearly blind me, and I flinch at the first pop of light. I blink rapidly to clear the black spots now swimming in my vision, heart lurching. Several photographers are scattered throughout the crowd, dressed in head-to-toe black and wielding cameras with practiced ease. The incessant clicks send fresh waves of discomfort coursing through me.

Of course, there are photographers. Why wouldn't there be?

"Good evening, friends," William's voice booms across the room, commanding attention without effort. He raises his arms in a gesture of welcome, and I can practically hear the smile on his face. "My family and I are delighted to host you all tonight for our annual silent auction."

His voice is steady and charismatic, the mark of a man who's spent decades perfecting the art of public appearances. As he speaks, his words carry seamlessly over the room, outlining the night's agenda and New Beginnings Housing Project's mission.

Meanwhile, my grip on Silas's arm tightens with each camera flash. The growing attention prickles across my skin, as though every lens in the room is aimed solely at me. The corners of my vision begin to blur, the crowd below blending into a haze of colors and faces.

I shouldn't be here.

The thought echoes louder than anything William is saying. If my picture makes it to the tabloids—and it will—it's game over. Peter will see it, and he'll use it. Twist it. Whatever illusion of control I've been trying to maintain will shatter, and I'll be left scrambling to salvage the contract on his terms instead of mine.

My pulse thunders in my ears, drowning out William's speech. I shift my weight from one foot to the other, trying desperately to distract myself, but the panic continues to creep in.

Just when I think I'm about to lose it, Silas leans down, his mouth brushing the delicate spot just below my ear. His voice is low and commanding, steady as a metronome. "Inhale for ten, exhale for ten."

I want to snap back at him, to reject his audacity to give me orders in a moment like this, but the words stick in my throat. My usual confidence, the sharp-edged armor I've perfected over years, has abandoned me.

Instead, I obey.

His warm breath lingers against my skin as I inhale deeply, counting to ten before exhaling with the same precision. He matches my rhythm, his chest rising and falling in sync with mine. His voice is soft now, muttering words I can't quite make out.

After a few rounds, the storm inside me begins to settle. The buzzing in my ears fades, and my racing heart slows to a manageable pace. My senses sharpen once more, and suddenly, I'm acutely aware of everything. The tickle of Silas's breath against my cheek, the faint spice of whiskey lingering on him, and the deliberate stroke of his thumb as it glides across the back of my hand.

I let out an uneven breath, roll my shoulders back, and shake my head slightly as if to clear away the fog.

"Good girl," Silas murmurs, straightening up beside me. The words wrap around me like a weighted blanket, and the heat crawling up my neck now has nothing to do with anxiety.

I don't look at him, refusing to give him the satisfaction of seeing how thoroughly he's just pieced me back together. Instead, I steady myself, my fingers loosening their grip on his arm just enough to regain a sliver of autonomy.

But as William's speech concludes and the applause begins, I can feel Silas's eyes lingering on me. I can't decide if his help was genuine or just another calculated move in whatever unspoken game he's trying to make me play with him.

The room begins to pulse with its usual energy as William descends the final steps, encouraging guests to enjoy themselves while continuing to support the auction and its cause. The applause fades as the Wells patriarch seamlessly transitions into working the room. He shakes hands, cracks quick jokes, and commands attention with the effortless charisma of a seasoned politician.

Silas and I follow behind, but his approach is markedly different from his father's. While William is overly engaging and warm, Silas's demeanor is cooler, more controlled. His polite nods and curt greetings create an invisible barrier between him and anyone daring to approach. The space around us shifts like water parting for a shark, guests instinctively stepping aside to clear a path and then filling in the gaps once we pass.

"I'm sorry," I whisper, my voice cracking as I finally find the courage to speak. Silas's profile remains impassive, his face a mask of practiced neutrality. His only acknowledgment is the faint upward tilt of his lips, more a smirk than a smile. "I've never clammed up like that before."

His head tilts slightly in my direction. "Before? Are you often on the arms of men hosting auctions?"

The warmth he'd shown moments ago is gone, replaced by the razor-sharp Silas Wells I'd met at Natalie's art exhibit. His comment feels like a challenge, and my irritation flares instantly. I pull my hand back from his arm, glaring at him. The glint in his eyes tells me he's enjoying this.

"You're not the first man to *charm* me into being their date at an event like this," I snap back, my voice tight with sarcasm.

Before he can retort, a server approaches with a glass of whiskey. Silas takes it with a nod, his movements fluid and precise, then gestures for me to order. After quickly requesting a tequila soda with lime, I wait for the server to disappear before continuing. "I should have known there would be cameras here," I admit, my voice quieter now. "I wasn't thinking. They freaked me out."

Silas doesn't respond immediately. His gaze drifts over the room, taking stock of the crowd. Natalie, Davey, and Jeremy have disappeared into the throng of guests, each absorbed in their own conversations. Even Jeremy looks less detached as he chats animatedly with a group of businessmen near a cluster of leather chairs.

Silas's hand remains steady at the small of my back, firm but unassuming as he guides me across the room. He steers me toward the paneled wall on the far side, away from the bustle of the crowd. Once we reach the quieter corner, he subtly shifts his hand, a gentle pressure to turn me until my back meets the cool surface. He steps in closer, his shoes nearly brushing mine, his presence overwhelming as the hum of awareness ripples through me.

I raise my eyebrows at him, trying to regain some semblance of control. "It's not polite to have your back to a room full of people waiting to speak with you," I point out, my tone teasing but edged with real concern.

He shakes his head slightly, as though warding off an intrusive thought. "Don't apologize for having a normal reaction to something," he says, ignoring my last comment completely. He adjusts his glasses with a quick push of his fingers. "I've been doing this my whole life, and even I can't stand the cameras or the publicity bullshit."

The server returns with my drink at lightning speed, and Silas takes the glass on my behalf, handing it to me with the same calculated precision as everything else he does. Our fingers brush briefly, and a flicker of heat crawls up my arm.

"Bullshit, huh?" I echo as I take a sip. The tequila burns less than his presence, though only just.

He shrugs, his expression relaxing slightly. "I'd rather just donate more money and skip the parties, but these events get other wealthy people to participate. The pros outweigh the cons."

His words catch me off guard, and I find myself studying him more closely. I hadn't pegged Silas as someone who would dislike the fanfare of wealth and power. Men like him usually thrive in environments like this. But his tone carries a weariness that feels genuine, and I can't help but feel the faintest thread of empathy.

"I didn't take you for much of a party guy," I say, tilting my head in mock contemplation. "But I also didn't think you'd hate them this much. Your family's business benefits from the publicity."

"There's good and bad in everything, Scarlett," he replies, my fake name rolling off his tongue. "I don't have to like it, just tolerate it."

"That's fair," I respond with a nod. Letting out a slow breath, I decide to steer the conversation back to safer territory. "As much as I love *not* making small talk with strangers, I don't need rumors going around about me seducing you at your family's charity event by hogging your attention in some dark corner."

Silas doesn't step back, but he straightens, offering me a sliver of reprieve from his pull. His expression shifts from contemplative to amused. "Is that the reputation you've earned since moving to Chicago? Gold-digging?" His words are a deliberate jab, accompanied by a sly sip of his drink.

My cheeks heat, and I grit my teeth.

Would it be inappropriate to deck him in front of all these people? Probably.

"Has anyone ever told you how absolutely insufferable you are?" I retort, my voice clipped.

His dark laugh rumbles between us, deep and unbothered. "Maybe," he says, his smirk growing. "But I have to say, you wear frustration beautifully."

I take a long sip of my drink, my fingers tightening around the glass as I glare at him. "Flattery will get you nowhere."

"Won't it?" he counters, his voice dropping just enough to make the air around us feel warmer. His glasses slide down his nose again, and this time, I don't even bother suppressing the urge to roll my eyes.

We both take a drink, the silence between us thick but not entirely uncomfortable. Curious eyes and hushed whispers flit around us like moths to a flame, the guests clearly trying to piece together why I'm here, on Silas Wells's arm no less. I catch sight of a few particularly bold onlookers and widen my eyes meaningfully, nodding subtly in their direction.

Silas follows my gaze and, with a faint but unmistakable flicker of irritation, pulls me gently by the wrist of my free hand. The motion is fluid but purposeful, turning us to face the crowd. He positions himself at my side, placing his hand firmly on my lower back, an unexpected display of decorum.

His tone is maddeningly nonchalant when he speaks again. "So, if it's not for my money, you must be here for my good looks." His eyes sparkle with mischief as he waits for my reaction.

I bark out a laugh, louder than I intended, the rim of my glass still pressed against my lips. "Your ego truly knows no bounds, does it?"

A slow smile spreads across his face, dangerously close to charming. "Would you like me to add humility to the list of things I'm insufferably good at?"

I shoot him a pointed look, my eyebrow arching with mock incredulity. "I think your humility got lost somewhere in that mansion-sized closet of yours. Right next to your collection of overpriced suits."

For a moment, his grin widens, genuine amusement lighting up his features. But our exchange is cut short as a group of impeccably dressed guests approaches, their shameless stares and eager expressions making it clear they're here for one reason only: to bask in even a sliver of Silas Wells's attention.

Silas rolls back his shoulders, demeanor shifting effortlessly. The teasing edge in his expression melts away, replaced by a perfectly neutral but undeniably commanding air. His hand doesn't move from my back, though it relaxes slightly, as if to remind me that, for now, I'm still part of his carefully curated image.

The guests begin their introductions with practiced ease, their voices a blend of sycophantic admiration and transparent opportunism. I plaster on a polite smile, watching as Silas navigates the conversation with undeniable ease. It's a masterclass in control; disengaged enough to keep them wanting more, yet just present enough to make them feel important.

As I stand beside him, I realize this isn't a game to him. It's second nature. A survival tactic for someone who's been surrounded by other predators his entire life. And while it's impressive, it also makes me wonder what it would take to see the real Silas Wells.

As it turns out, being Silas's date hasn't provided me with any groundbreaking revelations in the three hours since we rejoined the party. In fact, I've learned only two things. First, Silas has an uncanny ability to deflect or completely shut down any meaningful conversation. Second, he wields enough power that people simply let him do it without complaint.

After fielding advances from nearly every hopeful socialite or business connection who dared to approach him, Silas steered us toward the bar, where Davey and Natalie were already standing. William and Jeremy disappeared into adjoining rooms to mingle, and while William's absence is unremarkable, Jeremy's is a relief.

Silas remains close but detached, splitting his time between our small group and private conversations with guests of his choosing. Watching the interactions is like observing a dance: cautious glances, tentative approaches, and visible relief when Silas finally nods someone over to speak. His presence seems to unnerve nearly everyone in the room, and they tread around him as though he's a grenade with the pin pulled.

What's infuriating, however, is that he hasn't invited me to join him in any of these exchanges. Judging by the few passing glances he's thrown my way, the idea is off the table entirely. I'm left with no choice but to linger near Natalie, who has finally settled into the relaxed rhythm of the evening after greeting a steady stream of guests. Leaning one elbow on the marble counter of the bar, she blows out a long breath, visibly relieved as Davey excuses himself to the restroom.

"My brother is quite the date, huh?" Natalie's voice is dry, but there's a hint of amusement in her tone.

I shrug, popping the last bite of bruschetta from my small plate into my mouth. "Honestly, he's been more tolerable than most event dates I've had."

Her lips twist into a skeptical scowl, and I nod in understanding.

"I know. The bar is basically underground."

To be fair, in terms of typical dates, Silas has been nothing short of a gentleman. When he isn't engaging in business talk, he's attentive to me, Natalie, and Davey. The teasing, while ever-present, has been minimal, and he's carried the conversation effortlessly. I've heard stories about their childhood, his favorite and least favorite professors in college, and even a little about Wells Corp's upcoming foray into drugstore beauty products. In turn, they've asked about my upbringing, and though I keep my answers vague, I offer glimpses of the real me. Stories that feel like they belong to someone I used to know.

What I wasn't prepared for is the weight of Silas's attention. He listens in a way most people don't: intent and undivided. It's overwhelming to be the focus of someone so powerful, yet it also stirs something within me, a quiet thrill I'm not sure that I want to examine too closely.

A cool breath against my ear startles me. "Singing my praises over here, are we?" Silas's low, raspy voice sends a shock down my limbs. I jump slightly, bumping into his chest. The unexpected contact makes my skin prickle with a mix of heat and ice.

I spin around, craning my neck to look up at him as he towers over me. One hand braces on the bar top next to my waist, his empty whiskey glass within reach. His gaze, which has been thawing all evening, now carries a distinct warmth that stirs something in the pit of my stomach.

"You're doing a stellar job of leaving me alone," I say, patting his chest mockingly. His muscles twitch beneath his sweater, firm and defined under my palm. A satisfied smile tugs at my lips, but it's short-lived. Silas's eyes darken as he opens his mouth—likely to deliver some cutting remark—only to be interrupted by a smooth, unfamiliar voice.

"If that's the best compliment Silas Wells can get, I don't want to know how the rest of us will fare."

Silas's gaze sharpens instantly, and we both turn toward the source. A man stands a few feet away, dressed in a sharp charcoal-gray suit that looks tailored within an inch of its life. He's older than Silas but younger than William, with light-brown hair and piercing gray eyes. He's conventionally handsome, but there's a slickness to him, a too-perfect charm underscored by the kilowatt smile he flashes. The kind of man who could sell a glass of water to a drowning man.

"Martin," Silas greets coolly, his tone clipped and distant. He makes no move to shake the man's hand, nor does he bother with introductions. The casual authority in Silas's voice is enough to communicate that this man, despite his polished exterior, isn't a friend. "How respectful of you to join us as the party's concluding."

Sensing the tension, I force a respectful smile in the stranger's direction, silently assessing him. Whoever Martin is, it's clear that Silas doesn't trust him. And judging by the glint in Martin's eyes, he's not here to make friends, either.

"And you are his clearly enamored date?" Martin ignores his jab as his eyes settle on me with a glint of curiosity, hand extended in greeting. I take it, and like Jeremy earlier, he presses a soft kiss to my knuckles. The gesture, while polished, leaves me with the same undercurrent of restlessness Jeremy's did.

"Scarlett," I confirm with a polite nod as he releases my hand.

"A beautiful name for a beautiful woman." His tone is low, dripping with something just shy of inappropriate. A comment clearly meant to provoke, especially considering the host and my supposed date stand inches away.

Silas's hand, which had been resting lightly on the bar, moves to my waist, the pressure of his fingers firm. "There are a few auction items I think will interest you, Martin." Silas's voice is sharp but controlled. "Unfortunately, my time—and my date—aren't for sale." His words hold an edge, but the slight tug on my hip makes my stomach tighten, though whether from irritation or something else, I can't tell.

Martin's lips curl into an easy smirk. "Pity. I was hoping to discuss some business with you and your father."

"By all means," Silas replies, taking a measured sip of his whiskey. "Find the old man and bore him to death."

Martin tuts. "Now, we both know nothing I bring to the table is boring."

"Nothing you've ever brought me has been worth my time or money," Silas counters, his voice infuriatingly calm. "So forgive me for not caring to find a better word for it."

Watching this exchange is like seeing two panthers circling each other but unwilling to pounce just yet. Despite Silas's casual tone, his grip on my waist tightens slightly; a silent warning not to engage. Naturally, I do the opposite.

"I didn't catch your last name," I interject, feigning innocent curiosity as I shift my gaze back to Martin. Silas's thumb presses just a fraction harder against my side in subtle protest, but I ignore it. Hell will freeze over before I take direction from him without question.

A flash of amusement crosses Martin's face, his pride clearly stroked by my interest. "Shaw," he answers, as if expecting the name to carry weight.

Shaw. The name scratches at the edges of my memory. Have I come across him in a past job, or is he familiar because of my research into the Wells family? Either way, I can't place him. I tilt my head slightly but keep my expression neutral, allowing just the faintest trace of indifference to linger in my features.

"Shaw," I echo, as though the name means nothing to me, which, presently, it doesn't. Then I pivot slightly toward Silas, my decision already made. If there's one thing I've learned tonight, it's that Silas values loyalty. Earning his trust means staying on his side, even if it means ignoring someone who might be useful later.

Silas doesn't acknowledge my movement, but I feel the shift in his stance, a slight relaxation of tension in the hand still resting on my hip. Natalie, however, takes the opportunity to redirect the conversation. "I think my father is in the music room," she says, barely concealing her disdain. "I'm sure he'll pacify your request for an audience."

For the first time, Martin's gaze shifts to Natalie, and the look he gives her makes my blood boil. It's the kind of dismissive glance someone reserves for a piece of trash on the sidewalk, contemptuous and utterly dehumanizing. My fingers curl into a fist at my side, nails biting into my palm as a distraction from the rage bubbling beneath my skin. Natalie, to her credit, doesn't flinch. She holds his stare with unwavering defiance, her chin tilted just slightly upward in challenge.

"It's always a pleasure interacting with you... delightful Wells children," Martin finally sneers, straightening his tie. Without another word, he turns on his heel and stalks off toward the music room.

As soon as he's out of earshot, Natalie exhales a ragged breath, her mask of composure slipping just slightly. I press my back against the bar, angling myself to see both her and Silas at once.

"You're lucky Davey was in the bathroom," Silas hisses, his tone sharp enough to cut. He releases his hold on my hip to signal the bartender for another drink, his jaw tight with frustration.

"I've handled Martin before, and I'll handle him again," Natalie snaps, her voice lower and steadier now. She stares off behind the bar, her expression set in a way that dares anyone to question her capability. "I don't need my husband to rescue me."

The silence that follows crackles between them like static electricity. I make a mental note to dig deeper into Martin Shaw's connection to this family. Whatever bad blood exists between him and the Wells siblings runs deep, and William's apparent tolerance of him only adds another layer of intrigue.

The bartender slides Silas's drink across the counter, and I glance at my own glass, realizing it's nearly empty. "What time is it?" I ask, more to myself than anyone else.

"Five until ten," the bartender answers politely.

I sigh inwardly. The evening feels like a wash. If Martin Shaw doesn't amount to anything substantial, I'll leave this party with nothing but a full stomach and a lingering headache. I glance at Natalie, who finishes her cocktail with the air of someone hoping to drown the memory of the last few minutes.

She meets my gaze, and I can see the exhaustion in her eyes. She's putting on a brave face, but the cracks in her armor are visible if you know where to look. Something about that makes me like her even more.

"My car should be here in a few minutes. Want to walk me out?" I ask Natalie. A few minutes of cold air might be exactly what she needs.

"I'll do it," Silas answers before she can respond, cutting his sister off with a stern look. "Natalie is going to find Davey, let him know Martin's here, and make sure they stay as far away from him as possible."

"You act like Davey's an animal," Natalie retorts, crossing her arms over her chest. The subtle tension in her voice tells me that Davey, apparently, might loathe him more than anyone.

"When it comes to you? Yes." Silas's gaze doesn't waver. "Just do me a favor and handle it before it becomes a real problem. Go to the attic or the study. I'll find you after."

Natalie's jaw tightens, and it looks like she's about to argue, but I step in, cutting the tension. "Go find Davey," I say, offering her a small, closed-mouth smile. "I'll be fine. But behave, alright?" I tease, opening my arms for a hug.

She sighs, the smallest grin tugging at her lips as she steps forward and hugs me tightly. I pat her back reassuringly before she steps away and nods. "Alright, alright. See you soon," she murmurs, heading off to find her husband.

As she disappears into another room, I turn to Silas. "Is she going to be okay with that man here?" I ask, watching his expression carefully. Silas takes a sip of his drink, his shoulders sagging slightly as he exhales a long, tired breath.

"Natalie's resilient. She'll get Davey upstairs and away from Martin while I figure out how to deal with him." His voice carries the weight of exhaustion, and for a moment, I catch a fleeting glimpse of vulnerability behind his steadfast demeanor.

"Whatever Martin did, I'm sure he regrets ever becoming either of your enemies," I say, trying to lighten the mood. Silas's lips twitch, but his eyes remain distant as he nods toward the foyer, silently signaling for me to lead the way.

We weave through the thinning crowd; most guests left after the auction closed, but a fair number remain, lingering in small groups with their drinks. The foyer is quiet now, save for the soft chatter of two staff members at the coat check. I hand over my ticket, and they quickly retrieve my jacket. Before I can grab it, Silas plucks it from the staff member's hands and unfolds it, holding it open for me.

"You didn't have to do that," I mutter, turning my back to him and slipping my arms into the sleeves. Despite my words, there's a thoughtfulness to the gesture that I can't ignore.

"What kind of date would I be if I didn't help you with your coat?" Silas's voice is low, smooth, and entirely too close. When I turn to face him again, I realize just how close he's standing, and the intensity of his gaze nearly knocks me off balance.

The corner of his mouth curling into a look that could melt steel, but he doesn't say another word. Instead, he fastens the buttons of my coat, and the deliberate way his fingers brush against my body sets my skin on fire.

I swallow hard, forcing my expression to remain neutral even as heat blooms across my face. He buttons the last fastener near my collar, his fingers lingering for a moment, eyes as black as the void between the stars.

"Thanks," I manage, my voice barely above a whisper as I take a step back, trying to create space. My phone buzzes in my hand, and I glance down to see an incoming call from a local number, likely my driver waiting outside. I answer quickly, confirming I'm on my way out, and hang up. "That's my car," I say, more to myself than to him.

Silas doesn't move immediately. Instead, he reaches for my phone, the sudden motion freezing me in place. My heart stutters as I watch him open the contacts and add a number. Within seconds, he locks the screen and places the phone back in my hand, his touch lingering just a moment too long.

"You're giving yourself a lot of credit if you think I'll text you just because you added your number," I taunt, trying to hide the way my voice falters. Silas chuckles as he straightens out my collar.

"And to think, you were making fun of *my* ego earlier." His words are smooth and annoyingly charming.

He turns me toward the door, his hand guiding me gently by the elbow. A staff member holds the door open, and the biting winter air immediately nips at my face. I shiver, ducking my head against the cold as Silas leads me down the steps to the curb where my driver waits. Keith steps out and opens the door, but Silas is already there, his hand hovering to assist me. I ignore it, climbing in on my own.

When I settle into my seat, I glance up to see Silas leaning over me, one arm braced against the door frame and the other gripping the top of the door. His pink cheeks and windswept hair make him look impossibly handsome, a fact I hate myself for noticing. The scent of his cologne, woody and sweet with a hint of spice, lingers between us, and I struggle to focus.

"Text me when you make it home safe," he says, his voice soft but firm, a command disguised as concern. He steps back and closes the door with a decisive *thud* before I can respond.

I watch through the window as he strides back up the path to his house, his figure cutting an imposing silhouette against the glow of the streetlights. Letting out a breath I hadn't realized I was holding, I lean back in my seat, my pulse pounding in my ears.

Text him when I get home? What's next, sit, stay, roll over?

But as Keith pulls away from the curb, a small part of me—one I refuse to acknowledge—can't stop replaying the way he said it, like he actually expected me to listen.

102

CHAPTER 12

For what has to be the fifteenth time in three days, I find myself staring at Silas's texts, the words etched into my mind like graffiti I can't scrub away. The first two came in rapid succession after I arrived home from the auction.

Silas: Texting Natalie instead of me? Interesting choice.
Silas: I should've known you wouldn't follow my instructions.

The third, sent well past midnight, felt like an afterthought. Or maybe a calculated effort to unsettle me.

Silas: You're testing my patience, Ms. Page.

I imagine him lounging back in his study chair, feet propped up on the desk, smirking to himself as he crafted the perfect follow-up.

My lack of response is what he gets for stealing my number from Natalie's phone.

Yes, I purposefully texted her instead of him. Of course, I did. I assumed she'd pass along the message when she left for the night, sparing me the need to open the line of communication with Silas directly. Something about texting him felt... definitive. A step I wasn't ready to take. I didn't want to find out what it might mean. Or worse, what it might lead to.

I set my phone face down on my desk and push it out of reach. Whatever response he thinks I owe him can wait. If he's as curious and as arrogant as I think he is, he'll keep finding ways to put himself in my path. He can't help himself. That's how men like him operate. And if he keeps willingly pursuing me, then I can tell myself that I didn't push him into it. That it's not my fault. It won't stop the guilt entirely, but maybe it'll dull the edges when this is all over.

At least, that's what I tell myself.

I roll my neck, trying to ease the ache that's settled into my muscles from hours spent at my desk. I haven't left the apartment much in the last three days, choosing instead to bury myself in work. Leaving only to sleep or train with Jeff at the gym, I've avoided anything resembling a social setting. The thought of being recognized in public, of seeing those auction photos plastered across newsstands, makes my stomach twist.

Every major Chicago outlet had run the story, the headlines splashed with Silas's name and the phrase "mystery woman." They were vague, though whether that was due to Silas's influence or sheer laziness on their part, I couldn't say. Thankfully, I wasn't explicitly identified. The articles focused on the event itself, praising the Wells family for raising a staggering amount of money for New Beginnings Housing Project. There were glowing summaries of each sibling, though naturally, Silas stole the spotlight.

The photos, though, told their own story. One caught him leaning in close on the staircase, his mouth near my ear as I struggled through my panic attack. Another showed us mid-toast at the bar, glasses raised. And the candids? Me chatting with Natalie while Silas approached, the faintest hint of a smile tugging at his lips. To an outsider, it looked intimate. Like we were something.

The reality, of course, was far less polished. Less romantic. It had all felt so... normal. A little too normal.

Peter, naturally, had opinions. He'd called the morning after the auction when the photos were published, his tone dripping with satisfaction as he praised my "progress." I tried to explain that the images were misleading. That Silas and I could barely have a conversation without clashing, but Peter dismissed my concerns with unsettling ease.

"Doesn't matter," he says, his voice sharp and sure. *"What matters is that people are already seeing you together. You're in his orbit now. That's the leverage we need."*

I wanted to argue, to tell him he was wrong, but the words dried up in my throat. What could I say that he wouldn't twist back on me? I don't even know who hired Peter or what they're looking for. Are the Wells family innocent victims caught in someone else's crosshairs? Or are they just as guilty as the rest of the people I've dealt with in the past?

And then Peter did something that set my teeth on edge: he let it go. No rebuttals. No lectures. He simply moved on to another topic, his tone as casual as if we'd been discussing the weather. It wasn't like him to let things slide. Not unless he had a plan.

For once, I hope I'm wrong. But I'm not holding my breath.

In between researching the businessmen Silas spoke to at the auction, I've been digging deeper into Martin Shaw. His name had tickled something in the back of my mind the moment I heard it, and now I know why. I must have read it a hundred times while researching the Wells family.

For over a decade, Martin was the Chief Operations Officer at Wells Corporation and was widely rumored to be the interim CEO until Silas or Jeremy grew into the role. His departure from the company came not long after Natalie and Davey started dating, shocking nearly everyone in those circles. Officially, the decision to part ways was framed as amicable, but a few weeks later, Martin was announced as the President of NexBio Therapeutics in San Diego. A smooth landing, far removed from the empire he had helped build.

Outside of his career, Martin fits the mold of the stereotypical rich man: divorced multiple times, no shortage of money or connections, and an ego to match his net worth. But the dynamic I'd witnessed between him and the Wells siblings told me there was more to his story. Something significant must have happened for Natalie, Silas, and Davey to despise him so openly, yet not enough to sever his relationship with William. Of course, I wasn't getting past the Wells Corporation's airtight security to uncover his resignation details, and Martin's personal accounts I managed to access revealed nothing of substance. He's either exceptionally cautious or exceptionally boring.

My chair creaks as I stretch my arms over my head, the stiffness in my shoulders evident. Outside, the sun has disappeared behind the city skyline, casting long shadows across my sparsely decorated office. The quiet feels oppressive, a reminder of how isolated I've kept myself since the auction.

I flip on a few lights on my way to the kitchen, hoping dinner might offer some reprieve. The contents of my fridge are as uninspiring as my mood; just a flavored rice packet, some microwavable vegetables, and the remains of a rotisserie chicken I deboned earlier in the week. I toss the rice into the microwave and lean against the counter as it whirs, my mind wandering back to the Wells family and their tangled web of secrets.

My phone buzzes in my pocket, the vibration unmistakable. My pulse quickens, a mix of dread and anticipation flooding through me before I even glance at the screen. Only one person has that specific alert.

I take a steadying breath and press the phone to my ear. "Twice in one week. Are you calling because you missed the sound of my voice?"

Peter's laugh is sharp, humorless. "My favorite hacker. I still don't miss that attitude one bit. Have you learned anything else since we last spoke?"

"I've been looking into Martin Shaw," I reply evenly. "I don't think his departure from Wells Corp. was as clean as it seemed, but I haven't found anything concrete yet."

"And why does that matter?" Peter asks, his tone clipped and impatient, as if the answer should already be obvious to me.

"He and the Wells children don't get along, but he still has William's favor. I thought there might be something there."

"I doubt it," Peter says dismissively, his irritation palpable even through the phone. "Focus on the family. Martin Shaw is a distraction."

Of course, he would say that. Peter has never valued my instincts, no matter how often they've been proven right. Still, I know better than to argue. "Understood," I answer, tone flat.

As the microwave beeps, signaling the rice is ready, I swap it out for the vegetables and punch in a new cook time. Steam rises from the rice packet as I tear it open and dump it into a bowl.

"There's also the younger brother," I continue after a beat of silence. "He's a wild card. There are still some issues between him and the rest of the family, so I don't think he's fully trusted with company information."

"So, the oldest is our way in," Peter replies, his voice sharpening with interest. "Good thing you cozied up to him a few days ago."

"I mean, barely, but I guess," I say with a heavy sigh, stirring the rice absentmindedly. The silence stretches between us like a taut wire, snapping only when Peter's voice cuts through again.

"You sound upset," he states, his clipped tone making it clear he already knows the answer. "Is there something you'd like to share with the class?"

I lean my forehead against the cool granite countertop, my grip on the edge tightening. "You know my reservations about this part," I say quietly. "I'd prefer to stick to research."

"You had that once," Peter snaps, his voice rising. "Then you went and fucked it up. Who had to clean up your mess?"

My mouth goes dry, and the anger I try to keep in a tight ball in the pit of my stomach starts to unravel at what he insinuates by the word "mess." But I can't react. He's waiting for an answer, and I know he won't stop until I give him what he wants.

"You did," I whisper, pulling the phone away from my ear and setting it on speaker. Hearing his voice so close feels suffocating.

"That's right," he growls, his anger building with every word. "Me. Your lord and fucking savior. I was nice enough to give you a second chance, but there's no hiding behind a screen this time. If you screw this up, your ass is on the line. No one else's. Should I regret my decision?"

My fingers throb from the death grip I have on the edge of the counter. There's so much he's leaving out, so much he always leaves out. The years I spent working under him without a single complaint, doing everything he asked of me, giving him exactly what he wanted without hesitation. And, of course, he doesn't mention *her*. He never does. To Peter, she was nothing more than collateral damage. But I can't stop thinking about her. I never could. Not then. Not now.

The guilt claws at my chest, relentless and hollow, leaving nothing but echoes where my resolve should be. He's not wrong. It *is* my fault. All of it. I'm the reason I am where I am, and she's... where she is.

"No," I say, the word scraping against the inside of my throat. "I'll do it."

The words feel broken and jagged in my head, but they come out in the carefully practiced, indifferent tone I've mastered over the years. Somehow, I always let my composure slip with Peter. I walk into every conversation thinking, for once, I'll come out on top. That I'll have the upper hand. But we always spiral down this same path, the same script, the same moment where I lose.

"Good," Peter spits, his satisfaction like acid against my skin. "Now, find the information I need. I don't care if you have to fuck it out of the oldest one at this point, or even the sister's husband. Just. Get. It. Done."

Before I can force out the words that would seal my obedience for another day, he hangs up. The silence left behind is deafening, broken only by the soft hum of my microwave as it signals that my vegetables are done.

I stand there for a moment, staring at nothing, my mind a storm of regret and anger and shame. The smell of the microwaved rice and vegetables wafts toward me, but my appetite has long since disappeared.

I let out a slow breath, pushing away the sting of his words, the ache in my chest, and the memories that won't stay buried. It's just another conversation, another reminder of who Peter is and who I am under his thumb. And tomorrow, it'll be another task, another deadline, another step deeper into a hole I'm not sure that I'll ever climb out of.

With a shaky hand, I grab the bowl of rice and vegetables and place it on the counter. The act of eating feels like going through the motions of someone else's life. Like I'm not even here anymore, just a shadow of the person I once was. And maybe that's for the best. Shadows don't feel guilt. They don't feel anything at all.

Chapter 13

C hicago isn't exactly famous for warm springs, but this early April has brought an unexpected string of comfortable weather. When Natalie invited me over for dinner—just the two of us, since Davey was working late—I decided to walk from my apartment in Bucktown to her North Side townhome. It's a little over an hour on foot, but the fresh air and movement felt like the perfect antidote to a week spent holed up in the apartment.

As soon as I stepped out of the high-rise, my body fell into autopilot. I weaved through the bustling streets, dodging delivery drivers, bikers, and other pedestrians, all moving with that characteristic Chicago urgency. Even here in the city, the air felt light and crisp. Winter's grip lingered, but spring was beginning to force its way in with pockets of warmth and bright sunbeams slicing through the clouds.

Spring has always been my favorite season, especially in places like Chicago, where winter overstays its welcome. There's nothing quite like those first days when the sun does more than just shine. It thaws. People emerge from their homes like they're reborn, shaking off the lethargy of the cold months. For me, spring feels like the promise of a clean slate. A chance to shed the weight of whatever's been dragging me down and start over. With the sun warming my shoulders through my light jacket, I feel the pull of that promise.

The thought clings to me as I walk. Maybe I *can* start over. Maybe it's not too late. If I can just compartmentalize this job, keep my emotions in check, and remember why I'm doing this, then maybe, just maybe, I can find some semblance of redemption on the other side.

Natalie's invitation surprised me more than I care to admit. Not because of the opportunity it presented, but because I was actually looking forward to spending time with her. The excitement wasn't tied to what I might learn about Davey's access to information or whether Natalie might let something slip over dinner. It was the simple pleasure of her company that drew me. That realization sent an uncomfortable ripple through my chest. I've always been good at separating myself from these jobs. It's how I survive the work and justify the things I have to do. Turning people into tasks, into a checklist, dehumanizes them just enough to keep the guilt from drowning me. But Natalie? She's slipping through the cracks.

I push the thought away as I near their home. Tonight is about getting answers. If I can get a better sense of what Davey knows or if Natalie's aware of more than she lets on, this dinner will be a success.

A block from the Sinclair home, I stop at a boutique grocery store to pick up a few things: a small fruit platter, an overpriced bottle of wine, fancy crackers, and a specialty dip the cashier swears is a crowd favorite. By the time I leave, the panic bubbling under my skin has simmered down to a dull itch, manageable but persistent.

The Sinclair townhome looms ahead, an understated blend of charm and extravagance. It's not as massive as Silas's mansion, but it carries a quiet opulence that suits the Sinclairs perfectly. A brick fence with a black iron gate encloses a pristine front garden, and the grand steps leading to the entrance give the whole place an air of timeless elegance. The first story features the same white stonework as Silas's home, with arched black windows that transition to weathered antique brick on the upper levels.

Standing at the door, arms full, I press the doorbell with my knuckle and glance up at the security camera tucked into the corner of the alcove. I offer it a smile, friendly and unassuming, exactly the way I want to appear.

Natalie opens the door with a bright smile, immediately reaching for the bags in my hands. "I told you not to bring anything!" she scolds playfully, ushering me inside with a sweep of her hand.

"I'd never come empty-handed," I reply, stepping in. She lets out a small, amused huff, rolling her eyes before motioning for me to take off my jacket. As I shrug it off, she places the grocery bags on the steps of the grand wooden staircase in front of me. After taking my coat, she heads down the hallway to open a closet tucked beneath the stairs.

To my right is an oversized formal living room, outfitted with textured blue wallpaper and two light blue velvet love seats flanking a white-paneled fireplace. The space strikes a perfect balance between sophisticated and cozy, and just looking at it fills me with an unexpected sense of comfort.

I perch on the tufted ottoman near the door to slip off my boots, tucking them neatly underneath before standing. By the time I'm upright again, Natalie is gathering the grocery bags, nodding her head for me to follow.

"I can't believe the weather," she says over her shoulder as we walk. "Did you actually walk here?"

"I did," I answer, matching her pace as we move down a wide, white hallway. We pass a pristine powder room with bold, vibrant wallpaper and a dining room connected to the blue-accented living space through a cased opening. The dining room is neutral in tone but punctuated with blush pink details: artwork, a statement light fixture, and delicate glassware atop a solid wood credenza. "Did you decorate your home yourself?" I ask, genuinely curious.

She glances back at me with a small smile, nodding. "It's not everyone's taste, but it's mine."

As we step into her kitchen, my breath catches. Where the original exterior wall once stood, a massive island now bridges the transition to the new addition. Framed by two stately wood columns, the island anchors the space, its smooth countertop contrasting beautifully with the textured elements around it.

Muted green cabinets and dark-stained butcher block countertops start on the original kitchen walls before the lower cabinets seamlessly transition into the newer atrium-style section built off the back. Glass walls and a slanted ceiling stretch high above, with lush greenery visible from every angle. Open shelving with potted herbs and gleaming cookware decorate the atrium, while pendant lights hang elegantly overhead, casting a soft glow. Under the windows, the cabinets extend into a cozy built-in banquet tucked beside a glass door that opens to the backyard.

"Please tell me you designed this, too," I gasp, eyes wide.

Natalie's cheeks flush as she sets the bags on the island. "Well, I worked with an architect to make sure the house didn't collapse," she says with a dismissive wave.

I shake my head, ponying up to one of the black barstools at her side. "I knew your house would look like this, considering how you design events." I gesture toward the simple but elegant glass pendant lights overhead. "Why don't you work in interior design?"

She snorts lightly, waving off the suggestion as if it's absurd. "I don't think I'd be very good at it," she says, her face still rosy as she busies herself unpacking the food I brought. She comments that I picked a great wine, her tone shifting to polite deflection.

Watching her, I can't help but feel a pang of sadness. Seeing someone so outwardly confident and commands the attention of millionaires at events hesitate to give herself credit feels almost... devastating. Before I can stop myself, I reach out, placing my hand gently over hers to halt her movements.

"Stop brushing me off," I say, my voice soft but firm. Her hands still, and she looks up at me reluctantly. "You have real talent. Own it."

She blinks a few times, the sheen on her eyes betraying how much the words affect her. Finally, a small, grateful smile tugs at the corner of her mouth. "Thank you," she murmurs.

The pinch in my chest tightens, but I deflect the discomfort with a joke. "Remind me never to let you see my apartment. It's a cookie-cutter nightmare." I pat the back of her hand before pulling mine back to my lap.

Natalie laughs, her mood lightening, and moves to retrieve two wine glasses from a nearby cabinet. She uncorks the Sauvignon Blanc with practiced ease, pouring us each a glass. When I offer to help, she waves me off, insisting I relax as she plates the food I brought onto elegant dishes.

It's only after I've taken the time to fully admire her kitchen that I notice the mouthwatering aroma of garlic and the soft hum of the oven timer.

"Though my kitchen might suggest otherwise, I'm not much of a chef," Natalie says with a self-deprecating grin, noticing where my gaze has landed. "It's just feta pasta with tomatoes, spinach, and chicken. Oh, and there's a salad in the fridge."

"Sounds way better than anything I'd ever make," I admit, popping a piece of pineapple from the fruit platter into my mouth.

Conversation flows easily after that, as it always does with Natalie. Between discussing her next charity event, trading some half-truths about the types of "projects" I'm working on, and a few lighthearted stories from our pasts, the oven timer beeps. Natalie moves quickly, plating the pasta and salad, while I follow with our now-empty wine glasses and the half-drunk bottle of wine. She sets the dishes on the built-in banquette, motioning for me to sit as she grabs utensils and napkins.

"I don't care much for using the dining room," she admits, reaching to refill our glasses.

I swat her hand away, grabbing the bottle to do it myself. "I'd never want to leave this kitchen if I lived here either," I reply. She glances around, a faint look of pride flickering in her eyes, though she doesn't voice it.

Holding up my wine glass, I smile and tilt it toward her. She mirrors the motion, clinking her glass lightly against mine. "Remind me to thank Davey for working late," I joke.

Natalie huffs, shaking her head as she sits across from me. "As if that man needs encouragement to run himself more ragged than he already does."

I maintain a neutral expression as I cut into the chicken on my plate, ignoring the tightening in my chest. Lifting my fork to my mouth, I will away the ache and muster the courage to ask, "Does Davey work late often?"

My pulse quickens as I wait for her response, though Natalie doesn't seem to notice the slight tremor in my hand when I reach for my wine glass. She only rolls her eyes and stabs at her salad with her fork. "More often than I'd like."

I swallow hard, trying to dislodge the lump forming in my throat. *Get over yourself. Just do it.*

"It's difficult to separate this type of work from real life," I say, keeping my tone casual. "I'm sure it's even harder for him, working with family."

Natalie pauses, wiping her mouth with her napkin as she considers her response. Her eyes flicker with a mixture of appreciation and frustration, though I can't tell which is directed at me or Davey. "I'm grateful Davey works with my family. He's so good at what he does, but he thinks he has to prove himself more because he's married to me."

"Did he start working for your dad before or after you got together?" I ask, even though I already know he was a manager for two years before they crossed paths. Natalie's lips curve into a small smile, the signature Wells dimple appearing on her cheek.

"Before. But he's a director now. Though, he didn't accept the promotion right away; he thought my dad only offered it because we'd just gotten engaged. It took me an entire month to convince him to take it," she explains, sighing as she rubs her thumb along the stem of her wine glass. "Between that and Silas gearing up for my dad's retirement, they both barely sleep."

"I didn't realize your father's retirement was so close."

"He's been saying it for years, but he's finally serious now. The board has already voted in favor of Silas, and they recently set a date, signed and sealed. Silas has been hinting at nominating Davey as Chief Security Officer once he takes over, and I think that spooked him. So now, he's more focused than ever."

I process this revelation carefully. Silas wants to elevate Davey to a position just a step below his own? That's not just professional trust. That's a declaration of loyalty. If Davey is slated to become CSO, he must already have full access to the company's most sensitive information. Silas trusts him with his life, his family, and his entire legacy.

"Why doesn't Davey work from home a few days a week?" I suggest, testing the waters. "He can do his job from anywhere with the right setup."

Natalie shakes her head, her tone tinged with resignation. "He prefers his office. He says the systems are more secure there, and he doesn't want to bring his work here."

Her words confirm what I suspected. If Davey is that paranoid, any important information he handles is likely kept under lock and key at his workplace. This townhome might not hold any information I need.

"The Wells office isn't far from here, right? You could start having lunch or dinner with him on his late nights," I suggest, maintaining my easy tone.

She tilts her head, considering. "That's true. I'd just have to figure out which days he's at the downtown office or the satellite office."

My fork freezes midair.

Satellite office?

I school my expression, though my heart races. A second office, completely off my radar. How did they manage to keep it off both public and private records? Maybe it's owned by a separate business and I missed it because I didn't know to look for it.

"I didn't realize your family had more than one office in the city," I comment, taking a bite of salad to mask my curiosity.

Natalie shrugs, seemingly unfazed. "It's tiny. I think Davey and a few of his team members work there sometimes."

Her words strike me like lightning. I've been looking in the wrong place. If William or Silas has highly classified information, Davey would insist it be stored somewhere more secure than the cloud—somewhere accessible only on-site. This off-the-books office isn't just a workspace; it's likely where they house local servers.

With a strained smile, I encourage Natalie to create a schedule with Davey. By the end of the conversation, she's grinning hopefully, and I'm biting the inside of my cheek so hard I can taste blood.

If I can locate this satellite office, everything might change.

———

It's past eight by the time Davey walks in the door. I'm mid-motion, pulling my jacket from the closet when he steps inside. The look on his face tells me he's neither surprised nor pleased to find me in his home. Did Natalie tell him I was here? Or did he spy on the security cameras that undoubtedly cover every corner of this place?

The subtle security features are impossible to miss. The faint glint of a camera lens in the corner of the living room, the quiet hum of a system embedded somewhere in the walls. It's all so understated, yet unmistakably thorough, and fits Davey to a tee. And figuring out where that secret second office is without tipping him off will likely be the greatest challenge of my career.

"Headed out, Ms. Page?" he asks, his tone polite but not hiding the faint hope behind it.

Natalie, standing off to the side, scowls at him, her annoyance palpable.

"Yes, Davey. You can have your wife back for the night," I reply, slipping my arms into my jacket and pulling my hair out from under the collar. I step aside as he approaches the closet to hang up his own coat, but not before leaning into Natalie and planting a firm, lingering kiss on her lips.

Any trace of irritation she might've had vanishes instantly, melting away under his touch. The look Davey gives her when he pulls back is so intimate, so full of quiet devotion, that it feels like I've intruded on something private. I move towards the door, focusing instead on putting on my boots.

For all the reservations I have about him, there's never been any doubt about his love for Natalie. It's unwavering, absolute. His world revolves around her, and it makes Peter's earlier instruction to use Davey however I can make bile rise to my throat.

I stand and Natalie pulls away from her husband, skirting past him to see me out. "We're still on for Thursday?"

It hadn't taken much to convince her to plan weekly dinner dates, especially on nights she knows Davey tends to work late. Thursday, we're trying a new restaurant in one of the downtown hotels.

"It's a date," I confirm with a smile.

Natalie wraps me in a warm hug, the faint scent of her perfume brushing against me. "Are you sure I can't call you a car?" she asks, for what must be the third or fourth time tonight.

"I'll be fine," I assure her. The cold night air will do me some good. It's another chance to clear my head and think about how I might spend more time with her before Thursday.

After one last goodbye, I slip out the door and let it close soundly behind me. The sun has long since dipped behind the skyline, and the night air bites against my cheeks. Car tires crackle against the pavement, headlights cutting through the dim street as engines hum softly in the distance.

"Took you long enough."

The familiar voice works its way down my spine, low and smooth, like velvet drawn over steel. I turn toward the street, fighting the shiver that climbs up my body—a reaction I desperately wish I could blame entirely on the cold.

Under the glow of a streetlight, Silas leans casually against the passenger door of a sleek black sports car. His hands are buried in the pockets of his coat, ankles crossed, exuding that effortless confidence that's somehow both magnetic and infuriating.

Davey must have told him that Natalie had me over for dinner—probably the reason he dropped Davey off in the first place. Which means Silas didn't just stumble upon me. He came looking, just like I wanted him to.

Everything is going according to plan, right?

Swallowing the lump in my throat, I arch an eyebrow and muster my usual deflection. "If I realized I was making the King of Chicago wait, I would have taken my time." My legs feel unsteady as I descend the stairs, heat simmering in my veins with each step closer to him. His stubble is longer than it was the last time I saw him, that infuriating curl still hanging over the edge of his glasses. The chilly air has left his cheeks pink, and the gleam in his eyes looks eerily similar to the one he gave me when he deposited me in my car after the auction.

"Do you need something?" My tone is sharper than intended, but he doesn't seem bothered. If anything, he looks amused.

He shrugs nonchalantly. "I need plenty of things."

I unlatch the gate and step out of the Sinclair courtyard. Behind him, the street is lined with slowly moving cars, and to my left, the distant hue of red, blue, and white lights reflects off the nearby buildings. There must have been an accident further down the street.

"I can't imagine you need much," I counter, stuffing my hands into my pockets to shield them from the biting wind. It's colder than I anticipated, and I silently curse myself for not wearing a thicker jacket.

Silas pushes off the side of his Aston Martin, moving with the slow, predatory grace of a jungle cat. "You didn't text me when you got home after the auction," he says, cutting straight to the point.

"Ah," I begin, feigning casual indifference. "I texted Natalie. I'm sure she told you?"

"She did."

"Then I don't see what the problem is."

Silas pins me with a look so intense it feels like it's peeling back every layer I try to keep hidden. His eyes seem to pull me in, their darkness deepening as he takes a long stride toward me. It takes everything I have not to take a step back.

"I didn't ask you to text my sister," he says, his voice low and deliberate. "I asked you to text me."

The sharp edge of annoyance slices through the spell his proximity casts. Leave it to him to think I owe him something. I tsk and shake my head. "So demanding."

His lips quirk in response, but the gleam in his eyes shifts, glowing like embers stoked into a flame. He leans in slightly, his voice dropping. "You don't even know the half of it."

Heat coils low in my stomach at his words, and for a moment, my brain short-circuits. Just when I think I've got him figured out, he throws me off balance with that look. That vexing look that makes it impossible to remember what I'm supposed to be doing.

And that's the problem, isn't it? He's not just some stranger I can flirt with and forget. He's Silas Wells—intelligent, authoritative, and every bit the formidable man the world sees him as. He's also the one standing outside his sister's home, waiting for me, as if I'm the most pressing thing on his mind.

This is what you wanted, I remind myself, trying to tamp down the fire coursing through me. *Stick to the plan.*

The silence between us stretches, and my body sways imperceptibly toward his, as if pulled by an invisible string. His glasses reflect the faint streetlights, and for a moment, I catch my own image in them: parted lips, dilated pupils, and desire written all over my face.

The sharp honk of a car rips me out of the moment, cutting through the haze like a cold splash of water and reminding me of the chill in the night air. I shiver, taking a step back to put some much-needed distance between us. But before I can retreat further, Silas's hand darts out, his fingers curling around my elbow as a jogger passes behind me.

My skin burns under my jacket where his hand touches me. What the hell is wrong with me? I've faced down people who could destroy me with a single word, and yet here I am, unraveling over a man holding my elbow. This isn't me.

I clear my throat, glancing toward the distant flashing lights of the traffic jam. "I should get going."

His grip on my elbow tightens ever so slightly, his chuckle reverberating down my arm. "Get in the car, Scarlett."

The command jolts me back to myself. There it is. His arrogance.

I bristle, glaring up at him. "I'm perfectly fine walking home."

"I'm sure you are," he says placatingly, his grip remaining firm as he steps closer, closing the gap I just created. "But you're not going to. You can get in willingly, or I can put you in there and strap you in myself."

The quiet authority of his tone makes my heart stutter and my temper flare all at once. It's clear he's not bluffing, and part of me wants to push back and remind him I'm not someone who takes orders. But I know better. The smarter move is to let this play out, to spend more time with him and nudge him closer to trusting me. Still, I won't let him win so easily. If I'm getting in that car, it'll be on my terms.

Leaning into him, I rise onto my toes, steadying myself with one hand on his chest. His breath catches as my lips brush against his ear, and I whisper with sharp defiance, "Ask. Nicely."

His body goes rigid beneath my touch, the tension radiating off him in waves. For a moment, he's perfectly still, the only movement a subtle tick in his jaw. When he finally speaks, his voice is a low, gravelly growl. "Scarlett, please get in the car."

A triumphant smile spreads across my face as I pull back, patting his chest twice. "Now, was that so hard?"

His hand falls away from my elbow as I stride past him and yank open the passenger door. The warm interior of the car envelops me as I slide into the seat, the smell of expensive leather and cleaner filling my senses. I shut the door firmly before he has the chance to do it for me, cutting off any attempt at another word.

As I buckle, I watch him stand outside the car for a moment, his posture tense. He stretches his neck, the tight muscles pulling visibly under his skin, before finally making his way around to the driver's side. Whatever storm is brewing behind his calm exterior, I know one thing for sure: I've won this round.

The way he slides into the driver's seat is almost as intoxicating as the sharp, woodsy notes of his cologne that envelop the closed space. His fingers curl around the steering wheel, perhaps just a fraction too tight, the knuckles paling against the contrast of his dark, tanned skin. Then his gaze meets mine and, for a moment, it feels like all the air has been sucked out of the cabin.

The look in his eyes is a warning. It tells me I've crossed a line, that I'm teetering dangerously close to something I might not be ready for. But instead of cooling the fire raging within me, his intensity fans the flames. A spark bolts across my body, igniting that restless, defiant part of me that I thought I'd buried long ago.

There's something about riling this man up, about poking at his carefully constructed composure, that fuels a wicked, feral thrill deep inside of me. Maybe it's the power dynamic, the way he's used to bending others to his will, but has yet to figure out how to bend me. Maybe it's the way he looks at me, like he's deciding whether to argue or conquer. Whatever it is, I'm too far gone to resist the temptation to push further.

A slow, Cheshire grin spreads across my lips, and I lean back into the plush leather seat, crossing my legs leisurely. "Are we pretending you don't already know where I live, or can we just skip the part where you ask for my address?"

Chapter 14

S ilas doesn't answer my question about the address, opting instead to slip seamlessly into traffic between two cars. His movements are fluid, unhurried, like the city and its chaos submit to him. The frustration I'd sparked seems to dissolve as he settles into his seat, one wrist draped casually over the top of the wheel. He fits so perfectly in a car like this. Sleek, powerful, and undeniably expensive. My gaze lingers for a beat too long, and I quickly avert my eyes to the passenger window to keep myself from staring.

"Any clue what all that's about?" I ask, nodding toward the endless stretch of brake lights and the flicker of emergency vehicles up ahead.

His lips twitch, not quite a smile but close. "Your guess is as good as mine."

"Well, it can't be too bad if Davey didn't run into the house like a bat out of hell," I reply, leaning back and letting my eyes wander over the car's pristine, dark interior. Everything is polished and smooth, impossibly refined. Curiosity gets the better of me, and I trace my fingertips over the dash. It's just as soft and luxurious as it looks.

Silas breathes out a quiet laugh, the sound low and warm. "He's that easy to read, huh?"

"There's nothing subtle about Davey when it comes to your sister," I smirk, folding my hands in my lap. Silas nods in my peripheral vision, focus shifting back to the road as we crawl forward in the traffic.

"He loves her a lot," he says, as if stating an undeniable truth.

"No kidding," I snort. "It's sweet, though. She deserves someone who looks at and thinks of her that way."

His hand drifts through his already perfectly tousled hair, pushing it back as he exhales, the sound thoughtful. "Agreed," he says finally. "Natalie is the best of all of us."

I purse my lips at his words, my mind racing. She's the best of all of them? His family? Is that because she's not involved in whatever secrets or schemes he might be hiding? I don't dare push, though the temptation to dig deeper is a gnawing itch I can't quite scratch.

"She was telling me how much you both have been working," I venture instead, testing the waters. "Any chance you could tell Davey to get home in time for dinner a few days a week?"

"I do. Often." His chuckle is humorless, and there's a sharpness to his tone that catches me off guard. "That man is perpetually worried about work."

"Not the worst trait to have in your Director of Security," I reply lightly and watch the pedestrians on the sidewalk. They move briskly, heads down and jackets pulled tight against the cool night air.

"No, it isn't," he agrees, but there's an edge to his voice now, something that feels heavier than the conversation warrants. "But I also don't want work to be the reason my sister confides in new... friends about her marriage."

I turn my face to stare out at the slow-moving traffic. Even though I intrigue him, his guard is still up. And I can't blame him for that.

"She only told me she misses him," I say after a beat. "But I get what you mean. I figured you knowing was better than nothing."

The silence that follows feels stretched too thin, but I don't press. This isn't the battle I want to fight, and it certainly isn't the hill I want to die on. Eventually, the tension eases, and when he glances at me again, his eyes are softer, less guarded.

"Thanks," he murmurs, the word so quiet it almost gets lost in the hum of the engine.

"Sure," I whisper back, a tentative truce settling between us.

When he says nothing else, I reach for the radio, flipping through Silas's pre-set channels until I land on a nineties alternative rock station playing "Wonderwall." The familiar strumming of the acoustic guitar fills the car, and I lean back against the headrest, closing my eyes. This song always reminds me of one of the few high school dances I could afford to scrape enough money together to attend.

I'd been so nervous to dance with Danny O'Neil, palms sweaty against the back of his crisp, black collared shirt. I was sure he'd notice, but if he did, he didn't say anything. He just smiled that silly grin of his the whole time as we swayed awkwardly under the dim glow of the Christmas lights strung haphazardly across the gym ceiling. When the slow song ended, I bolted to the bathroom to wipe my hands on the paper towels, mortified. Later, he kissed me on the cheek, and I walked home practically skipping, clutching that memory like a treasure through the turbulent years that followed.

"I didn't take you as an Oasis fan," Silas's voice cuts through the haze of my thoughts, snapping me back to the present. I blink, the glow of passing headlights illuminating the faint smile playing on his lips.

"My dad wasn't good for much," I say without thinking, my tone softened by the unexpected vulnerability of the memory. Then, realizing I might've said too much, I quickly tack on, "But he had great taste in music."

To my relief, Silas doesn't pry. Instead, he nods and says simply, "Alternative rock is my favorite, too." His tone is appreciative, and I'm grateful for the reprieve.

Laughing lightly, I tease, "I wasn't expecting that. I figured your parents only let you listen to Mozart and Bach."

A hint of amusement tugs at the corner of his mouth. "You're not entirely wrong. But I went to boarding school, so they couldn't do much about it."

"Wow, a little rebel," I say with exaggerated mockery. "Did you also eat candy after brushing your teeth?"

He rolls his eyes, but the slight darkening of his smile doesn't go unnoticed. "That smart mouth," he breathes, as though he's speaking more to himself than to me.

"What about it?" I taunt, unable to resist poking at the crack in his composure. I lean back in my seat, my gaze fixed on him. Though he doesn't look directly at me, I can feel his attention like a physical force.

"It never knows when to stop," he replies, his tone cool but with an edge of challenge.

"There isn't much that would make it stop," I counter, pushing just a little further.

Without warning, Silas veers sharply to the right, peeling away from the crowded roadway and onto a side street. The sudden shift presses me into the seat, my stomach lurching as the car accelerates. My fingers instinctively clutch at anything I can grab; one hand gripping the door pull, the other landing on the center console. Silas doesn't slow. He weaves seamlessly between cars, the engine roaring with each turn, buildings and streetlights blurring into streaks of color.

The rational part of my brain registers the danger, the recklessness of his driving, but another part of me—the part I don't want to acknowledge—can't help but feel exhilarated. My pulse thrums, and a heat unfurls low in my stomach, spreading through my body like a tidal wave.

Why does this feel like more than just adrenaline?

I clamp down on the thought, willing myself to focus. My breaths come fast and shallow, but I force my face to remain calm, refusing to give him the satisfaction. This is a game to him, a test to see if I'll yield like all the others who've likely sat in this very seat. He won't get that from me. I don't care how captivating he looks with his wild eyes and easy control of the wheel.

Finally, the car jerks to a stop at a red light, the engine humming in the sudden stillness. My chest heaves, but I fight to steady my breathing, nostrils flaring as I exhale slowly. The radio is still playing softly in the background, the only other sound is the faint ringing in my ears.

Silas doesn't move. He watches me intently, gaze dragging down to my chest and lingering for a moment too long before snapping back to my face. The crimson glow of the traffic light casts harsh shadows across his features, highlighting the curve of his jaw and the smirk that tugs at his lips, dark and dangerous.

My fingers ache from the grip I've maintained on the door pull and the center console. It's only then that I realize my left hand is wrapped tightly around Silas's forearm, his muscles flexing beneath my touch. The realization sends a jolt through me, and my grip falters, fingers brushing against the hard lines of his arm before I pull away. His gaze flickers down, catching the movement, and something in his eyes shifts that makes my breath hitch.

The pounding of blood in my ears hasn't stopped, but I somehow manage to find my voice. "Who taught you to drive like that? Vin Diesel?"

A noise escapes from Silas's throat—a mix between a laugh and a bark. The sound is so unexpected that it startles me, and before I can process it, he reaches over, his fingers wrapping firmly around my wrist. My breath catches as he pulls it toward himself and presses his thumb against the inside of my wrist.

"What are you doing?" I snap, trying to tug my hand back, but his grip tightens ever so slightly, keeping me in place.

He doesn't answer immediately. Instead, his focus sharpens, the corners of his mouth twitching as he counts the beats of my pulse. The seconds stretch unbearably long, the sensation of his thumb resting against my skin heightening the fire flowing through my veins. I don't know what's worse, the intimate hold or the fact that my heart is pounding so hard I'm sure he can feel every erratic thrum.

When he finally lets out a low chuckle, it's rich and infuriatingly smug. "Not as tough as you let on," he remarks, his nearly black eyes cutting to mine. The fingers at my wrist linger for a second longer, running softly down the side of my arm before falling away completely.

The moment of contact leaves a jolt of electricity in its wake, and my head spins, both from the sensation and his sheer audacity. I open my mouth, poised to retort, but the light turns green, and before I can utter a single word, he forces the car back into motion just enough to make my head snap back.

"All The Small Things" begins playing over the speakers, and I can't think of anything to say that won't come out breathy and nervous. My mind is a tangle of scattered thoughts, caught somewhere between irritation, adrenaline, and something far more confusing.

I steal a glance at him, trying to steady myself. Silas looks as calm as ever, his posture relaxed as he shifts gears and navigates the nearly empty road with precision. But there's a hint of a smirk playing at the edge of his lips, and I realize with growing frustration that he knows exactly how much he's gotten under my skin.

Determined not to let him win, I cross my arms over my chest and lean back in my seat, feigning indifference. "You're insufferable, you know that?"

The smirk grows, his eyes flicking toward me for a split second before returning to the road. "So I've been told."

I roll my eyes, my pulse finally beginning to slow, though the warmth in my cheeks lingers. "What exactly was the point of that little stunt? Are you trying to give me a heart attack or prove something?"

He shrugs, the movement effortless. "Maybe I just wanted to see how you'd handle it."

"And?" I challenge, arching an eyebrow, though my voice is still slightly shaky.

His smile deepens. "You're still here, aren't you?"

I bite the inside of my cheek to keep from snapping back, unwilling to give him the gratification of riling me further. Instead, I turn my gaze out the window, watching the city blur past, though my attention is painfully aware of every subtle shift in his demeanor.

The steady rhythm of the streetlights casts alternating shadows over Silas's profile, sharpening the lines of his face and creating an almost cinematic contrast. His voice cuts through the quiet, casual and confident. "I went to Columbia, by the way."

I blink at him, caught completely off guard. "Huh?"

His white teeth flash as he smiles, a flicker of amusement dancing across his face. The cold, calculated Silas evaporates, replaced by the flirtatious, easygoing man who had greeted me at Natalie's doorstep earlier. It's dizzying how effortlessly he switches between personas.

"You never gave me the third degree when we were having lunch a few weeks ago," he says, voice teasing. "Since you clearly have no interest in who I am, I'm assuming you still haven't looked into me," he pauses, turning slightly toward me, his tongue sweeping over his bottom lip. "Or have you?"

My eyes widen. *Is this guy for real?* "We weren't having lunch; *you* interrupted *mine*. And that's what you're thinking about right now?"

"That's not a no."

I open my mouth, ready to rebuff him, but nothing comes out. Again. The satisfaction in his expression grows as he catches my hesitation, and with a huff, I cross my arms over my chest before turning toward the window. The heat pumping from the car vents feels stifling now.

Does he have a personality disorder?

"You held me hostage at a charity auction less than a week ago," I finally reply, trying to regain control of the conversation. "I have every right to look into my kidnapper."

"Is that how you describe being wined and dined as the date of the host?" he counters, turning onto a main road. My apartment building is just a few blocks away now.

"Wined and dined? That's generous," I scoff. "I spent most of the night with your sister and brother-in-law, who hates me, while you talked business with the other rich men in Chicago."

"You didn't seem to mind." His smirk sharpens. "Didn't you say I did a fantastic job of leaving you alone that night?" he adds, his tone overconfident.

He's not wrong—I'd give him that much. Silas had been perfectly polite, letting me roam freely most of the evening. But now? Now I have no idea which version of him is the real one. Is he the composed, charming host, or the reckless maniac who races through Chicago streets? Is this just an elaborate act to keep me on my toes?

As my building comes into view, I instinctively reach for my seatbelt, but before I can unbuckle it, Silas's hand lands on mine, his calloused fingers pressing lightly against my skin. I glance up at him from under my lashes, but he keeps his gaze firmly on the road, his brows furrowed with a seriousness I wasn't expecting.

"Wait until I'm parked," he commands. As if I'm going to open the door to tuck and roll.

I gape at him. "That's funny, coming from the guy who just Tokyo Drifted across the city."

The corner of his mouth twitches, his smirk impossible to hide. "You seemed to like it plenty."

Before I can argue, I notice the subtle slide of his fingers across the back of my hand. A deliberate, lingering touch. My brain feels deep-fried, unable to process his many moods or my body's infuriating response to his presence. The car slows as we pull up to my building, and he releases my hand, leaving my skin cold where his warmth had been.

I fumble with the seatbelt and turn to grab the door handle, but I can't stop the words that tumble out of my mouth. "You seriously think I liked that?"

The sharp edges of my voice are dulled by breathlessness, and I hate that I've revealed even a sliver of how rattled I am. A cool gust of air hits me as I push the door open, grounding me for a moment. I step out into the night, desperate to escape the suffocating pull of this man.

But I can't help myself. I turn back toward him, determined to have the last word. His face is bathed in the soft light spilling from my building, his eyes shimmering with that dangerous, knowing glint. He leans lazily, one arm draped behind the passenger headrest, and his curls frame his face in a way that makes him look effortlessly disarming.

"Let's not pretend," he murmurs, his voice low and intimate. He cocks his head to the side, his smile a razor-sharp tease. "You liked that as much as I did."

The prickle of heat rises on the back of my neck, but I set my jaw and glare at him. Without another word, I slam the door shut, my boots clicking angrily against the pavement as I stalk toward the entrance.

From behind me, his voice rings out, playful and dripping with arrogance. "I don't like liars, Ms. Page."

I glance back briefly to see him ducking toward the now open window to see me, my own smirk curling at the corners of my mouth.

If that's the case, you're in for a real treat, Mr. Wells.

CHAPTER 15

I'm typing the final lines of a new script to probe unprotected access points in the Wells cloud when my phone pings. Blurry-eyed from hours of staring at monitors, I blink a few times to bring the notification into focus.

Harrison.

My fingers freeze mid-keystroke. I haven't heard from him since before the auction. I assumed Peter sent him away as punishment for the fiasco, but I should've known better. Peter doesn't waste resources lightly, and Harrison's misstep probably wasn't big enough to warrant permanent removal. Worst case, they'd just have to replace me. Still, his silence had been a small reprieve from Peter's constant watch.

The notification sits on my screen, but I let it linger, savoring a moment of quiet control before turning back to my monitors.

Natalie's offhand mention of that satellite office has been gnawing at me. I've gone back into the Wells cloud for another pass, scouring for blueprints, access logs, correspondence, anything that could hint at its existence. But the search came up empty. No mentions, no anomalies. It's as if the place doesn't exist.

Natalie mentioned it so casually, with no awareness of the secrecy surrounding it. She probably doesn't even realize this office might be a closely guarded secret.

I've taken things further than I usually do. Last week, I tailed Davey every day, hoping to catch him making a detour or breaking his routine. But he never did. Every morning, he drove straight to the flagship office downtown, parking in the underground garage reserved for upper management. He didn't leave until well after seven or eight in the evening, heading directly home. If he's accessing this secondary location, he's doing it during the day, and likely in another vehicle as a backseat passenger. Short of hiding myself in his briefcase, there's no safe way to pinpoint when or where he's going.

The level of confidentiality surrounding this office leads me to an unfortunate conclusion: the location and purpose of this site are likely buried in the highly encrypted files I've been avoiding. Files that Peter insisted I decrypt alone.

I've delayed long enough. I'm good at what I do: penetration testing, bypassing firewalls, exploiting vulnerabilities, and social engineering. But cryptography? That's different. I can manage, but there are others who are far better—experts Peter has on retainer.

When I asked Peter, for the second time, if I could loop in one of those associates for this, he nearly bit my head off and asked why he even bothered picking me for the job if I couldn't handle a simple task.

His words still echo in my mind, laced with disdain. In the past, he's had no problem letting me pull in specialists when necessary. Now, his refusal feels deliberate, like a setup. If I fail, he'll have an excuse to punish me. That's Peter's way: always keeping the power dynamic skewed in his favor, always reminding me that I'm replaceable.

So, my days have been spent researching.

After hours scouring darknet forums, I found whispers of a small vulnerability in the framework the Wells's encryption system uses. The script I'm writing is designed to exploit that vulnerability. Once finished, I'll test it in a sandbox environment that mimics the Wells system as closely as possible. If it works without setting off alarms, I'll be ready to deploy it. It's a long shot, but it might be enough. My palms sweat at the thought. Success means gaining access to their most protected files. Failure means triggering every red flag in their arsenal.

My phone buzzes again. Harrison. His name flashes across the screen, breaking my focus.

Harrison: You're joining me for dinner downtown.
Harrison: 7:30 at the Gilded Sear. Formal dress code.

The clock on my phone reads 5:26. My skin prickles with frustration as I toss the phone onto my desk and sink back into my chair, staring at the ceiling. There's no reason to respond. Harrison knows I'll be there. Peter knows I'll be there. I always show up. It's not a choice. It hasn't been for a long time.

Six years ago, I wouldn't have believed this would become my life. Back then, I was living in a modest apartment in Chandler, Arizona, working remote gigs Peter sent my way. The pay was steady, the work manageable, and I was content. Drew and I spent our days dreaming about the house we'd buy together—a little place with enough room for a garden, a dog, and the kind of peace I'd never known growing up. We were happy. It felt like we were finally getting ahead, finally building something solid.

Until it all crumbled.

Thinking about Drew is like walking barefoot through broken glass, no matter how much time passes. I avoid it when I can, but in moments like this, when Harrison and Peter's demands corner me, she's all I can see.

For years, I could recall her face perfectly: her sun-kissed skin, the medium brown waves of her hair, the green eyes so vibrant they could outshine a forest. But now, the edges are fuzzy. Did she have freckles across her nose or just on her cheeks? Were her bottom front teeth as crooked as I remember, or has my memory warped them over time? Even her laugh—her uninhibited, musical belly laugh—feels distant, like it's slipping away.

I close my eyes and try to hold on to her for just a moment longer.

We met during my freshman year at Arizona State. Same computer science program, same overwhelming lecture halls, and the same desperate need for a friendly face in a sea of strangers. Drew was bright, magnetic, and impossibly kind. By the end of our first month, we were study partners. By the end of the second, we were inseparable.

But we didn't become *Drew and me* until she found me crying in the back of the library, buried under the weight of everything I couldn't carry. I'd hit a wall—financially, emotionally, and physically. My job at the diner barely covered rent, let alone anything else. I was living on leftover scraps and overdrafted accounts, and it still wasn't enough.

Drew didn't judge me. She didn't pity me. She just held me, stroking my hair and whispering that I wasn't a failure. That I'd done everything I could, and it wasn't my fault. And then she started to fix it.

She called the housing office and terminated her dorm contract. She told me she was moving in. No arguments, no hesitation. We'd make it work, she said. Between the two of us, we could afford the rent. She even made a joke about the studio apartment being like a permanent sleepover.

She gave me a kind of love I'd never known before.

Growing up, my parents were too busy hating each other to love me. Their marriage was a mistake, an accident born from an unplanned pregnancy, and I was the physical reminder of everything wrong between them. My father always said I had my mother's "sharp tongue," and my mother never missed a chance to call me "useless" like my dad. I tried for years to earn their approval. To make myself small, agreeable, perfect. But nothing worked.

When I was fifteen, my mom nearly spit in my face for drinking the last of the milk. That small moment snapped something inside me—or, maybe, it welded itself shut. The pain, the longing for their love, it all vanished. I became hollow, numb. After that, I treated our relationship like a business transaction. I paid them rent, bought my own groceries, and avoided them entirely.

When ASU accepted me, I saw my escape. My ticket to freedom. I didn't care that they refused to co-sign my student loans or told me I'd never make it in computer science. I packed my bags, left without a goodbye, and never looked back.

It wasn't easy. My federal loans barely covered tuition, and the part-time job I picked up didn't keep me afloat. I was drowning in bills, skipping meals, and running on fumes. By the time Drew moved in, I didn't have a single penny to my name.

But she made it work. We made it work.

Drew became my family. My person. She saw something in me that no one else ever had, not even myself.

And then she was gone.

The chime of my phone snaps me out of the spiral.

Harrison: Don't be fucking late.

I arrive a block from the Gilded Sear at 7:27 and take my time walking the street toward the upscale restaurant, letting the cool April breeze calm my nerves. By the time I step into the elevator and reach the 15th floor, the clock has just ticked over to 7:33. I approach the hostess desk, waiting behind other guests as the clock turns to 7:34. That small rebellion satisfies something deep within me. A tiny act of defiance that warms my body from the inside out.

By the time the young hostess in her neatly braided hair guides me toward Harrison's table, I can't stop the satisfied smile from spreading across my face.

The Gilded Sear is every bit as luxurious as its reputation: coffered ceilings, rich wood paneling, and buttery leather-bound booths bathed in the soft glow of crystal chandeliers. The muted lighting and flickering tea candles on every table add to the moody, elegant atmosphere. Even on a Friday night, the restaurant hums with the steady buzz of patrons and waitstaff, each moving with practiced precision.

And then there's Harrison.

Sitting at a corner table, facing the entire room with the perfect vantage point. He looks every bit the polished gentleman he wants the world to see. His dark blue suit is tailored well, his long, dirty-blond hair combed back into a sleek bun, and even his stubble is neatly trimmed. It's a facade, just like everything else about him. But I'd be lying if I said this isn't the best I've ever seen him look.

Of course, that doesn't stop the way his eyes darken the moment he sees me. The grin he plasters on as he stands is so exaggerated it borders on comical. There's something immensely gratifying about making him wait and forcing him to play the part of a doting gentleman in public.

"Scarlett," he calls out, his voice loud enough to draw the attention of nearby diners. Arms outstretched, he steps forward, his every move a performance. I force a bright smile, nodding politely to the hostess as I step into his embrace.

It isn't optional. Nothing ever is with Harrison.

I wrap my arms around his neck with the barest enthusiasm, but he isn't having it. His hands grip my hips through the thin silk of my dress, yanking me flush against him. My body stiffens as his head dips to the side of my neck, his lips brushing the skin below my ear.

"I told you not to be fucking late," he hisses, venom punctuating every syllable.

It takes everything I have not to pull away. Instead, I plaster on a sweet smile, my voice dripping with mock innocence. "Sorry I kept you waiting. The hostess was busy helping other guests."

I count to three before untangling myself from his hold. Harrison steps back, gesturing to the chair directly beside his, rather than the one across the table. His pointed look makes it clear there will be no argument. I sit, but not without rolling my eyes when my back is to him and the room for a brief moment.

Harrison follows, pushing his chair closer to mine until our knees bump beneath the table and making my skin crawl. Through gritted teeth, I mutter, "Is there a reason you're practically sitting in my lap?"

He ignores my question, instead grabbing both of my hands from my lap and placing them between us, fully visible to the rest of the restaurant. The grip of his fingers is rough, bordering on painful, and I resist the urge to yank away.

"You're only to look at me," he says, his tone low and sickly sweet, a perfect contrast to the disgust in his icy blue eyes. One of his hands releases mine, only to move to my face, his dry palm brushing my cheek with calculated gentleness. "And it better be with those fuck-me eyes I saw you give that Wells kid in those auction photos."

Rage bubbles in my chest, but I can't afford to let it surface. His expression dares me to defy him, to challenge his authority here and now. Instead, I lean into his touch, a hollow smile stretching across my lips.

"I'm going to fucking kill you," I whisper through my teeth, the conversation around us masking the threat.

His grip on my hand tightens painfully, his mocking grin widening. "Not if I kill you first."

Our stare down is interrupted by the arrival of the waiter. Taking the opportunity to break contact, I feign embarrassment, withdrawing my hands and ordering a glass of wine from the sommelier's recommendations. Harrison orders a craft beer before the waiter leaves with a curt nod.

Once he's out of earshot, I turn my attention back to my so-called date. "What's your name tonight, and what the fuck are we doing here?" My question doesn't have the same heat it would if I could talk at a normal volume.

"Tristan," he says easily, swirling his water glass. "And we're here as a favor for Peter."

"What kind of favor involves you pawing at me like I'm a fucking chew toy?"

"You'll see."

"When?"

"When I say so," he shoots back, a fake smile plastered across his face.

I press my lips together, my free hand reaching for the menu as a distraction. Harrison still hasn't let go, his grip loose but possessive, a silent reminder that I'm exactly where he wants me. I force myself to focus on the neatly printed dish names, skimming over them without actually processing a single word.

I want to look up. To glance around the room to find whatever it is we're here for, but I don't. I already know the rules and what will happen if I break them, especially if this dinner is a favor for Peter.

The minutes drag, stretched thin by the weight of his touch and the suffocating silence between us. When the waiter finally returns with our drinks, Harrison doesn't reach for his beer right away. Instead, he looks directly at me.

Knowing I can't ignore him, I glance up from the menu once again. My eye contact is invitation enough for him because he leans in too close, yet again. With lazy, deliberate movements, Harrison brushes my hair off the shoulder closest to him. As I hold my breath, he makes a fanatical show of perusing my décolletage with his eyes, dipping lower and lower until he is just blatantly staring at my chest. My teeth clench as I fight the urge to recoil. The hand resting under his on the table is fisted so tight, I swear my nails are breaking through the skin of my palm.

As if sensing he is walking a dangerous tightrope with my patience, Harrison presses his lips to the shell of my ear, the heat of his breath turning my stomach.

"If you don't start acting like you're into me, we're going to have some problems," he hisses. "Now, fake a laugh."

I close my eyes, and all I see is red. Anger. Blood. The roses on his future casket. I never want this disgusting human to touch me again. The sheer audacity of his words makes every muscle in my body tenses with the effort of not reacting.

But I have to endure this. It's just one night. Actresses worse than me have faked liking men. Gold diggers constantly do it. I can do this. I *have* to do this.

The giggle that escapes my lips isn't my own. I don't know where I pull it from, but it works because Harrison pulls back just enough to meet my eyes, his diabolical smile widening with satisfaction. It's a smile that tells me he knows he's winning this round, and the knowledge only makes my blood boil hotter.

Without another word, he reaches for his beer and holds it up to me in a toast. I force myself to mimic his relaxed posture, even when my hand shakes slightly around the stem of my glass as I touch it to his. It takes every ounce of self-control not to drain the wine in one go to numb the anger, but I can't afford to lose my focus. Not tonight. Not when I have no idea what else he has planned.

The rest of dinner is an excruciating performance. Harrison keeps up the charade, leaning in too close, his hand constantly on the back of my chair, brushing against my bare shoulder. Every move is meant to provoke me while ensuring I can't lash out. Our quiet threats are hidden behind fake smiles, and every once in a while, I have to force a giggle just to satisfy his growing need for control.

And then comes dessert.

The crème brûlée I ordered sits mostly untouched on my plate as Harrison leans in, grabbing my chin with his hand. His grip is harsh, fingers digging into my skin with enough force to leave a mark. I know what's coming before he even moves.

"Harrison, don't—"

But it's too late. His mouth crashes into mine, his hand moving to the back of my neck to hold me in place. I freeze, panic seizing my limbs. His stubble scrapes against my skin, and the moment I feel his tongue at the seam of my lips, I want to scream.

When I don't immediately comply, his free hand finds my thigh under the table, squeezing hard enough to make me gasp. That's all he needs to force his way in, his tongue invading my mouth with violence, and bile rises in my throat.

I want to fight him. I want to shove him back and storm out, but every movement, every place he's touching me, has a purpose. He isn't going to let me go until I play along.

Though my body fights me, I force myself to relax, loosen my jaw, and escape to the recesses of my mind. This isn't the first time I've endured something like this. But it sure as hell will be the last.

Eventually, he pulls back and the fingers on my legs unclench, though he holds my face close to his by my nape. "You're going to excuse yourself to the bathroom," he says quietly, breath hot against my lips. "And when you get back, we're leaving."

He lets me go, hand falling to his lap as he leans back with an arrogant, fake grin. My chest heaves as I force myself to stand, smoothing out the front of my dress. My face burns with fury and humiliation, but I turn and walk calmly toward the bathroom, every step fueled by a singular thought.

How fucking dare he.

Remembering I passed the restroom on my way in, my feet carry me in that direction while my vision tunnels. But I don't allow it to take me. He will not break me. Not after this many years and not over a kiss, even if I want to scrub the memory from the folds of my brain.

Just get through the next ten minutes.

Once inside the opulent, empty bathroom, I bypass the stalls and go straight for the sink, twisting the hot water on full blast. Without hesitation, I shove my mouth under the spout, letting the scalding water hit my gums and tongue. The burn is a welcome distraction, a cleansing pain to erase the taste and feel of that vile man from my insides. I swish until every inch of my mouth feels raw, spitting it all into the basin below.

The soap dispenser tempts me. God, it tempts me. But how do I explain that if someone walks in and catches me scrubbing my mouth like I'm trying to disinfect a crime scene? Especially if it's someone I know or who just witnessed that farce of a dinner. I shake off the thought and brace my hands on the cool edge of the sink, forcing myself to stare into the mirror.

My reflection mocks me. Glassy eyes threatening tears, lips swollen from Harrison's assault, hair mussed in a way that screams "attentive date" to onlookers but makes my skin crawl. My silk dress is wrinkled and clings in all the wrong places, a casualty of his unyielding hold. If you don't look too closely, I'm a woman who's hopelessly smitten, but I know the truth. He knows the truth. My fingers curl against the porcelain, wishing it were his windpipe beneath them.

Breathe. In for ten. Out for ten.

Silas's gravelly whisper from the auction floats into my mind. It surprises me, but it also smooths the jagged edges of my thoughts. His words loop in my head as I force myself to follow the rhythm. Inhale. Exhale. Again. And again.

The minutes tick by as I fix myself in the mirror, willing my composure to return. My eyes clear. The redness on my lips starts to fade. My hair is smoothed back into place. The dress is a lost cause, but the solid, concrete wall I've built over so many years begins to reform, brick by painstaking brick.

By some miracle, I manage to walk back into the dining room with my shoulders rolled back and my head high. In my absence, Harrison has retrieved my coat from the coat check. A flare of annoyance surges through me, knowing he had to rummage through my purse for the coat ticket, but I take solace in the fact that he was forced to wait on me. After what he just pulled, he should be groveling at my feet, cleaning the bottom of my heels with his fucking tongue.

Harrison holds the coat open for me, and my mind flashes to Silas doing the same just weeks ago. I cling to that memory, imagining Silas's steady hands on my shoulders as I reluctantly accept Harrison's offering, turning around to put it on.

Before I can button the coat, Harrison's arm snakes around my stomach, pulling me back against him. I stumble, catching myself on his forearm just as his face buries into my hair, his nose skimming the side of my neck. My jaw clenches so tightly I half expect my molars to crack.

"Look up," he commands, his voice sharp enough to cut through the surrounding chatter. Against my better judgment, I follow his direction. My gaze sweeps the room until it lands on the table directly across from us, where a familiar face sits among a group of men in suits.

Silas.

His posture is casual, almost lazy—legs splayed, one hand circling the rim of his crystal whiskey glass. But his eyes... His eyes burn, like molten steel just before it hardens. And they're fixed solely on me.

The pieces of the puzzle fall neatly into place. The reason Harrison demanded I act as his doting date. The reason we're seated at this specific table. We weren't here to watch. We were here to *be* watched.

Of course. Peter saw those auction photos, and he found a way to weaponize them. Why did I ever think he wouldn't? And now, he's forcing me into his scheme with no warning, crossing boundaries I swore I'd never allow, all because I haven't been "efficient" enough for him. Because I refuse to crawl into Silas's bed and try to seduce my way into his secrets.

The realization fuels a life-altering rage. One that I can't even put to words. My heartbeat pounds in my ears, and my fingertips tingle with the effort of keeping it all contained. But even that fury is nothing compared to his.

Silas isn't just angry—he's seething, a storm barely leashed, his rage so potent it warps the air around him. This isn't the kind of anger that cools with time. This is the kind that burns. If I blinked, I swear I'd see the steakhouse engulfed in flames, reduced to ash under the sheer force of his fury. And it's all for me.

I don't even know whether it's directed *at* me or *because* of me, but it doesn't matter. Either way, it hurts. And that pain only fuels my mounting fury, molding it into something even more reckless and volatile.

Push it down. Swallow it whole. Funnel it into the black void where all your emotions go to die.

In a blink, the shock on my face melts into neutrality, a mask as believable as it is empty. I avert my gaze to the ground, retreating behind my fortress of composure.

Harrison's grip loosens, and he takes my hand, guiding me toward the restaurant's entrance. I don't need to look back to know Silas is still watching. The weight of his stare follows me into the elevator, into the street, and onto the busy sidewalk where Harrison finally lets go to stand next to me.

He reaches into his pocket, pulling out a pack of cigarettes and a lighter as he speaks, but I can't hear him. People pass by, their presence a shield, their indifference a quiet encouragement.

I finally let the anger win.

Spinning on my heel, I drive my knee into his groin with every ounce of force I can muster. Harrison doubles over with a groan, his hands instinctively clutching at the point of impact. My nails dig into his shoulders as I lean in, savoring the tremble in his breaths as he wheezes out insult after insult at me.

"If you or Peter ever pull that shit again," I hiss, my voice venomous, "it'll be the last thing either of you ever do. Follow me home, and I'll *kill* you."

I push him back, and he stumbles into the side of the building, his curses cutting through the cold night air. Without a backward glance, I stride toward the curb and hail a cab.

It's only when I'm several blocks away, safe in the back seat of the taxi, that the tears come. Silent and hot, they spill over, each drop burning a path down my cheeks as I let myself break.

Chapter 16

I t's been too quiet since my "date" with Harrison last Friday.

I expected him pounding on my door the same night, ready to beat me to a bloody pulp. Or Peter to materialize at the foot of my bed in the dead of night. But there's been nothing. No ominous figures lurking in my hallway, no attempts to nab me on the street during my gym sessions with Jeff, no bullets to the back of my head in the grocery store.

Not a single word.

I've hated every second of it.

My head's been on a swivel for six days, every creak of a floorboard or passing glance from a stranger sending jolts of adrenaline through my system. If the constant paranoia about Harrison or Peter rounding every corner isn't enough, my thoughts keep drifting to Silas. Late at night, after I've triple-locked my apartment door with the deadbolt, the portable lock, and the steel bar jam, his silence creeps in, as deafening as everything else.

It's been hard not to relive the memory of his eyes that night. So many emotions flashing across them in rapid succession: surprise, fury, disgust, something I can only describe as betrayal. If I weren't still grappling with my own emotions about Harrison's assault, I might have more room to feel livid about the quiet judgment Silas hurled at me from across the restaurant.

What gives him the right to look at me like that? For being on a date? For kissing someone else? He doesn't own me. Hell, he doesn't even know me, not really. To him, I'm still his sister's new friend. The shiny new toy that wasn't handed to him on a silver platter.

Now, it's Thursday night, and I'm sitting across from Natalie at a Thai restaurant. The sun is just beginning to set, casting a golden glow over the city. Its reflection dances off the windows of the towering buildings outside, including the front doors of Wells Corporation, gleaming just across the street. I didn't realize how close the restaurant was to their headquarters until my ride-share pulled up, my heart lurching at the proximity. It's far too close for comfort. But then Natalie saw me from the window, waving with that bright, beautiful smile she always wears when we meet. There was no turning back after that.

My eyes keep darting to the glassy blue-tinted doors behind her head, heart thudding erratically at the thought of Silas walking out to climb into one of the sleek town cars idling in the curbside pull-off. It's a little before seven. Prime time for him to leave the office.

"What do you think?" Natalie asks, pulling me back to the table.

Blinking, I realize she's been talking to me. "Sorry. Run that by me again?" I say, sheepishly. Her forgiving smile reminds me too much of Drew. My grip on my fork tightens instinctively.

"This Tristan guy," she repeats. "I'd love to meet him. Maybe you two can come over for dinner? Davey's usually good about keeping weekends open."

The fork freezes midway to my mouth. Over my dead body would I let Harrison anywhere near Natalie or her home. I force myself to take a bite of my Pad Kra Pao, using the food as a momentary shield while I gather my thoughts.

Natalie texted me on Sunday to let me know an acquaintance of hers—some nosy attorney named Kiera Lawson I've met in passing—had seen me "on a date" and gushed about how passionate and intimate it looked. I lied through my teeth, telling her "Tristan" was someone I'd been set up with by an old client who knew I'd moved to Chicago. I breezed past the part about the kiss, downplaying it as much as I could, and Natalie took it all in stride. She didn't mention Silas seeing me and for some reason, him not saying a word to her stings worse than if he had.

I swallow my bite, even though it suddenly feels like sandpaper. "I don't think I'll be seeing him again."

"No?" Natalie's eyebrows knit together. My silence fuels her curiosity as she toys with the food on her plate. "I didn't want to pry, but Kiera said he couldn't keep his hands off you and that you both looked... really happy. You're not into him?"

There's a note of disappointment in her voice. She's probably wondering why I didn't tell her about "Tristan" sooner. Guilt twists in my stomach.

"He's definitely more into it than I am," I hedge. It's not entirely a lie. Harrison's always been more committed to Peter's schemes than I'll ever be. "The date was fine, but he wants more, and I don't. Plus, he really turned me off when he kissed me like that in the middle of dinner. That's far too bold for a guy I've only seen a handful of times, don't you think?"

Her lips pressed into a line as she mulls over my words. Maybe she thinks I'm sparing her feelings, or Kiera's description doesn't match what I'm saying. Either way, she doesn't press. Instead, she exhales softly and nods.

"That's fair," she says, though the tinge of sadness in her eyes gives her away. Before I can stop myself, I reach across the table and place my hand on hers.

"I don't date casually, Natalie. I didn't plan to mention him because I knew it wasn't going anywhere. I want to be sure about someone before introducing them to my friends. So, if I ever find someone worthy of that, you'll be the first to vet them."

The small gesture earns a small laugh from her, easing some of the invisible weight on her shoulders. But it doesn't do much for the nausea threatening to rise in me. How am I supposed to keep using this woman to get what Peter wants? How am I not going to destroy her in the end? And how is this not going to ruin *me*?

Just as my thoughts spiral into that familiar pit, Natalie sits up straighter, plucking the drink menu from its holder on the table. The apprehensive smile she wore just a moment ago morphs into a devious smirk.

"I'm in the mood to drink," she says, eyes gleaming with mischief. "How do you feel about being violently hungover tomorrow?"

I should say no. I should lie and tell her I have an early meeting tomorrow. But there's something about that spark in her eyes; it's too familiar. It's the same look Drew used to give me on rare Fridays when we both had the night off, and she wanted to drag me out for a night of fun, refusing to take no for an answer. If I squint just enough, Natalie's hazel irises could almost look like Drew's vibrant green.

Instead of doing what I should, I find myself saying, "Shots or cocktails?"

———

After migrating to the bar, downing several fruity mixed drinks, ripping a few tequila shots, and laughing far too much, Natalie and I have officially been cut off.

We probably should have known we were at our limit when the idea of ordering a light beer suddenly sounded like a good one. But the bartender just chuckled at us while wiping down glasses and promised to print our tab before bringing over a pitcher of water. The restaurant has mostly emptied since we moved from our table, leaving just a handful of diners at their tables and a few others scattered along the far end of the bar.

I can't remember the last time I was cut off. Maybe senior year of college after finals? The thought makes me laugh.

"Do you ladies have a ride?" the bartender asks as he sets down the water pitcher. He's an older man with thick glasses and a kind smile that makes me think he's seen plenty of drunk, giggling women like us in his years behind the bar.

"What time is it?" Natalie taps the top of her phone to light up the screen. 8:57.

"We don't close until 10:30, so you're welcome to sit and sober up," he offers, clearly amused before nodding toward the other end of the bar. "I'll be down there if you need anything."

"Thanks," I say, grinning lazily as Natalie salutes him with the same enthusiasm. As soon as he's out of earshot, I burst into full-on laughter. "Holy shit. I'm drunk."

"Same," Natalie snorts, leaning her shoulder against mine. "Thanks for doing this with me. Not the drinking—though, yeah, that's been fun—but dinner, you know?"

"Why are you thanking me for that?" I ask, raising an eyebrow at her. "I'm the one who asked you to do this every week."

"You know why," she says softly, smiling in that earnest, almost bashful way of hers. "It just still means a lot to me."

The nausea I felt earlier at dinner returns in full force, and I can't decide if it's from the lychee martinis or my guilt. I grab the glass of water in front of me, holding it to my lips as I grumble, "Stop acting like I'm doing you a favor." I drain the glass in one go before setting it back down with a little too much force.

Natalie rolls her eyes but lets it slide, instead downing her own glass and pointing at the pitcher of water. "Refill those while I go to the bathroom?"

Her tone makes the request sound like a question rather than the mild command it should be, and it strikes me again how different she is from her brother. Silas would have demanded it without hesitation.

"You got it," I say with an exaggerated gesture that makes her laugh. She hops off her stool and heads toward the back of the restaurant, swaying slightly as she walks.

Left alone, I busy myself pouring water, finishing my glass, and refilling it again. While I sip the third glass more slowly this time, I check my phone for messages from Peter or Harrison, half-expecting to find something lurking in my inbox that wasn't there before.

Nothing.

The empty screen taunts me, and I slide the phone back into my pocket with a sigh. Harrison would have already come for me if he was allowed to. He's a creature of instinct: simple and brutal. He doesn't wait. He acts. Peter, though? He's a different kind of devil. Calculated. Patient. Sadistic. If he wants me dead, he'll make sure it hurts first. My past mistakes have taught me that much. Whatever's coming, it's going to be creative, diabolical, and drawn out.

Lost in my thoughts, I jolt when Natalie reappears, clumsily hoisting herself onto her stool. She mutters something under her breath, suddenly drunker than before, but I manage to convince her to finish a second glass of water before she starts pouting. Only after I'm sure she's secure in her seat do I excuse myself to the restroom.

The narrow hallway to the bathrooms is dimly lit, the walls painted in vibrant colors that swirl and blur in my vision. My head spins slightly as I walk, and I giggle quietly, still surprised at how much the alcohol has hit me.

Once in the restroom, I wash my hands and glance at my reflection in the mirror. My messy ponytail is still intact, but my eye makeup is smudged, and my sweater looks a little disheveled. I use some water to clean up my eyeliner, smoothing out my appearance as best I can.

Satisfied, I push the door open to leave, eyes cast down as I adjust the hem of my sweater.

"Ms. Page."

The sound of his voice freezes me mid-step, and the door swings shut behind me, bumping me further into the hallway.

It takes a moment for my vision to focus, but there he is. Silas, leaning against the opposite wall with his hands in the pockets of his tailored trousers. His suit jacket is unbuttoned, and his tie is gone, giving him a slightly disheveled appearance that only adds to his infuriating perfection.

"Silas," I breathe.

His chocolate eyes track the movement, lingering on me for a moment too long. His jaw tightens as he speaks, tone far too polite to be anything but seething. "Having a nice evening with my sister?"

The edge in his voice sobers me instantly. I straighten my back, crossing my arms over my chest as I lift my chin. "I am. Why are you here?"

"Natalie called Davey for a ride. We were still at the office."

"That doesn't explain why *you're* here."

"Call it curiosity." His lips curl into a mockery of a smile. "Where's the new boyfriend tonight?"

My stomach drops. He's nothing if not direct.

"I don't have a boyfriend."

"So, you just go around making out with random men at five-star restaurants?"

God, he's blunt. My cheeks burn and I tighten the grip I have on the fabric of my sweater as I force myself to hold his gaze.

"You have no idea what you're talking about," I snap. "And you know what? It doesn't matter. I don't owe you an explanation."

His humorless laugh echoes down the hallway as he pushes off the wall to take a step closer. Despite his casual posture, there's nothing relaxed about the way his eyes bore into mine.

"Is that all you have to say?" he taunts, his voice low and dangerous.

"Oh, fuck you and your holier-than-thou attitude," I bite back, the alcohol loosening my tongue. "I should knee you in the balls like I did to him."

His expression shifts instantly, disgust morphing into something darker, sharper. But I'm too far gone to care.

"You think because you had your little sidekick run a background check on me that you know what type of person I am? You don't know anything." My voice shakes, but I keep going. "So, once again—fuck you."

I turn to leave, my movements unsteady, but I only make it one step before his hand slams against the wall beside my head with a loud *thud* and I flinch. The silence between us grows like a vine, curling tighter and tighter around my chest.

"Why did you knee him?" he demands, his voice a low growl.

I glare at his arm, refusing to look at him. "Move."

"Did he do something you didn't want him to?"

"You don't get to act concerned now you've suddenly decided I'm not some whore," I snap, looking up at him again. The wrath in his eyes dims when he sees the same emotion reflected in mine, shifting from pitch black to a stormy midnight brown.

"I didn't say that."

"You didn't have to. It's written all over your face." My voice cracks slightly, but I steel myself, refusing to break under his scrutiny.

Silas's ramrod-straight arm finally relaxes, his elbow bending as he leans closer. The air around us pulses, like the hum of a plucked wire stretched to its limit. Before I can brace myself, he consumes every inch of my vision, every thought. Instinctively, I roll my back onto the wall to create some semblance of space, but it doesn't stop him from leaning closer, just enough that I can see my distressed reflection in the sheen of his glasses.

"Did he do something you didn't want him to?" he asks again. His voice is barely above a whisper but carries a severity that pins me in place.

I can't stop the shudder that ripples through me. My eyes drop to our feet, nearly toe-to-toe, and I swallow hard. "I'm not seeing him again."

"That's good to know," he says with less venom. "But it's not what I'm asking." His free hand lifts, tilting my chin with deliberate gentleness, forcing me to meet his gaze. His thumb brushes the edge of my lower lip. My resolve wavers as his features, so achingly close, blur the line between threat and tenderness. "What did he do?"

His cool breath grazes my skin, sharp and minty, and for a fleeting moment, I falter. Silas Wells, a man who could have anything or anyone, is standing here, demanding to know what happened. He cares. To what extent or why, I don't know, but he does.

For a heartbeat, the longing hits me like a tidal wave. The urge to tell him everything—Peter, Harrison, Drew—claws at my chest. What would it feel like to lay it all bare? To let someone like him, someone who seems unshakable, hear the full weight of my truth? Could he help me? Would he?

But then reality crashes back, glacial and merciless. What would happen if he learned my name isn't Scarlett Page? That I've been using him and his sister, drawing closer to their family with every step while holding the knife Peter wants me to twist in their backs? He'd hate me. Natalie would hate me. And then, there'd be no running. I'd have to face the wrath of the Wells family *and* Peter.

The dream of freedom dissolves as quickly as it appeared, leaving behind the cold, hard truth: I can't trust anyone.

I press myself harder into the wall, my jaw tightening. Silas's thumb twitches against my chin, waiting for something I can't give him. I swallow the lump in my throat and force out the only half-truth I can manage. "Nothing I wasn't able to handle."

He exhales slowly, his breath heavy with frustration, and the hand at my face falls away. My chest aches as I watch him make the conscious choice to let it go and draw his own conclusions.

There's a long, heavy pause before he finally speaks, his voice quieter now, almost hesitant. "Will you let me drive you home?"

The weight of his question is not lost on me. Silas Wells, a man used to taking what he wants, is asking me for permission. My heart stumbles over itself, the cracks in my defenses widening with each passing second. Every cell in my body screams at me to say yes, to let him lead me out of here and into his car. To feel the rush of him speeding down the city streets, teasing me with that dark, untamed energy that's as intoxicating as it is infuriating.

But I can't.

If I say yes, if I let him take me home, I'll be proving what I already fear—I can't trust myself around Silas. And that's exactly what Peter wants. He'll eventually learn I've crossed the line I swore I never would.

Even if Silas kicks me to the curb two minutes later, Peter will have already won, and he'll savor every second of making me watch him dismantle these siblings I've grown to care about.

And deep down, I know I can't deny the current pulling me toward Silas. It's always there, quiet at first, then relentless and unyielding, dragging me deeper every time we're in the same room. Peter saw it in those auction photos—the way Silas leaned into me on the staircase. He saw it and waited, biding his time, knowing exactly how to push us both toward this moment.

Peter is handing Silas to me on a silver platter, daring me to take him. And I can't. Even if I don't fully understand Silas's role in whatever secrets these servers hold, I can't do this to him. I won't.

"I think... I think it's better if Davey and Natalie take me," I finally say, the words scraping against my throat.

Silas stiffens, his confusion fleeting but blunt. His stare narrows, lips pressing into a thin line. He waits, as if giving me a chance to change my mind, but when I don't, his eyes harden.

Brick by brick, I watch as he fortifies the walls I've spent months trying to quietly tear down. He steps back, creating a chasm between us that feels more final than I'm ready to accept.

My ears ring in the silence. I wrap my arms tighter around myself, holding everything in.

Silas nods toward the front of the restaurant, his expression painfully cold and detached. I lead us back to the table, painfully aware of the space he's put between us, his footsteps echoing further behind mine than they normally would.

The current that always seemed to pull us together has shifted. Now it's an ocean, and we're on opposite shores.

Chapter 17

J eff lands a counter jab, this time on the side of my temple, snapping my head to the side. Pain lances through my skull, and I grunt, blinking away the white splotches dancing on the edges of my vision.

My arms fall for a split second before I raise them again, nodding at him to keep going. My breaths coming out ragged now and drowning out the upbeat rhythm of the radio Jeff always keeps running in the background. Somewhere in the corner of the gym, a couple of people are sparring on their own, while others alternate between weights in their circuits.

"For fuck's sake," Jeff growls, pausing mid-stride. He lets his punch mitts drop to his sides, disappointment radiating from him. Not a single drop of sweat glistens on his inked skin, and the lack of exertion on his part feels like salt in my wounds. "That was an easy block. Where the hell is your head?"

Natalie and Silas's faces surface in the corners of my thoughts. They always do. They've seeped into the fabric of my mind, woven into the very threads of my existence. No matter how hard I try, I can't stop seeing their faces, my betrayals, the collision course of all of it. It plays on repeat in my head, an unrelenting loop.

I shake my head violently, as if the motion alone could dislodge them. "At the other end of your mitts, apparently," I snap, trying to mask my turmoil with sarcasm.

Jeff's scowl deepens. He strips off his mitts with practiced ease before spitting the guard out of his mouth and letting it drop into his palm.

"Sit," he orders.

"Come on, J. I'll do better." The bravado in my voice falters, the exhaustion bleeding through. My guard stays up anyway, a futile attempt to convince him—and maybe myself—that I'm still in this.

Jeff rolls his eyes, the muscles in his tattooed neck straining as he points firmly to the mat. "You aren't focused, and I'm not about to haul your ass to the hospital. You can take a breather, or we're done for the day. Your choice."

Normally, I'd argue and push until he gave in. But today? Today, I drop to the mat without a word, lying flat on my back with my knees bent. As the adrenaline fades, the ache of Jeff's earlier hits settles in—a pulsing heat in my sides, temple, left cheek, and thigh.

A water bottle appears in my peripheral vision, Jeff holding it out without a word. I grab it and set it beside me, the cool plastic pressing into my palm. He mutters something about hydrating, but I don't respond. Instead, I stare up at the industrial ceiling, its black paint stark against the fluorescent lights humming overhead. The brightness stings my already watering eyes, but I can't bring myself to look away.

Jeff drops himself onto the mat with a *thud* near my feet. The force jolts my soles off the floor, but he says nothing. After a few moments, he shifts, stretching out parallel to me, his tattooed arms folding behind his head.

"The hell is going on with you?" he finally asks, his tone a mix of exasperation and concern.

"Nothing," I reply curtly, pulling my mouth guard out and wiping my lips with the back of my glove.

"Nothing, my ass." He grunts, sliding closer until his head is turned toward me. His gaze burns into the side of my face, but I refuse to meet it. I keep my eyes locked on the ceiling, counting the fluorescent lights in an attempt to focus on anything else. "Come on, kid," he mutters, softer this time.

The concern in his voice weighs on me more than I want to admit. What can I even say? Jeff has a knack for pushing my buttons—sometimes to the brink of madness—but I care about him. He's become this weird, tattooed uncle-figure in my life, and the thought of him getting caught in the crosshairs of my mess is unbearable.

But I'm exhausted. Of keeping everything bottled up. Of pretending I have control. Of carrying this weight alone. It's selfish and reckless, But right now, I just need someone who isn't tangled in this chaos. He doesn't need the full truth—just enough to remind me there's someone who still cares.

"I can't tell you," I admit in a whisper. "I can't tell anyone."

Jeff stays silent beside me, his presence grounding in its simplicity. He's always been acutely observant, ever since our first session together. I used to make vague requests for specific skills, asking to learn ways to protect myself that wouldn't make sense for an average thirty-something woman working in tech. No matter how odd my scenarios sounded, he never questioned me. He'd just nod, answer, and show me exactly what I needed to know. It was as if he understood, even without the details, that there were things I couldn't say. Instead of prying, he poured everything into teaching me, pushing me harder on the mat, preparing me in the only way he could.

I suspect Jeff knows a thing or two about trouble himself—probably got into his fair share. But just as he's never asked about my past, I've given him the same respect in return.

"Are you in danger?" His voice is low, careful. A reminder that the gym isn't empty; there are still a few others training on the far side of the room.

I consider my answer carefully before matching his tone. "Baseline? Always to some degree. Right now? Absolutely." I hope the vague honesty makes sense to him.

Jeff's exhale is a slow, heavy sound, and I see him glance at the ceiling in my peripheral vision. "Shit."

A strangled laugh escapes me, teetering on the edge of hysteria. My vision blurs. "I know," I choke out.

"What can I do to help you?"

"You already have," I reply earnestly, my voice softer now. "Multiple days a week for months."

A beat of silence passes, heavy and full of unspoken things. Then, without meaning to, the words I've been dying to say out loud come tumbling out. "My work is... complicated. I have to do things I don't agree with and the job I'm on now involves people I like a lot. And when it's over, what I do might destroy their family."

Jeff is quiet for a moment, digesting my words. Then, he asks, "Your work *makes* you, or you *choose* to?"

Peter's furious face flashes in my mind, and a shiver runs down my spine.

"Makes me," I whisper, closing my eyes as a few stray tears slip from the corners, trailing down toward my ears. Jeff hums in understanding, his voice steady and calm.

"Do these people deserve to be destroyed?"

I shrug, half-heartedly, unsure if he's even looking at me anymore. "I don't know this time. But I... I think they're actually good. I don't want to hurt them."

"And there's no option for you to walk away?" The resignation in his voice tells me he already knows the answer.

Another strained laugh bubbles out of me, bitter and hollow. "I won't be able to say no to this kind of work for a very long time."

The confession I rarely admit, even to myself, steals the breath from my lungs. My body shakes as I struggle to hold back the sob clawing its way up my throat.

Jeff's hand grips my forearm firmly, his fingers nearly wrapping all the way around. He holds me there, steadying me. It's a simple gesture, maybe the closest thing to affection a man like him will ever openly offer someone who isn't his wife, but I know what it means. He's here, sitting with me in this unbearable moment, and though it's all he can give, it's enough.

"I'm so sorry," he says gruffly, clearing his throat. His thumb brushes against my skin in a show of comfort. "I don't think I have the right connections to help you."

"I don't think anyone does," I murmur with a small, sad smile. "They'd find me, anyway."

Finally, I turn my head toward him, catching his thoughtful expression through the haze of leftover tears. His blue eyes are clouded with concern, his brows pulled together as he thinks.

"If there's anyone smart enough to figure a way out of this, it's you," he says firmly. The sentiment is sweet, but it only makes me deflate further into the mat.

"I wish I had a choice," I admit softly, chewing on the inside of my lip.

"It might not feel like you do," he counters, his voice quiet but resolute. "But you can always choose yourself, Scarlett. That's always an option." His fingers tighten briefly around my arm, and he gives me a crooked smile that softens the scar on his upper lip. "If you choose yourself, and it's the end of the line for the rest of it? Come find me. I'll do whatever I can to keep you safe."

The conviction in his voice slices through me.

"Thanks, J," I say finally. There's no point in arguing with him, no use in trying to convince him otherwise. I'll let him hold on to the hope that I'll come to him in my hour of need. But deep down, I know the truth. If it comes down to it, no one else will suffer because of me.

"You got it, kid," he replies, giving my arm one last squeeze before letting go.

Chapter 18

"**Y**ou've got to be kidding me," I mutter under my breath, staring down at my phone.

I've been sitting on this damp bench, two blocks from the Wells office, for over twenty minutes. The rain from earlier this morning still stains the sidewalks a deep gray, and the lingering clouds make sure the sun doesn't get a chance to dry them. It's a cool spring morning. Perfect weather, really, other than the text that just ruined my day.

> **Luis:** They've already flagged the breach.
> **Me:** What? How?
> **Luis:** Their system caught the injection point almost immediately. I'm guessing someone on their team spotted the vulnerability you used and patched it.
> **Me:** So, no shot?
> **Luis:** I could try to mask the traffic better next time, but they're already on high alert. The good news is, I didn't touch the video feed yet, so they don't know what we were after.
> **Me:** Damn it. Okay. I'll have to figure something else out. Thanks, Lu.
> **Luis:** Anytime. Let me know if you come up with a Plan B.

I sit back and exhale sharply, letting the phone rest on my knee. My pulse is pounding in my ears. Luis is good. *Really* good. But even he couldn't get more than two minutes before Wells's system flagged the intrusion. It doesn't matter how they caught it at this point. My plan is a complete bust.

Luis and I met on a job in California three years ago when Peter paired us to dig up dirt on a District Attorney. At first, I'd been prepared for the usual, especially when I learned he was seven years older than me: a guy throwing his weight around, acting like he knows more than he does. But Luis? He's nothing like that. Straightforward, kind, and respectful right off the bat. He even let me pick which desk I preferred in the cramped apartment Peter rented us.

We worked side by side for five days, and by the end, I was showing him my wireless network exploitation techniques while he introduced me to some of the best reverse-engineering software I'd ever seen. For the first time in a long time, I didn't hate every second of a job.

When it was over, and we handed Peter the DA's skeletons—money laundering, of course—we exchanged information. It was just a "you never know" kind of thing, but since then, we've kept in touch. A handful of times, we've been each other's second set of eyes, just like today.

Except today didn't go as planned.

I lean forward, resting my elbows on my knees, and rub the bridge of my nose between my thumb and index finger. My skull pounds, blossoming into the beginnings of a full-blown headache. The honking downtown traffic grates on my ears, sharp and jarring, as if the entire city decided to conspire against me.

The plan had seemed solid this morning. Luis would disable the exterior feeds, loop the cameras in the underground garage, and keep watch while I slipped in through the side entrance using the key FOB I swiped from the booth attendant yesterday. I'd noticed the employee always leaves it dangling visibly from his belt loop—an easy enough target. When he ducked into a nearby sub shop on his lunch break, I followed. I brushed past him as he reached for a napkin dispenser, my hand quick and precise, lifting the FOB in a single smooth motion. By the time he turned back toward the counter, I was already out the door.

The rest of it was supposed to be quick and clean. I'd even set up a coffee date with Natalie half a block away in thirty minutes, so I'd have a perfectly innocent excuse to be in the area.

But now? Now the system's on high alert, Luis is locked out, and I've got nothing but a useless garage key. A few minutes of video looping wouldn't have been enough, anyway, not with how tight the timing was.

I sit back and glance at the cloudy sky, exhaling through clenched teeth.

"Plan B," I mutter, though I have no idea what that looks like yet. My mind races with alternatives, but nothing feels as solid as the original plan. Peter left me with few choices, and looping Luis into this job was already a risk. One he isn't even aware Peter would flay me for taking. Still, Luis is the only one I trust with something this critical.

A part of me wants to call him back, ask him to try again, but I know it's pointless. Lu wouldn't have walked away if there was another option.

After my run-in with Silas last Thursday, reality has crashed down on me with full force. For months, I've been trying to find Peter's information, but I've also been playing it safe. Partly because I'm cautious to a fault, but mostly because I started to like it here.

I can't believe I ever thought Natalie would just be a means to an end. I hadn't realized how badly I needed someone like her—someone unwavering and kind—until she was right in front of me. Once I had her friendship, I didn't want to let it go. Being selfish with Natalie also gave me something else: Silas. Or maybe, it cursed me with him. Time spent with her gave me the chance to let this insurmountable attraction between us grow, to learn more about his family, and to question whether they're truly the villains in this story. Now, I'm so tangled up in them that I hadn't even noticed the noose tightening around my neck until it was too late.

It's time to cut the cord. It'll hurt less if I do it now.

Not that I can, though. Because I've accomplished nothing. Luis is already out of their system, but Davey's team is now fully aware of the breach. They're locking down every weak point even tighter, likely patching any chance I had of exploiting them again. I should've known better. I acted too quickly, didn't test the software thoroughly enough, and now I've tipped them off. Stupid. Amateur.

I thought I'd be crawling under a few cars by now, planting trackers and gathering data. But instead, I'm sitting here. My laptop is back in my apartment in Bucktown, and there's no way I'll make it there and back before I need to meet Natalie for coffee.

I could reschedule. Rain check on the coffee and head to Bedford Park or Little Village instead. From my research and the satellite images, both areas are just outside the city and their warehouse districts seem ideal for servers. The Wells might be renting space within a larger warehouse as a cover. At the very least, it's worth sneaking around to cross them off my list. Natalie will be disappointed, but she'll understand.

Just as I lift my phone to type out an apologetic message to her, someone sits down on the three-person bench directly next to me several inches too close.

Most days, something like this wouldn't bother me. Men invading a woman's space is nothing new in a city like Chicago. Intentional or not, it happens all the time. But for some reason, the hair on the back of my neck stands on end.

My fingers hover over my screen, contemplating whether I should tell the guy to back off. It wouldn't be the first or last time I've had to put a man in his place, but before I can find the words, he speaks.

"You're a hard woman to find alone," he says, his tone too casual. Like he knows me.

My head snaps up. Sitting next to me is an unassuming white man, probably in his late twenties or early thirties. Short brown hair, light-brown eyes, medium build. His features are plain, and he's wearing a black sweatshirt, dark jeans, and gray sneakers—so nondescript he might as well be invisible.

The kind of man you'd struggle to pick out of a lineup.

My stomach sinks, dread settling heavy in my chest.

163

"Peter or Harrison?" I ask, my voice hitching at the end. That small sign of fear must amuse him because his smile widens, and he chuckles softly.

"They both send their love," he replies casually before standing and dusting off his jeans. "Come on."

I stiffen, my pulse hammering in my ears. Does he really think I'm just going to stand up and follow him like a lamb to slaughter? To whatever hell awaits me at the end of this little walk?

My hesitation irritates him. He sighs, shoving his hands into the front pocket of his sweatshirt. As the fabric stretches away from his body, I spot it: a handgun, its profile unmistakable against the soft material.

My heart stops.

A mother and her young daughter walk past us, hand in hand, oblivious to the weapon inches from their unprotected backs. Would this man do something so crazy in broad daylight?

"Are you really going to make this more difficult than it needs to be?" he asks, his tone laced with thinly veiled impatience.

An unforgiving chill runs down the entire length of my body. I glance at the duo disappearing around the corner, and my decision is made for me. It's not worth the risk.

I swallow hard and stand slowly, still gripping my phone in my hand. The crowd around us flows on, oblivious. In a place like this, people tend to mind their own business, eyes fixed on their phones or the sidewalks. Not one of them notices the man beside me adjusting the bulge in his sweatshirt pocket with his free hand, his posture casual but precise.

"Where are we going?" I demand, forcing more strength into my voice than I feel. My question hangs in the air unanswered. Instead of responding, he starts walking, gripping my upper arm harshly as he passes. His touch burns, the kind of grip that leaves fingerprints. Even his scent is indistinct—clean clothes smelling faintly of cheap detergent. He doesn't speak, doesn't even look at me, but his hold tightens just enough to keep me in step.

As we move upstream, away from the corporate district, he adjusts his grip. It's swift, calculated. Before I can react, his hold shifts to my opposite arm, and his steps sync with mine as he slides slightly behind my shoulder, pressing his side into me. From a distance, we might look like a couple taking a casual stroll, his arm draped protectively around my back, keeping me one step ahead for protection. But hidden between us, his sweatshirt pocket conceals the truth: the cold, unyielding barrel of his gun pressed firmly against my ribs.

Every step we take away from downtown grinds that barrel into my side, a reminder of who's in control. I focus on the pavement in front of me, measuring my steps, but even the slightest misstep earns me a punishing shove of the gun against my skin. My breaths come shallow, but I force them to even out, counting each inhale and exhale. Panicking won't help me.

Minutes pass, and I realize he isn't leading me to a car. He's walking too deliberately, taking turns that suggest a destination within the city itself. Parking down here is a logistical nightmare; even seasoned criminals wouldn't gamble on securing a spot nearby. That leaves one grim possibility: wherever he's taking me, it's close enough to walk.

For almost two weeks, I've been bracing for this moment. I knew Peter would retaliate. I just didn't know when. After what I did and said to Harrison, I knew this was coming. He's killed people for less. But even with all my preparation, I didn't expect it to feel like this. Like I'm walking to my own grave, step by step, with no way out.

I've imagined Peter a thousand ways in my head: furious, smirking, gloating. But the truth is, he's not here. Peter never does his own dirty work. He hides behind money and power, letting others carry out his orders. And now, this unremarkable man gripping my arm and shoving a gun into my ribs is his executioner.

I hate that my pulse thunders in my ears. I hate the acidic, consuming fear gnawing at my insides. Most of all, I hate that Peter will know. He'll know that even though I didn't beg, I wanted to. God, I want to beg. But

I won't. I'll never give him or this asshole the satisfaction of thinking I regret anything I've done.

The stranger yanks my arm, wrenching me out of my spiraling thoughts as we veer into an alleyway. I stumble but manage to keep up, barely. The world shifts as we step into the shadows. The brightness of the cloudy day dims almost instantly, the alley shrouded in darkness cast by the towering brick buildings on either side.

The air reeks of decaying food, piss, and whatever else people have discarded here. The narrow passage, barely seven feet wide, is cluttered with overflowing dumpsters. Their contents spill out in bloated, blackened bags, creating an obstacle course of filth. He pushes me forward, uncaring, forcing me to weave through the mess. The stench churns my stomach, and bile rises in my throat, but I swallow it down, focusing on my footing.

Just when I think he might shove me into one of the dumpsters to execute me—less mess to clean up, after all—we step into a cleared area farther back. The space is quiet, eerily so. The alley narrows slightly, with no windows or doors to be seen. The other end is boarded up by a weathered wooden fence. We're completely cut off, trapped in this desolate space.

My heart sinks. *Fuck.*

The man shoves my shoulder, forcing me to spin toward him as he casually pulls the gun out of his pocket. My stomach drops at the sight of the silencer attached to the barrel. His slimy smirk is the kind that makes my skin crawl, and my body goes rigid as he extends his free hand toward me, palm up, fingers curling.

"Open your phone and give it to me," he commands, his tone flat, as if he's tired of even having to say it.

"Why?" I ask, my grip tightening around the device, unwilling to relinquish it so easily. His smirk fades, replaced with an expression of irritation. He curls his fingers again, gesturing for the phone.

"Jesus. You're as annoying as they said you'd be," he sneers. "Just do what I fucking say."

I take a deep breath through my mouth to avoid inhaling any more of the rancid alley air. His face betrays the same disgust at the stench, but he picked this spot for a reason. With the relentless city noise and our location deep in the alley, no one would notice us unless they came right up to it. It's the perfect spot for whatever he's planning.

Reluctantly, against every instinct screaming at me not to, I unlock my phone and place it in his outstretched hand. His fingers close around it, and he immediately starts rifling through my settings with the kind of ease that tells me he knows what he's doing.

For a moment, I stand still, waiting for an opportunity to move, but he's expertly splitting his attention between me and the screen. My body is nearly vibrating as I try to figure out my next move. "Great. Thanks," he mutters after a few minutes, slipping my phone into the back pocket of his jeans with a relaxed shrug.

And then it happens.

Pain explodes across the front of my face. My vision goes white, and the world tilts violently as I hit the ground. My teeth rattle from the impact, and I blink furiously, trying to focus. Something warm drips into my eyes. I swipe at it with the back of my hand, only to gasp at the sharp sting as my fingers brush over my forehead. When I pull my hand back, a smear of blood confirms what my throbbing head already knows.

Did he just punch me?

The question barely registers before his hand tangles in the hair at the crown of my head, yanking me to my knees with brutal force. My scalp burns in protest, and a scream rips from my throat, echoing off the narrow alley walls.

Do something, you idiot! Jeff's voice thunders in my mind, and suddenly, I'm back on the mat with him, hearing his no-nonsense instructions.

With the man distracted by the deadweight he's hauling up by my hair, I drive my fist into his gut with every ounce of strength I can have. He grunts, doubling over at the waist and releasing my hair. Relief washes over me as I collapse to the ground, but I don't stop there. With adrenaline surging through my veins, I reach for the space behind his knees with both hands and rip them back.

The move works. He loses his balance, crashing onto his back. I'm on him instantly, my focus zeroed in on the hand still gripping the gun. I grab his wrist and slam it against the pavement over and over, ignoring the searing pain in my knuckles as the force jars my arm. He curses and thrashes while still disoriented, my blood dripping onto his face. After a few desperate attempts to hold on, the gun finally clatters free, skidding across the ground toward one of the dumpsters.

I don't even have time to breathe before his hands find the ground. With his palms braced against the asphalt, he uses his legs to launch me off his chest, the sheer force of it sends me hurtling over the top of his body. My chest slams into the brick wall. Stars burst behind my eyes as I try to push off it, but he's on me before I can fully regain my footing.

A sharp blow lands between my shoulder blades, and my cheek slams against the unforgiving brick. The air is forced out of my lungs in a painful gasp. His hand clamps down on the back of my neck like a vice, and his full-body weight presses against me, pinning me in place. My chest burns as I struggle to draw even the shallowest breath under the pressure of his grip.

The stench of garbage and decay is overwhelming, mingling with the metallic tang of blood dripping into my mouth. I try to move, to kick out with my legs, but the angle is wrong. He's pressed so tightly against me that I can't gain the leverage I need.

The man lets out a frustrated laugh, his hold on my neck tightening with each huff. "You put up a better fight than I thought you would," he mocks.

In my peripheral vision, I catch the twisted curve of his smug smile. "Fuck you," I spit through gritted teeth, though it only seems to amuse him further.

His grin widens as he leans in closer, his free hand reaching behind his back. For what? A second gun? A knife? A condom to leave less DNA behind before killing me? My mind spirals, each possibility worse than the last.

Why didn't I scratch him? At least the police would have something under my nails to use as evidence.

"Be quiet now," he murmurs, almost lazily, as if savoring my panic. "The fun's about to begin."

I brace myself, every muscle locked as I wait for the worst. But instead of the cold press of metal against my skull or the sound of a zipper being undone, I hear something faint. A ringing. It takes me a second to realize the sound is coming from a phone.

He's calling someone.

"Hello?" A voice filters through, familiar and warm. My stomach drops into a black abyss as the realization hits me.

Natalie.

Every cell in my body screeches to a halt. The world stops spinning. Time itself stops. My heartbeat freezes mid-thump, replaced by a deafening silence that reverberates through my skull.

No. No. No. *NO.*

I don't even register when the desperate words begin tumbling from my mouth, pouring out in a frantic, incoherent plea, bouncing off the walls like an angry echo. He shoves me harder against the brick, growling at me to shut the fuck up, but it only makes me scream louder.

"Scarlett? What's going on?!" Natalie's voice is panicked and distant through the phone's speaker, a lifeline tethered to me by the slimmest thread. I can barely hear her over the rush of blood in my ears, over my own sobs that are now uncontrollable.

The man leans closer, his breath hot against my skin, and taunts me in a low, venomous voice. "Answer Natalie. What *is* going on?" He holds the phone close to my face, tilting it just enough for me to see her name glowing on the screen of my phone. This is real. He called her.

Why? To lure her here? To kidnap her? Kill her? None of this adds up. Peter wanted this job done quietly. What is this man thinking?

Or maybe it's not about the job at all. Maybe this is solely about punishing me—because what's a better punishment than making me witness another friend's death?

The thought detonates in my chest like a bomb, ripping apart whatever is left of my composure. My brain screams at me to move, to fight, to do something.

With him so focused on keeping me pinned, he doesn't account for my feet. Grasping for every ounce of strength I have left, I lift my knee and slam the heel of my boot down on the top of his foot as hard as I can. His grip falters, just for a second, but it's all I need.

With a snap of my neck, I rear my head backward. The impact is sharp, cracking against his face. I don't even feel the pain—adrenaline numbs everything. He curses loudly, and the phone crashes to the ground near us.

I don't hesitate. Spinning, I use the momentum to drive my knee up into his groin. The move that worked so well on Harrison two weeks ago delivers again. His guttural wail is a symphony to my ears as he crumples to the ground, clutching himself in agony.

Blood trickles down my forehead, blurring my vision, but I don't take any more time to look at him. I wipe it away with the back of my hand as I turn and stagger toward the alley's mouth. My breaths come in ragged gasps, each step heavy and unsteady. My legs are like jelly, wobbling beneath me as though they might give out at any moment, but I force them to keep moving.

Just get to the road.

I shuffle through the garbage-strewn alley, my boots dragging through the muck and piles of rotting trash. I don't dare lift my feet too high for fear I'll lose what little balance I have left. My heart pounds so violently in my chest it feels like it might crack my ribs, the rhythm deafening as the opening of the alley grows closer.

The city sounds hit me like a tidal wave the moment I stumble out onto the street. Honking cars. Chatter from pedestrians. The dull roar of a bus engine. The normalcy is disorienting, almost surreal.

But I keep moving, my gaze darting around for anyone who looks suspicious, for any sign that he's recovered and followed me.

An old woman gasps at my side, her hand flying to her chest as she takes me in. Her wide, horrified eyes rake over the blood on my face, the disheveled state of my clothes, but I don't stop. I can't stop. Distance is the only thing that will keep him away from Natalie. I don't have the luxury of explanations or reassurances.

Without a word to her or the other bystanders beginning to slow their steps to stare, I half-walk, half-stumble down the sidewalk, legs wobbling under the weight of my exhaustion. I need to get farther. Safer. I need to call Natalie and tell her I'm okay before she does something reckless like try to find me herself.

I should have grabbed my phone off the ground.

My blurred vision makes it easier to block out the curious, concerned eyes around me. I only speak when one brave woman about my age steps directly into my path, hands hovering at her sides like she's not sure if she should touch me or not.

"Are you okay?" she asks gently, but the question only irritates me. I interrupt her before she can say anything else.

"What street am I on?" My voice is hoarse, dry, like it's been scraped against sandpaper.

Her eyes flutter in surprise at my question, but she answers quickly. "You're on Monroe, heading towards the lake." She steps closer, placing a light hand on my forearm, her expression softening. "Can I help you? Should I call 911? You really need to get to an emergency room."

Her kindness is almost enough to crack me, and for a brief moment, the invisible weight pressing on my shoulders feels just a little lighter. But I shake my head and pull my arm from her grip.

"No," I mutter, shaking my head again as if to dislodge her words. "Thank you." It's barely a whisper, but I can't stop. I have to keep moving. Silas's building is only a few blocks from here.

Each step grows heavier; the adrenaline that carried me this far is fading fast, leaving me empty and vulnerable. The sluggishness creeps in, dragging me down like quicksand. My vision narrows, but I force myself forward, focusing on the itching sensation of the drying blood on my face to keep from succumbing to the darkness clawing at the edges of my mind.

By the time I reach the towering Wells Corporate building, I'm barely moving. Everything feels distant, blurred, like I'm watching myself from outside my own body. I blink, and suddenly, I'm inside, standing in the pristine ground-floor reception. The bright lights sting my eyes, and the polished marble floors feel like they might swallow me whole.

"Ma'am?" A deep voice calls out, and I flinch at the sound. It feels like it ricochets inside my pounding skull. An older man is walking around the counter, his brows furrowed in concern. His suit is immaculate, his demeanor professional but cautious, like he's not sure whether to approach me.

"Silas," I rasp, barely audible. I swallow and try again, my tongue thick in my mouth, words slipping away as fast as I can grasp them. "Davey. I need... I need them to call Natalie."

The man's brows knit tighter. "Why don't you sit down?" He gestures toward a sleek leather couch a few feet away, his voice kind but firm. I nod numbly, my body moving before my mind registers. My steps are uneven, unsteady, but somehow I make it to the couch and sink onto the cold leather.

A woman who had also been behind the counter hurries out, clutching a handful of napkins. Her mouth moves, words spilling out, but I can't make sense of them. My focus is locked on the man.

"Silas and Davey," I repeat, more of a mumble now as my head tilts back against the cushion. "I'm Scarlett Page. Natalie's friend. She's worried."

Even in my haze, I see his hesitation. His eyes dart between me and the other people in the lobby—business professionals, delivery personnel, a few suited security guards—all now stealing glances at me from their respective places. Who wouldn't?

I must look insane.

"Please," I whisper, the word cracking on my lips. It's barely audible, but it seems to break something in him. He nods stiffly, murmuring something about notifying them before retreating to his desk. I can see him pick up the phone, speaking quickly, his eyes flicking back to me every few seconds.

The woman kneels beside me, her presence warm but distant, pressing the napkin gently against my forehead. Her voice is soft, instructing me to lay down. The words barely register, but I press myself deeper into the couch. My chest heaves with shallow breaths, and I'm vaguely aware of the man hanging up the phone, nodding in my direction as if to reassure me that he's done what I asked.

I can't hold on any longer. My body collapses further into the sofa, and my head rests against the bottom cushion. The last thing I register is the faint, distant hum of voices in the lobby before I give in completely to the darkness.

Chapter 19

"**S**carlett," a low, velvety voice says near my ear, breaking through the dense fog of my dreamless sleep. "I need you to wake up."

Almost as soon as I surface, the pain follows, spreading like wildfire. Pressure pounds behind my eyes, the throbbing in my forehead intensifying with every relentless heartbeat. I inhale shakily, but the air feels like knives against my raw throat.

Where am I?

Blinking doesn't help. Something is covering my eyes, pressing lightly against my skin. A prickling sensation starts in my fingers and toes, crawling up my limbs as my body wakes up piece by piece. Panic rises in my chest.

Did the man come back? Did he find me in the lobby and take me somewhere else? Am I somewhere I'd recognize so he blindfolded me?

Dread pools in the pit of my stomach, cold and heavy. My breaths come faster, quicker, teetering on the edge of hyperventilation.

"Easy," the voice speaks again, softer now, but firm. There's a weight on my chest, but it doesn't feel threatening. It's grounding, almost comforting. "It's okay. You're safe."

I know that voice. It's the same one that whispered to me on the steps of his mansion weeks ago, pulling me back from the edge.

Silas.

Relief surges through me, bursting out in a strangled, half-choked cough. My body relaxes all at once, sinking further into what I now realize is a soft, cushioned surface. The panic ebbs, giving way to awareness—the cool, damp cloth on my face, the absence of bindings or re-straints, and the unmistakable cedarwood cologne that lingers in the air.

Hands trembling, I pull the cloth off my eyes, flinching at the brightness that stabs at them like tiny needles. With a curse, I throw the back of my hand over my face, accidentally bumping my forehead. The pain feels like a lightning strike, and a whimper escapes before I can stop it. My head feels like it's splitting in two.

"Should've warned you that might hurt," Silas mutters, almost to himself. His voice is close, like he's sitting right beside me, but I don't have the energy to check.

Eyes closed, throat raw, I croak, "How long have I been out?"

"About half an hour." His voice softens further as I feel the faintest touch running tenderly over the top of my head and through my tangled hair. "Are you able to sit up? I have water."

Somehow, I manage to comply, though it feels like my entire body is moving through sand. Every motion is slow and excruciating. Silas braces my upper back with a steady hand, guiding me upright with surprising care. My head feels impossibly heavy, like I'm balancing a brick on my shoulders.

The second my feet touch the floor, I hold out my hand instinctively. A bottle of water is placed in my palm. I don't even check to see if the cap is off before tipping it toward my lips. To my relief, it is. Cool water streams down my throat, soothing the rawness. It's heavenly. I force myself to sip slowly, knowing that guzzling it all at once will only make me sick.

Lowering the bottle, I cautiously blink. It takes several tries before I can tolerate the brightness. My head still aches, but the pain is manageable now, a dull throb instead of a sharp spike. Each blink sharpens the room around me—its dark wood accents, rich earth tones, and meticulous organization. This isn't a hospital.

This is Silas's office.

I take in the sprawling bookshelves that dominate the far wall, neatly arranged with leather-bound volumes and labeled file boxes. The large desk in front of them is pristine, not a single item out of place. A wall of windows to my left, partially obscured by light-filtering shades, offers a breathtaking view of Millennium Park and Lake Michigan. The furniture is sleek and modern—a long, comfortable couch where I'm sitting, flanked by two cigar chairs and a sturdy metal coffee table.

My gaze shifts to the man beside me. Silas sits on the edge of the couch, elbows resting on his knees, hands clasped loosely in front of him. His white button-down is slightly wrinkled, his tie loosened but still in place. There's a faint smear of blood where his pec and shoulder meet, as if my head rested there at some point. His usual calm, polished appearance is marred only by the tension in his forehead and the slight curve of his lips pressed into a thin line. Those mocha eyes, however, are what hold my attention. They're filled with something I rarely see directed at me: concern.

He doesn't speak, doesn't push. He just watches, waiting for me to come back to myself.

"Where's Natalie?" I rasp, voice shaky.

Silas carefully takes the water bottle from my trembling hands, capping it and placing it on the coffee table in front of us. He moves like every motion is calculated to steady the moment. To steady me. "She's here," he says evenly. "Davey took her to his office so she could calm down. You needed to rest before Doctor Carrow got here."

My eyebrows furrow, and the sharp movement sends a wave of pain through my forehead. I wince. "Who?"

"Our family physician," he explains with a slight shrug. The casual tone almost masking the tension coiled in his body. "He'll be here soon."

"Your family physician?" I echo in disbelief and clear my throat. "That feels... excessive. An ambulance to the emergency room would have been fine."

I'm not even sure if that's true. My gun-toting kidnapper probably already thought of that. If he's brave enough, he'll call Peter to figure out which hospital I checked into. Or worse, he's already racing to find me before Peter realizes what happened. Either way, I probably wouldn't have been safe there.

Silas's jaw ticks, his earlier patience replaced with something sharper. His knuckles faintly whitening as his hands tighten on his knees before he forces himself to relax. "Scarlett," he says, his voice low, each word deliberate. "You were passed out in my lobby, bleeding, asking for me. Do you really think I would throw you in an ambulance to be dumped at some random hospital?" He pauses, his jaw working, then exhales through his nose, clearly reigning in the fraying edges of his temper. When he speaks again, his voice softens. "Dr. Carrow is always available. And he's the best in the city."

My cheeks burn with embarrassment. My intentions *had* been good. I truly wanted to make sure Natalie didn't come looking for me, but that doesn't change the fact I made a scene. Not only had I stumbled in looking like death warmed over, but I'd also begged for the most important man in the building to come save me in front of God knows how many people.

"I'm sorry," I whisper, my gaze dropping to my lap. My voice feels small, like it belongs to someone else. "I'll pay to have the couch cleaned, and I'll apologize to your receptionists."

In an instant, Silas no longer at a distance but sitting directly in front of me on the edge of the coffee table, one knee wedged between mine, the other bracketing the outside of my left leg.

With a warm and steady hand, Silas tilts my chin until my eyes meet his. The touch is gentle, but there's a tension radiating from him that feels like a physical force. "Do you really think I'm worried about anything besides you right now?" His eyes burning into mine, searching. A small, crooked smile tugs at the corner of his mouth, though it doesn't quite reach the rest of his features. "The couch, Mr. Harris, and Mrs. Voss are the least of my concerns."

The intensity in his expression is almost too much, and I lean back instinctively, trying to create space to catch my breath. His hand drops and finds a new home on my knee, the movement so casual it's as if it's always belonged there.

"How freaked out was Natalie?" I manage.

He exhales, his eyes narrowing slightly as he considers the question. "Pretty freaked," he admits, jaw clenching again. I can almost feel the effort it's taking him to keep his composure. "Can you tell me what happened?"

I hesitate. As much as I want to tell him every last terrifying detail, I can't. Peter, Harrison, and their cronies are still out there, lying in wait. But if Davey or Silas decides to gain access to the surrounding security footage, they'll likely see what happened to me right until I entered that alleyway, anyway.

My punishment will come eventually. I know that. But not at the expense of someone who hasn't done anything wrong. Not Natalie. So, I decide on another half-truth. Just enough to keep her safe.

"Some guy held me at gunpoint."

Silas's entire body stills, but the sharp inhale that flares his nostrils gives him away. The hand on my knee moves back and forth across the torn fabric of my jeans. The touch is instinctive, intimate, like it's the most natural thing in the world.

"Do you know what he wanted?"

I snort, focusing on the veins and tendons in his hand as he moves. "We didn't get into the pleasantries before he punched me in the face." My tone is dry, but it's a thin veil over the exhaustion and fear. I don't allow the silence to linger before continuing, "I think he's seen me with Natalie and wanted to use me to get to her."

The moment the words leave my mouth, the soothing motion of his thumb slows, then stops altogether. The weight of his stare bears down on me like a physical force and I look up to look back at him. His eyebrows draw together, concern carving lines into his otherwise flawless features. The muscles in his jaw tighten with a tension that radiates through his entire frame.

"What makes you think that?" he asks, his tone low, measured. Controlled. But not calm. Never calm. Despite that, his hands remain steady, one still on my knee, the other now resting firmly on the outside of my thigh, as though he's anchoring me—or himself.

"I thought he was going to rape me or kill me..." The words come out in a rush, tumbling over one another, and I have to swallow hard before I can continue. "Or both." My voice catches on the last word, and I let out a shaky breath. "But instead, he took my phone, called her, and taunted me with it. I don't know how he planned to lure her there because I fought back and he dropped the phone, but I just can't think of any other explanation."

Silas doesn't speak immediately. He doesn't need to. The transformation in him is terrifyingly visible. His face darkens with each word that passes through my lips, his gaze hardening into something so lethal it almost hurts to look at him. The composure he wears like a second skin isn't breaking—it's shattering, but not in a chaotic way. No, this is precision rage, the kind that implodes instead of explodes, calculated and deadly.

This isn't the calm and collected businessman or the annoying yet charming adrenaline junkie I've seen before. The silence is more unnerving than any outburst could ever be, and I realize that he's not just thinking of how to protect Natalie. He's planning how to annihilate anyone who even dared to threaten her.

For a moment, I'm struck by the sheer intensity of him. I should be scared—after all, I'm part of the threat. But not where Natalie's physical well-being is concerned, and I think he knows that. At least, I hope he does. I meet his eyes, unflinching, letting him see the sincerity in mine.

He lets out a slow, controlled exhale, the muscles in his shoulders shifting as though he's forcing himself to dial back his anger. The grip on my knee remains there, hot against my jeans.

A knock echoes through the office, and I jump, the sudden sound sending a sharp bolt of pain through my head. I grunt in discomfort as I close my eyes tightly.

Silas's grip on my knee and thigh tightens with firm but gentle reassurance. "Try to breathe. Deep and slow," he instructs, his voice softer now. It's the Silas I recognize from the auction, the one who talked me down when my panic had threatened to consume me. The one I trust, whether I should or not.

I do as he says, my breaths shaky but slowing as I follow his lead. His hands linger a moment longer before he stands, leaving me feeling oddly bereft in his absence.

He moves to the door, his strides purposeful but silent, and speaks in hushed tones to whoever is on the other side.

A man in his fifties with salt-and-pepper hair and a neatly trimmed goatee enters the room. He's dressed in a crisp striped dress shirt, dark tie, tailored dress pants, and an open petticoat. In one hand, he carries a medical bag, and a leather briefcase hangs from the opposite shoulder.

"Hi, Dr. Carrow," I greet him softly, figuring that breaking the ice might get this examination over with faster. "I'm Scarlett. Thanks for coming to see me."

"I wish we were meeting under better circumstances," he replies with a sigh, giving me a polite, practiced smile. I'm not sure under what better circumstances I'd ever meet him, but I don't bother to ask. He strides further into the room with an air of familiarity, dropping both bags onto one of the open cigar chairs and draping his coat neatly over them. "Can I ask you a few questions before I take a look at you?"

"Of course," I respond, though my throat protests the words.

He rifles through his briefcase, retrieving a leather-bound notebook and pen. Settling into the other cigar chair, he clicks the pen a few times as he flips to a clean page. "As long as you feel comfortable with it, it would help me if you could recall as many injuries as possible and their causes. I'll give you a head-to-toe examination regardless, but this information will give me a good starting point, so I know we won't miss anything."

The thought of recounting every moment of this morning sends a shiver down my spine, but there's no way around it. Silas remains silent, but I can feel his presence like a furnace at the edge of the couch. He's watching, waiting, holding on to whatever storm is brewing inside him.

I take a shaky breath and begin, starting from the split skin on my forehead. My voice is measured, clinical. As if detaching myself from the details will make them easier to speak aloud. By the time I finish recounting every ache and injury, my voice is barely a whisper. Dr. Carrow listens intently, jotting down notes, occasionally pausing to nod or ask for clarification. His face betrays flashes of surprise and concern, though he remains professional and calm.

Silas, however, is a different story. By the time I'm done, he's standing completely still, his arms folded so tightly across his chest I'm surprised the fabric of his shirt hasn't torn. The restrained anger radiating off him is tangible, like standing too close to a live wire. It's not directed at me—I know that much—but the intensity of it is almost overwhelming.

Dr. Carrow finally closes his notebook, slipping it back into his briefcase before standing and reaching for his medical bag. "From the sounds of it, you handled yourself well," he says kindly, though there's an edge of astonishment in his tone. Then he turns to Silas. "Can you help Ms. Page to the bathroom?"

Before I can protest that I don't need help, Silas is at my side, his touch surprisingly gentle as his fingers fold around the crease of my elbow. He pulls me upright with ease, taking most of my weight as my legs threaten to buckle beneath me. His other hand slides across the small of my back, steadying me before carefully finding my opposite hip. The heat of his palm seeps through my clothes, centering me in a way I didn't expect.

"Lean on me," he murmurs, his voice low but certain. "I've got you."

For some reason, I don't doubt it—just like I didn't when I stumbled into his lobby earlier. But nothing would have prepared me for this drastic and sudden change in our dynamic. It's almost giving me whiplash.

Silas isn't teasing me, making pointed jabs, or trying to rile me up. He isn't even angry at me like the last time I saw him. I half expected him to be, even knowing he'd take care of me. Instead, he's treating me gently.

Not in a condescending way, but as if he's trying to keep me together without drawing attention to the cracks.

The Silas I've gotten to know doesn't do gentle. He needles, provokes. Enjoys getting under my skin. But this? This is different, and the shift is so stark it leaves me reeling. Yet, as unsettling as it is, I can't deny that it feels... nice. Steadying.

Giving in, I allow myself to lean into him, my body protesting the movement with every step. My knees ache, a deep, throbbing soreness that makes me wince, and my knuckles sting where the skin has split. Even the simple act of shifting my weight sends a dull pain radiating all over. Silas doesn't comment, just adjusts his grip, steady and sure, as he guides me toward the bathroom with an ease that makes me wonder how many people he's had to carry like this.

The light in the bathroom is almost too bright, and I squint against it as Dr. Carrow begins unloading his bag onto the counter. The space is as immaculate as Silas's office and home—a modern blend of dark wood, black tiles, and warm beige walls. An upholstered chair sits next to the sink, facing a blank wall, clearly prepared for me.

"I apologize for the brightness," Dr. Carrow says with a grimace, gesturing toward the overhead lights. "It makes it easier for me to examine you. Can I have you change into a gown?"

I nod, resigned. Silas guides me into the small toilet room, ensuring the lid is down before lowering me onto it as though I weigh nothing. The effortless way he handles me would be almost irritating if it weren't so reassuring.

Silas kneels in front of me, folding himself into the cramped space. One hand rests lightly on my knee, the other holding the folded hospital gown Dr. Carrow must have handed him.

"I'm going to stand right outside the door." He nods to the wall next to the opening. "If you need help or feel dizzy, just say my name. I'll hear you."

The kindness woven into every word is almost too much, scraping against the fragile walls I've built around myself. I can feel them bowing under the weight of his care. Incapable of handling this tender side of Silas Wells any longer, I force a smirk onto my face, desperate to deflect the attention.

"If you wanted to see me naked, you could have just asked," I quip, my voice hoarse, but there's an undeniable teasing edge.

It takes him a second to process my words, and when he does, a low chuckle rumbles from the back of his throat, deep and rich. He squeezes my knee briefly before letting go, and rising to his full height as he places the gown in my lap.

"That mouth," is all he says, his molten gaze lingering on mine for a moment longer than necessary. Then, he steps back and slips out of the room and shuts the door so quietly that I barely hear the latch click into place.

As quickly as my battered body will allow, I strip off my dirty clothes, every movement sending small jolts of pain through me. I shove the ruined garments into a corner with a foot, the action more cathartic than it has any right to be, and slide the hospital gown over my shoulders. The fabric is cool against my skin, a stark contrast to the heat still radiating from every bruise and scrape. It's a strange comfort, and I focus on that sensation rather than letting my mind spiral into the chaos of what happened earlier.

It would be nice to have more time to process this. Time to sit and think and let myself unravel just a little. But I know better than to indulge in that. If I give myself even an inch, the floodgates will open, and there's no way I can afford that right now. Compartmentalization has been my survival strategy for years, and I can handle this too. It's just one more thing to lock away for later.

Taking a deep breath, I place a hand on the cool metal of the door handle. My fingers tremble slightly before pulling the door open. I step out into the bright bathroom, my back straight despite the muted throb in every inch of my body.

Silas is waiting just outside, leaning casually against the wall, as though he hasn't been silently standing guard the entire time. He steps forward, his hand hovering near my elbow, ready to steady me if needed but giving me the space to move on my own.

"Let's get this over with," I mutter, more to myself than anyone else, and Silas's lips quirk upward in the faintest hint of a smile. He doesn't say anything, just stays close as I return to the chair near the sink. Dr. Carrow is already waiting, his expression calm but focused as he pulls on a pair of gloves.

———

According to Dr. Carrow, the split on my forehead isn't as bad as it looks. Head wounds tend to be "dramatic" and bleed excessively, he assures me. It has already started clotting on its own and thanks to Silas's help while I was sleeping, the dried blood on the rest of my face had been gently wiped away with a clean washcloth. This made it easier for Dr. Carrow to clean the area, apply an antiseptic, and place steri-strips to encourage the cut to close. He assures me the scar should be minimal.

The scratches on my cheek, hands, knees, and fingers have been meticulously cleaned. Dr. Carrow had to remove tiny pieces of debris—likely crumbling brick—from my face. He warns me to keep an eye on it for signs of infection. My throat appears fine but might stay sore for a few days, and he advises me to see my doctor if the pain persists. The last thing he examines is the lump on the back of my head.

"All things considered, you made it out of an unfair fight relatively intact," Dr. Carrow remarks, a trace of admiration in his voice that makes my cheeks flush. "Do you take self-defense courses?"

I manage a small smile, trying to ignore the warm pride blooming in my chest. "I train in Jiu-Jitsu and a few other combat sports."

The doctor chuckles softly as he examines the lump on my head, moving my hair gently from side to side. After a few more minutes of prodding, questions, and shining a light into my eyes, he steps back in front of me with a satisfied nod. "Judging by the welt, I'd be surprised if you didn't break his nose. Your training probably saved your life."

His words hit me harder than I expect, a sudden wave of validation for all the hours I've spent preparing for moments like this. Hearing a stranger acknowledge the work I've put into protecting myself feels like a small victory amidst the chaos.

"So," Dr. Carrow begins, crossing his arms and meeting my gaze. "Your injuries are manageable. My biggest concern is the concussion, which you'll need to monitor closely. I want you to take some acetaminophen before I leave, and someone needs to keep an eye on you for the next forty-eight hours to ensure your symptoms don't worsen. Is there anyone you'd like me to call to stay with you?"

The warm pride in my chest immediately twists into something sharp and uncomfortable. The shame of not having anyone to call in these moments has never dulled over the years. I force a half-smile and shake my head, barely moving it to avoid aggravating the throbbing in my skull. "No. I'll be okay. Thank you, though."

Dr. Carrow opens his mouth, likely to press me on the issue, but Silas's voice cuts through the room like steel. "She won't be alone."

I glance at Silas, taken aback by the quiet conviction in his voice. His arms are crossed, his posture stiff, but his eyes leave no room for argument. As much as I want to push back, I don't have the energy for it, and I definitely don't want to bicker in front of the doctor. I nod my agreement, and Dr. Carrow exhales softly.

"Very well," he says, turning back to his bag and packing up his instruments. Between movements, he hands me two acetaminophen tablets and explains the over-the-counter regimen he wants me to follow, along with a list of concussion symptoms to watch for. He ends with a recommendation for a follow-up appointment with my own physician. After writing everything down in his notebook, he tears out the page and hands it to me.

"I'm glad you're alright, Scarlett. Please don't hesitate to call me if you need anything at all." He places a comforting hand on mine for a moment, giving it a reassuring squeeze before releasing me. I thank him again, and he waves me off, telling me I'm free to go change.

Silas, who's been silent but watchful from the far wall, steps forward as Dr. Carrow grabs his things. "Thank you, Dr. Carrow. Send Leslie the invoice, and she'll handle it."

"I can pay—" I start from the doorway of the toilet room, but Silas's sharp gaze snaps to me.

"No, you won't." His tone firm and final

Though my skin burns under his commanding stare, I relent with a roll of my eyes. Silas, satisfied, turns back to Dr. Carrow. "If Natalie's waiting in the hallway, let her know I'll come get her when Scarlett's ready for visitors."

"Of course." Dr. Carrow offers me a kind smile as he leaves, murmuring, "Nice to meet you, Ms. Page. Silas has my number if you need me."

After I close the door behind myself, I notice something new in the corner of the bathroom. My old, bloodied clothes are gone, replaced with a neatly folded pile of fresh clothing on the top of the closed toilet—a pair of leggings, slip-on shoes, socks, a sports bra, a fitted t-shirt, and a quarter-zip with the tags still attached. My head throbs too much to piece together how Silas managed this without me noticing or who he sent out to purchase them, but the sight of the clean clothes stirs an unexpected wave of emotion. Tears prick the corners of my eyes and I blink them away, unwilling to let them fall.

Once dressed, I step into the rest of the bathroom, feeling slightly more human. Silas is leaning on the edge of the counter, his sharp gaze lifting to meet mine. He nods toward me, a silent invitation to join him. My feet seem to have a mind of their own, carrying me across the room.

Unwilling to face my reflection in the mirror behind him, I gingerly hoist myself onto the counter, my legs dangling over the edge. Silas watches me for a moment, his expression unreadable, before he stands straight and turns to face me. My pulse quickens, and I swallow nervously.

"Do you want me to dispose of your clothes or have them cleaned?" Silas asks simply, his tone neutral, giving no hint of preference for either option.

"Burn them," I reply instantly. His eyes flicker with understanding, and he nods once, resolute.

"Done."

The counter in this bathroom is unusually tall, clearly designed for someone with Silas's stature. It makes our faces closer than they've ever been when I'm standing, and for the first time, I'm acutely aware of the height disparity between us. At almost 5'8", I've always felt relatively tall for a woman, but Silas's sheer presence—his unyielding, consuming energy—makes me feel impossibly small.

Clearing my throat for what feels like the hundredth time, I break the silence. "Why can't Natalie come in yet?"

He leans forward, placing his hands on either side of my thighs, gripping the edge of the counter with enough force to turn his knuckles white. His slightly hunched shoulders bring his face close enough that I could count the faint freckles scattered across his nose if I wanted to.

"I have a few more questions," he murmurs, his breath cool as it brushes against my skin. A shiver runs down my spine despite the warmth radiating from his body.

"Okay," I manage to say. "Let's hear them."

One hand leaves the counter and reaches for the hair draped over my shoulder. He twirls the strands between his fingers, his eyes fixated on the movement as if studying every detail before shifting his attention back to me, his gaze sharp and unreadable.

"Are you okay?"

I blink in surprise, the question catching me off guard. "Huh?"

Silas raises an eyebrow, his previously expression softening just slightly. "It's one of my questions. Are you okay?"

The words tangle in my brain, leaving me momentarily speechless. When I first woke up, I expected Silas to demand answers, to dissect what had happened with his characteristic focus and precision. It's how he operates, and I prefer it that way. But this sudden shift leaves me fumbling.

"I'm fine, Silas," I finally say, though my voice lacks conviction. "Tired and sore, but fine."

The creases in his brow deepen, jaw tightening like he's holding back from arguing with me. "Can I get you more water? Something to eat?"

I reach up, wrapping my fingers gently around the wrist of the hand still toying with my hair. His skin is warm and steady. "I'm good right now. Thank you."

His hand moves slowly, sliding up the side of my neck, causing my own hold to fall away. His fingertips brush over the bruises there with a feather-light touch, lingering, as though trying to absorb the pain for himself. He stops on my uninjured cheek, thumb grazing my skin so gently it feels like a whisper.

The noise in my head—the endless static of worry, fear, and exhaustion—fades under his touch. His scruff is slightly longer than it was a few days ago, adding a rugged edge to his otherwise polished appearance. It's a subtle difference, but it does something to me I can't quite name. For the first time in what feels like hours, the world narrows to just this moment. To just him.

"What made you come here?" he asks, his voice low and the question loaded.

My stomach twists, the weight of his question pressing heavily on me. I take a shaky breath and force myself to speak. "I heard Natalie panicking on the phone. I wasn't thinking clearly, but I was worried she might try to find me, since we were supposed to meet for coffee nearby. When I got out of the alley and back to the main road, I realized how close I was to this building. I thought if I could talk to you or Davey, you could call her so she wouldn't do anything dangerous," I pause, debating whether I should say what I'm really feeling. Against my better judgment, I decide to be honest. "And I... I knew I'd be safe here. That you'd take care of me."

Silas's lips part, his pupils dilating behind the glasses perched on his nose. His hand slides further back, into my hair, his fingers curling into the strands with a tenderness that contradicts the tension in his body. His chest rises and falls with uneven breaths as he takes in my words.

"Fuck, Scarlett," he mutters, his voice rough as his forehead dips forward, nose brushing against the side of mine. The intimacy of the gesture steals the air from my lungs. "What are you doing to me?"

His free hand presses lightly against the small sliver of skin exposed at the base of my spine, his touch both comforting and electrifying. My body responds instinctively, leaning into him despite the soreness radiating through my limbs. Every nerve ending feels like it's on fire, hyper-aware of the man standing between my knees, holding me like I'm something precious.

I can't think. His lips are so close that I can almost taste him, and I know with certainty that if he leans in, if he decides to take what he wants, I won't stop him.

Without letting up his grip, Silas lifts his head, his eyes still clouded with emotion but sharpened by something more calculating now. "Do you have any idea who the man was?" he asks. The question is enough to pierce through the haze clouding my mind.

"No," I reply, shaking my head slightly.

"Where did he first approach you?"

Even though I don't intend to contact anyone, I try to divert his attention from the details, if only for a moment. "Shouldn't we call the cops for this?" I ask, watching for his reaction.

His eyes narrow. "The cops aren't going to do what I need them to. If you want to call them for your own peace of mind, of course, we can do that," he says, his voice softer now, though it carries a definitive edge. "But I'm going to have my own team look into this."

My eyes widen in surprise. That's news to me. "Your own team?"

Before he can elaborate, there's a knock at the office door. It's quiet, almost hesitant, but the interruption feels like a ripple in the stillness between us. We both know it's Natalie. And if I've learned anything about her, it's that she's not going to go away. Silas sighs deeply, as though he's been expecting this.

189

"She'll kick the door down soon if I don't let her in," he says, a faint trace of amusement in his voice. Then, as if it's a given, he adds, "We can talk more at home."

"Home?" I repeat, confused.

He chuckles softly before leaning in to press his lips against my hairline. The gesture is so gentle, so unexpectedly affectionate, that my heart stutters in my chest.

"You need to be watched for forty-eight hours," he explains, taking on a matter-of-fact tone. "And either you lost your purse and keys, or the asshole stole them. We'll need to contact your apartment and have the locks changed. I'll help you cancel your cards, too."

I hadn't even noticed my small cross-body bag was missing. In all the chaos, it didn't even cross my mind. It likely fell off during the struggle, but if my attacker did take it, it's not like the fake ID or my keys would be a real issue. Peter has his own set of keys to my place, and if he wanted to make a move, he wouldn't hesitate. Still, the last thing I need is to insist on staying home, have Natalie come with me, and then face an unexpected visitor in the middle of the night.

"Awfully presumptuous of you to think I'm going to stay with you instead of Natalie," I joke weakly, attempting to lighten the mood.

The corner of Silas's mouth lifts in a slow, knowing smile as his hands slide from my hips to hook under my arms, pulling me gently to the edge of the counter. My body slides down the front of his with maddening slowness until my feet touch the floor, but he doesn't step away. The steady beat of my heart thunders in my ears, making my headache worse.

"She's going to visit Cecilia in Los Angeles for the weekend," he says casually, as if we're discussing the weather. "Once Davey hears the details, I wouldn't be surprised if he charters the plane tonight instead of tomorrow morning."

Shit. I'd completely forgotten about Natalie's trip. She'd mentioned visiting her best friend until Sunday, which means I'd be left to either stay with Silas or, worse, be offered a room at Davey's place. The latter sounds like a nightmare, and I can't imagine Silas letting me choose his best friend over him without a fight.

As if sensing my hesitation, Silas adds, "Once we know you're safe, you'll be free to go."

I don't miss the way he phrases it—"safe," not "healthy." My lips press into a thin line, giving him a look that says I'm onto him, but he doesn't seem the least bit phased.

"Doesn't sound like I have much of a choice," I mutter, though there's no real bite to my words.

His smile widens, his lips tugging up at one corner in that infuriatingly confident way of his. Finally, he steps back slightly, leaving one hand resting on the small of my back to guide me toward the door. "I'm not so arrogant to think I can make you do anything," he answers. "But I want to. And I think you want me to, too. Let me do this for you."

The exhaustion is starting to settle deep in my bones, making every step feel heavier than the last. The idea of someone taking care of me, even for a little while, is more tempting than I want to admit. And this version of Silas, the one who looks at me like I'm more than just a puzzle or a challenge, is someone I'm not ready to say goodbye to just yet.

So, against my better judgment, I let him win. "Okay," I whisper.

Just this once.

"Scarlett's been through enough today," Natalie insists, her sharp tone cutting through the tension in the room. Her glare at Davey's back could level mountains, but he doesn't turn around. Her husband stands at Silas's floor-to-ceiling windows, his hands in his pockets, shoulders taut with frustration.

"It's not adding up," Davey mutters, almost to himself, his focus trained on the skyline beyond the glass. "You have other friends. No one's ever gone after them to get to you. Why now? Why her?"

The ice pack chills my forehead, but his words cool me to the bone. He isn't wrong. For over an hour, he's been drilling me with questions—careful, precise, probing for any loose thread in my story. Davey has never trusted me, and now, with a potential threat tied to Natalie, I'm under his microscope more than ever.

The man is as paranoid as he is brilliant. And that makes him dangerous. If I make one mistake, give him even the smallest inconsistency, Davey'll tear my story apart piece by piece. My heart races with the need to run, but I stay rooted in place. Running won't solve anything. It'll only confirm whatever suspicions he has.

Peter's motives are no clearer now than they were in that alley. I'd assumed the man with the gun was sent to get rid of me: simple, clean, efficient. But this? This was something else entirely. Why would he go to the trouble of calling Natalie? What was the plan? To kidnap her and use her to pressure the Wells family into giving Peter what he wants? Or was it worse? Something designed to remind me of the leash around my neck and what happens when I test its limits? The uncertainty grates at me. All I know for sure is that Natalie cannot be in the line of fire.

If I get Peter what he wants, if I find the servers and deliver the blackmail, maybe it'll be enough to stop all of this. Silas can handle whatever fallout Peter has planned; his strength, his influence, his sheer force of will make me believe that. But if Peter takes Natalie the same way he took Drew, I won't survive it. And neither would the two men in this room.

I've done my best to steer Davey's interrogation toward Natalie, keeping his focus there. His love for her is my best weapon. If he's preoccupied with protecting her, the rest of my carefully crafted half-truths won't matter.

"Agreed," Silas says, his voice cutting through the tension. He leans back in one of the leather cigar chairs. "Scarlett needs rest."

From the couch, Natalie grips my forearm gently. Silas looks between us, his focus landing on me before continuing, "Leslie's canceled my meetings for the rest of the day. I'll be taking her back to my house after this."

Natalie's head snaps toward her brother, her eyebrows pinching with frustration. "Why are you acting like I'm not staying in Chicago to take care of her?" she demands.

"Because you aren't," Davey answers before Silas can, turning from the windows to face us. "You've been looking forward to this trip. And it'll be good for you to get some distance while we figure this out."

Her aggravation is palpable as she looks between her husband and brother, but I intervene before she can argue further by patting her hand. "You've been talking about seeing Cecilia for weeks. And Davey's right. It'll be safer for you if you're away from here for a few days."

"You're hurt because of me," she murmurs, her golden eyes glistening with unshed tears. The guilt in her voice twists something deep in my chest, but I shake my head firmly.

"No," I say, my voice steady despite the ache in my head. "I'm hurt because *some asshole* wants to hurt *you*."

"Scarlett's right," Silas interjects and stands to his full height to begins to button the front of his suit jacket, commanding attention without effort. "You're not responsible for someone else's actions. But he made a mistake underestimating her, and that will cost him."

Silas's voice is calm, but the conviction behind his words sends a shiver down my spine. When his eyes meet mine, the heat in them softens just slightly, but the promise remains. His words are as much for me as they are for the room: a vow of retribution.

"Scarlett needs to rest, and you need to pack," he reiterates, looking at his sister. "She'll be in good hands while you're gone."

Natalie hesitates, her stubbornness flaring again as she bites the inside of her cheek. But as she glances between the three of us, she finally relents, shoulders slumping in a mix of defeat and reluctant acceptance. "I know she will be," she murmurs softly. "Okay. Let's get going."

She squeezes my arm one last time before standing, and for a moment, her eyes meet mine. There's so much emotion there—guilt, care, worry—and it takes everything in me not to crumble under the weight of it.

Chapter 20

The ride to Silas's home is meticulously planned, efficient, and oddly soothing. We exit the office through a private elevator leading to the underground garage, the hum of city life entirely shut out. Davey's Lincoln and a luxury SUV I'd never seen before are already idling at the curb when the doors open.

Natalie wraps me in a tight hug, her whispered promises to check in makes my throat tighten, and I manage to thank Davey despite the calculating glint still lingering in his eyes. Through it all, Silas hovers at my side. The coolness of his palm under the base of the sweatshirt on my lower back is startling, but I don't pull away. Instead, I let it anchor me as we exchange our goodbyes and head toward the SUV.

There's no recklessness, no thrill-seeking edge in the way Silas handles the wheel this time, only steady precision. His silence isn't oppressive but intentional, a rare moment of quiet in a day that's been anything but. His hand rests on my thigh as he drives, his thumb tracing lazy, reassuring circles over the fabric of my leggings. I should pull away, remind him of my boundaries that we both know we're ignoring, but I don't. Instead, I let the steady rhythm of his touch ease the tension in my body as I lean back into the plush seat.

Sleep doesn't come, but the quiet allows the ache in my body to subside just enough to keep me present. Only when the warmth of Silas's hand disappears do I open my eyes. The wrought-iron gate to his home is sliding open, and we pull into the privacy of his four-car garage, tucked away from the main road. The hum of the garage door shutting behind us feels oddly final, as though I've just crossed into a space I won't easily leave.

Once the SUV is in park, Silas turns to me, his eyes scanning my face. "What do you need?" The simplicity of his question, paired with the sincerity in his voice, catches me off guard. My chest aches at the unspoken promise behind his words.

He'll get me whatever I ask for.

I rub the ends of my dirty hair between my fingers, grimacing. "Dr. Carrow said I can't get the steri-strips wet, but I'd like to wash my hair and... just clean up in general." My voice is small, almost shy. "And maybe eat something too."

"Done and done," he replies without hesitation and circles around to my door before I can reach for the handle. His hand extends toward me, palm up, and I take it, the roughness of his calloused skin brushing against mine.

He leads me through the garage bays and into his home through a side entryway near the kitchen, pausing briefly to unlock, disable, and re-arm the alarms. The movements precise and practiced. "Kitchen's through here," he says, gesturing toward the open space beyond. "I'll give you a proper tour when you're feeling better." His fingers flex around mine comfortingly. "You can get cleaned up, and I'll make you some lunch. Do you have any allergies or dietary restrictions?"

I blink at him, processing the question a beat too late. "You cook?" I ask, surprised. It's the only response I manage.

He huffs out a soft laugh, the corners of his mouth lifting in a way that sends warmth skittering through my chest. "I can fend for myself when necessary," he answers. His grin deepens as he glances down at me, his full lips only inches away. My throat tightens, and I muster a small smile in return.

"No allergies or restrictions," I reply, the words finally finding their way out.

"My favorite kind of woman," he teases, stepping away slightly, but not before giving my hand a small, reassuring tug to pull me closer to his side.

He leads me through the house with an ease that feels oddly intimate, like he's walked this path with me a hundred times before. Most of the spaces we pass were filled with staff during the auction, leaving me with no real sense of his home's layout. But now, I can tell that it's a pretty straight shot from the side entry to the familiar back staircase I snuck up weeks ago.

"You're familiar with this area," Silas remarks, waving his free hand around the stairwell as we ascend. His playfulness and relaxed smile makes me roll my eyes, which only encourages him further.

On the second floor, he takes me past his office and into an unexplored hallway with several doors on either side. He stops at the furthest one on the right and opens it, revealing a guest room that's somehow both cozy and impossibly luxurious.

The walls, trim, and ceiling are all painted in a soft moss green that feels calming, while the dark floors and black accent furniture add a rich depth to the space. A king-sized bed with crisp white bedding dominates the room, flanked by linen curtains over the two oversized windows. Opposite the bed, an original dark wood fireplace with antique tiles catches my eye, its craftsmanship a testament to the home's history. Two inviting chairs sit nearby, clearly meant for quiet moments and maybe a book. The warm glow from the bedside lamp illuminates the space, making it feel like a haven.

"Closet and bathroom," Silas says, nodding toward the two doors on either side of the bed before walking toward the one farther away. He flips the light switch as he steps inside, motioning for me to follow.

The bathroom is just as stunning, a seamless extension of the bedroom's understated elegance. White marble covers the surfaces, reflecting the soft lighting overhead. A claw foot tub sits near the far wall, a standing shower large enough for a crowd next to it. Double vanities painted the same green as the bedroom walls complete the space, each detail perfectly curated.

"Thank you," I whisper, my voice barely audible as I take it all in. The enormity of his generosity, of his care, presses in on me from all sides. Without a word, Silas releases my hand and steps out of the bathroom, disappearing around the corner.

I blink after him, listening to his retreating footsteps. He doesn't return. For a moment, I feel the weight of the silence, a rare moment of solitude after everything that's happened. Maybe he thinks I need this—a chance to breathe, to process. He's probably right. And yet, his absence feels stark and unsettling.

Just as I reach for the door to close it, Silas reappears. My hand flies to my chest, startled. In his hands, he's carrying a simple black wooden chair. His brow furrows, but he says nothing, simply placing the chair on the floor between us.

"Sorry," he murmurs, his voice softer now. "I wanted you to have a place to sit."

My hand slides down from my chest to rest at my side. "Sit for what?"

"To wash your hair," he says matter-of-factly, as though the answer is obvious.

I tilt my head, a small, confused smile tugging at my lips. "I'm not sure I'm following you."

"You're not going to be able to wash your hair comfortably on your own," he responds, chin jutting toward the shower. "You shouldn't be moving your head around like that anyway. We can wash it in the shower. It's plenty big for both of us and the chair."

The casual cadence of his voice feels almost disarming, the striking contrast to the vulnerability of what he's suggesting. My throat tightens, and the words catch before they can leave my lips. "You're going to wash my hair?" I finally manage.

The question settles between us, and he watches my reaction before pushing the chair to the side to close the small distance between us, one hand rising to my face. His fingertips rest just under my chin and those dark eyes lock onto mine, searching. Steady.

"Yes," he says with quiet conviction. "I told you earlier—I've got you."

For a moment, the world tilts as the reality of his words settles over me. This isn't just kindness or obligation. This is better than any version of him I've encountered. This is the Silas I never dared to imagine, and I'm completely undone.

"You barely even know me," I whisper, my voice cracking as my eyes grow glossy. I don't mean to sound so vulnerable, but the day has worn down my walls.

Silas's glasses glint under the bathroom light as he offers a quiet, closed-mouth smile. His dimple peeks out just slightly beneath the growing scruff on his jaw. "But I want to," he says simply.

"Why?" The question comes out before I can stop it, loaded with confusion and the worry I can't quite contain. Silas doesn't shy away from it. He just keeps his eyes on mine, his hand sliding down to caress the side of my neck, thumb brushing gently over my skin.

"Because I like what I *do* see," he murmurs, and I struggle to keep my composure.

This man is going to break me. Just like Natalie being hurt would break me. I'm in so far over my head that I'm drowning, but for the life of me, I can't seem to push him away.

Silas takes my silence as acceptance, touch shifting down to my shoulders. He turns me gently toward the shower, as if we have all the time in the world. "Come on, you should relax. Take off your sweatshirt, and I'll set up the chair."

Grabbing the wooden chair, he moves it into the walk-in shower, positioning the seat to face away from the shower head. With meticulous care, he rolls up his sleeves, folding each section neatly until his forearms are exposed. The muscles flex subtly as he moves, the veins faintly visible beneath his skin. For the first time, I catch a proper glimpse of his tattoo. The bottom half is a detailed landscape—a dark, winding river beginning at the top of his wrist, carving its way through rugged terrain flanked by small clusters of trees. Their sparse branches stretch toward the base of his elbow, their leaves delicate against the stark scenery. The suggestion of mountains disappears under the cuff of his shirt.

I'm so distracted by the ink that I blurt out, "We're both going to get soaked."

Silas stills, and when I look up at him, I realize he's caught me staring. My cheeks burn under his knowing gaze, and his pupils dilate.

"I've had worse things happen to me," he replies smoothly.

A breathy laugh escapes me, breaking the tension. "Oh, grow up," I shoot back, rolling my eyes despite myself.

His lips curve into a lopsided grin, the warmth behind it making my stomach twist in ways I can't explain. "Never," he counters without missing a beat. Then, with a slight nod toward me, he adds, "Take the sweatshirt off. Shoes and socks, too."

For a brief moment, I consider insisting I can handle it myself, but the idea of arguing with him feels exhausting and my head aches. So I give in. After peeling off my sweatshirt and draping it over the sink, I kick off my shoes into the corner along with my socks.

When I glance back up, Silas has done the same. He's standing barefoot, the shower hose in his hand, looking entirely unbothered. There's something startlingly intimate about seeing him this way; barefoot and at ease in his own home, his usually polished exterior stripped down to something quieter and softer. I avert my gaze, trying to ground myself as I plop into the chair.

Wordlessly, he turns on the faucet, focusing entirely on adjusting the temperature. The sound of the rushing water fills the room, and I close my eyes, letting the noise wash over me. Once satisfied, Silas leans down as he instructs, "Sink back into the seat and let the back of your neck rest here." A towel is placed over the top edge of the chair, cushioning the hard surface.

Following his directions, I slide lower into the chair until the middle of my neck rests comfortably against the towel. My head hangs back, hair falling freely, and I'm left staring up at the ceiling.

Once I'm settled, he holds the shower head close to my scalp, and I groan in relief as the warm water trickles through the strands and across my skin. He's considerate as he moves, lifting my hair gently to saturate every piece and being mindful of the welt near the base of my skull, which rests just above the chair's back.

For a minute, I revel in the quiet, the rhythmic sound of water filling the space between us like a balm. Then Silas's soothing voice breaks through. "What do you train besides Jiu-Jitsu?"

With my eyes still closed, I smile faintly. "I've tried just about everything. I started with boxing, but Jiu-Jitsu has always been a favorite. Muay Thai, kickboxing, MMA, Krav Maga."

"I like kickboxing too," Silas admits, shutting off the water momentarily. Behind me, I hear the faint sound of a bottle cap popping.

"Is that why your hands are calloused?" I ask.

He chuckles. "Yes, and from weightlifting."

There's a gentle touch to the side of my head before his fingers begin to massage in the shampoo. I've always noticed his exceptional dexterity, but nothing prepared me for the sensation of those skilled hands working through my hair. His touch is firm yet careful, his fingers coaxing the tension from my scalp with a tenderness I didn't know I needed. The breath I release is loud, shaky, and embarrassingly unguarded, but I refuse to hold it in.

"Was that something you did as a kid, or did you pick it up as an adult?" he asks.

"Adult," I answer, keeping my eyes closed to focus on the way his hands move. "I never could've afforded it back then."

"Ah." His response is soft, almost self-conscious. "Money was tight growing up?"

It might be the concussion or the exhaustion, but I decide to go with a half-truth instead of outright lying. After all, what's publicly known about Scarlett Page's upbringing isn't far from my own, so it's easier for me to remember. "Nonexistent is more like it."

"That must have been hard."

I shrug, more focused on his touch than the question. His fingers slow for a moment. Too soon, he reaches for the shower head to wash out the suds, and I feel the warmth of the water cascade down my scalp again. "I figured it out," I answer, my tone deliberately light but hiding the weight behind the words.

"What do you mean *you* figured it out? Where were your parents?" His voice is calm, but there's a thread of curiosity.

Contemplating my words, I settle on, "My parents weren't exactly thrilled about one another—or about having me."

He hesitates. "Did they abandon you?" His voice is tinged with disbelief, as if the concept is utterly foreign to him.

"Emotionally, yes. Financially, mostly." My response is straightforward, stripped of feeling. This is just a fact, a piece of my past that I've grown used to explaining away, even to myself.

"Jesus," he mutters, his voice heavy with something I can't quite identify. Anger, maybe, or pity. "I'm sorry, Scarlett."

The last time anyone expressed genuine empathy for my upbringing was my high school IT teacher and Drew. I even spared Natalie the details of why I don't speak to them. The emotion feels foreign now, almost uncomfortable. But as foreign as it is, it's also... freeing. To speak the words aloud to someone who isn't judging loosens something tight in my chest.

"It is what it is," I say with a small shrug. "I haven't seen them since I left for college. It's better this way. They were poor and miserable, and they took it out on me. We've all moved on."

Silas hums, a low sound that feels like it carries more meaning than just agreement. I can't tell if he's protesting the idea or simply processing what I've said. But before I can analyze it further, he turns off the water again and combs conditioner through my hair with his fingers. The small tugs on the ends of the strands send shivers down my spine, momentarily wiping away any coherent thought.

After a long pause, I find myself asking quietly, "How was your childhood?" I want to know more about him, to peel back another layer of this version of him who's still so enigmatic yet unexpectedly warm.

His hands pause for a moment, fingers still tangled in my hair, as if he's debating how to answer. Finally, he speaks, his voice slower, more thoughtful than before. "It was good, mostly. My parents got along, and my mom always prioritized us and our activities. We didn't see my dad much, but that was to be expected."

There's an ease to his words that draws me in, the faintest trace of nostalgia softening his tone. "We traveled a lot when we were little, and then we went to boarding school outside of Chicago. Our high school years were a little different from most kids', but they made it to the major events. Everything was... good."

His voice falters slightly as he continues, a shadow passing over his expression. "Things fell apart for a while after my mom was diagnosed with ovarian cancer and eventually passed. But we've mostly been able to work a lot of that out among ourselves since then."

There isn't a hint of deceit in his voice, no attempt to paint a picture that isn't true. He doesn't mention the trouble Jeremy brought to their table, but his vague references are enough for me to fill in the blanks. For all their losses and struggles, they appear to be a relatively happy family, at least, compared to what I've known. That realization settles deep in my stomach, twisting something raw and unfamiliar.

What I would have given to have a sibling. Just one person to be in the trenches with me while dealing with my parents. I never knew what that kind of love and loyalty felt like until Drew. And hearing Silas speak so casually about the foundation his family gave him, even in the face of grief, leaves me aching for something I've never had.

"You're lucky," I whisper, more to myself than to him.

His fingers still, then continue their careful work. "I know," he murmurs, his voice heavy with understanding. "But it doesn't mean it wasn't messy."

A heavy silence blankets the room, punctuated only by the soft trickle of water as Silas rinses the last of the conditioner from my hair. He works with quiet precision, squeezing the excess water from the ends before reaching for a towel. The tenderness in his movements feels overwhelming, and when he finally wraps the towel around my head, gently securing it in place, the final frayed piece of composure I've been clinging to unravels. It's all been too much. This day. This conversation. This man.

Hot tears slip silently from the corners of my eyes, tracing cool paths down my temples. They pool in the hollows near my ears as I release slow, shaky breaths, desperate to calm the ache in my chest.

I know he sees the tears; they're impossible to miss. But he doesn't comment. Instead, his touch becomes even gentler, his thumbs sweeping across my cheeks in slow, deliberate strokes to wipe away the evidence of my emotions. The quiet acceptance of my breakdown makes everything better and worse all at once.

"Thank you," I whisper, my voice raw and trembling. I open my eyes to find him standing over me, his expression masked through the blur of my tears. His hands remain on either side of my head, the touch is so delicate that it threatens to break me all over again.

Squeezing my eyes shut, I fight to rein in the wave of emotions threatening to consume me. I need to pull myself together, to find solid ground. But as I sit there, lost in my own thoughts, I almost miss it—the softest, briefest press of lips against the corner of my mouth.

It's so fleeting, so impossibly tender, that for a moment, I convince myself I've imagined it. But then I feel the warmth of his breath against my skin, the faint brush of his nose along my chin. My heart pounds in my chest, every nerve in my body alight and screaming for more. I want to close the distance, to pull him back to me, but he lingers only a moment longer before drawing away, just enough to meet my gaze.

His eyes lock onto mine, deep and unrelenting, as if he's drawing out every shadow I carry and making them his own. And when he finally speaks, it's so certain that it feels like a law of nature. An absolute truth.

"Whatever you need, you can have it."

Chapter 21

"What made you go into IT?" Silas asks, setting a steaming cup of herbal tea on the counter next to me.

It's almost midnight, and we're in his kitchen. Like every other room in this home, it's immaculate. Solid wood cabinets stretch from floor to ceiling, paired with white marble countertops that reflect the soft glow of pendant lighting. It's a space any at-home chef would dream of, with a commercial-grade gas stove boasting eight burners, a double oven, two deep sinks, and a sprawling ten-foot island made for both prep work and hosting. It's a kitchen designed to perfection, much like the man leaning against the counter across from me.

After lunch—a grilled cheese Silas insisted on making while I took a body shower—I'd found myself pulled into his den with several ice packs in tow. He put on a docuseries, settling into the couch beside me with his laptop, pillows and blankets stacked on the coffee table. It wasn't lost on me that the cozy setup was likely a ploy to get me to nap, and if it was, it worked. I was out for most of the afternoon.

When I woke, groggy but more rested than I'd felt in days, I wandered into the kitchen just in time to see him plating a dinner of roasted chicken, asparagus, and rice. He caught me staring and smirked when I asked if he made it himself before telling me it was his secret to keep.

While we ate, Silas filled me in on what he'd handled during my nap. He contacted my apartment building, explaining the situation with the stolen key. I wasn't thrilled to hear he convinced the manager to act without my permission, but I couldn't deny how relieved I felt when he told me the building had already arranged for a locksmith to change the locks in the morning. Meanwhile, maintenance had installed a lock cover on my door.

Now, I find myself perched on one of the barstools while Silas leans casually against the cabinets next to the sink, sipping his own tea. Sleeping for most of the afternoon has left me restless, and Silas, ever attuned, has taken it upon himself to keep me entertained with a steady stream of questions.

At first, they were simple, easy—my favorite color, my death-row meal, my birthday, if I ever had pets growing up. Those were safe or simple lies. I learned just as much about him in return. He prefers green, his last meal would definitely be steak and eggs, his birthday is November sixth, and his family always had Cavalier King Charles Spaniels. But then his questions started to dip into more personal territory—where I grew up, what my parents did for work, places I'd lived.

It's trickier navigating those. Scarlett Page can share some pieces of my past, some of the hardships, but not all. The real me is a risk he can't uncover. If he starts digging too deep, I don't know how I'd survive the fallout.

"I was good at coding and had an IT teacher who saw potential," I say carefully, wrapping my hands around the warm mug. My words come slower, not because they aren't true, but because the dull ache in my head makes it harder to think on my feet. "He recommended I take a few of the free college courses the high school offered." I shrug, keeping my tone casual. "And IT is a field where you can make good money, so I stuck with it."

Silas nods, a small smile tugging at his lips. "Davey did something similar," he says, leaning more comfortably against the counter. "He applied to Wells when he was twenty-one with a master's degree. We thought he lied on his resume at first, but turns out he'd graduated from high school with a ton of college credits." He chuckles, his dimples showing faintly. "He's always been the overachiever in our family."

I can't help but smile, picturing a young, eager Davey trying to talk his way into a Fortune 500 company. "Somehow, I can't imagine anyone in your family being anything less than impressive."

"Impressive, maybe. A little insane, definitely," Silas jokes.

The herbal tea lets off soft tendrils of steam. I blow gently on the surface before taking a tentative sip. "Did you like studying business administration?" I ask, not bothering to act like I don't already know his degree. Silas doesn't seem fazed by my familiarity. Instead, he shakes his head, his expression unreadable.

"It was fine," he admits. "I didn't love it, but I didn't hate it. I was good at it, so it came pretty easily to me. I enjoyed my time outside of class more than in." His lips curl into a playful smile, his hand braced casually on the counter beside his hip.

"Did you choose your major," I venture, tilting my head, "or was it decided for you?"

The question catches him off-guard, his dark eyes narrowing slightly, though I can't tell if it's out of offense or surprise. For a moment, I wonder if I've overstepped, but then he answers.

"It was expected of me to get some kind of business degree," he answers with quiet honesty. After crossing his ankles, he clarifies, "I think I would've done it regardless. I want Wells to stay in the family for as long as possible."

Knowing what I do about Jeremy, Silas likely didn't feel like he had much of a choice. With his brother's addictions spiraling out of control and Natalie uninterested, Silas became their last hope to pass the reins to another Wells.

The realization hits me harder than I expect. "That's a pretty selfless mindset," I remark quietly.

His brown eyes narrow further, but his smile remains, soft and amused. "Why are you so surprised I acted selflessly?"

Ignoring his question, I roll my eyes with a grin, deflecting. "Was there anything else you wished you could have studied?"

He shrugs, his shoulders rising and falling with a kind of resigned acceptance. "Not really. I knew I'd get a business degree, so I didn't let myself consider anything else. What good would that have done?"

The simplicity of his statement nearly takes the wind out of me. I went to school for computer science out of necessity, driven by a need to survive and escape the crushing cycle of generational poverty. Silas, on the other hand, came from endless opportunity and resources, yet his path was no less predetermined. In his world, the weight of family expectations shaped his future just as survival shaped mine.

It's strange, this thread of commonality between us. Though our circumstances are worlds apart, we both know what it's like to have dreams sacrificed. Neither of us had the freedom to imagine what might have been. In the most messed-up, roundabout way, we've been dealt similar hands. That realization makes the space between us feel smaller, warmer, more tangible.

"Good thing you're already freakishly good at the CEO thing, then," I joke, taking another sip of tea. It's floral and slightly earthy, a blend Silas had explained promotes sleep. I'm not sure I entirely buy into it, but the taste is pleasant enough.

He lets out a short breath. "Yeah, that is a plus."

"And so humble."

He takes a sip of his tea, speaking over the rim of the mug. "Am I supposed to be selfless *and* humble?"

"They don't need to be mutually exclusive."

"But imagine how much more insufferable I'd be if I was this handsome, rich, cared about others, *and* refused to admit how great I am?" I arch a brow as he sets his mug back down.

"You're right. You'd be unbearable."

Silas smirks, the dimple in his cheek making a rare appearance. "Exactly. People need me to be a little flawed. Otherwise, it just isn't fair."

"How generous of you," I quip. "You really are doing the world a service."

He chuckles, his eyes sparkling with amusement. "I knew you'd understand."

"Of course," I tease back. "Someone should really start a foundation in your honor. Maybe it can be the beneficiary of next year's silent auction."

He nods, playing along effortlessly. "I'd donate to that."

I tilt my head, pretending to consider it seriously. "Only if the CEO is humble enough not to plaster his face all over the promotional materials."

"Now you're just trying to take all the fun out of it."

Shaking my head, I let out a laugh and place my now half-empty mug on the counter. When I look back up, Silas is watching me, his expression soft, warm. The banter fades, leaving a quieter, heavier silence between us. For a moment, we just look at each other, neither rushing to fill the space.

At some point earlier this evening, Silas had changed into a pair of sweatpants and a plain t-shirt, trading his usual polished armor for something far more casual. Seeing him like this, in his own home under the warm glow of the kitchen lights in the middle of the night, chips away at some of the walls I've built around myself. Every hour we've spent together today has felt like peeling back another layer of him, and I find myself drawn to what's beneath.

I had wanted there to be something unappealing about him, some fatal flaw that would make it easier to keep him at arm's length. But the deeper I go, the harder it is to find anything that pushes me away. Gone is the disinterested, stand-offish future CEO I'd met months ago. In his place is a man who cares deeply for his family, whose dry humor rivals my own, and protects those he holds close with a ferocity that feels unwavering. And right now, for some reason I can't fully wrap my head around, that includes me.

The reminder of everything else I need to worry about—Natalie's safety, Peter's inevitable punishment for the ways I've defied him, and the simple fact that I've been lying to Silas and his sister for months—presses down on me like an invisible hand around my throat. Where do I even begin to untangle this mess? Should I focus on finding the servers Peter wants, hoping it's enough to keep him from coming after Natalie? Or should I tell Silas everything and risk his so-called "team" doing something even worse to me than Peter ever could?

The questions rattle around my head, threatening to split my skull open. But I shove them down, burying the uncertainty for another time. This isn't a problem I can solve today. There are too many moving parts, too many variables, and I need to recover before I make any decisions. I can't afford to let emotions cloud my judgment.

Still, as much as I know I should be keeping my distance, I'm not ready for Silas to stop looking at me the way he is right now. Like I'm the most fascinating person in his world.

Not yet.

CHAPTER 22

When I wake up the next morning, a wave of unease washes over me. The bed feels too soft, the pillow is uncomfortably thick, and the comforter carries a scent I don't recognize. It's not unpleasant—fresh linen, crisp and clean—but it's not the familiar lavender detergent I use.

Groggily, I open my eyes and blink. Almost as quickly as the confusion and panic sets in, it melts away as I take in my surroundings. There's a soft glow illuminating from the cracked bathroom door in the otherwise dark green bedroom, and a sliver of morning light peeking through the edges of the thick, drawn curtains.

The day before comes rushing back and lingers on the final memory of the night; Silas walking me to the guest room, pausing just outside the door. His hand found my nape, warm and firm, as he pulled me close and pressed a kiss to the uninjured side of my temple. Against the side of my face, he'd whispered for me to come to him if I needed anything before stepping into the room directly across from mine—the one that was so obviously his bedroom.

My head aches all over, the skin on my forehead feels tight, and my body is heavy with the remnants of exhaustion. All things considered, though, I slept like a rock. My body clearly needed the rest, but as I drifted off last night, I had a fleeting thought that probably helped me relax: Peter can't reach me here. Even with my portable door jammer and travel lock at the apartment, I've always known he could get to me if he really wanted to. But here, in this house, I feel a kind of safety I haven't felt in years. Knowing that I'm beyond his reach, even if only temporarily, brings an unfamiliar sense of relief and makes me cry all over again.

Unsure of what time it is, I peel myself out of the luxurious sheets and pad over to the bathroom. There's a double window with sheer curtains barely containing the bright morning sun. After using the toilet and washing my hands without looking up, I brace myself against the counter. I never ended up looking at myself yesterday. It was all too overwhelming, and I couldn't bear to confront the reality of my injuries and the scars that might linger long after this is over. But today is a new day, and the only way forward is to face it head-on. Reluctantly, I lift my amber eyes to the mirror and wince.

The diagonal cut on my forehead is about halfway between my left eyebrow and hairline. Thanks to it being shallow and the skin splitting evenly, Dr. Carrow's steri-strips seem to be doing their job well, even if they're stained a faint red.

What's more jarring is the giant lump beneath the cut and the dark purple bruising that's pooled mostly under my left eye and in my right tear duct. The discoloration, mixed with my pale skin and the road-rash-like scratch across my cheek, leaves little to be desired. Luckily, the other injuries are less noticeable, especially the welt hidden beneath my long, brown waves.

There's nothing to be done about it anyway. The cut will heal, the bruises will fade, and the lump will shrink in a few days. I made it out of that alley alive, and that's what matters right now.

I cast the thoughts from my mind and distract myself by getting ready. The bathroom is fully stocked with new toiletries and the over-the-counter medications Dr. Carrow instructed me to take, so I take my time brushing my teeth and washing my face, careful not to disturb the steri-strips since they need to stay on for at least a week. The brush Silas had taken out from a drawer under the sink last night is still on the counter, so I run it through my tangles before tying them back in a ponytail with the hair elastic around my wrist, and then pop two acetaminophen into my mouth.

When I re-enter the bedroom and open the curtains, something stacked on the black dresser near the door catches my eye. After moving closer, I realize it's a neatly folded stack of clothes: several pairs of jeans, a sweatshirt, pajamas, sweaters, and t-shirts, all with the tags still on. To the side of the clothes is a paper bag containing underwear, socks, wired bras, and sports bras. On top of the stack is a folded piece of paper with my name written on the front in a bold, masculine font.

As I reach for the note, my foot accidentally kicks something at the base of the dresser. I glance down and spot two pairs of shoes tucked neatly under the edge: white sneakers and black boots. Shaking my head with an incredulous huff, I pick up the letter, my curiosity piqued.

I considered picking something out myself, but I like my balls right where they are. Natalie handled it instead. Left these here for when you wake up. Come downstairs and have breakfast with me when you're ready. – SW

I snort out a laugh, folding the letter neatly and setting it aside. A wave of gratitude washes over me for Natalie's thoughtfulness. I wish I had a phone to text her a thank-you. That's just another thing I'll need to get sorted today.

Glancing at the clothes again, I decide on a pair of jeans and a sweater. Stripping off the pajamas that had mysteriously been placed on the bathroom vanity last night, I toss them into the hamper next to the dresser and carefully slipping the sweater over my head, I wince at the slight pull against my forehead. When the jeans bunch at my knees, pressing against the bruises there, I let out a small whimper but push through. Once I'm dressed, I grab a pair of socks from the paper bag, pull them on, and slip into the sneakers that fit like a glove.

Taking a deep breath, I step out of the bedroom and head toward the kitchen, unsure of where Silas might be. The faint aroma of something savory and warm guides me. I stop short in the entryway, taken aback by the sight of an older woman in a crisp white chef's coat standing at the island. She's strong, with broad shoulders and short blonde hair tucked neatly behind her ears. Her hands move with precision as she dices vegetables, the sound of her knife against the cutting board rhythmic and efficient. As if sensing my stare, she glances up and meets my eyes. Her sharp nose and soft blue eyes give her a kind yet no-nonsense appearance, but she offers me a welcoming smile, not the slightest bit deterred by the wounds on my face.

"Ms. Page?" she asks, her voice professional, though not unkind. She doesn't stop her dicing, which stresses me out a little. How do chefs manage not to chop off a finger while talking?

"Hi," I respond awkwardly, feeling the heat rise to my cheeks as I step further into the kitchen. My eyes dart toward the stove, where a sauce simmers gently, releasing a rich, savory aroma. A colander of fresh fruit sits by the sink, still dripping with water, and several bowls filled with colorful ingredients surround her workspace. The oven clock reads 8:23.

"Mr. Wells is on the enclosed terrace," she says, nodding toward the other doorway. "I planned on making a vegetable and turkey sausage omelet with fruit and toast. Does that sound okay?"

"That sounds delicious," I admit, clasping my hands in front of me.

"Wonderful. Can I get you a cup of coffee to take out there with you? How do you take it?" She finally sets down the knife, wiping her hands on the towel draped over her shoulder, and moves toward the impressive coffee station in the corner.

As much as I want to tell her I can do it myself, something about her presence tells me this isn't a battle I'll win. "Sugar and almond milk, usually, but I'm okay with any type of milk."

"Got it." She nods briskly and gets to work. In less than a minute, she stirs the sugar into the steaming cup and places it in front of me.

"Try it and let me know if you need anything added," she instructs, tossing the spoon into the sink behind her.

I lift the mug to my lips, testing the temperature before taking a sip. It's smooth and balanced, exactly how I like it.

"It's perfect," I say, lowering the mug back to the counter without letting go of it. A sudden wave of self-awareness hits me. "I'm sorry, I'm being rude. Can I ask your name?"

Her brows furrow slightly as she looks up from transferring the diced peppers into a stainless-steel bowl, as if she wasn't expecting the question.

"My name is Kendall. I'm Mr. Wells's residential chef."

"Hi, Kendall. It's nice to meet you," I reply with a smile. "I'm sure Silas asked you to call me Ms. Page, but please just call me Scarlett." I pause, holding the mug closer. "Thank you for the coffee and for making us breakfast."

Kendall's expression softens further, her small smile widening. "It's nice to meet you, too, Scarlett."

"I won't distract you any longer, but thanks again."

"It's my pleasure," she replies, dipping her head in acknowledgment before turning back to her work.

Cradling the coffee, I leave the kitchen through the entrance on the opposite side, assuming the enclosed terrace is the outdoor space I saw at the center of the rooms I was in during the silent auction. I navigate the house, taking in the quiet elegance of the space. After one wrong turn and a brief moment of disorientation, I finally spot the main staircase and use it as a point of reference.

The French doors connecting the terrace to the formal dining room are propped open, allowing the cool morning air to drift into the house. Silas sits at a round metal table, glasses sliding down the bridge of his nose as he reads from a tablet resting in his lap. He's dressed in a black sweater, brown tapered pants, and white sneakers. A steaming cup of coffee sits in front of him, wisps of vapor spiraling upward before disappearing into the crisp morning air.

Seeing Silas in pajamas last night hadn't prepared me for what casually dressed Silas would look like. Heat simmers beneath my skin and threatens to spill over when he glances up. I'm prepared for him to grimace at my injuries now that they've had time to settle, but there's no hint of disgust in his expression. Instead, his eyes sweep over me, pausing at every visible mark before returning to my face with a soft, disarming smile.

"Good morning," he greets, his voice gruff with the remnants of sleep. A sound I wish I could bottle that sound and save it for later.

"Morning," I reply, stepping further into the dining room and out onto the terrace. The late April air is brisk, but the warmth radiating from the house provides just enough reprieve to make it tolerable.

There's only one other chair, positioned to Silas's left against a stone wall draped with climbing vines just beginning to turn green. I take the seat, scooting closer to the table before setting my coffee down.

Once I'm settled, I glance over at him. Without hesitation, he leans forward, fingers brushing lightly over the side of my temple and tracing down toward the dark bruise under my left eye. The contact is nearly weightless, but it still makes my heart thunder against my ribs.

"How are you feeling?" he asks, his espresso-colored eyes scanning my face with a mix of concern and something else I can't quite place.

I shrug, trying to appear unaffected by his proximity. "Honestly, not terrible. Everything hurts, but I expected that. My head's the worst to-day—just sore."

"Resting definitely helps," he agrees, his lips curving into a small, lopsided smile. "You were sleeping like the dead when I brought in those clothes."

"Is sneaking into your guest's bedroom a hobby of yours, or am I just special?" I tease, arching a brow to mask the heat rising to my cheeks at the thought of him watching me sleep.

His fingers slide down the curve of my jaw to rest on the tip of my chin, holding me in place with the faintest pressure of his thumb. My breath catches, eyes widening as he leans in just slightly as he murmurs, "That fucking mouth."

The words send a shockwave through me, my stomach flipping as he holds my gaze, his expression a mix of heat and playful challenge. My mind scrambles for a response, but his thumb lingers just long enough to leave me speechless before he pulls away.

Instead of taunting him further, I lift my coffee and take a sip, desperate for something to occupy my hands and focus. That's when I notice the two smartphones sitting side by side on the table.

"The one on the left is for you," Silas says, seeing where my attention has shifted. "It's not attached to a provider yet. I figured you'd want to handle that yourself."

I gape at him, sitting back in my chair. "That's too much."

"It's too much to replace your stolen phone?"

"Absolutely."

He tilts his head slightly, studying me like I've just said something absurd. Picking up his coffee, he takes a slow drink before setting it down alongside his tablet. "Would it make you feel better if I said you could pay me back?"

I set my coffee down. "It would," I answer firmly, crossing my arms.

His response is a low chuckle, one that sends warmth curling through me. A stray curl falls across his forehead as he leans forward, elbows resting on the table and fingers threading together. His expression is so calm, so sure, it's almost maddening. "Okay."

My eyes narrow suspiciously. Something about his tone tells me that even if I went out of my way to pay him back by slipping cash into every crevice of this house, he'd find a way to return it all.

"You're irritating."

Silas smirks just as Kendall walks through the formal dining room toward us. She carries a tray with the precision of someone who's done this a thousand times. Without so much as a clink of the dishes, she sets the tray down on the opposite side of the table and begins serving.

First, she places two perfectly portioned omelets in front of us, each loaded with colorful vegetables and turkey sausage. Next comes a small basket of whole wheat toast accompanied by a butter dish, two bowls of vibrant fruit salad, neatly arranged utensils, and four glasses.

Kendall disappears briefly, returning moments later with another tray that holds pitchers of orange juice and ice water, an insulated coffee pot, a sugar bowl, and a creamer filled with milk. Her timing is impeccable, almost as if rehearsed.

How in the world did she make this so fast?

"Thank you, Kendall," I murmur, my eyes wide as I take in the spread. Silas, mid-reach for a piece of toast, freezes for a second, his eyebrows shooting up. Did he really think I wouldn't ask for this woman's name after she made me coffee and prepared a feast?

"Yes. This looks incredible, as always. Thank you," he echoes, offering her a kind smile. Kendall nods, her small grin softening her otherwise sharp features, and excuses herself back into the house.

"How often is Kendall here?" I ask, aiming for casual curiosity, though it feels like such a ridiculous question. But this is the world Silas inhabits.

"Every day except Mondays and Tuesdays," he answers, slicing into his omelet. "She usually preps meals for me to take to the office or reheat when I get home."

I pluck a piece of toast from the basket between us, spreading a small amount of butter over the warm slice. "So, I can safely assume you *weren't* the one who roasted that chicken last night?"

Silas laughs mid-bite. He swallows quickly, his dark eyes glinting with humor. "I could've done it, but why ruin the fun of keeping you guessing?"

We fall into easy conversation, sharing stories of our favorite meals to cook and how Silas's mother raised all three of her children to have those basic life skills. Despite the enclosed terrace blocking the direct sun, the morning gradually warms, the breeze carrying a hint of spring. The atmosphere is calm, almost domestic, and for a moment, I allow myself to enjoy it.

But just as we're finishing our meal, Silas's phone vibrates on the table, its screen lighting up with an incoming call. His easy demeanor sharpens instantly, hand stilling as his eyes flick to the screen before picking it up. Even without saying it, I know it's about me.

"Go ahead," Silas answers, sharp and professional. My stomach tightens as I shift uncomfortably in my seat. I glance down at the remnants of my breakfast, suddenly losing any remaining appetite.

Silas notices. Of course, he does. Without missing a beat, his hand finds my thigh. The warmth and steadiness of his touch quell some of the rising panic in my chest.

"And nothing was caught on camera?" His voice dips lower, jaw tightening as he listens. His thumb begins to move in slow, deliberate circles against my leg, the motion a silent reassurance. It's absurd how much comfort such a simple gesture brings me.

I take a shaky breath, the sound barely audible but enough to catch his attention. His gaze lifts to meet mine, his expression softening slightly despite the tension radiating off him, silently asking me if I'm okay.

I give him a faint nod, unable to trust my voice.

On the other end of the line, light chatter buzzes faintly, too muffled for me to make out. Silas listens intently, his eyes narrowing as he stares at the stone wall over my shoulder.

"Okay," he finally says, his voice clipped but calm. "We'll head that way in a few minutes. If you haven't already, have Paul do a sweep of the building before we get there."

The nausea churns harder in my stomach as he ends the call. His fingers tighten briefly on my thigh before retreating, leaving me feeling unmoored.

He sets the phone down and exhales quietly, his tone softening just slightly as he speaks. "Some of my team met the locksmith and your apartment manager to ensure the lock change went smoothly." His voice carries that same calculated calm, but his eyes flick to mine with careful intent. "When they got there, the police were pulling up because they received a call from one of your neighbors. The lock cover was busted and someone broke in."

My chest tightens. I sit up straighter, my pulse thundering in my ears. Silas's eyes stay locked on mine, watching every micro-expression as I try to process the weight of his words.

"They think whoever it was might have been looking for something," he continues, his voice steady, yet heavy with implication.

He doesn't say it. He doesn't have to. We both know what—or who—they were looking for.

Me.

CHAPTER 23

The car ride to Bucktown is cloaked in a tense silence. Moments after Silas hung up his first call, he was already dialing Cillian, instructing him to bring the town car around. The speed with which Cillian arrived made me wonder if he'd been lurking somewhere in the mansion, or if he was simply close by. Either way, just minutes later, the sleek black vehicle was in the driveway. Silas ushered me into the back seat with practiced efficiency, pulling me into the middle seat once the door shut behind him.

I half-expect Cillian to make some snarky remark about how far I've come since sneaking around the back stairwell of Silas's home, but he remains laser-focused on the road, scanning our surroundings. Silas, too, seems preoccupied, one elbow resting on the window ledge, chin propped on his palm as his thumb absently brushes over his lower lip. His other hand rests on the inside of my knee.

My head throbs, the dull ache amplified by the events of the past few days. Peter's fury has finally landed squarely on me, a terrifying weight I've been anticipating but hoped to avoid. And then there's Silas—his presence in my life transforming in a matter of hours from distant and skeptical to something intimate and protective. It's all too much to process, the speed of it dizzying.

The ride takes longer than expected thanks to traffic. When we arrive at the front of my apartment building, the sight of several police cars parked along the curb sends my heart into overdrive. Silas exchanges a few hushed words with Cillian as we're getting out of the car, who nods and drives off, likely to park somewhere discreet. Silas clearly doesn't want to leave the car unattended. Not when the break-in might be a prelude to something bigger, and certainly not if someone is keeping watch.

With the fluidity of someone accustomed to avoiding attention, Silas maneuvers us through the lobby with surprising efficiency. He keeps his hand on the small of my back, gently guiding me forward as we pass a small group of residents gathered near the entrance. They're deep in conversation with a member of the building staff, all eyes darting toward us as we walk by. Some look curious, others suspicious. I'm not sure if they're wondering whether I'm the tenant whose apartment was broken into, or if they recognize Silas's face. Either way, I don't stop to find out.

Their stares follow us as we reach the elevator. Silas presses the button, we step inside, and I hit the button to my floor instantly. The doors slide shut, mercifully cutting off their gazes. I exhale slowly and stare at each number lighting up as we ascend.

"They're just scared it might happen to them," Silas murmurs.

I nod stiffly, unable to shake the growing knot in my stomach. I want to ask him if his team has shared any specifics about the break-in, but the words cling to the back of my throat, paralyzed by the reality of what we might find. I know what Peter is capable of and have seen the destruction left in his wake before. When he aims to make a point, he makes sure it hurts.

The elevator dings, and the doors slide open far too quickly. My unit is at the end of a side hallway, but even from here, I can see a police officer stationed at the corner we need to turn down. His posture straightens as we step out, his watchful eyes assessing us as we approach.

"I'm Scarlett Page," I blurt out, the words tumbling from my lips like an automatic defense mechanism. As if my name alone can explain everything.

The officer's expression hardens slightly, skeptical. "Do you have ID to confirm that?"

My heart sinks. "The person who likely broke in is the same person who did this," I say, gesturing toward my bruised and battered face. My voice is sharper than I intended. "He also stole my bag with my wallet and apartment keys."

The officer doesn't look convinced. His eyes dart briefly to Silas, as if trying to determine whether I'm someone worth entertaining. Before I can spiral further, Silas steps in with the composed authority that seems to radiate off him in waves.

"Officer Jensen, is it?" Silas asks smoothly, squinting at the nameplate on the officer's chest. He doesn't wait for confirmation before continuing. "My name is Silas Wells. I have a few associates who were overseeing the lock change this morning when the broken lock cover was discovered. If you've gathered most of your evidence, would it be possible for us to enter? Scarlett would like to collect a few belongings and something to confirm her identity, at the very least, given the circumstances."

His tone is polite but firm, leaving no room for debate. The weight of his presence shifts the dynamic entirely. Officer Jensen hesitates, then nods slightly, his skepticism softening into reluctant compliance.

"Alright," Jensen says, waving us along to follow him.

We're escorted down the hallway to my apartment door, where a small hive of activity unfolds. Several officers mill about, along with Julie, one of the building managers I've met before. She stands off to the side, speaking quietly with the locksmith, who's crouched by my shattered lock. His toolbox is open, a screwdriver in hand. Two men in well-tailored suits hover nearby, their sharp gazes lifting when they spot Silas. Their shoulders relax slightly, acknowledging him with subtle nods.

Julie steps forward, her expression stiffening when she takes in my battered face. "This is Scarlett," she confirms to Officer Jensen, barely able to take her eyes off me. "This is her unit."

Silas seizes the opportunity to pull aside his team. I catch fragments of their conversation; references to yesterday and details they've shared with law enforcement. But their words become muffled background noise as my attention shifts to the wreckage beyond my apartment's open door.

The entryway is destroyed. Coats from my closet are strewn across the floor, their fabric sliced open, dirty footprints staining the fabric. My heart sinks as I spot the small side table where I used to leave my keys and mail—it's splintered, its legs broken, pieces of torn envelopes scattered like confetti. The ceramic bowl that used to hold my spare change is nothing but shattered fragments, glinting under the dim hallway light. Beyond the entry, three officers are walking through the living area, speaking quietly to one another as they document the space with photos and evidence markers.

Julie's voice pulls me back to the moment when she places a gentle hand on my upper arm. "I'm so sorry this happened, Scarlett. The locksmith should be done soon, but if you'd prefer, we can discuss moving you to another unit entirely."

I force a small smile, though I'm unsure of where I'll even be living in a few days. "I'll think about it," I say vaguely. "Am I allowed to grab some of my things?"

Hearing my question, one of the officers inside the unit looks up. "Both bedrooms, the bathroom, and the hallway have been documented," he informs me. "You're free to collect belongings from those spaces."

I nod, offering a quiet thank you before stepping carefully around the locksmith and into the apartment. The destruction before me saps what little energy I've managed to gather since yesterday.

The hallway is even worse upon closer inspection. My sliding closet door hangs slightly ajar, revealing my coats piled haphazardly on the floor. Most of them are ruined, slashed with what looks like a box cutter or knife. I wince, reaching up for the stack of reusable grocery bags I keep on the top shelf. By some miracle, they're untouched. I shake one out, clutching it tightly.

The bathroom is the first door off the hallway, and though it initially seems mostly intact, a closer look reveals the mirror over the sink. Its surface is a spiderweb of cracks, the impact point a jagged hole in the center, reflecting misshapen fragments of the ripped shower curtain. I carefully step over the shards scattered across the floor, crouching down to open the cabinet beneath the sink. Relief floods through me when I reach for the inconspicuous tampon box tucked toward the back.

I open the false bottom, my heart pounding, and exhale shakily when I see my real passport, the debit card tied to my real name, and the additional fake IDs and credit cards Peter had made for me. Every piece is accounted for. With trembling hands, I shove the items back into the hidden compartment, fish around for a few unopened essential toiletries, and step out of the bathroom.

The next room off the hallway is my bedroom, and when I reach the doorway, my heart sinks further. My mattress is flipped against the wall, its fabric torn in places, exposing foam stuffing. The drawers of my dresser are pulled open, some of them broken where the joints meet, and my clothing is everywhere. Shirts, pants, and dresses litter the floor, cut to shreds. I wonder if Peter gave Harrison this honor.

My hands tremble as I sift through the mess and try to salvage anything of use. I find a pair of leggings, several socks, and little else. My phone charger is still plugged into the wall by the bed somehow. The side tables have been beaten with one splintered leg hanging precariously, and my personal phone that used to sit in one of the drawers is nowhere to be seen. The few sentimental items I kept on them are smashed.

The tears come unbidden, stinging my eyes, but I blink them away furiously. *These are just things*, I remind myself. Insignificant in the grand scheme of what's happening. I've survived with next to nothing, and I've rebuilt my life more times than I care to count. I can do it one more time.

At last, I enter my office, bracing for the worst. Holes pepper the walls and closet doors, chunks of drywall scattered like confetti across the floor. The desk and chair I had painstakingly picked out for their perfect balance of function and aesthetic have been hacked apart, as though someone took an axe to them in a blind rage.

How did my two neighbors not get woken up by this and report me to the leasing office?

What unsettles me the most, though, is the absence of my laptop and computer. No shattered monitor, no toppled tower, not even a stray keyboard. It's as if they were never here at all. The cold realization sinks in; if Peter has my laptop and computer, it means someone is combing through my files, my research, my entire digital footprint. He's taken the information I've gathered for himself, removing the middleman he no longer trusts. And Peter doesn't just let loose ends walk away.

My gaze shifts to the emerald velvet couch behind my desk, the one I used to curl up on to bask in the morning sun. It's been gutted, the back and cushions sliced open, stuffing spilling out like the aftermath of a brutal fight. Above it, taped to the window, is a photograph torn cleanly in half. It's the only photo I ever kept in this apartment.

I approach it slowly, the sunlight catching on the glossy paper and deepening its colors. A blood-red X slashes across the image, cutting through Drew's radiant smile. Her hair falls in soft curls around her shoulders as she sits at a bar table, arm wrapped around someone whose presence is lost to the torn edge. I don't need the missing half to know what it showed: an equally happy version of me.

A cold dread pools in the pit of my stomach. With trembling hands, I peel the photo from the window. My thumb runs over Drew's face, willing the ink to disappear. But the red is permanent, soaked into the fibers of the paper. It's stained. Tainted. Just like everything Peter touches.

Just like everything I touch.

A droplet of water lands in the center of the photo, blurring the edges of the ink. Startled, I reach up to my face, only to realize I'm crying. My chest tightens as panic flares; hot and suffocating.

What the ever-loving fuck am I going to do?

"Scarlett."

Silas's voice cuts through my spiraling thoughts, startling me. I whirl around to face him in the doorway, his broad frame blocking the destruction of the common area. His hands are clasped behind his back, taking in the mess and then locking his attention on me. His expression is mostly unreadable, but his eyes are a swirl of contradiction: concern and barely contained fury.

I hastily wipe the tears from my cheeks, jamming the torn photo into the tote bag hanging from my elbow. "There isn't much that's not destroyed," I manage to say hoarsely.

His jaw flexes, the tendons in his neck taut. He nods once, assessing me from head to toe. "Things are replaceable," he answers softly, a gentle reminder rather than a dismissal.

"They are," I echo, nodding, though my heart isn't in the words.

Silas breaks the invisible barrier between us, stepping into the room and into the space I've used to work against his company for months. Guilt crawls up my spine, an insidious virus spreading through my limbs, but I don't move away. I can't.

When he's close enough, his hand lifts to the side of my neck, his fingers warm and steady as they rub back and forth. "The security here is shit," he declares, frustration dripping from every syllable.

I flinch inwardly, knowing all too well that he's right. The building's security was one of the reasons Peter chose it. Their cameras are mediocre, and the network laughably easy to infiltrate. It made my comings and goings seamless, made it simple for Harrison to slip in and out unnoticed. It was perfect for the facade I needed to maintain as Scarlett Page. But now? Now it feels like a ticking time bomb.

"It doesn't help that someone stole my keys and ID to know where I live," I add, the lie slipping out smoothly as I gesture to the mess at our feet. Anything to deflect attention from the glaring security lapse it would be strange for someone in my profession to overlook.

Silas's thumb nudges my chin upward, forcing me to meet his gaze. His eyes burn with quiet intensity, but his touch remains soft. "I don't feel comfortable with you staying here."

I blink, startled by the declaration. Before I can respond, he continues, "You can stay with me until we find you a place with better security. It shouldn't take more than a few weeks."

His words hang in the air, heavy with finality, and something inside me bristles. I don't know if it's Silas's demand, the thought of losing the first space that's been my own in years, Peter's calculated brutality, or all of the above. My arms cross tightly over my chest as I take a deliberate step back. "I'm not going anywhere."

Silas's expression remains calm, but I see the flicker of irritation in his eyes, sharp and fleeting. "Scarlett. Be reasonable."

"I am," I shoot back, and my voice cracks slightly. "You think uprooting my life is going to solve this? That throwing me into some high-rise fortress with guards at the door is the answer? That's not happening."

He exhales slowly, as if trying to keep his composure. His voice, when it comes, is low and steady, though I can hear the strain beneath it. "I'm not throwing you anywhere. I'm trying to make sure you're safe."

"I *am* safe," I snap, though it's missing some of its usual bite. My eyes dart to the broken remains of my desk, the gutted couch, the holes in the wall. This isn't safety, and we both know it. "This is my home."

His gaze sharpens, his mouth tightening into a grim line. He doesn't raise his voice, but the weight of his words is crushing. "Safe?" he repeats, gesturing pointedly to the wreckage. "Someone attacked you, stole your keys, and tore this place apart. That's not safe. That's a warning shot."

A chill freezes the words in my throat. He's so spot-on it's terrifying. But instead of admitting it, I let my stubbornness, pride, and deep-seated need for independence take over. "I can handle myself," I answer rigidly.

"Can you?" Silas's tone hardens, though it doesn't lose its edge of care. "Because it wasn't *me* who showed up at my office yesterday, bleeding and beaten in broad daylight."

The truth of his words cuts deep. I glare at him as my guilt coiling tight in my chest like a vice. My fists clench at my sides, nails digging into my palms. "You don't get it," I mutter, shaking my head.

"You're right," Silas says, his patience thinning as exasperation seeps into his words. "I don't. All I know is that you're in danger, and I'm not going to let you sit here and wait for whoever did this to come back. Whether you like it or not, you're leaving."

"You don't get to decide that for me." The words come out harsh, but I can't take them back.

He runs a hand through his hair. "This isn't about me deciding for you, Scarlett. This is about someone targeting you to get to Natalie. I won't stand by while you act like everything's fine. You're not fine."

My pulse thunders in my ears. The truth is suffocating, but I can't let him know just how right he is or why.

Silas takes a steadying breath, his voice softening as he closes the gap I've created between us. "Look," he says quietly. "I get that you feel like this is your problem to solve, but it's not just you anymore. I'm involved now. Natalie's involved. I need to know you're somewhere safe, or I won't be able to focus on anything else."

The guilt twists sharper, stealing my breath. I look at him, *really* look at him. The exhaustion is etched into his features, the tension in his shoulders like a coiled spring. He's scared. For me. For Natalie.

"Scarlett," he says softly, his hand reaching for my arm. "Please."

The plea undoes me. My shoulders sag, the fight draining out of me as I stare at the floor. The broken bits of wood, the debris, the shattered pieces of the little life I created. I can't do this alone, not right now. I can't let him shoulder this burden either, but for now, I don't have a choice.

"Fine," I whisper, my voice barely audible. "I'll go."

Relief flashes across his face, softening the hard edges. "Good."

"But I'm not doing this because you told me to," I add quickly, clinging to a shred of control. "I'm doing it because I don't want to deal with this mess right now."

He tilts his head slightly, a faint trace of warmth in his voice as he replies, "Whatever you need to tell yourself."

I don't respond, my arms tightening across my chest as I look past him at the destroyed space that used to be mine. Silas doesn't push me further, and for that, I'm grateful.

Because the truth is, Peter didn't just send a message with this break-in. He sent a promise. And until I know what he's planning, staying close to Silas and Natalie might be the only way to keep them safe. Even if it means convincing Silas that I'm not the very danger he's trying to save us from.

CHAPTER 24

We spent another two hours at my apartment complex finalizing the termination of my lease and giving the police any remaining details that Silas's team hadn't already provided. Since the only three units in my hallway belonged to me and two neighbors who worked nights—one as a trauma surgeon, the other as an airline pilot—no one had heard the break-in when it happened. It wasn't until one of them came home after their shift and found my door open that the police were even called.

Silas insisted on hiring a team to clear out what was left of my place after the investigation wrapped up. I agreed. There wasn't much worth salvaging anyway. With all my equipment gone, the false-bottom tampon box in my possession, and any remaining important documents locked away in a safe deposit box in Arizona, there was nothing left for anyone to find.

When the police asked to speak with me alone, I was relieved. At least Silas wouldn't hear my answers if the questions took a strange turn. But before they could begin, they asked me to come down to the station. Silas immediately intervened, arguing that I was in no condition to leave and needed rest. He stated that he could both vouch for and prove my whereabouts the night before, making a trip to the station unnecessary. If they wanted to question me, they could do it here or schedule a time when I was in better shape. Surprisingly, they agreed and for once, I was grateful for Silas's incessant need for control.

They brought me into my office and asked Silas and the others to step into the hallway outside of the apartment. Once the doors shut behind them, the questions started, and many of them the ones I expected. But they were instantly focused on the photograph of Drew taped to my office window. My best friend. My *dead* best friend.

I told them who she was, keeping the details vague.

Eventually, they got to the question I dreaded. Did I think there was a connection between her, my attack in the alley yesterday, and now this? I said no. The detectives didn't look convinced, but it didn't matter. They weren't going to find who did this. No one ever would.

The two officers asking the questions let me go not long after, handing me their cards and telling me to call if I thought of anything else. Then they sent me on my way so they could finish processing the crime scene.

By the time we leave, exhaustion drags at my limbs. I don't look back as we step into the car, don't spare a glance at the apartment I'll never return to.

After a quick pit stop to pick up a new SIM card, we return to Silas's home. I excuse myself to the guest room under the pretense of setting up my phone and calling my credit card providers. Silas agrees easily, mentioning he has a few calls to make, including one to Davey for an update.

With my tote bag of belongings in hand, I take the back staircase to the guest bedroom, shut the door, and quietly lock it. Dropping the bag to the floor, I meticulously comb over every inch of the space: the furniture, floorboards, molding cracks, even the air vents. I don't find a single sign of surveillance. No cameras. No microphones. Nothing. Silas, for all his protective tendencies, seems to trust his guests enough to grant them privacy. I'll need it if I'm going to keep staying under his roof.

The next couple of hours pass in a blur of technology. After thoroughly inspecting the new phone, I find Silas only opened it to add his number and Natalie's new one. A quick dive into the phone's settings allows me to encrypt all stored data and set up my VPN. By the time I'm done, the phone feels like an extension of me, a fortress of digital safety in the middle of chaos. The familiarity of it calms me in a way nothing else has since this mess began.

Contacting the banks to cancel my credit cards is quick and painless, mostly because I know I can never use them again. Those cards were Peter's tools, connected to identities that don't truly exist. They were my safety net for jobs, a layer of separation between me and the information I sought. But now they're compromised, like everything else.

Needing something to occupy my restless mind, I unpack the reusable grocery bag. The socks and leggings go into a dresser drawer, and my preferred toiletries replace the ones Silas provided. Opening the stash box, I pull out a spare Scarlett ID and replace it with the ripped photo of Drew before tucking it carefully in the back of the bathroom vanity under the sink.

By the time I finish, the clock reads 3:42. Silas has been on calls for as long as I've been busy, likely catching up on the work he's pushed aside for me these last few days. I'm left to my own devices in a house I was once instructed to infiltrate. The realization hits me like a tidal wave, sinking me deeper into the guilt that's been threatening to drown me for weeks.

Silas doesn't deserve this. None of it. But Natalie doesn't deserve Peter's wrath, either. I've seen firsthand what Peter's capable of. The message he left, etched across my life with Drew's defaced photo pinned to my window, was loud and clear. I can't let him turn his attention to Natalie to punish me. Peter can do whatever he wants to me. That much, I can take. But he won't touch her.

Getting into Silas's office undetected will be next to impossible, but there is still a chance the servers exist somewhere in this house. If I have to break whatever fragile trust I've built with Silas to find out, so be it. My happiness will never outweigh Natalie's safety. I just have to move quickly and cleanly: get in, get out, and minimize the damage.

At least, that's what I tell myself. I glance around the room and my chest tightens. A flicker of doubt presses against the back of my mind.

I *hope* fewer people will get hurt.

Before I can talk myself out of it, I square my shoulders and unlock the bedroom door. Security cameras cover every inch of the communal spaces; I noticed them during the auction and in the past day. If Cillian or anyone else is monitoring the feed, they need to believe I'm just being nosy, not looking for anything in particular. That shouldn't be difficult to sell, considering how our first encounter went a few weeks ago.

The hallway is still and the silence presses on my ears. I keep my footsteps light, moving with deliberate slowness to appear as though I'm wandering aimlessly. My heart, however, is racing, each beat a countdown I can't ignore.

The first thing that catches my eye is the staircase leading to the attic, its entrance tucked into a corner between another bedroom and Silas's office. If the servers exist anywhere in this house, the attic seems like a good place to start. Its seclusion would make it ideal for housing sensitive equipment.

At the top of the stairs, I'm shocked to find a cozy movie room instead. A massive sectional sprawls across the center of the space, its plush cushions draped with soft blankets. A vintage popcorn machine gleams in one corner, shiny and clearly used. Recessed lights cast a warm glow over the room, and a wall-mounted screen dominates the far end, framed by slated ceilings. It's comfortable and completely at odds with the rest of the house's polished formality.

However, there's nothing useful here. No servers. No equipment. Just an unexpected glimpse into a part of Silas I didn't know existed.

I back out quietly, retracing my steps to the second floor to continue my search past Silas's office and the main staircase. Though I peeked into some of the other rooms at the auction, it might seem odd if I walked straight past them now.

I take a moment to peer into each one, looking for anything unusual like locked closets, hidden panels, even oddly placed outlets. But each room is what it seems: a bedroom.

Finally, I reach the end of the hallway, where the back stairwell comes into view. I glance into the half-bath and the laundry room, chuckling at the absurd size, just as I had the first time I saw it.

"Looking for something?"

The voice behind me sends a surge of adrenaline straight to my chest. I spin around, nearly tripping over my own feet in the process. Silas stands at the corner of the hallway with his hands in the front pockets of his pants, one brow lifted in question, and his lips tugged up into a lopsided smirk.

"You're creepily quiet, did you know that?" I blurt, scrambling to deflect. Straightening, I plaster on what I hope passes for a sheepish smile.

"I'll add that to my resume," he teases. "Right under 'freakishly good CEO.'" He straightens and strides toward me. His chest brushes against my shoulder as he leans past me to look into the room. "So," he starts, "what's so funny about my laundry room?"

"Everything," I reply without hesitation, waving my hand toward it. "Who in their right mind needs five washers and dryers?"

"Someone who hosts visitors," he counters smoothly.

"And who are you hosting? The entire Royal Family?" I quip, arching a brow.

Before I can fully process the playful gleam in his eye, Silas grabs the hand I gestured with, his grip firm but not painful. In one fluid motion, he twists my arm behind my back and pulls me flush against him. I gasp sharply, my pulse hammering in my ears. The hard planes of his chest and stomach press against my back, the warmth of his body radiating through our clothes.

He leans down, his nose grazing the shell of my ear. My eyes flutter shut instinctively, savoring his closeness for just a moment too long. Then he whispers, voice low and dripping with that confidence that makes me want to punch him and kiss him all at once. "Has anyone ever told you that mouth is going to get you into trouble?"

Every time he brings up my mouth, I feel like every vein in my body is about to burst. It seems to be his favorite line when it comes to my attitude. Or maybe it's mine.

"Some rich asshole has told me once or twice," I manage to reply, my tone deliberately flippant. But I know the effect he's having on me, and so does he.

Lust wins over my better judgment for a fraction of a second, and I tilt my head, exposing the column of my neck to him. The movement makes Silas rumble in approval, his free hand sliding down to squeeze my hip.

"Would you like a tour," he murmurs, his lips hovering millimeters from the sensitive skin beneath my jaw, "or do you prefer snooping around on your own?"

All I can think about is what it would feel like if he pressed those lips against me, tasting me. He's the kind of man who knows exactly how to use his tongue; I can tell just by looking at him. The thought alone sends a shiver down my spine.

I exhale a shaky breath, forcing myself to focus. This is dangerous territory, and I can't afford to lose myself in it. Not now. Not when I need to stay sharp. This tour could be the perfect opportunity to scope out the areas he's avoided showing me so far, to test his reactions and see if any of my questions hit a nerve.

With every ounce of willpower I can muster, I swallow the desire bubbling up inside me and say, "I'd love a tour."

Silas freezes, clearly caught off guard by my honest answer. Slowly, he releases my hand from behind my back, his fingers trailing down my wrist before intertwining with mine. Then, he spins me around so we're face-to-face, chest-to-chest. His eyes burn into mine, dark and smoldering like molten chocolate.

"Where haven't you looked yet?" he asks, his voice softer now. His glasses slide slightly down the bridge of his nose as he stares at me, his expression unreadable. Without thinking, I reach up with my free hand and push them back into place.

The intimacy of the gesture doesn't hit me until it's too late. His jaw tightens, the corner of his mouth twitching as though he's fighting a smile. A faint flush creeps up my neck.

I drop my gaze to his Adam's apple, my palm suddenly feeling sweaty against his. "First floor and basement," I admit.

"So you went into the attic?" A faint note of curiosity laces his tone as he guides us toward the back stairs. As we begin to descend, his elbow locks securely, ensuring I'm steady.

"I have to admit," I say, glancing at him from the corner of my eye, "that was a bit of a surprise. I didn't peg you as the cozy-movie-room type."

Silas raises a brow, a flicker of amusement playing across his features. "What exactly does that mean?"

"I mean, the vintage popcorn machine kind of gave you away," I tease. "It's a little too wholesome for the guy I assumed reads business magazines in his sleep."

He lets out a chuckle, shaking his head as though the image genuinely entertains him. "Maybe I like stories that don't involve quarterly reports or board meetings," he replies, his voice dipping into something more honest. "It's nice to escape somewhere else for a little while."

I blink, caught off guard by his candor. We reach the landing in the middle of the stairs and turn down the next set. "Huh. Silas Wells, movie buff. Who would've thought?"

"You don't have to sound so shocked," he retorts, tilting his head as he looks at me.

Grinning, I press on. "What's your favorite movie?"

For the first time, I see something that might resemble a faint blush tinting his sculpted cheekbones. He shrugs, his usual confidence momentarily replaced by something almost bashful. "*Inception.*"

I stop short at the bottom of the stairs, twisting to face him fully. "Wait. Seriously?"

"Is that judgment I hear?" His tone is laced with mock indignation, though the faint blush lingers, betraying his amusement.

"I just didn't see you as a fan of dreams within dreams and spinning tops," I say quickly, fighting to keep a straight face. "I bet you're the guy who pauses the movie to give everyone a lecture on the layers of the plot."

Silas huffs out a low laugh, his thumb absently brushing against my knuckles. "What can I say? I like movies that make you think."

I narrow my eyes at him, as though studying him anew. "I also bet you think the top is still spinning at the end."

He leans in ever so slightly. "And what do *you* think?"

Matching his energy, I tilt my chin defiantly. "I think *you* want it to keep spinning because you can't stand the idea of not having all the answers."

Delight sparks in his eyes, and the edges of his lips tug upward in a half-smile. "You're a piece of work, you know that?"

"You invited me here," I remind him, smirking as I step ahead of him.

"That I did," he murmurs, his voice low and rich. "And what about your favorite movie?"

I pause, weighing my options before letting out an exaggerated sigh. "Fine. *The Devil Wears Prada.*"

Silas's brow quirks. "And you're giving me grief about *Inception*?"

"Don't knock it," I defend, crossing my arms. "It's a great story. And, honestly, you'd probably relate a lot to Miranda Priestly."

His grin widens, slow and dangerous. "Would I?"

"Tell me your employees don't know when you're pissed off with a single look," I say, mimicking Meryl Streep's icy stare. "She could have been created in your image."

Silas laughs outright this time, the sound echoes down the darker hall-way. "I think I liked it better when you were snooping around quietly."

"Too late," I reply, tossing him a triumphant smirk.

He exhales a small sigh, rolling his eyes as he motions toward the hallway I hadn't explored before. Without missing a beat, he flips on the light to the first room, the warm glow spilling into the hallway as he steps inside. "Alright," he says over his shoulder, his tone tinged with both amusement and exasperation. "Let's start your tour."

Silas's tour lasted over thirty minutes as he walked me through every inch of his sprawling home. We skipped the rooms I had already seen—the kitchen, garage, entry, den, formal dining room, two formal sitting rooms, and terrace—but paused briefly in the music room, now free of the silent auction items. Without the clutter of displays, the space felt more intimate, its soft lighting and polished piano evoking a quiet elegance.

He showed me a small office on the first floor, a space I imagined he reserved for conversations with colleagues he wasn't comfortable bringing into his study upstairs. The room was sparse, devoid of personal touches, with only a writing desk, a few chairs, and minimalist decorations. There were several bathrooms scattered throughout, storage rooms for his staff that held linens and glassware, an oversized library, and a billiards room complete with a sleek wet bar and vintage cues displayed on the walls.

The basement was just as impressive. The stairs opened up to a striking wine cellar, its walls lined with bottles that looked like artwork. A hallway branched off to the side, leading to two additional spaces: a fully equipped gym with a sauna that rivaled any luxury fitness club and a security office that was more of a fortress than a workspace.

The office was self-sufficient, complete with a small living area, a full bathroom, and a kitchenette. In the back corner was the surveillance room, its walls lined with over a dozen monitors displaying security footage from every corner of the mansion, both inside and out. Cillian was seated at the main desk, flipping through paperwork, utterly unfazed by our sudden presence. I didn't fail to notice that none of the video feeds were in bedrooms or bathrooms. Confirmation of a subtle yet deliberate boundary I appreciated more than I expected.

Throughout the tour, I kept my focus on Silas, asking a few pointed questions about his security setup. He answered each one without hesitation. There was no caution, no suspicion. Just an openness that burned through me, making me acutely aware of how deeply I was burying my own truths.

We finish just outside our bedroom doors, and Silas gives me a mischievous smile, his hand paused on the handle of his room. "Did you snoop through my bedroom before I found you?"

I roll my eyes at him, leaning back against the wall. "Contrary to popular belief, I do have boundaries."

"You do?" He arches a brow.

"I do," I insist, crossing my arms. "Someone else here is the one intent on breaking them."

His grin widens, wicked and unrepentant. Without a word, he pushes open the door to his room, stepping aside and waving me in with a dramatic flourish. "Be my guest."

Hesitantly, I take a step over the threshold, instantly enveloped by everything that is Silas Wells.

The room is as vast as I expected, but its understated décor makes it feel cozier. Against the pale gray walls stands a bed with an upholstered headboard in a muted rust color. The charcoal-gray duvet is folded back in the meticulous way you'd find in a luxury hotel, exposing crisp white sheets beneath navy-blue accent pillows. Above the bed, two framed pieces of art hang in perfect balance: one a serene landscape, the other a brooding portrait of a man with sharp features and, between them, a round wooden clock that ties the space together effortlessly.

Flanking the bed are matching wooden nightstands, each adorned with a lamp featuring pleated shades, a small stack of well-chosen books, and a single potted plant. The floor-length curtains in deep olive drape heavily over the tall windows, their fabric pooling on the dark hardwood floors. Beneath the bed, an ornate rug in faded patterns of muted blues and creams soften the dark tones of the polished wood.

At the foot of the bed sits a leather bench, positioned to face the period -appropriate fireplace directly across the room. Tucked in the corner is an oversized chair in dark blue with a matching footrest. I can easily imagine

Silas sitting on it at the end of a long day, elbow resting on the arm while his hand rubs at his temples.

"This is beautiful," I breathe out, twisting slowly as I take it all in. It's not at all what I expected: warmer, softer, more personal. But in a way, it makes perfect sense. Nothing about Silas has been what I expected.

"I agree," Silas murmurs, his voice low and steady. I glance back at him, expecting to see his gaze sweeping across the space, taking in its understated beauty. But he isn't looking at his perfectly decorated bedroom.

He's looking at me.

My breath catches, his expression so precisely focused that it sends a ripple of heat through me. He leans casually against the door frame, arms crossed, one ankle over the other, as though he has all the time in the world to watch me.

Silas's words linger in the air for only a moment before he starts to move, pushing off the threshold and taking a step closer. "I've thought about you being in this room a lot," he says, his voice low and warm, each word wrapping around me like a velvet tether. "Somehow, it's already better than what I imagined."

The gravity of his admission and my heart hammering drown out any rational thought. His coffee-colored gaze locks onto mine and darken when I don't immediately bolt, but I can't even feel my legs enough to move. This isn't the usual teasing flirtation or passing touches. It's a promise—not just to take what he wants, but to tip us both over the edge, the culmination of every subtle push that's brought me here.

"Silas," I begin in an unsteady attempt to maintain control. "Don't say things like that."

"Why not?" He closes the space between us. "It's the truth."

Only when we're inches apart does his hand snake around my back, palm pressing firmly against the fabric of my sweater, drawing me closer. I inhale sharply, shaking my head as though it'll lessen the tension crackling in the air. "This isn't a good idea," I whisper, though my words lack conviction.

"No?" His tone is a soft challenge as his free hand brushes a stray piece of hair from my scraped cheek. His fingers graze the edges of my bruise. "I think it's the best idea I've had in a *very* long time."

"It'll mess everything up," I say, my voice barely audible. My hands hover awkwardly at my sides, unsure whether to push him away or pull him closer. His thumb traces lazy circles against my lower back, sending sparks skittering across my skin.

"You really think that?" His forehead tilts toward mine, the warmth of his breath brushing against my lips. The closeness is intoxicating, and I feel my resolve fraying with every second. His hand trails slowly up my neck, the pads of his fingers sliding just behind my ear before curling into the base of my hair. The touch is electric, his grip mindful to avoid the welt near my skull.

"Yes," I manage.

For a long moment, he doesn't move. His gaze drops to my mouth, then back to my eyes, searching, waiting. "Tell me to stop," he murmurs, his voice tense, like a coil wound too tight and ready to snap.

I should. I should tell him to stop. But my thoughts are muddled, my willpower faltering. My gaze roams his face, tracing the lines of his jaw, the stubble that shadows it, the slight crook of his nose, and finally, his lips; full, slightly parted, and devastatingly close. My hesitation stretches into silence, and that silence is all the permission he needs to press his lips to mine.

He begins slowly—exploring, learning. Testing. Tasting. It's everything I expected and nothing like I imagined. As if he's savoring the moment, committing every detail to memory. But when his tongue grazes the seam of my lips, seeking entry, I part for him, and the moment I do, my world tilts on its axis.

His tongue sweeps inside, demanding and relentless. Fingers tighten in my hair, threading deeper, a possessive hold that angles my head just where he wants it. His other arm locks tighter around me, evaporating the space between us until I can feel every hard, unyielding inch of him.

Then his teeth catch my lip, a sharp bite that blurs the line between pain and pleasure, unraveling every rational thought in its wake.

My hands, once hesitant, now clutch at the front of his sweater. Every nerve in my body is on fire, responding to him like it already owns his. He feels like home and chaos all at once. A guttural sound escapes my throat, and it only seems to spur him on.

The surrounding air grows thin, and I'm lost in the taste of his mouth, the strength of his hold, the way he consumes me without hesitation or apology. I knew he would feel like this—like being rewritten from the inside out. His touch almost hurts as it engraves itself on my skin, burning a path that embeds itself in my DNA. He's everywhere. Everything.

But then, as if the universe conspired to pull us back to reality, the sharp vibration of his phone cuts through the haze. The sound jolts, and I pull back, trying to take a shaky step away. Silas doesn't let me move more than a centimeter. His hands linger in my hair, holding my forehead to his as we both catch our breath.

The phone continues to ring, and he exhales sharply, the sound laced with frustration. His hand at my waist moves to retrieve the device from his pocket. "It's Davey," he mutters, his jaw tightening. He looks up, something unspoken flickering in his expression: regret, longing, maybe both. "I have to take this. Stay here. I'll be back soon."

Before I can respond, he presses a final, fleeting kiss to my lips before turning and answering the call. "What is it?" His tone is clipped, all business, as he strides out of the room and down the hallway toward his office.

As the door clicks shut behind him, the silence rushes in, deafening. My heart pounds in my ears, drowning out my thoughts as I lean back against the edge of the bed.

How did I let it come to this? I know better. I've always known better. This is wrong. A betrayal. Not just of him, but of the fragile boundaries I swore to maintain. How had I let myself fall so far?

The answer is bitter and unavoidable: Because I'm selfish. I let him because I wanted this.

But there's no world where this ends well. I'm the storm that will tear through everything he's trying to keep safe. And yet, here I am, adding fuel to the fire.

So, I do what I do best.

I run.

Pushing off the bed and crossing the room, I grab the door handle with shaking fingers and slip across the hall to the guest room, shutting and locking the door behind me without looking back.

CHAPTER 25

T hirty hours. That's all it took for my carefully constructed walls to crumble under Silas's relentless persistence. I've been lying to myself, pretending I had my feelings under control. Every lingering glance, every subtle touch, every quiet word chipped away at my defenses, and I let it happen. Now, I'm stuck ten feet from the one person I can't trust myself to be near and have never wanted more in my life.

The texts started not long after I locked myself in the guest room. His knock on my door was soft and tentative, but when I didn't answer, he tried the handle. The click of the lock stopping him felt like a line drawn in the sand, one I hoped would hold. But his shadow lingered under the door for what felt like an eternity. Then the messages came, each one a reminder of how far I've fallen.

Silas: Why did you leave? I told you to stay. I meant it.
Silas: I'm sorry it took longer than I expected. Davey needed to go over the footage from the day you were attacked.
Silas: Don't tell me you regret what happened, Scarlett. Because I don't.
Silas: I know you're reading these messages. Don't shut me out. Talk to me.
Silas: I'll give you space for now, but we're going to talk about this. Soon.

He finally left, but not before making it clear that he isn't letting this go. Relief and disappointment tangled in my chest as I listened to his footsteps retreat down the hallway. I spent the rest of the afternoon wrapped in blankets, trying to untangle the mess I created. By dinner, a knock sounds on the door.

An unfamiliar, female voice filters through the cracks. "Ms. Page? Mr. Wells asked for me to bring you dinner. I'm going to leave it outside the door. Place the tray out here when you're done, and it'll be collected."

I wait several minutes before cracking the door to retrieve the tray. Chicken parmesan over penne pasta, a side salad, and a bottle of diet cola. My death-row meal. I don't know whether to laugh or cry. Damn him. Damn Silas for giving me space and knowing exactly how to play this game better than I ever could.

As much as I want to hurl the tray against the wall, my body has other plans, stomach growling at the sight alone. The scent of marinara and melted cheese overpowers my defiance, and I sink to the floor at the foot of the bed, devouring every bite. Kendall deserves a damn raise.

The quiet while I eat it all gives me time to think, but none of it brings peace. I need to regain control. I can't keep pretending this is real, can't let myself believe I belong here. This life isn't mine. It never was. I'm not Scarlett Page. I'm not a successful business owner. These are not my friends. This is not my home.

None of this is real.

The pain sharpens me, beginning to carve away the illusions I've let take root. I can't keep delaying this. It's time to finish what I started.

Grabbing the debit card hidden in the bathroom, I sit on the bed and place several online orders. A laptop, bags, clothing, and supplies; everything I'll need to run when it comes to that. My escape plan isn't perfect, but it's a start. I need to be ready to leave at a moment's notice, especially once Natalie returns from California. I'll ask to stay with her temporarily. Davey will protest, but I can't stay here any longer. Not with Silas.

By the time I finish, night has fully settled over the house. The tray from dinner has been placed outside the door, but I don't dare check if it's been taken. Instead, I head to the bathroom, stuffing a towel under the door crack and locking it. I turn the shower on full blast, letting the sound of rushing water drown out the chaos in my head.

With trembling fingers, I dial one of the few numbers I have memorized. The line rings, each tone like a hammer striking my resolve.

"Luis," the voice on the other end answers sharply, the familiar tone bringing an unexpected comfort. For the first time in hours, I smile, picturing Luis surrounded by his usual chaos: half-drank cups of coffee and protein bar wrappers scattered around his desk, and his ever-present keyboard.

"Hey, Lu, it's me," I say, settling on the closed toilet lid.

There's a brief pause before he speaks again. "Marilyn? Why are you calling me from a new number?"

I roll my eyes at the nickname. On another job, Luis found endless amusement in Peter's attempts to have me coerce men through sex. First, because Peter thought he could talk me into it and second, because I'd never be good at it, given my shining personality. Since then, he's taken to calling me Marilyn Monroe at every opportunity.

"That's actually why I'm calling," I sigh, my shoulders sagging under the weight of everything I haven't said yet.

"What happened? Did you get caught?" His keyboard clatters louder, his concern clear.

"Not quite," I admit, picking at a loose thread on my pant leg. "Do you have time to talk?"

"For you? Of course. What's going on?" Luis's reassurance is so firm, it plants a small seed of hope in my chest.

"You might want to write this down," I warn.

"I'm ready."

And just like that, it all comes spilling out. I lay everything bare: the past three months condensed into a relentless torrent of words. I tell him about Peter's mounting demands, Harrison's faux date and subsequent assault, the destruction of my apartment, and the missing laptop. I don't exclude a single detail: my interactions with the Wells family, the clues I've uncovered about the local servers, and my fear that I've finally pushed Peter to the edge with my defiance. My throat burns by the time I'm done, and I stumble to the sink for a drink of water, the phone still pressed to my ear as I place my mouth under the faucet.

"And you haven't talked to Peter?" Luis finally asks, his voice deathly quiet.

I straighten, wiping my mouth with the back of my hand. "I... I've been too scared to call him."

"Fair."

"Part of the reason I'm calling is to see if he's reached out to you about me." We both know what I'm really asking: Has Peter put a target on my back?

The silence stretches, heavy with meaning, before Luis snorts, incredulous. "Do you think I'd take that job at all, let alone not tell you if he asked?"

A shaky laugh escapes me, relief breaking through the tension like a sliver of light. "I hoped that was your answer, but I can't be too careful right now."

"He hasn't called me in weeks. Last I heard, he was busy with Clarissa in New York." Luis pauses. "But nothing you've said sounds good."

I swallow the lump forming in my throat. "Do you think I should confess everything to Silas and Natalie?" I bite down on my nail, the polished edge snapping off under the pressure.

Luis exhales deeply. "Honestly? I'm not sure. They have just as many resources as Peter, so it's a gamble. I don't know them well enough to judge how they'd react."

That's always been the problem. I know Natalie would want to forgive me, maybe even let it go and never speak to me again. But Silas... Silas is different. He's fiercely protective, willing to burn the world to keep his family safe. I've observed that darkness in him, the same ruthlessness Peter wields like a weapon. I wouldn't be an exception to that destruction.

I press my fingers into my closed eyes, leaning my elbows on my thighs. "Lu, I don't know how much longer I can keep this up. If I don't tell someone, the truth will eventually die with me." I breathe out. "There's something else I need you to know."

"It's not going to come to that," Luis says firmly, though his voice softens. "But I'm listening."

My breath hitches as I try to find the words. Memories flood back, unbidden, overwhelming. The sound of her laugh, her unwavering support, the way she made me believe I could be better. *Drew*.

Clearing my throat, I force myself to start. "When I was in college, I had a best friend and roommate. Her name was Drew Bennet. She was smart, selfless, beautiful. And she's the reason I didn't drop out of college."

"She sounds great," Luis says cautiously. "What happened?"

Tears already sting my eyes as I finally say the words I've kept buried for so long. "Peter killed her."

The silence on the line is deafening, until Luis asks, "Come again?"

As I start talking, my grip on the phone tightens, as if holding it will keep me from slipping into the past completely. "I originally found Peter on a forum when I was in college and desperate. My bills were piling up, I couldn't make rent even after Drew moved in with me, and dropping out of school felt inevitable. I needed work that paid well, and someone connected me to him. You know how it goes from there."

I pause, wiping at the tears spilling over. Luis says nothing, letting me continue uninterrupted.

"At first, the jobs were legitimate and relatively easy. For the first time in my life, I could cover my half of rent, groceries... I thought I was finally getting ahead." My voice wavers, and I close my eyes, forcing myself to press on. "But then the jobs started to change, and I convinced myself it was still worth it. It was the first time I had anything to my name, and I wasn't ready to let go of the steady income."

I swallow hard, my throat dry despite the tears. "I lied to Drew. I told her I'd gotten a paid, remote internship that turned into a full-time offer after we graduated. She believed me. And things were fine until the day I left my desktop on accidentally."

Luis stays silent, letting me unravel the story I've kept secret.

"She saw, Lu. I don't even remember which job it was, but it wasn't good. She flipped out. Said she couldn't live with the knowledge of what I was doing. She wanted to report me, to turn me in." My breath hitches, the memory of Drew's angry, devastated face hitting me like a punch to the gut. "I begged her not to. I told her it wasn't what she thought, that I'd stop, but she wouldn't let it go.

I panicked. I told Peter, thinking—God, I don't know what I thought. That he'd calm her down, maybe scare her into staying quiet. I just wanted to protect what little life I had carved out for myself. I never thought..."

My voice cracks, holding my head in my free hand. "The next morning, I went grocery shopping, and when I got back, the apartment door was cracked open. I thought Drew had left it open by mistake."

I still can't say it all out loud. Can't put words to the way her green eyes stared, dull and lifeless, at the ceiling. The way my knees hit the floor so hard I barely felt it over the icy shock crashing through me. The smell of copper was so overwhelming it burned my nose. My hands, slipping in blood as I tried to press my palms to her chest, tried to force breath into her lungs even though I knew she was gone. My own screams tangled with the 911 operator's voice in my ear, but I couldn't stop, couldn't let go, couldn't accept that she was already cold beneath my fingers.

A shuddering breath escapes me. "The place was trashed, and Drew... Drew was on the couch. She'd been stabbed. Twenty-six times."

There's a sharp intake of breath on the other end of the line, but I can't stop now. "The police eventually wrote it off as a home invasion gone wrong. No DNA, no leads. The knife was one of ours, and her wallet and a few personal items were missing."

The guilt crashes over my body so violently, it feels like it's choking me. "A few days later, Peter called me. He was so calm. Told me it wasn't just about cleaning up a loose end. It was a punishment for my carelessness.

He said I should be grateful he made it look like a random robbery." My voice trembles with anger, despair, and the crushing weight of my own culpability. "He blamed her and said it was her fault for threatening his operation."

The silence on the other end is deafening, but I press on, my voice barely above a whisper now. "I told him I wanted out, but he just laughed. Said I owed him for almost ruining his business. That if I stepped out of line again, I'd be next. And after what he did to Drew, I believed him. This was five years ago. I've been doing his dirty work for five years because I knew he'd destroy me if I didn't."

I wipe my face, but it's useless. The tears won't stop. "It's my fault. All of it. If I hadn't involved Peter, Drew would still be alive. And now..." My voice breaks. "Now I can't let him hurt Natalie, too. If I find the servers and give him the information, maybe he'll leave her alone. If he kills me, fine. But she will *not* end up like Drew."

Luis finally speaks, his voice low but firm. "Holy shit, Marilyn. That... that's a lot to unpack."

"It's all my fault," I whisper, my voice hollow. The shame is suffocating, and for a moment, I can't breathe.

"I had no idea that's why you worked for him. I thought... I thought you were like the rest of us," he admits. I squeeze my eyes shut, unable to respond.

I envied the other contractors I've met—people like Luis, who managed to live their lives outside of Peter's grasp, keeping parts of themselves hidden, untouchable. They were careful, calculating, and free in ways I could barely comprehend.

But not me. I got caught in this too young, dragged in before I even knew what freedom really meant. My life ended the moment I told Peter about Drew, and I've been running on borrowed time ever since. The girl I used to be, the life I used to have, all feels like a story I made up.

"Listen to me," Luis says sharply, snapping me out of my spiral. "First of all, this is not your fault. Peter is a monster. He did that to Drew. Not you. Do you hear me?"

I don't respond, knowing he's wrong but not having the energy to argue with him about why Drew isn't here anymore.

"Second," he continues, his tone softening slightly, "you're not going after those servers. Not while you're staying in that house. I'll figure it out, but you're not putting yourself in more danger."

"I can't just sit here," I protest weakly, my voice shaking.

"You can, and you will," Luis grits out. "If Peter is targeting Natalie to get to you, handing him what he wants won't stop him. It'll only make him bolder. We need to figure out what he's really after and how we can use it against him. Until then, you stay put. Stay close to Silas and Natalie, keep your head down, and let me handle the rest."

"I don't want to drag you into this," I whisper.

"You didn't drag me into anything," he says firmly. "I'm here because I care about you, and I'm not going to let Peter ruin your life any more than he already has."

His words wrap around me like a lifeline, pulling me back from the brink. I don't deserve his help, his loyalty, but I cling to it anyway.

"Okay," I murmur, my voice barely audible. "Okay."

"Good," he says, his voice softening further. "We'll figure this out. Together."

But even as I nod to myself, a small, cynical voice in the back of my mind whispers that this might be a battle neither of us can win.

Chapter 26

I t's almost embarrassing how long I spend drafting a text to Natalie on Monday afternoon, trying to find the right way to ask if I can stay at her place.

Me: Hey! I hope you had a good trip. Sorry I didn't answer your messages, I was trying to stay off my phone, but I hope Davey filled you in on everything. I was wondering if maybe I could come stay with you for a little while I get my apartment situation figured out?
Natalie: You're alive! No worries, I know they say to avoid screens for a few days and you needed to rest. We have so much to talk about. Of course you can, but is everything okay? Did Silas do something?

I bite my lip, searching for the most inconspicuous wording.

Me: Oh, no. He's been great. I just don't want to overstay my welcome.
Natalie: You can stay with us for as long as you need. Davey and I are going on a date, but I'll text Silas that we're coming over for a nightcap and then you can come home with us.
Me: That's okay, I can let him know when I see him next.
Natalie: No worries, we're texting already, anyway!

I stare at my phone like it's a ticking bomb, waiting for Silas's inevitable message. My stomach twists as I reread my conversation with Natalie.

I've spent the better part of two days holed up in this room, waiting for Luis to call with an update and trying to convince myself that staying away from Silas is the right thing to do. But he's made it almost impossible. The meals, the snacks, the thoughtful gestures: popcorn, sour candies, cheddar broccoli soup, a BLT—everything I told him I love. It's infuriatingly sweet. Yesterday, Dr. Carrow called me out of the blue to check in on my symptoms, which I have no doubt was orchestrated by the controlling man sleeping across the hallway. Silas said he'd give me space, and he's kept his promise, but I know it's only a matter of time before he pushes again. And now, he knows I'm planning to leave.

My phone vibrates. Of course, it's him.

Silas: You're not leaving until we talk about Saturday.

I stare at the screen, willing myself to stay calm. At least he's open to the idea of me leaving. Eventually. But his condition for it is exactly what I was hoping to avoid. I need to shut this down before Natalie and Davey show up and make everything ten times more awkward.

Me: We don't have anything to talk about. It was a mistake.

The reply comes almost instantly, as if he'd been waiting for it.

Silas: Don't lie to me, Scarlett.

My jaw tightens as I type out another response, my fingers moving faster now.

Me: Natalie is my friend, and I don't want to ruin that by getting involved with her brother.

Silas: That's a nice excuse.

I clench my teeth.

Me: It's not an excuse. She's important to me, and I don't want to complicate things.
Silas: You think avoiding this will make things less complicated?
Me: No, but I'm asking you to respect my boundaries.
Silas: I respect you, but I don't buy that this is about Natalie. You're scared.

The accusation hits harder than I expected. I swallow hard, hesitating before I respond.

Me: I am not. I just don't want to do this with you.
Silas: We'll settle this tonight.
Me: There's nothing to settle!
Silas: Keep telling yourself that. Maybe you'll believe it by the time I see you.

His confidence is maddening. I toss my phone onto the bed, far out of reach, and bury my face in my hands. Why does he have to be so relentless? So sure of himself? It's like he's incapable of accepting no for an answer.

But what makes it worse and makes my chest ache with something far too dangerous to name, is that he's not entirely wrong. I *am* scared.

Because he's not really chasing me. He's chasing Scarlett Page, the carefully constructed version of me that doesn't exist. He's drawn to a mirage. A woman who's equal parts truth and deception, her allure built on a foundation of half-truths that will crumble if he dares to look too closely. And when he finally does find out that I'm nothing but a fraud...

I shudder.

Needing to occupy my mind and keep my hands busy, I pop up from my seat and begin packing my new backpack and duffel bag. The action feels purposeful, even comforting, as I fold and stack the few belongings I have, leaving room in one of the interior pockets of the backpack for the Arizona debit card and my IDs still hidden in the bathroom. In the walk-in closet, I discover several deep-set drawers built into the cabinetry; likely meant for bulky winter sweaters. I place the bags in the bottom drawer, pushing them as far back as they'll go. There's a sense of security in knowing I'm ready to leave, no matter what happens.

For a few fleeting minutes, the preparation calms me. But soon enough, the uneasiness creeps back in, gnawing at the edges of my mind. Unable to slow my racing thoughts, I lounge on the bed with my phone, looking aimlessly through listings and forums, researching places I might go if Luis can get me out of here. Maybe the mountains of North Carolina? The isolation might be nice. Or perhaps southern Texas. Ranch hand jobs in that area often come with housing and don't ask too many questions. I could blend in, work under the table, and lie low until I figure out my next move.

Lost in my scrolling, I nearly jump out of my skin when a knock on the door jolts me back to reality. My surroundings blur into focus, the soft orange glow of the setting sun filtering through the windows. The room is several shades darker than it had been the last time I looked up. I glance at my phone—6:27. Shit. I've been planning my escape for far longer than I realized.

"Ms. Page, here's your dinner," the now-familiar female staff voice calls through the door, her tone quiet and polite. After a brief pause, she adds, "Mr. Wells wanted me to tell you that Mr. and Mrs. Sinclair will be here in an hour, and he'd like you to meet them in the billiards room."

For the first time in days, I respond, my voice low and raspy from disuse. "Thank you." Whether she hears me, I'm not sure, as her footsteps fade away without another word.

I glance at the tray she's left outside my door; a hearty Caesar salad with perfectly grilled steak, the aroma tempting. In any other world, I'd already be devouring it. But now? My stomach twists into a tight knot. The realization sinks in like a stone: in an hour, I'll have to face Silas.

As I enter the billiards room, I'm relieved to find it quiet and empty except for Natalie. The space is bathed in a warm amber glow, the soft hum of music playing over the speakers. Her back is to me, a glass of clear liquid resting on the lip of the table as she leans over to line up her next shot. The quiet *clack* of the cue ball echoes softly in the room as she sinks a stripe into the corner pocket with practiced ease.

"Nice shot," I say from the doorway, my voice breaking the silence.

Natalie turns, a smile spreading across her face. "Scarlett," she says, setting the cue down and walking toward me. She pulls me into a quick hug, the faint trace of her perfume surrounding us. When she steps back, her eyes sharpen, scanning my face. "How are you feeling?"

"Better," I reply, forcing a smile. "A little bruised, but nothing I can't handle."

Her hazel eyes linger on the steri-strips still stuck to my forehead and the purple and blue bruises beneath. "Have you been back to the doctor yet?"

I shake my head, waving a hand dismissively. "No need. It's been days, and I've had no other side effects."

"You should still go," she presses, her tone taking on that maternal edge I've come to expect.

"Noted," I say lightly, desperate to steer the conversation elsewhere. "Now, are we playing while you tell me about LA, or do you want to mother me instead?"

She exhales, clearly unimpressed but relenting, picking up her cue and handing me another. "Fine. But I'm not going easy on you just because you're injured."

"I wouldn't expect anything less," I say, lining up my first shot while glancing around the room. I half-expect Silas or Davey to walk through the door at any moment.

As if reading my mind, Natalie leans casually against the edge of the table, swirling her drink. "Silas and Davey are in his office. They said they'd be down soon," she says, her tone casual, though she keenly observes me.

I nod, her words sending a ripple of unease through me. It's likely about me; it always is about me these days, isn't it?

Pushing the thought aside, I focus on Natalie and ask about her trip. She recounts her and Celicia's horseback ride through Malibu's canyons, yoga overlooking the Pacific, and a private viewing at an exclusive Beverly Hills gallery. I nod along, offering the occasional comment, but my mind feels distant, foggy.

Mid-sentence, she pauses, setting her drink down and studying me. "Are you okay?" she asks, her voice tinged with concern.

My grip tightens on the cue. I bend to line up another shot, avoiding her gaze. "Just tired, I guess."

Natalie doesn't buy it. "Did something happen between you and Silas while I was gone?" she asks gently, her voice surprisingly understanding. "If it did, I wouldn't be mad."

I miss the shot entirely, the cue ball barely grazing its target. Straightening, I force a laugh. "Why would you ask that?"

She sighs, moving around the table with her cue in hand. "Because I've known my brother my entire life and I see the way you both look at each other. Plus, you're acting like he's going to jump out of the walls."

My throat tightens. Leaning the cue against the table, I cross my arms. "It's complicated."

Natalie smirks faintly, setting up her next shot. She hits the cue ball with precision, sinking her target into the middle pocket. "It doesn't have to be," she responds, standing straight and stepping closer to me. "Scarlett, Silas... he's not perfect. But he's *good*."

I open my mouth to respond, but the words don't come.

"He doesn't let many people in," she continues, her tone firmer now. "But when he does, he's loyal to a fault, and the people he chooses get all of him—no hesitation, no half-measures. You don't see it, but he's been showing you how much he cares in every way he knows how."

Her words sound so nice, but there's just no world where Silas treats or cares about me, a virtual stranger, anywhere close to how he would Natalie or Davey.

She pauses and, when unconvinced by my reaction, picks her glass back up and her voice drops to a whisper. "Do you want to know why we hate Martin Shaw?"

I blink, caught off guard. "Natalie, you don't have to—"

"No," She cuts me off, her expression hardening. "I'm telling you this because you need to understand the way Silas protects the people he cares about."

She lets out one measured breath before beginning, "Martin's been a family friend for as long as I can remember. When I was in my early twenties, he started making advances. Compliments, standing too close, lingering hugs. I ignored it for years, but after I started dating Davey, it became... more obvious. Silas and Davey noticed too, but none of us knew how to confront him because his actions were still subtle enough to leave room for doubt. I decided that it wasn't worth the drama it might bring them or my father at work."

Her grip on the glass tightens. "Then one summer, during one of my father's parties, Martin cornered me in the hallway. He forced himself on me. I didn't even have the chance to scream. But somehow, Silas was there before he..." she trails off, straightening her back as she shakes the memory away. "He pulled Martin off me and pinned him against the wall, threatening to ruin his life if he ever came near me again. Martin resigned within the week."

The weight of her words presses down on me. She doesn't have to explain to me, another woman, why she didn't go to the police. It would've gone to court, her word against his, likely with no evidence beyond the three of them. The lawyers would've twisted the story, painted her as some kind of whore who led him on, and the publicity would have destroyed her. Martin would've walked away unscathed, and Natalie would've been left to pick up the pieces of her life. Instead they chose to keep the truth close, using it as leverage to keep Martin far away.

The courage it must have taken for her to keep that secret, to live with it, to protect her family while enduring the weight of what happened. My heart physically aches for her.

"I'm so sorry that happened to you," I whisper, my voice barely audible.

She exhales, her knuckles white around the glass. "Thank you," she says softly. Then, more firmly, "It was my decision not to go after Martin legally, but Silas was ready and willing to do anything I asked of him. That's who he is."

I can only nod, her words burying themselves deep in my chest.

We stand in silence for only a few heartbeats before her breath hitches. She sets her glass down with a sharp *clink* and walks toward the door. "I... I need a minute," she murmurs, disappearing into the hallway.

I stay rooted in place, wanting to follow her but knowing better of it. She needs a minute to collect herself, and she deserves that much. Instead, I move to the bar and make myself a tequila soda with lime, ignoring the pang of unease as I realize everything I need for the drink is conveniently waiting for me on the counter, as though someone knew I'd need it.

The sound of the door opening behind me breaks the silence. I turn, glass still raised to my lips, as Davey steps inside.

"Scarlett," he says, his voice carrying a note of severity that immediately puts me on edge. His gaze is sharp as it rakes over my face, and I lower my glass slowly.

"Davey," I reply, my voice guarded.

He glances around the room, his expression unreadable. "Where did Natalie go?"

I hesitate before nodding toward the hallway. "She stepped out for a moment. Said she needed to use the restroom."

Davey's eyes linger on me for a beat too long, as if trying to read something in my expression. Finally, he nods. "Thanks. I'll wait for her." He carries himself further into the room, taking hold of Natalie's abandoned cue, rolling it in his palms. "In the meantime, you and I need to talk."

I swallow hard, bracing myself. "About what?"

Davey's jaw tightens, and his gaze locks onto mine.

"You know what."

CHAPTER 27

The blood rushes to my head, and I reach for my cue stick with my free hand, fingers curling around it for something to hold onto. Davey doesn't look away, his piercing gaze locked onto mine. He sets his cue back on the table with deliberate ease, then crosses his arms and shifts his weight onto one leg, posture deceptively relaxed.

"I find this whole situation... funny," he says, pausing as if savoring the word.

I lift my cocktail to my lips, the condensation trickling down my fingers as I take a measured sip. The tequila burns on the way down, offering me a moment of reprieve. "What's funny about it?" I ask, my voice steady despite the unease coiling in my chest.

He tilts his head, scrutinizing me. The furrow between his brows deepens. Even his usually immaculate auburn hair is disheveled. He's been stewing over this, probably since the moment I showed up at Natalie's art gala.

"You," he says finally, his tone sharp but calm. "You show up out of nowhere, befriending my wife and bewitching my brother-in-law. We've known you an all of, what? Three months? And suddenly, our worlds spin as if you've always been in it."

The weight of his accusation is like a stone thrown into still water, rippling outward. I force my fingers to relax, even as heat prickles at the back of my neck. He knows nothing. He's just trying to rattle me.

I place my glass down and hold on to the edge of the pool table before letting out a soft, dismissive laugh. "You're making me blush."

Davey raises a brow, unimpressed. "That's an interesting way to respond to an accusation."

My fingers tap a steady rhythm against the cue stick as I shrug, feigning nonchalance. "I take all accusations seriously." I force an easy smile. "I befriended Natalie because she approached *me* at an event. I was there to meet people, and Natalie is the kind of person anyone would want as a friend. Wouldn't you agree?"

For a moment, his fist clenching so subtly it's almost imperceptible. But I notice. After a beat, he shakes his head, letting out a dry chuckle. "You're good," he mutters, a touch of incredulity coloring his tone.

I tilt my head slightly. "I'm just being honest," I reply, my grip on the table tightening. "And as for the second half of your accusation—what exactly have I done to 'bewitch' Silas?"

Davey rolls his eyes, his annoyance barely masked. "As if you don't know exactly what you're doing."

I don't fully deny it. I can't. Instead, I deflect. "I genuinely want to understand. What have I done that makes you think I've put Silas under some kind of spell? Honestly, I never thought he was even capable of being seduced."

"He isn't," Davey responds almost too quickly. His hands drop to his sides, sliding into his pockets. "And that's precisely why I want to know what you're playing at. Why you're doing all of this."

Something about his words strikes a nerve, more than I expect it to. Maybe it's his relentless suspicion, his constant needling, or maybe it's the way he reduces everything between me and Silas to a ploy. As though my feelings—real, messy, complicated feelings—don't exist.

The words that leave my mouth are laced with frustration. "All of what, Davey? I moved to Chicago and met both of them. I've kept to myself, accepted invitations when given, and tried to build a life here. I'm not sure why you think so little of Natalie, but there are a million reasons I want to be her friend. None of which have anything to do with her family."

His eyes darken at my insinuation, anger flashing across his features like lightning. It's a low blow, and regret creeps along my spine for even bringing Natalie further into this conversation. But I'm too far in now to back down.

The silence between us stretches, heavy and suffocating, until he chooses to ignore my comment and instead presses, "And what of Silas?"

Before I can stop myself, the memories flood in. Silas's intense, dark eyes heating during our banter. The way his grin transforms him when he bests me, and the way his jaw ticks when I best him. The raw fury in his gaze at the restaurant, and the tenderness in his touch as he tended to my injuries in his office. The way he moved against me in his bedroom, his lips commanding mine like he was memorizing me.

I blink rapidly, dragging myself back to the present. My throat feels dry and I swallow hard, avoiding Davey's gaze by staring at the scattered billiard balls on the table.

"Silas isn't like anyone I've ever met before," I admit quietly, my voice barely above a whisper. Silas does something to me I can't explain—he quiets the chaos in my mind. Steadies everything in the most unconventional way. For someone like me, who thrives in controlled disorder, that calm feels like a luxury I can't afford.

I square my shoulders, and meet his stare. "I don't know what more I can say other than I like being around them."

When I meet Davey's gaze again, his expression has shifted, so subtly I could have missed it. The hard edge in his eyes softens just enough to let me know he won't push this subject further. At least not tonight.

"People don't fall into the Wells family without reason," he says quieter now, almost reflective.

I nod, swallowing down the things I can't tell him. Instead, I offer him another half-truth, one I can stand behind without it breaking me. "I'm sure, in most cases, you're right."

Davey reaches down, picking up a billiard ball in front of him. He pushes it slowly across the table, letting it roll until it comes to a complete stop near the center of the felt. His movements are deliberate, like everything else about him.

"It goes without saying," he begins, his voice low and deadly serious, "but if you ever do anything to hurt Natalie..." He trails off, leaving the threat hanging in the air. His eyes blaze with a fierce protectiveness as he speaks of his wife, and if it weren't obvious enough already, I'm reminded of the depth of his devotion.

I nod again, unable to promise him anything but my understanding. "I know," I say softly, the weight of his words settling heavily on my chest.

The faint hum of music is the only sound in the room. I hold my breath, refusing to break eye contact, even as my grip on the pool cue tightens once more.

After what feels like an eternity, Davey glances at his watch and, without warning, steps away from the table and heads toward the door. "I'm going to make sure everything's okay with Natalie," he says over his shoulder.

I don't respond, and he doesn't expect me to. In his perfectly tailored suit, Davey strides out of the room without a second glance, leaving me alone with the echo of his footsteps.

The heavy wooden door clicks shut behind him, and only then do I exhale, the breath rushing out of me in a shaky gasp. I bend at the waist as the tension I've been holding on to floods out of me all at once. My grip on the pool cue loosens, fingers cramping as I flex them to regain feeling. With my free hand, I pinch the bridge of my nose, willing myself to calm down.

I'm so, so fucked.

"He's right, you know." The sound of Silas's smoky voice fills the room, and I jump, clutching the cue stick like a lifeline.

I whip around, heart pounding, to see him in the shadows of a barely visible doorway. He's leaning casually in the frame of what, I assumed, was a closet door next to the bar. My mind registers the existence of the passageway, filing it away for later, but my attention is immediately drawn to him.

He looks disheveled in the most infuriatingly attractive way: dark dress pants, a slightly rumpled white button-up, and a tie hanging loose around his neck. His unruly dark curls frame his face, and his rolled-up sleeves reveal the ink swirling over his left forearm. My blood feels molten in my veins.

"You scared me," I manage to say, forcing a weak half-smile. He smirks, but it does little to mask the frustration etched into the rest of his expression.

"Boo," he says mockingly, his smile growing so much that it's all teeth.

I sidestep to maintain the distance between us, trying to keep my composure even as he draws closer purposefully.

"Are there any trap doors I should be concerned about falling into?" I joke halfheartedly, nodding toward the door he came though in an attempt to break the tension.

"Not to my knowledge," he replies, stopping far too close for comfort. I can feel the heat radiating from him as he leans against the side of the pool table, his eyes locked on me. "Did you have a nice conversation with Davey?" His tone is taunting, daring me to rise to the bait.

I don't answer. Instead, I focus on the pool table. "How is he right?" I ask, steering the conversation back to his earlier remark.

Silas pauses, considering his words. "It's unusual for someone to infiltrate our family so easily," he finally answers.

I force myself to meet his gaze, offering a closed-mouth smile. "Infiltrate, huh? Like a spy?" I try to lighten the mood, but he doesn't bite. His lips press into a thin line as he pulls a handkerchief from his pocket and takes off his glasses to wipe the lenses with slow, deliberate movements.

Everything about him is calculated, every action intentional. That's part of what draws me to him. He knows exactly what he wants and how to get it. And no matter how much I try to convince myself otherwise, he's made it abundantly clear that, for now, what he wants is me.

"You've been avoiding me," he says finally, sliding his glasses back onto his face and returning the cloth to his pocket. His tone is calm, but his sharp gaze pierces me, leaving no room for escape.

My throat tightens. I reach for my glass, taking a sip to steady myself. His eyes remain fixed on my lips. Heat blooms in my chest, and I set the glass down, gripping the cue stick with both hands as if it can ground me.

"I told you how I feel about everything." My voice is strained but steady.

"You fed me your lies earlier, yes." His casual delivery of the accusation grates on my nerves.

"They weren't lies, Silas. Saturday was a mistake."

One of his brows arches slightly, his expression unreadable but no less intense. "Why are you fighting this so hard?" he asks, stepping closer, his presence overwhelming.

"Because I don't want it," I respond, my voice rising as my grip on the cue stick tightens.

"So you felt nothing when I touched you?" His voice dips, rough and tantalizing. "Kissed you?"

Fingers curls around the wrist of my free hand and pull me against him, his body warm and solid. Our chests rise and fall in the same rhythm, pressing the pool stick between us. His other hand brushes the corner of my lips, his thumb lingering there, and I can barely breathe.

"Say it, Scarlett," he murmurs, his mouth so close to mine that his breath becomes my own. "Tell me it meant nothing."

The hand on my wrist slides lower, fingers brushing my palm before intertwining with mine. The touch is a silent challenge, daring me to pull away. The warnings screaming in my brain, for some reason, don't reach my mouth.

"You can't, can you?" he whispers, his lips curving into a faint, knowing smirk. His eyes blaze with unspoken promises, every sinful thought he's ever had laid bare. "Because you don't want me to stop."

A sharp sting of clarity cuts through the haze. "Fuck you," I snap, shoving hard against his chest. He releases me instantly, the smirk vanishing as I put distance between us. My heart pounds like a war drum.

For a moment, neither of us speaks. But even as I struggle to collect myself, he doesn't back down. I can see the determination brimming in his eyes.

"That doesn't answer my question," Silas says, recovering far too quickly, his voice infuriatingly confident as his gaze tracks my every move.

"I don't care," I snap, wrapping both hands around the pool stick again like it's armor. I turn my body perpendicular to his, hoping to shield myself from even a fraction of the pull he always has on me. "I'm telling you no."

"And I'm telling you to stop being a coward."

A sharp, bitter laugh escapes me before I whip my glare over my shoulder at him. "I'm not a plaything, Silas. You don't get to decide for the both of us. I'm not ruining my friendship with Natalie for sex."

"Who said it's just sex?" he counters smoothly.

"Oh, please." I roll my eyes, my voice dripping with disdain, desperate to keep him at bay.

"Please, what?" There's tension in his jaw now, the muscles flexing under his stubble.

"The sweet-talking won't work on me. I'm not stupid. You just can't handle being told no."

His laugh is low and humorless, sharp enough to cut glass. "You really think I do this with just anyone?"

"Honestly? Yes," I fire back, my words like venom. "And I'm not one of them."

"Hate to break it to you, Scarlett, but you already are."

Any shred of patience I had left goes up in flames. "You are fucking impossible." My voice rises, bouncing off the walls. If he isn't going to relent, then I'll make him. I'll make him hate me. So, I reach for that part of me I keep hidden, the part of me that knows how to hurt. "Just stop. I'm not some desperate woman pining for scraps of attention from you. You're a spoiled, self-absorbed—"

Before I can finish, a sharp pressure tugs at the end of my ponytail, forcing my head back. A startled gasp escapes my lips as my body is yanked back against his with ease, the hard plane of his chest pressing into my back. The cue stick in my hands feels like a lifeline, but my grip falters as his presence consumes me.

With a precise twist of his wrist, Silas tightens his grip, his fingers threading through my hair as he holds the back of my head against his shoulder, suspending me between defiance and submission. My vision adjusts, and when it sharpens, I meet his gaze: dark, endless, and brimming with something unrestrained and dangerous.

His nostrils flare, a single measured exhale passing through his parted lips. The surrounding air thickens, becoming something tangible. It presses down on me like a shadow, suffocating and intoxicating all at once, but it's darker than anything I've ever encountered before. More visceral. It pulses between us, like a wire stretched to its breaking point.

"*That fucking mouth*," Silas growls, his tongue sweeping over his front teeth as he studies me, his eyes blazing with heat.

My own gaze betrays me, drifting to the sharp line of his jaw, the freckles scattered across the bridge of his nose, the way his glasses frame those piercing eyes. I cling to the pool stick, the only thing keeping my knees from buckling.

When I try to speak, nothing comes out, my voice caught somewhere between my chest and throat. Silas takes my silence as surrender, pulling a little harder on my ponytail, just enough to make me arch further into him. Heat radiates from the base of my scalp, igniting every nerve ending down to my toes. The sharp pull of his grip shouldn't feel this good, but it does.

God, it does.

I feel the solid wall of his chest, the unyielding press of his thighs against the curve of my hips, fitting against me like a glove I didn't know was made for me.

Sensing my unraveling, Silas leans forward, his nose skimming the side of my cheek. I jolt at the rough scratch of his beard against my skin, a friction that sends sparks shooting down my spine.

"It's one of my favorite things about you, Scarlett," he murmurs, his voice dripping with depravity. "Even if it makes me violent."

The grip on my hair loosens slightly, just enough for my head to fall to the side, baring the length of my neck. His lips hover near my ear, each word a velvet dagger.

"You're not staying in the guest room tonight."

My heart releases a traitorous thump against my ribs. I manage to find my voice, though it's lacking all its regular conviction. "I'm not staying here *at all*, Silas. I can't be with you like that."

A low, throaty laugh escapes him, the sound wrapping around me like smoke. His hand slides from my ponytail to my waist, pulling me even closer, the possession in his touch clear. "You can't?" he repeats, his voice heavy with skepticism. "Or you won't?"

"Both," I bite out, though my words falter. "I told you."

His hand moves to cup my jaw, tilting my face upward, forcing me to meet his gaze. His dark, espresso eyes bore into mine, saturated with lust. "You're in my house, Scarlett. You've already crossed that line, whether you want to admit it or not."

I try to pull back, to create even the smallest amount of distance, but his hold tightens just enough to keep me rooted in place. "This isn't right," I whisper, hating the way the words sound so weak, so uncertain.

A faint, predatory smile curves his lips. "It feels right to me," he counters smoothly, his thumb brushing over my bottom lip. "And it feels right to you, too."

I shake my head, desperate to cling to the remnants of my crumbling resistance. "I can't sleep with you."

The hand on my waist flexes, his grip firm yet not painful. "Do you really think I let anyone into my life, into my home, into my bed, like this?" he asks, his voice a low hiss, as if I've insulted him.

Hope, heat, and devastation swell in my chest, his presence suffocating and overwhelming me. I open my mouth to argue, to tell him he's wrong, but my voice betrays me, leaving me at a complete loss for words.

"You can fight this all you want," he continues, his tone softening, though it remains edged with unyielding steel. "But we both know you're staying."

His other hand slides down my arm, his fingers brushing against mine as he gently loosens my grip on the pool cue. He plucks it from my hands and places it on the edge of the table without ever breaking eye contact. "Say it," he murmurs, his voice softer now but no less commanding. "Say you're staying."

"I—" my voice cracks, and I look away, unable to bear the weight of his gaze any longer. Any remaining strength is slipping through my fingers like grains of sand.

"Say it," he repeats, his thumb tracing the line of my jaw, coaxing me to turn back toward him. When I do, when I finally meet his gaze again, I know I'm lost.

There's something in his expression I've never seen before, a vulnerability that takes me by surprise. It's a look that both demands and pleads, as though he's utterly certain I'll say yes but bracing himself for the possibility I won't. He's stripped himself bare, his usual confidence and control set aside, leaving him raw and exposed. It's a kind of trust I don't know how to handle.

"Okay," I whisper finally, the word barely audible, but it seals my fate nonetheless.

His smile is a mix of satisfaction and something deeper. "Okay," he repeats, his tone quieter now, like a promise.

I hate the way I've let him rob me of my own autonomy, the way I've surrendered with almost no fight. But the worst part, the part that burns hotter than any frustration or anger, is that I want this. I *want* to give him this power over me. I want to surrender to him, to let him take the control I've never been able to hold on to. And that truth—that undeniable, complete truth—scares me more than anything else ever could.

Chapter 28

I t's 9:07, and we're standing in Silas's dimly lit kitchen, just like we did Friday night. But this time, instead of tea, Silas is fixing us both drinks. His back is to me, broad and impossibly distracting, as he moves with an unhurried grace. My spine presses against the edge of the island, the stone countertop digging into my palms where I brace myself for balance.

Natalie and Davey left only minutes ago. When Silas announced that I'd changed my mind and decided to stay, I could barely bring myself to look at them. Natalie's grin was brimming with approval, while Davey's narrowed gaze drilled into me. It was as though he could see right through me, searching for the hidden strings that tied me here. For once, he was wrong. I have no fucking idea what I'm doing or why I stayed.

All I know is the way Silas looked at me in the billiards room, his gaze a perfect blend of conviction and vulnerability, held me fast. Every rational part of me screamed to leave, to create distance, to flee before it was too late. But those parts fell silent in the face of the pull between us, an undeniable gravity I can't escape. I know how this will end: heartbreak. Mine, maybe his. It doesn't matter. He's stripped me of logic.

"Talk to me."

Silas's low, steady voice pulls me from the whirlwind in my head. He glances at me over his shoulder. Those beautifully cosmic eyes glint in the warm, dim lighting, cutting through the fog in my mind.

At some point, while Natalie and Davey were still here, Silas excused himself to change. Now, he's in sweatpants and a plain t-shirt that clings to him in all the ways that make it impossible not to look. The muscles of his shoulders and back shift subtly as he moves, and his glasses are gone, leaving his face sharper, more striking. It makes me wonder if he wears contacts sometimes, or if he just doesn't need them for what comes next. My pulse quickens at the thought.

"What do you want me to say?" I ask quietly.

He turns fully then, holding two drinks. One is filled with dark amber liquid, the other is clear and bubbling, condensation trailing lazily down the glass. He steps closer, handing me the clear drink and his fingers brush mine, sending a flicker of warmth up my arm. He lifts his own glass in a subtle toast, his eyes never leaving mine. "Tell me why you're so scared."

I bite the inside of my cheek, holding back the tidal wave of truths that threaten to spill. The real reason I'm here. How I promised myself that I'd never let it get this far. The inevitability of it all crashing down, destroying not only this fragile thing between us, but also my relationship with Natalie. How I'll have to leave, sooner rather than later, and he'll hate me when he finds out the truth. But instead, I cling to a simpler answer. The safest one.

"I don't sleep around," I reply.

It's not entirely untrue. On the rare occasions I stayed in one place long enough to date, I occasionally said yes when asked out. But I never slept with them before getting to know them, and I certainly didn't move into their house—however temporarily—before doing so. And while I feel like I know Silas better than I knew any of those men, none of them ever felt like *this*.

The weight of his gaze deepens as he considers my words. Without breaking eye contact, I raise my glass, reaching across the small space between us to tap it softly against his. The quiet *clink* reverberates in the stillness.

"And you assume I do?" Silas asks as we both take long sips. His eyes linger on me over the edge of his glass.

I give him an incredulous look, one eyebrow arching. He smirks, lowering his drink as his tongue flicks out to swipe along his lower lip. The sight sends a ripple through me, one I try to suppress by taking another sip of my drink.

"Silas," I finally say, my voice edged with disbelief.

His smirk softens as he steps closer, setting his glass down on the counter beside me. The sound of the glass meeting stone feels sharp, final, like he's just declared something.

"You still think I'm like this with everyone." His voice is almost teasing, but there's an undercurrent of seriousness that's hard to miss.

I press my lips together and hold his stare, trying to find cracks in his armor. "Am I wrong?" I challenge, the words sharper than intended.

He leans forward then, close enough that his scent—clean soap and cedarwood—wraps around me, heady and intoxicating, a reminder of how easily he overwhelms my senses.

"Scarlett," he murmurs, his voice low and intimate, sending shivers down my spine. "I don't think I've ever looked at anyone the way I look at you."

For a moment, I can't breathe. I don't know how to respond. So, I do what I always do; I retreat behind silence, raising my glass again and using it as a shield, a barrier between us.

Undeterred by my retreat, Silas reaches for a loose strand of my ponytail that's fallen over my shoulder, his touch so light it feels like a whisper against my skin. He rubs the lock between his fingers, his eyes fixed on it like it holds all the answers he's searching for. "Whatever you think I've done before, this isn't the same," he says simply. "*You're* not the same."

His words send a jolt through me, almost mirroring the thoughts I was just having moments ago. The fact that he feels it too only seems to tighten the invisible thread between us. And that scares the shit out of me.

I dart my eyes anywhere but at him, nursing my drink until the glass is nearly empty, desperate for anything to keep me planted in reality. Silas doesn't move until I set the glass down on the counter with trembling hands. Only then does he shift, sliding the glasses further away and gripping the edge of the island on either side of my waist, caging me in. There's a sliver of space between us now, just enough for me to tell him no if I choose.

But I don't.

Instead, I press my hands behind me, locking them against the small of my back, as if that will stop the urge to touch him. My pulse pounds in my ears, each beat echoing louder than the last, drowning out the frantic warnings in my head.

Silas hums softly, the sound deep and thoughtful. His eyes flick back and forth, studying me, and I can't help but wonder what he sees. Watching his mind at work has always been one of my favorite things about him, and now, more than ever, I wish I could crawl into his head and see how the cogs turn.

"How about this?" he finally says, his voice a low rumble that feels like it's vibrating through me. His face inches closer. "We'll run a few tests to see if Saturday was just a fluke. If it was, we'll pretend none of this ever happened."

"Tests?" I whisper as my throat tightens. His gaze dips to my neck, tracking the movement as I swallow.

"Yes," he breathes, his voice dropping further, rich and velvety. His lips hover just above mine. "Just be a good girl and sit still."

His mouth is light and tentative, like he's waiting for me to pull away, but the heat of him engulfs me, incinerating every last ember of resistance I had left. It's reckless, inevitable—like stepping into a fire and knowing I'll burn, but wanting the flames anyway. I lean into him, and the moment I do, his restraint shatters.

He claims me with a confidence that shakes my foundation. Hands move to the underside of my jaw, holding me in place as he presses his weight into me with a firm, possessive grip. When his teeth pull against my lower lip, tugging just enough to make me gasp, I fist the front of his shirt, as if letting go would pull me back into reality.

This isn't the exploration of Saturday night. This is a declaration, a confession, a collision of everything we've both been holding back. He's drinking from me, taking what he wants, and I know I should stop, but I can't. Not when he kisses me like I'm the only thing he's ever wanted.

We could have been like this for three minutes or thirty—I lose all sense of time. Everything else fades away until there's only Silas. There's no room for anything else.

He pulls back first, his breath ragged, but he doesn't let go. His forehead rests against mine, his dark eyes smoldering, rich and intense like freshly brewed coffee, swirling with untamed heat.

"That was a really good test," he murmurs, his lips brushing mine as he speaks, the words laced with both satisfaction and longing.

"It was," I manage to whisper, my voice shaky. My own breathing is embarrassingly heavy, every inhale causing my chest to brush against his, amplifying the tension between us.

Why can't I have this, just this once? Why can't I enjoy the thing I want most when it's standing right in front of me?

Almost as if he can sense my final surrender, his fingers trail up the back of my head, tangling in the base of my ponytail. Then, with deliberate precision, he pulls sharply. The burn on my scalp is a delicious contrast to the heat pooling low in my stomach. A soft, involuntary moan escapes me before I can stop it.

His response is instant. A groan vibrates in the back of his throat, sending a jolt of electricity straight through me. Taking full advantage of my exposed neck, he leans down, his teeth grazing my skin as he leaves a trail of biting kisses that are just on the edge of pain. The friction is intoxicating, and I shudder against him, my fingers clutching him harder, desperate for more.

"I'm going to fuck you on this counter," he promises in a low growl as his teeth sink into the spot where my neck meets my shoulder.

I tilt my head back, sighing at the sensation. His hands slide down my sides, pausing just below my ass before lifting me onto the cold stone of the island. My legs part instinctively, making room for him to step between them. Before I can take another breath, his mouth is on mine again. Rougher. Hungrier.

I submit to him, letting him take control, letting him consume me. Right now, I'm his, and he can have anything he wants. Anything at all.

His palms move up and down the sides of my thighs, hands warm against my skin. My fingers find the hem of his shirt and I slip underneath, savoring the heat of his hard, toned body beneath my touch.

"Do you have any idea what you do to me?" He mutters against my lips, rough and unsteady. The words sending a rush of warmth through me and I run my tongue over his bottom lip, earning a low, almost desperate curse from him.

Then his movements quicken, his need for me evident in every touch. Hands grip the bottom of my shirt, and with one fluid motion, he pulls it over my head as if it were nothing more than an obstacle in his way. My bra is next, unclasped and discarded with the same efficiency. Only then does he pull back slightly, his gaze trailing over my now-bare chest. His jaw tightens as he takes me in, fighting a losing battle with his control.

"Fuck, Scarlett," he whispers, his eyes roam over me, savoring in every inch. The way he looks at me addicting, a blend of hunger and reverence that sets my skin ablaze.

"It's only fair if I can also see what I'm working with." I lean back on my hands, trying to steady my breath. My tone is teasing, but the anticipation pulsating through my body is anything but.

Silas doesn't hesitate. He grabs the hem of his shirt, pulling it over his head and tossing it aside without a second thought. The sight of him is breathtaking. His chest and stomach are just as I imagined—defined, strong, and entirely distracting. The tattoos on his arm extends to his shoulder, depicting a snowy mountain landscape, while another intricate design wraps around his side, hinting at a story I can't quite decipher from this angle.

I realize I've stopped breathing when Silas steps closer, his devilish smile making my heart skip. "What's the verdict?" he asks, his hand trailing lightly across my abdomen, creeping upward with featherlight strokes that send shivers across my skin.

"I'll have to see how the lower half holds up, but I feel pretty good about the odds," I quip, leaning into his touch.

The sound of his laugh wraps around me like silk. "You're such a brat," he says with mock exasperation before leaning down to capture one nipple between his teeth.

I arch into him instinctively, a sharp inhale escaping as the sensation shoots through me. His tongue follows, soothing the bite with warm, wet strokes before his lips close over the sensitive peak. His free hand teases the other, brushing lightly before rolling the nipple between his fingers, drawing a soft moan from my lips.

"Si," I breathe, the nickname slipping out without thought as my fingers thread through his tousled hair. It's softer than I imagined, but the realization is lost in the storm of sensations coursing through me.

He groans, his breath hot against my chest. "I love hearing you call me that."

Moving slowly, he worships my body before his lips close over my other nipple, I let out a shaky exhale, my back bowing to press myself further into him. The way he touches me, so deliberate and precise, feels like he's playing an instrument he's spent a lifetime mastering, and I'm powerless against it.

"Please," I whisper, grinding my lower body against him, desperate for more.

He releases my nipple and pulls my upper body closer, his nose brushing against mine as his lips hover just a breath away. "Please, what, princess?" he taunts, his voice a low, dangerous whisper.

"You know what," I reply breathlessly, though my impatience bleeds through. His expression shifts, a feral look overtaking his features that steals what little resolve I have left.

"You're going to be the death of me," he growls through clenched teeth, his fingers digging into my thighs as he pulls me closer to the edge of the countertop. "Do you want me to fuck you, Scarlett?"

The question, spoken in that rough, commanding tone, should have made me hesitate. It should have reminded me of every reason why this is a terrible idea. But instead, it only fans the flames, obliterating any semblance of doubt.

"Yes," I breathe, my voice steady despite the chaos within me. My hands reach for the waistband of his joggers, desperate to close the space between us.

But Silas stops me, his hands catching mine and gently redirecting them to the counter. His focus shifts to my jeans, and with deft fingers, he unfastens them before lifting me slightly to slide them down my legs, along with my panties. The air against my bare skin is a shock, but his hands are quick to follow, fingers trail lightly along the crease of my thighs, lingering just enough to make my breath hitch.

"We can take our time with all the niceties later," Silas mutters, almost to himself, his voice rough with restraint. I commit the moment to memory—the way he looks at me like he's just taken the first hit of a drug he's craved his whole life.

"This is a one-time deal," I manage to say, though my voice lacks conviction.

He gives me an infuriating, knowing grin. "We'll see," he murmurs, as he slowly lowers himself to his knees. His hands trail down my thighs, leaving a blazing path in their wake.

Without breaking eye contact, he spreads my legs wider. Fingers dig into the soft skin and he pauses as if daring me to look away. But I don't. I feel laid bare before him, vulnerable in a way I rarely let myself be.

A slow, satisfied smirk tugs at his lips. "That's my girl," he murmurs, his gaze dropping between my thighs. The rich brown of his irises fades, overtaken by black. "Look at you. So pretty and ready for me." His head dips to press a kiss to the inside of my calf, but his eyes stay locked between my legs—transfixed, as if he can't bear to look away.

For a moment, panic grips me as I remember the cameras scattered throughout the house, including the ones here in the kitchen. My body tenses, my gaze darting around the room, but before I can say a word, Silas notices.

His movements slow, his breath warm against my skin as his lips brush the inside of my thigh. "They're off," he murmurs, as if he's plucked the thought straight from my mind. "Do you really think I'd ever let anyone else see you like this?" His mouth drags higher, the next kiss lingering. Possessive. "This," he continues, a whisper away from where I ache for him, "is only for me."

The absoluteness of his words washes over me, dissolving the fear that flickered to life. I believe him. I believe every word because I know Silas would never allow anyone else to have this. Not when his claim is absolute.

I exhale, tension melting from my body as I ease back onto my elbows, in surrender. His hands inch higher, the touch slow and deliberate, each kiss a silent vow. Heat coils low in my belly as his lips trail closer, teasing, until his nose grazes my clit. The contact is fleeting, barely there, but it's enough to rip a whimper from my throat.

"You're so fucking wet." His voice thick with satisfaction, breath fanning over me before his tongue follows in a slow, methodical taste. The sensation detonates through my body, sharp and overwhelming, making my vision blur.

"You might think this is a one-time deal," he muses, his words a dark promise, "but your pussy already knows better. It's begging for me to do it again."

The taunt is filthy, but I can't respond. I can't think. I can only gasp as his tongue moves in devastating, calculated patterns, each stroke designed to unravel me. My hands slap against the cold marble, unable to ground myself against the onslaught of pleasure.

The sound fuels him. His grip is unyielding, holding me open, keeping me exactly where he wants me. Then, he slides one hand between my legs, teasing at my entrance before pressing a single finger inside with unbearable slowness. I gasp, back arching, but he drags it out, savoring the way I react. When he adds another, stretching me, my hips jerk against his mouth, seeking more.

"So responsive," he mutters against me in a low, wicked drawl. He flexes his fingers, curling them deep before setting a steady rhythm, each stroke in sync with the relentless flick of his tongue.

It's too much and not enough, the tension winding tighter inside me with every calculated movement. My body is no longer my own. Right now, it belongs to him and it's like he knows every hidden trigger, every spot that will break me apart.

"Please," I whimper, my voice wrecked with need. "Please, *please*..."

Silas chuckles like the devil himself, reveling in my undoing. "Impatient," he muses. Then, as if to punish me, he presses deeper, curling his fingers just right—hitting the spot that makes my entire body seize. "Say my name again."

"I swear to God—" my threat dissolves into a moan as his pace increases, his mouth and fingers working in tandem.

"How about another 'please'?" he taunts, flicking his gaze up at me. His lips glisten as he smirks before he curls his fingers again.

My orgasm crashes through me, violent and all-consuming, pleasure so intense that for a moment, I forget how to breathe. My entire body shakes, thighs clamping around his head as I come apart beneath him.

"Si," my voice breaks as my hands find him, fingers tangling in his hair, pulling hard. He growls against me, the sound low and primal, vibrating through every overstimulated nerve.

He doesn't stop. Not until the last aftershock fades, not until I'm slumped against the counter, boneless, my chest heaving and limbs molten. Only then does he rise, pulling me upright with a firm grip on my wrist.

"I guess I'll have to wait for the 'please' next time," he retorts, thick with amusement, though his uneven breath is proof of how much he enjoyed ruining me.

I huff out a breathless laugh, but it dies the moment Silas's hand slides from my wrist to my throat. His thumb strokes the skin there, a tender contrast to the intensity of everything else.

Lips, swollen and slick from his own destruction, curve into a sinful smile before he yanks me forward and crashes his mouth against mine.

The kiss is a fresh onslaught, his tongue sweeping past my lips to claim and dominate. He kisses like he owns me—like he's branding me from the inside out. Normally, I'd push back, fight for control. But with Silas, it's different. With him, surrender feels like freedom. It feels safe.

But I want *more*.

My hand slips between us, determined to finish what he started as I free him from his pants. The heat of him is undeniable, searing against my palm as my fingers wrap around his length, stroking once. His breath hitches, his kiss faltering for the first time, and the sharp exhale that follows sends a thrill racing through me.

I steal a glance between us, my breath catching in my throat. Jesus. Silas is confident for a reason. He's more than I expected, thick and heavy in my grasp, and for a moment, all I can do is marvel at the sheer size of him before dragging my thumb over the tip, smearing the bead of wetness there.

"Fucking hell," he grits out, his voice raw. His head tilts back slightly, the muscles in his jaw ticking as he fights for control. A losing battle. "I'm not going to be gentle with you."

"I wouldn't dream of it," I murmur, squeezing him just enough to make his hips jerk into my hand. My reward is immediate—a deep, guttural moan that sends heat pooling low in my stomach.

There's something untamed about his messy hair, dark eyes blown wide, skin flushed with heat. He looks almost feral, like a man barely holding himself back. If I didn't know better, I'd swear he *was* under some kind of spell.

"I'm clean," he says, his voice steady despite the tension radiating off him in waves. "Are you?"

"Yes," I breathe. "And on birth control."

His eyes burn hot at my admission, the fire in them threatening to consume me whole.

Fuck.

Scooting closer to the edge of the counter, I tilt my hips, guiding the thick length of him to my entrance. It's enough to reignite the flames licking at my stomach, sending anticipation clawing up my spine.

Leaning in, I drag my hand down his chest, tracing the sharp ridges of his muscles, feeling the way they tense beneath my touch. My lips hover over his, so close our breaths tangle. "Were you serious about not being gentle?" I ask, my voice a low, teasing challenge. A dare.

His fingers flex around my throat, his lips curling deviously. "You'll see just how serious I am."

Then he thrusts forward.

The sudden, brutal stretch steals the air from my lungs. It's a delicious, unbearable burn, but my body welcomes the invasion, softening, adjusting, desperate to take him. A choked sound escapes my throat as my nails dig into his skin, every nerve alight with pleasure laced with the sharpest edge of pain.

He doesn't move. Not yet. We stay like that, bodies locked, breathless, chests rising and falling in sync. The moment stretches, the tension unbearable.

"Jesus Christ," he hisses through his teeth, eyes locked on the spot where our bodies are joined, watching the way we fit together. "So tight."

I clench around him, and his fingers tighten around my throat, followed by a sharp inhale. His lips twitch into a strained, wicked smile—like he enjoys the torment just as much as I do.

"Remember," I manage to whisper, my mind already slipping into the haze of pleasure. "Not gentle."

The challenge ignites in his eyes. "Not gentle," he repeats, voice pure sin.

Then, without warning, he lifts me by his grip on my throat and hip, controlling every movement, only to slam me back down onto him. The force of it steals my breath, knocks the air from my lungs in a silent scream.

The sensation is devastating. Overwhelming. Pleasure ignites like wildfire as he repeats the motion, dragging me up just to bring me crashing down again, each thrust deeper, harder, more merciless than the last.

The sound of it—the obscene meeting of our bodies—fills the space around us, mingling with our desperate breaths. My head spins, vision swimming at the edges. The pressure of his hold around my throat is a reminder of who is doing this to me as I close my eyes.

"Faster," I rasp, my hands gripping the counter for support as I roll my hips against him, meeting every thrust.

A curse rumbles from his chest before he gives me exactly what I asked for. His movements turn brutal, each snap of his hips tearing through me like a shockwave, leaving me trembling, gasping. He guides me effortlessly, owning every moan that spills from my lips.

The pressure builds, blinding in its intensity, but it's not enough. Not yet. And Silas notices. Of course, he does. His dark gaze drops between us, watching the way my body takes him, his breath shuddering as he devours the sight.

Then his hand slides between us, fingers finding my clit with unerring precision. The sharp pinch sends a bolt of electricity through me, detonating the pressure that's been building.

Pleasure crashes over me in almost painful waves, my body seizing around him, dragging him deeper into my release. Silas lets out a strangled moan as his hands slip beneath the backs of my knees, pulling me closer, spreading me wider, opening me completely for him.

He ruts into me, desperate, possessed—like he's pouring every unspoken word, every ounce of longing from the last three months into my body. It's erratic until finally, he buries himself to the hilt, his entire body going rigid as his release floods through me.

His weight pins me there. Like I'm the only thing keeping him tethered to reality.

Holy fucking shit.

For a few moments, neither of us move. Silas's body is draped over mine, his breath warm against my chest where he rests, each slow exhale fanning over my flushed skin. My back is pressed firm against the cool marble, a stark contrast to the lingering heat still humming through my body.

My fingers slip into his hair, nails dragging lightly over his scalp, and he exhales, his muscles unwinding against me. The hands that once held me with bruising force now soften, his touch slow, reverent.

Eventually, our breathing evens and the fog of ecstasy slowly begins to clear, but neither of us speaks. Silas shifts first, pushing himself upright, but instead of pulling away, he takes me with him. The movement feels effortless, as if gravity bends for him and the world has always tilted to his will.

When we're both upright, his hand slides to my nape, fingers threading through the damp strands at the base of my skull, careful to avoid my injury. He pulls me into a kiss that's slower. Savoring. Like he has all the time in the world to taste me.

My eyes flutter shut, and I let myself sink into him, the lingering spice of his scent, the possessive weight of his hand holding me steady.

As the kiss begins to fade, I can't help myself and catch his bottom lip between my teeth, biting down just enough to make him feel it before releasing him. When I open my eyes, he's already watching me. His gaze glassy and laced with something I can't quite name.

"Those tests were very enlightening," he says, voice rough. The slow, menacing smile that adorns his face sends a jolt of both excitement and dread through me. "I think we're going to need a few more trials."

A laugh slips from me, though it's more air than sound. I try to ignore the way his words settle low in my stomach, stoking embers that haven't fully burned out. "That good, huh?" I tease.

Instead of answering, his hand drifts from my neck to my chin, tilting my face up. His thumb brushes over my lips, pressing lightly, and without thinking, I part them, welcoming him in. He slides the pad of his thumb past my lips. I bite down, not hard, just enough to make his pupils blow wide with something dark and pleased.

But his control doesn't waver. If anything, it sharpens. "Better than good," he murmurs, his tone soft but thick with intent. His thumb presses further, dragging against my tongue. "Maybe enough to ruin me."

CHAPTER 29

The muted warmth of sunlight creeps through the heavy curtains, pooling across the bed like a soft golden blanket. For a moment, there's peace. A fragile, weightless calm that cradles me in unfamiliar comfort. But the faint scent of cedar and linen wraps around me, a quiet reminder of where I am and who I'm with. Memories seep in of what we did in the kitchen and then in this bed, persistent and unyielding.

I sit up, pulling the gray duvet tighter around me, as though it might shield me from the storm brewing in my head. Silas stirs beside me, his body shifting lazily before his hand slides across the bed to rest over my lap. He doesn't bother opening his eyes, his voice thick with sleep.

"Don't do that," he murmurs. "Don't ruin this by overthinking."

"I'm not," I lie, though my voice cracks, betraying me.

One of his eyes opens, blinking against the soft morning light as he props himself up on his elbow. His hair is mussed, a dark halo of unruly curls, and the stubble on his jaw looks darker in the sunlight.

"Yes, you are." He looks at me with a small, knowing smile tugging at the corner of his mouth. "I can see it all over your face."

I look away, but Silas doesn't let me retreat. He leans over, the mattress dipping beneath his weight as his hand slides beneath my back, pulling me down until I'm lying flat. The other hand moves to my hair, his fingers threading through the strands with a gentleness that makes my heart ache.

"Scarlett," he whispers my name, his lips brushing the edge of the injury on my temple. "I like you. Too much, probably. But I want to see where this goes. Just... let me show you what this could be."

I don't say yes, but I don't say no either. Because what can I say? I can't leave, and he knows it. And maybe worse, I don't want to. Not yet. His thumb traces slow, absentminded circles against my back.

"You're safe here," he murmurs, his lips brushing the corner of my jaw with an unhurried tenderness. "With me."

I want to tell him that safe isn't the same as right, that we're teetering on a precipice that promises only ruin. But I don't. Instead, I close my eyes and let myself sink into the warmth of his touch and the quiet reassurance of his voice. His lips find mine, tasting of promise and something more profound than I can name. His hand tightens in my hair, angling my face closer, as his other arm wraps around me, pulling me flush against him.

When he finally pulls back, his mouth hovers just over mine. His breath is warm against my lips as he whispers, "Stay in bed with me for a while."

I laugh softly. "You've already been out of the office for days," I say, brushing a stray curl from his forehead. "You don't have to babysit me. I'll survive if you go back to work."

He groans dramatically, the sound rumbling deep in his chest, and rolls onto his back, pulling me with him so I'm curled against his side. "Don't remind me," he mutters. "If I have to sit through another pointless board meeting, I might lose my mind."

"Pointless?" I tease, tilting my head to look at him. "What's going on over there?"

He sighs, his hand trailing absently along my shoulder. "I missed one yesterday. Apparently, my father decided to throw his weight around like he still runs the place." His jaw tightens, the frustration barely contained.

"What happened?" I ask hesitantly, unsure if I'm treading on dangerous ground.

"The same old story." His tone is clipped. "He undercut me on a vote I've spent months securing. He was the deciding vote and he shot it down, despite backing it two weeks ago. How am I supposed to establish authority if he keeps undermining me at every turn?"

I prop myself up slightly, resting my chin on my hand as I study him. "When is he officially stepping down?"

"At the end of the year," Silas says, quiet but firm. "And not a moment too soon. He runs everything like it's still the nineties, refusing to adapt or listen. I want to make the changes this company needs, but he's fighting me every step of the way."

There's a weight to his words, an edge that tells me there's more than he's letting on. I trail my fingers lightly across his bicep, offering what little comfort I can. "You'll get your chance soon," I murmur. "And then you'll make it better."

His hand cups my face, guiding my gaze to his. The intensity in his eyes sends a pang through my chest, but then his lips curve into a small, genuine smile. "Thank you," he says softly, before leaning in to kiss me again.

We fall into a comfortable rhythm after that, neither of us in a rush to leave the sanctuary of the bed. The minutes stretch into an hour, the light shifting across the room as we talk about nothing and everything. Silas lies on his back, one arm tucked behind his head, while I rest on my stomach, propped on my elbows, tracing idle patterns along his chest with my fingertips.

The air between us is light and easy with the outside world temporarily forgotten. For the first time in weeks, I let myself relax, surrendering to the quiet intimacy of this moment. I know it won't last. There's no place for this when there are consequences waiting beyond this room. But for now, I let myself have it.

Eventually, Silas rolls, glancing at the clock on the nightstand. "If I don't get up now, I never will."

"You make it sound like that's a problem," I tease, falling back to bury my face in the pillow with a sigh.

He chuckles softly and leans over, pressing a lingering kiss to the sensitive space just below my ear, his lips warm against my skin.

I feel the bed shift as he slides out from under the duvet, the absence of his warmth immediate and unwelcome. I peek up from the pillow just in time to see him stretching, his broad shoulders rolling as his arms reach toward the ceiling.

Holding out his hand to me, he says, "Join me for a shower."

I raise an eyebrow, feigning indifference even as my heart skips a beat. "Is that an invitation or a command?"

His lips curve into a sultry grin, his hand still extended. "Take it however you like. Either way, I'm not leaving this room without you." His gaze never wavers and I savor the way he watches me as I take his hand, the oversized t-shirt I stole from his drawer rides up, baring more of my thighs as I rise to stand.

Silas leads me into the bathroom, and I'm struck by its sheer elegance. The warm glow of recessed lighting dances across marble floors that stretch out like liquid gold, and the soft curves of the freestanding tub catch the light in a way that feels almost ethereal. Large mirrors framed in brushed bronze reflect the double sinks, each adorned with delicate vases of flowers I'm sure are replaced every few days.

Without a word, he guides me forward to the large shower on the far end, his lips brushing my nape as he reaches past me to turn it on. Water cascades down in a perfect, soothing stream from the ceiling.

When I turn back toward him, he's a few steps away, stripping his legs of his sweatpants, and his shirt already discarded on the floor. With his attention elsewhere, I take a moment to admire him in the daylight.

Silas is the kind of man you can't help but notice; all tall, lean power. There's a faint trail of dark hair starting just below his navel, leading downward that feels deliberately tempting. A thin scar curves along his ribs and to his torso, barely visible beneath the tattoo I hadn't been able to see in its entirety in the daylight until now.

It's a compass rendered in fine black and gray ink. Each of the four cardinal directions is carved in elegant, serif-style lettering, and needle points slightly off-center, suggesting a departure from the expected path. Surrounding the compass are fractured cracks, inked in a way that makes them appear as though they're radiating outward from the center, like shattered glass.

When I lift my eyes to his again, his lips twitch into a knowing smirk. "See something you like?" He teases as he steps out of his sweatpants entirely. My cheeks flush, but I don't look away. I'm too far gone to pretend otherwise.

I take a step forward, my fingers skimming over the tattoo on his side, tracing the edges. "What does it mean?" My voice is quieter than I expect.

A wry chuckle escapes him as he places his hand over mine, holding me against his warm skin. "It's a reminder," he says simply. "That even when I was forced onto a path I didn't choose, I could still find my own way." His fingers flex as he looks down. "I got it in college when I was feeling particularly rebellious. My parents hated it." His grin turns sharp at the last part, but there's something else there too.

My gaze shifts to his sleeve, taking in the beautiful landscape that stretches the length of his arm. "And this?"

His expression changes and hesitates, just for a second, before turning his arm slightly so I can see it better.

"This is a place I used to go with my mother when I was a kid," he says, his voice rougher now. "Lofoten, in Norway. She loved it there."

The tattoo is a sweeping landscape that starts at his wrist—a river winding through a valley, the water dark and endless—before climbing to jagged, snow-capped mountains near his shoulder. The peaks are stark against a pale sky, inked in delicate gradients of black and gray.

"She always said it was the one place that felt untouched," he continues, his voice quieter now. "No city noise. No obligations. Just... peace." His thumb brushes absently over the river, as if tracing its path. "She took us every year until she couldn't anymore."

I don't ask when that was. I already know.

I look at this piece of her he carries with him, inked into his skin like a permanent keepsake. "That's a really beautiful way to honor her," I say softly, meaning every word.

His gaze flicks to mine, searching, like he's waiting for something else. Pity, maybe. But there's none of that in me. Just understanding.

Whatever he sees on my face makes something in him snap.

His fingers slip beneath the hem of my shirt, his jaw tight as if restraining something within him. "Come here," he murmurs the command. With practiced ease, he strips the fabric over my head, leaving me bare beneath his hungry gaze.

I barely have a second to catch my breath before he's guiding me backward into the shower, like he knows exactly how he plans to have me. His mouth is on mine before the water even touches us.

The warm spray cascades over our heads, steam curling around our entwined bodies like a cocoon, blurring the edges of reality. Silas's hands roam my skin with reverence as he traces every curve and dip. As if he's committing me to memory.

I melt into him, fingers dragging over the hard planes of his chest, his skin slick and hot beneath my palms. The muscles beneath my touch flex in response and a quiet shudder ripples through him as I press closer, as if the space between us is offensive.

I don't care that my steri-strips are soaked. All I care about is this and the overwhelming, all-consuming need to crawl under his skin and stay there.

Without hesitation, I sink to my knees, the warm water now cascading over Silas's back, wrapping us in steam and heat. My hands glide over his hips, slow, teasing, before wrapping around the thick base of his cock. My fingers tighten, just enough to test him, just enough to make his breath hitch. A sharp inhale, a shuddered exhale.

I drag my tongue along the sensitive vein that runs the length of him, tracing a slow, deliberate path to the tip. When I reach the head, I press my tongue against it, savoring the faint taste of him—salt and musk and something uniquely Silas. The flavor spreads across my tongue, sending a jolt of heat through me.

Silas groans, the sound vibrating through the small space, curling around us with the steam. One of his hands slams against the shower wall, steadying himself, while the other buries into my wet hair, fingers threading deep, tugging just enough to remind me who's in control.

But he doesn't push. He waits.

I hollow my cheeks, letting him feel every slick, heated inch of my mouth. He fills me completely and each time I pull back, it's only to torture, to leave him wanting—to watch his control fray at the edges.

"Scar," he rasps, his voice little more than gravel.

God, I'd never wished Scarlett was my real name more than right now.

Still, a rush of satisfaction floods me, spurring me on, and I take him deeper, pushing my limits and his. His hips jerk slightly, restraint thinning with every slow drag of my tongue, every hollowed breath around him.

But just as I settle into a rhythm, his grip in my hair tightens. Not rough. Not punishing. But decisive. With a sharp tug, he pulls me back and I look up at him.

Water beads along his skin, slipping down the sharp lines of his jaw, his chest rising and falling in heaving breaths.

Before I can process the shift, he hauls me to my feet, a hand locked under my jaw, the other gripping my hip. The world spins as he lifts me, pressing my back against the tiles. Instinctively, my legs wrap around his waist, locking him in place.

Silas aligns himself with me, pressing the thick head of his cock against my entrance. My breath hitches, anticipation thrumming in my veins. His eyes meet mine—starving, merciless. Like he plans to devour me whole.

He shifts beneath me, guiding me into place before he thrusts up in one smooth, powerful motion. A strangled cry rips from my throat, my head falling back, fingers clawing at his shoulders as he fills me completely.

His movements are relentless. Each thrust is intentional, forcing me to take all of him, to feel the full weight of whatever this is between us. It's intoxicating, searing, leaving no space for thought.

"You feel so fucking good," he grunts, his voice rough, unsteady, barely tethered to control. His gaze drops between us, dark and molten, watching the way my body swallows him.

The sight alone is too much.

"More," I whimper, my heels digging into his back, urging him deeper.

His eyes flick up, locking onto mine and blacker than I've ever seen them. The next thrust is brutal, devastating, and the sound that spills from my lips only encourages him.

"Perfect," he breathes, almost like I'm unraveling him in ways he never expected.

His rhythm shifts, his movements turning precise, like a hunter finding his mark. He angles his hips just right, dragging me higher with every stroke, making sure I feel him everywhere as he pulls me to the edge. It's a slow, torturous climb until pleasure coils so tightly that I can't hold back any longer.

I come apart with a muffled cry, my release rushing over me in blinding, pulse-shattering waves. My nails dig into the taut muscles of his back, entire body trembling around him as I ride the high.

Silas follows moments later, his pace faltering, grip tightening, fingers digging in as his jaw goes slack. With one final, desperate thrust, he buries himself deep, pressing me harder against the wall as he comes undone.

My name falls from his lips like a surrender, his forehead dropping to the crook of my neck as he shudders through the last remnants of pleasure.

We untangle slowly, the moment stretching between us as the warm water beats down, washing away the sweat and passion. With an easy strength, he lowers me to my feet, but the moment I sway, his hold tightens, steadying me. His smirk is nothing short of smug as he watches me find my footing, eyes dark with satisfaction, knowing exactly what he's done to me.

Then, without prompting, Silas reaches for the body wash and pours a generous amount into his hands before trailing them over my skin. There's a quiet intimacy in the way he touches me, and I return the gesture, my hands moving over his chest and shoulders, tracing the lines of his tattoos and the faint scar along his ribs. We take out time like this, not a word spoken.

When we're both clean and wrapped in fluffy white towels, I persuade Silas back to reality, reminding him that we both have work waiting for us. Reluctantly, he agrees that he could spend a few hours in his study. With a lingering kiss, he releases me and watches as I slip out of the bathroom. Quietly, I make my way across the hallway to the guest room and lock the door behind me.

My mind is still spinning, a mess of contradictions and emotions I can't untangle. I need space, clarity, anything to pull me back to center. Forcing myself to move, I dress quickly, pulling on jeans and a t-shirt. As I tug the fabric over my head, my phone lights up on the nightstand I left it on the night before. Even from a distance, I recognize the number flashing across the screen: Luis.

The last time we spoke, I wasn't sure how far he'd get, especially with the limited information I could provide. I grab the phone, rushing into the bathroom and shutting the door behind me as I answer.

"Lu?" I say, my voice tight with anticipation. "Tell me you have some good news."

There's no preamble. "Depends on your definition of 'good'," Luis says, his voice low and rough, as though he hasn't slept. "We've made progress, but it's... complicated."

I perch myself on the edge of the claw foot tub, clutching the phone tighter. "Who's 'we'?" I ask, suspicion creeping into my tone.

He exhales sharply, the sound static in my ear. "You were right. The encryptions were a nightmare. I pulled in some friends—experts in cryptography. We managed to decrypt some of those files you flagged in their cloud. The bad news is it's fragmented as hell. Someone went to extreme lengths to split the data apart and bury it under layers."

"What's the good news?" I ask, bracing for an answer I already know won't bring comfort.

Luis exhales, his voice dropping lower, as if he fears someone might overhear. "The files mention something called 'secondary operations.' It's frustratingly vague. Whoever designed this system went to extreme lengths to ensure no one could easily figure out what it is."

I swallow hard, my thoughts spinning. "Secondary operations," I repeat, the words foreign and heavy in my mouth. "Do we know what it refers to? Is it a department, a project...?"

Luis hesitates, his frustration evident. "Not exactly. There are scattered mentions of encrypted servers but no concrete details about their locations or access points. The language is so obscure it's practically unreadable. Placeholder terms, internal codes, references to protocols... nothing clear. It's like trying to solve a puzzle when you're missing half the pieces."

My fingers press into my temples, the familiar weight of exhaustion creeping over me. I was right: the servers have to house the information Peter is after, and I'd still bet my life they're located in the satellite office Natalie mentioned. "So, that's what he wants; details on these secondary operations," I murmur, straightening slightly.

Luis doesn't respond immediately, letting the silence stretch for a beat. "I can't imagine he's looking for anything else," he finally says.

Whatever this is, it's big. Big enough to justify the level of encryption Luis and his team are struggling to crack. Big enough that Peter, ruthless and methodical, is willing to move mountains in the most chaotic way to get his hands on it.

"Can you tell who has access to the files you've decrypted so far?" I ask, the question spilling from my lips before I can fully form it.

"Not yet," Luis replies, irritation bleeding into his tone. "The permissions are layered in a way that makes it almost impossible to identify users without breaking through additional encryption. Whoever set this up wasn't playing around."

I drop my head into my hands, the heels pressing against my eyes. My thoughts circle back to Davey. As head of their IT team, he must be aware of the encrypted files' existence. But does he know their contents? The idea sends a cold wave rolling through me. Davey is a straight arrow, the kind of guy who sticks to the rules, no matter what. He's loyal to Wells, but I can't imagine he'd knowingly put his wife at risk.

It's not uncommon for IT professionals to secure sensitive data without knowing what's inside—especially when strict confidentiality policies are in place. Davey seems like someone who wouldn't ask questions if he was told not to. But if that's true, then the responsibility of knowing rests higher up the chain.

Luis's voice pulls me out of my spiraling thoughts. "You still with me?"

"Yeah," I say quickly, though my head feels like it's spinning with too many unanswered questions. "If it's not Davey, then..." My voice trails off, my mind shifting to the man who casts a shadow over everything at Wells Corp. William. The one who holds all the strings.

What is he hiding? And why has he gone to such lengths to keep it buried? It can't be good. You don't build encryption this deep for charity work or harmless side projects. Unless... unless others know about it, too. People William would trust, like his sons.

My gaze drifts to the door as unease crawls up my spine. Memories of Silas from this morning flash through my mind—his frustration with his father, his desire to take over and fix things. Could this be what he was referring to? Is this the problem he wants to solve once William steps down? Or was he talking about something else entirely?

I chew the inside of my cheek, my chest tightening. If Silas knows about this, would he allow it to happen? Would he cover it up, justify it somehow? Or is he just as much in the dark as Davey?

The thought that Silas might be complicit in whatever this is sends a sharp pang through me, but I shove it aside. No. Silas wouldn't willingly endanger people—especially not Natalie or Davey. But if he doesn't know, what will happen when he finds out? And what will I do if it comes down to choosing between telling him the truth and walking away?

Luis interrupts my spiraling thoughts again, his voice low and urgent. "Marilyn, whatever this is, it's bigger than we thought. If Peter's willing to kill for it, imagine what the people behind it will do to keep it hidden."

"I know," I whisper, the words barely audible, their weight suffocating. But now that I've gotten a glimpse of the edges of this thing and what it might mean if Peter gets his hands on it, there's no turning back. I can't unsee it.

Luis lets out a defeated sigh. He knows what my response means; that I won't walk away. "I'll keep digging, but you need to be careful," he says, his tone heavy with concern. "Peter's dangerous, but so is whoever built this system. These aren't people you can outmaneuver on a whim."

"I'll be fine," I say automatically, but the words ring hollow, even to me. I've repeated them so many times now they've lost all meaning, a mantra I chant to keep myself upright. "Keep me updated."

"Will do," he replies after a pause, the hesitation in his voice unmissable. Then the line goes dead.

The silence that follows is deafening, amplifying the weight pressing down on my chest. I lower the phone into my lap.

William. Silas. Davey. Jeremy. Their names loop through my head, growing louder with every beat of my racing heart. If William orchestrated all of this, how much does Silas really know? How deep does his loyalty run? Is Jeremy part of this tangled web, or is he just another pawn? And Davey—if he's protecting these files without knowing the truth, how much danger is he unknowingly putting himself and Natalie in?

I have more questions than answers, and that alone should be reason enough to keep Silas at bay. But even now, I know it's pointless. As long as I'm here, he's a force I can't ignore. A pull I'm clearly powerless to resist.

Chapter 30

O ver the next few weeks, life settles into a strange rhythm. Each day blends into the next, the quiet routine of Silas's house is both comforting and suffocating at the same time. The morning after Luis called with updates on the decrypted files, I somehow convinced Silas to return to the office. It wasn't easy, but I reassured him I'd be fine. Truthfully, I needed the space to figure out just how much Silas knows about William's secrets, and having him here all day made it impossible to think clearly.

Meanwhile, Silas and Davey have grown increasingly frustrated with the lack of progress in finding my attacker. Their tension is palpable, building with each passing day. Every evening, I watch Silas's jaw clench when their daily reports come in with no new developments, aside from the limited footage they managed to obtain of the path where the attacker took me. I sit there quietly, pretending to share their concern, while guilt churns in my gut.

Talks of me finding a new apartment have been completely tabled. Silas is adamant that I stay under his roof until my attacker is found, and I haven't even fought him on it. Luis was right: Peter won't risk exposing himself by coming after me while I'm here, under constant watch. So, when Silas told me he wanted me to wait before signing a new lease, I conceded. It was easier than arguing.

I also reluctantly agreed to the rest of his security measures, the most notable being that someone from his team accompanies me whenever I leave the house. Cillian is the one who usually shadows me. He drives me everywhere I need to go and keeps a watchful, silent presence nearby. Because of this, I've kept my outings minimal. Most of my time is spent between Silas's house and visiting Natalie at her home. She's under the same security measures as I am, though she accepts them with far less resistance.

This past Monday, I finally returned to the gym to train with Jeff after getting cleared by Dr. Carrow; with restrictions, of course. I hadn't expected Jeff to be thrilled about my long absence, but his reaction caught me off guard. He grilled me, demanding to know where I'd been and why I hadn't called. When I told him about how his training had saved my life, his anger deflated almost instantly. Still, he gave me a sharp, knowing look when I mentioned that my attacker hadn't been caught and only had a half-assed explanation of why I was targeted by this "random" man. Training felt good, though. Even with Cillian looming at the edge of the gym like a watchful shadow, it felt familiar, like I was reclaiming a part of myself I thought I'd lost.

Despite everything else going on, there are moments where life with Silas feels almost... normal. As if we were always meant to exist this way. Silas wakes up several hours before me to workout in the basement and is at the office until the evening. During the day, I work from the guest room, collaborating with Luis on decoding the files. Progress is agonizingly slow, but it's something. By the time Silas gets home, we've fallen into a routine: dinners at the kitchen island, conversations about his work and the changes he wants to make when he takes over Wells, late nights watching movies in the attic, and long, lingering kisses that start innocently enough but always end with us tangled in his bed.

He's thoughtful in ways I hadn't expected, like calling between meetings to check in or surprising me with my favorite takeout when I'm too distracted to eat. His edges are still sharp, but Natalie was right: Silas *is* good. He's better than I gave him credit for. The more time I spend with him, the more convinced I am that he doesn't know what's hidden on those servers. I can't imagine the Silas I've come to know being complicit in whatever his father is doing. He's too principled, too loyal to the people he cares about.

And yet, no matter how certain I feel, that lingering doubt never fully disappears because I've never had something this good without it slipping through my fingers. Nothing in my life has ever stayed untouched by betrayal or consequence, and I don't know how to believe this will be any different. It's the last thread holding me back, the one thing keeping the truth locked inside me. Because if I'm wrong, if I misjudged him, it could seal my fate. If Silas decides I'm too much of a risk, this knowledge could die with me.

Yesterday, Silas surprised me with a last-minute request to attend a gala with him. The way he mentioned it over dinner made it clear he wasn't exactly excited about the event. It's hosted by one of the city's most influential families to support the expansion of medical access to underserved communities. He explained that he hadn't intended to go, but he learned earlier in the day that his entire family would be in attendance and decided it was important for him to be there as well.

The tension in his voice when he mentioned his father was unmistakable, but I didn't press him, because despite everything, I can't seem to say no to Silas. Not when he looks at me like he did when he asked.

Now, as I blink away the spots in my vision from the flurry of photographers outside, the grand entrance of the gala stretches before us. The towering downtown building is a masterpiece of elegance, its arched doorway framed by cascading lights that shimmer like stars. Silas's hand rests lightly at the small of my back, guiding me forward. His touch is a quiet reassurance as we step into the lavish event space. The soft hum of conversations mingles with the gentle notes of a string quartet, the faint scent of roses and champagne wafting around us.

Men in tailored suits and women in flowing gowns glide effortlessly across the floor, their movements fluid and rehearsed. This world isn't foreign to me anymore; not the polished grandeur, the staged smiles, or the subtle glances sweeping over every arrival. My pulse quickens, but not because of the attention we attract. I'm used to the hushed whispers and speculative looks that follow Silas wherever he goes. No, it's the knowledge that William Wells is somewhere in this room, and I'll have to interact with him knowing everything I'm trying to uncover.

A waiter approaches with a tray of bubbling champagne flutes, lowering it in front of us with a practiced smile. Silas and I each take a glass, murmuring our thanks before the waiter moves on. I catch two women nearby, close to my age, blatantly staring at Silas. I don't blame them. He looks beautiful in a tuxedo perfectly molded to his body, his dark curls styled just enough to be polished without losing their natural edge. His glasses catch the light, the sharp frames accentuating the piercing intensity of his gaze.

Turning to him, I clink my glass lightly against his, the crystal ringing softly between us. His palm remains a brand at the small of my back, even through the crimson fabric of my dress. The asymmetrical neckline and cut-out at my waist feel elegant, but the way Silas's eyes rake over my body makes the dress feel like less of a statement piece and more of a weapon forged specifically against him. His gaze lingers as he takes a slow sip of champagne, his dark eyes smoldering.

I smirk, raising an eyebrow. "Can I help you with something?"

His lips curve into a filthy smile as he leans in closer, his breath brushing the shell of my ear. "You already are," he murmurs, his hand pressing more firmly against me. "But if you're offering, I can think of a few things."

A sudden flush of heat washes over me. I give him a pointed look, trying to mask the way my heartbeat picks up. Silas chuckles, low and quiet, taking another sip of his drink as his gaze sweeps the room.

But then his attention shifts, and I catch the subtle tightening of his jaw. I follow his line of sight and hear it before I see it. A distantly familiar voice, loud and dripping with exaggerated amusement. The blonde woman I've only seen in passing at previous events is holding court a few feet away, theatrically discussing my now infamous date at the Gilded Sear. Her words are laced with ridicule as she wonders aloud if I'm "seeing two men at the same time." And the women around her laugh.

The delicious warmth from Silas's previous comment simmers into something hotter. My hands twitch at my sides, but instead of turning toward her and risking a scene, I rest my palm on the elbow of the arm wrapped around my waist, the touch deliberate and possessive. Silas's gaze flickers down to me at the movement, his expression softening just slightly.

"You look handsome," I whisper, my fingers brushing over the smooth fabric of his tux jacket. "Like, distractingly handsome."

The compliment seems to snap Silas out of his thoughts. His eyes lower to mine, the remaining tension in his face melts away, lips curving into a smile. Full, genuine, and so beautiful it makes my toes curl in my heels.

Releasing his hold on my waist, he takes my hand, and lifts it to his lips, kissing the pulse point on my wrist.

"And you," he says against my skin, his voice a quiet rumble that sends a shiver down my spine, "are breathtaking."

The warmth of Silas's mouth remains, even after he pulls away. For a fleeting moment, I almost forget we're standing in the middle of a crowded room filled with sharp eyes and sharper tongues. But the reprieve is short-lived. His gaze moves past me, his posture stiffening ever so slightly.

I follow his line of sight and immediately spot them: his siblings and William, clustered together near a group of important-looking attendees. Natalie's bright smile lights up the space effortlessly as she chats animatedly with someone I don't recognize. Davey stands beside her, his expression more reserved, though there's a kind smile on his face. Jeremy is mid-conversation with William and another man, gesturing subtly as he speaks. William, ever the patriarch, listens with an air of authority, nodding occasionally. The man they're speaking to looks captivated, his gaze flicking between William and Jeremy like he's absorbing every word.

Silas exhales softly beside me, his fingers sliding into mine. "Looks like it's time to play nice," he murmurs, his tone dry. "Come on."

As we weave through the crowd toward his family, I can feel the tension radiating off him. He doesn't have to say it, but I know the last board meeting, where William publicly undermined him, still lingers like an open wound. I squeeze his hand lightly, hoping the gesture will offer him some measure of reassurance.

William is the first to notice our approach. His sharp brown eyes flick to Silas, then to me, and his lips curl into a practiced smile. It's polite, almost warm, but there's a detachment that feels like it's been fine-tuned for public appearances.

"Silas," William greets smoothly, his voice laced with paternal familiarity. His attention shifts to me, and the smile widens just enough to feel deliberate. "Scarlett. I'm glad to see you looking better. I trust you're recovering well."

The air stills, just for a moment, as his words settle. Of course, William would be aware of the attack, even if the marks are no longer visible on my face. He's too deeply involved in his family's affairs not to know, especially with Davey working alongside Silas to identify the culprit. But the knowledge feels heavy in my chest, like it's being wielded as a subtle reminder of how closely he watches everything. I return his smile, careful to keep my tone neutral.

"I'm much better, thank you," I reply, my voice steady. "It was a difficult few weeks, but Silas has been incredibly supportive."

William's gaze lingers on me for a beat too long, and something flickers in his eyes. It's quick, almost imperceptible, but distinctly calculating. Like he's weighing every word I've just said. Then, he turns back to Silas, his expression unreadable.

"My son, ever the protector," he says, his tone light but pointed.

The comment feels like a double-edged sword, cutting at both ends. Is it a jab at Silas's need to step into roles William sees as unnecessary? Or is it a backhanded compliment? Either way, the tension in Silas's hand as it

302

tightens around mine tells me he's not thrilled. I part my lips to respond, but Natalie's voice cuts through the moment, bright and disarming.

"There you are!" Natalie exclaims, breaking away from her conversation with a radiant smile and pulling me into a warm hug. The scent of her light and floral perfume fills the space between us. "You look incredible. How do you always make it look so easy?"

I laugh softly, her warm voice easing some of the tightness in my chest. "I could ask you the same thing," I reply, letting the natural rhythm of our friendship take over. I glance at her glass, using it as an excuse to steer the conversation away from William. "What are you drinking?"

She grins, holding up her glass with a mock flourish. "Some sort of elderflower champagne concoction. Want me to grab you one?"

I shake my head, smiling. "Maybe later. I'm still working on this one."

Natalie laughs, lifting her glass in a playful toast before returning to her conversation. Davey gives me a polite nod, his expression measured, while Silas exchanges a brief handshake with him. Jeremy offers a faint smile before re-engaging with the man he and William had been speaking to. With everyone momentarily distracted, Silas takes the opportunity to guide me away, his hand finding its place at the small of my back once again.

We move through the crowd seamlessly, exchanging pleasantries with other guests as we go. Silas's presence is magnetic, drawing attention wherever we stop. He keeps me close, his hand never straying far from mine or my waist, a quiet but undeniable claim. The warmth of his touch is steadying, even as the din of the room threatens to overwhelm.

When my champagne glass empties, I lean toward him, touching his arm lightly to get his attention. "I'm going to run to the restroom," I say, offering a small smile. "I'll meet you back here."

He nods, taking the empty glass from my hand without question. "Take your time," he says, his voice low and even.

I step away, weaving through the crowd toward the hallway lined with restrooms. As I move, I can still feel the weight of Silas's gaze, a tether that anchors me even as I put distance between us.

The noise of the gala fades behind the heavy restroom door, replaced by the muffled echo of my heels on polished marble as I move toward the sink. The quiet sanctuary is a welcome reprieve from the chaos outside, the warm lighting and cool surfaces offering a moment to collect myself. I smooth my dress, reapply a bit of lipstick, and meet my own gaze in the mirror, willing my heartbeat to slow.

When I step back into the hallway, the distant hum of the party barely registers. The corridor is empty except for one figure standing just a few feet away, leaning casually against the wall. William.

His posture is deceptively relaxed, hands tucked into his pockets, but his sharp eyes track my every move with precision. My instincts scream at me to keep walking, to ignore whatever he's about to say. But something about his stillness demands attention, pulling me forward.

"Scarlett," he greets, his voice calm and almost cordial. The faint smile on his lips doesn't reach his eyes. "I thought I might find you here. Taking a moment to escape the chaos?"

It's not really a question and the subtle undertone of scrutiny is impossible to miss. But I still force a polite smile, keeping my voice measured. "Just a quick break. It's been a busy evening."

William hums, a noncommittal sound as he straightens to rock slightly on his heels. "I have to admit, I was surprised when Silas told me he was bringing you tonight. He isn't one to use the same date twice."

The barb slices cleanly through the air between us but I refuse to let the insult land. Instead, I tilt my head slightly, letting the smile linger on my lips. "Maybe I'm the exception."

His smile hardens, though his gaze remains cool. "Perhaps. But I must say, you've made quite an impression on my family in a remarkably short time. First, there's your... unfortunate accident, then Natalie suddenly needs heightened security, and Silas is consumed with playing the hero." He pauses before delivering the final blow. "And you, Scarlett. You have a real talent for finding yourself at the center of it all, don't you?"

The calm mask I've been wearing threatens to crack under the weight of his insinuations. My mind races, panic flashing like a warning light. Does he know? Has he pieced together why I'm really here?

But his tone is too measured, his words too carefully vague. He's not accusing me outright. He's testing me, watching for a slip, a tell.

I latch onto the simplest assumption, the one that serves both of our purposes: he thinks I'm a gold digger. I let out a light laugh, as though his comment amuses me rather than infuriates me. "I promise, William, I'm not trying to shake up your family. Being in the middle of things just kind of... happened. Not exactly something I planned."

"Is that so?" he asks, his tone calm but cool, the hint of a smirk playing on his lips. "Because from where I'm standing, it all seems rather convenient. A sudden accident, Silas rushing to your side, and now you're living with him and fully integrated into a world most people would kill to be part of."

I meet his gaze head-on, summoning every ounce of composure I have. My smile doesn't falter, but there's steel in my voice now. "With all due respect, I don't need Silas or anyone else to integrate me into anything. I've done quite well for myself long before I met him."

His expression shifts, his smile tightening as he takes a step closer, his presence looming without being overtly threatening. "And yet, here you are."

"And yet, here I am," I echo, lifting my chin. "Because I care about Silas."

The silence that follows stretches thin, taut as a wire. William studies me, his sharp gaze flicking over my face as if cataloging every nuance of my expression. My heart pounds in my chest, each beat reverberating in my ears, but I hold his stare without flinching.

"Well," he finally says, his tone clipped, the faint smile never leaving his lips. "I suppose time will tell."

"Is there a problem here?"

I turn toward the sound, my heart leaping as Silas approaches with long, purposeful strides. His expression is calm, but his eyes burn with

305

barely restrained anger. Before I can blink, he's at my side, his hand settling firmly on my hip. The gesture is subtle but unmistakable: a warning and a reassurance all at once.

William's polished smile doesn't falter, though I notice the brief flicker of something colder in his eyes as he meets his son's gaze. "Not at all," he replies smoothly. "Scarlett and I were just having a friendly conversation."

Silas's fingers flex slightly against my side, his voice a controlled, razor-sharp edge. "Funny," he says evenly. "It didn't sound friendly, *Dad*."

William shrugs, the picture of indifference. "Just a misunderstanding, I'm sure." As he finishes the words, he steps forward and pats Silas's shoulder. The gesture is light and almost paternal, but intentionally crosses the invisible boundary Silas has placed between him and me.

Silas doesn't move, doesn't respond. The tension between them is a silent battle of wills that feels far older than this moment. The Wells patriarch only lingers a moment longer. He withdraws his hand, straightens his cuffs with an air of nonchalance, and steps back, leaving the friction simmering in his wake.

Once William is out of sight, the breath I'd been holding escapes me in a shaky exhale, and my shoulders sag slightly as the weight of the encounter begins to lift. Silas turns to me immediately, his hand at my side tightening as he searches my face.

"Are you okay?" His voice is softer now, the anger from moments ago replaced by concern.

I nod quickly, forcing a smile. "I'm fine. Really. Thank you."

He studies me for a moment longer, his brow furrowing, as if he doesn't entirely believe me. Then, with a gentle squeeze at my waist, his expression softens. "Come on," he murmurs. "Let's get out of this hallway."

Silas guides me back toward the ballroom. The hum of the gala wraps around us as we step inside, the music swelling and mingling with the murmur of laughter and conversation. I find myself clinging to him just a little tighter, my fingers brushing against his wrist to keep him close. He leads me directly to the dance floor just as a new song is about to begin.

Without a word, Silas takes my hand and pulls me into a waltz, his other hand resting gently on my waist. Quickly, the room blurs around us, the crowd and their watchful eyes fading into the background as his focus remains solely on me. He doesn't speak, only guides me through the dance with effortless precision, his grip steady, though I can tell he's grappling with what he wants to say to me.

Only a minute into the waltz, I can't stand the silence between us any longer. "Thank you for standing up for me," I whisper, my voice barely audible over the music. I hesitate, struggling to find the right words. "I hope you know that what he said... I don't..."

"Stop," Silas interrupts gently, his voice firm as he slows our movements. We come to a complete stop on the outskirts of the dance floor, his hands releasing me to frame my face. His thumbs brush against the sides of my jaw as he holds my gaze, his dark eyes steady and unrelenting. "You don't need to justify yourself to him or anyone else. I know who you are, Scar. I see *you*."

The weight of his words hits me like a tidal wave, threatening to sweep me under. My throat tightens, and I blink hard, fighting back the sting of tears. Every part of me aches to tell him the truth—to let him see me for who I really am—but fear holds me hostage.

Silas's hands linger on my neck, his thumbs brushing lightly against my jaw. For a moment, it feels like he's on the verge of saying something, but he doesn't. His lips press together, and he exhales sharply through his nose, the sound heavy with frustration.

"Scarlett," he says, his voice strained, like he's forcing the words out. "I—" he stops, looks away for a moment, then meets my gaze again, his eyes blazing with conviction. "I'm in this. You and me. I want this."

The simplicity of his words gut me. He's choosing me without hesitation. Without fear. It's overwhelming, and the ache of knowing I can't choose him back feels like it's tearing me in two.

I open my mouth to respond, to say something. Anything. But the words won't come. Instead, I lean into his touch, my voice breaking as I whisper, "Silas..."

"Just know it," he says, his grip on me unfaltering. "That's all I need you to do. Just know it."

The music swells around us, seeming to match the rhythm of my own racing heart. Silas doesn't wait for me to respond. Instead, he leans in, his lips brushing against mine in a kiss that feels like a declaration. He doesn't care who's watching or what they might think. His thumbs caress my cheeks as his mouth moves against mine, slow and achingly tender, taking his time savoring me.

His words replay in my mind, over and over, as guilt and warmth battle for space in my chest. And for now, just for a little while longer, I let the warmth win.

CHAPTER 31

S **ilas:** Have you seen the photos from the gala?

My thumbs hover over the keyboard, hesitating before I finally type a response.

Me: No. Why? Should I?
Silas: You should. Look them up.

I bite my lip, dread and curiosity warring inside me. Something about the way he says it feels like I'm walking into a trap, but I still pull my laptop onto my thighs, open a new browser, and type "Carter Annual Gala" into the search bar. My stomach flips as the results load. The headlines jump out at me.

Silas Wells and Mystery Date Steal the Show at Annual Gala
A Romantic Waltz for Wells and His New Partner

My chest tightens as I click the first article, and there we are. Photo after photo of the two of us at the event.

Silas walking beside me, his hand splayed protectively against the small of my back as we entered. Silas and I laughing with his friend Gordon, my smile brighter than I remember it feeling. Silas guiding me across the dance floor, his expression softened in a way that's undeniably intimate. And then the kiss.

His hands cradle my face, his lips pressing against mine with a gentleness that borders on reverence. Around us, the other dancers blur into streaks of color and motion, their forms indistinct, as though we were the only ones who mattered. The photo captures everything I've been trying to deny, laid bare for the world to see.

Further down, there are older photos from the silent auction in March, paired with speculative headlines suggesting we've been in a secret relationship all along. This time, however, they've identified Scarlett Page. The articles dive into her life, breaking it down into succinct, impersonal bullet points. The words feel clinical, like they're dissecting a version of me I barely recognize anymore.

My phone buzzes in my hand, snapping me back to reality. Another text from Silas.

Silas: What do you think?

I blink, trying to gather my thoughts. I sit up on the guest room chair I've been sunk into for hours, contemplating my words. But all I can manage is the truth.

Me: I think I don't love the whole world speculating about my life.

His reply comes faster than I expect.

Silas: That's not what I asked.

I pause, my heartbeat quickening.

Me: What do YOU think?
Silas: I like them. They make it clear.

I blink, my brow furrowing, and type back quickly.

Me: Clear?
Silas: That you're mine.

A short, disbelieving laugh escapes me. I shake my head, typing back with a smirk.

Me: That's very caveman of you.
Silas: Very.
Me: You don't care at all, do you?
Silas: When it comes to you? Never.

The ache that's been growing in my heart only deepens as I reread his response. For all his arrogance and bravado, there's an undeniable truth to the way he claims me, unashamed and unflinching.

My fingers move on their own, typing out a confession before I can overthink it.

Me: You know, I wasn't lying when I said how handsome you looked.

The response takes a little longer this time.

Silas: Good. I wasn't lying either.

My lips twitch despite myself, and I lock my phone, leaning back against the seat. Beneath the browser tab I just closed, several terminal windows and programs are running, most of them tools Luis and his friends Ben and Corey set up to help with decryption. The scripts are efficient but not mine, so I've been reverse-engineering them to make sense of the process. Some of the metadata hints at something connected to New Mexico, but we're not sure what yet.

This process has been like dismantling a minefield—tedious and dangerous if we overlook even a single line of corrupted data. Progress has been slow, but Luis thinks we're close, and I do too.

My phone pings, but it's not the familiar sound of a text message; it's my email. I freeze. Since the alley attack, I've created new accounts for everything, including a new email. I meticulously went through all my important accounts, changing login details to this new email or canceling them entirely. No one has this address besides Luis and he has yet to use it for any reason.

I open the app, and my stomach drops. An anonymous email glares back at me like a ghost materializing from my past.

Subject: Are you having fun playing house?

The body is nearly empty, save for a single line:

Don't forget who you work for. Time is running out.

Beneath it is an attachment. A photo of Drew. The same one they used on her memorial card. Bile rises in my throat. Her face, frozen in time, still haunts me.

I slam my laptop shut, as if the image might seep out and consume me. My phone buzzes a moment later. Another email from the same thread.

The Wells boy isn't the only one with secrets. Let's talk before I decide to share yours.

My fingers shake. I don't have time to think this through. I push the unease aside and type out a single word in reply:

Fine.

It's less than a minute before I receive a response.

Call me in ten minutes.

They include a number, but I don't need to memorize it. I already know it's Peter.

Ten minutes stretch into an eternity as I move to sit on the edge of the bed, checking the security on my devices out of instinct. Both scans on my phone and laptop come back clean. My VPN and firewall are next, both show no unusual activity.

The seconds tick by, each one a countdown to something I'll regret. I take a shaky breath and dial the number, my heart threatening to flat line.

It rings once before Peter's smooth, almost cheerful voice cuts off the tone. "I was starting to think you'd forgotten me."

I grit my teeth, clutching the phone tighter. "What do you want?"

"Straight to business. I admire that." He chuckles, low and patronizing. "Let's not pretend this is anything other than that: business. You still remember how to handle business, don't you?"

"You tried to have me killed," I snap. My voice trembles with barely restrained fury. "Why would I listen to anything you say?"

He exhales, long and deliberate, like I'm being unreasonable. "You've always been a little too stubborn for your own good, and I needed to remind you who's in charge." He pauses, and I can hear the smirk in his voice when he adds, "And it pushed you right into the Wells boy's arms. It worked out for all of us, didn't it?"

The realization settles under my skin instantly. Peter gambled on how I'd react. How Silas would react. Weeks ago, he'd already set his trap, and I walked into it willingly, perfectly. My cheeks burn with a mix of fury and humiliation.

"You're delusional," I spit, though my pulse quickens, betraying the doubt gnawing at me.

"Am I?" he counters, his voice sharpening into something darker. "You think Silas and his family would still have you if they knew the

313

truth? If they knew who I am? What I've done for you? What *you've* done for me?"

The blood drains from my face. My grip on the phone tightens. "You don't scare me, Peter."

"Maybe not," he says, his tone hardening. "But you should be scared for them. You think I won't go through them to get what I need? You *know* how far I'll go. After all, your little college friend didn't just fall into my lap."

His words light a fire in my veins, rage overtaking the fear. "Don't you dare—"

"I wouldn't have to if you'd stop playing games," he snaps, cutting me off with the sharpness of a blade. "But I will if you keep pushing me. I know about Luis. Did you really think I wouldn't?" He scoffs. "You're getting sloppy, Scarlett. And worse— you're getting sentimental." His voice drops lower, colder. "Finish the job, or I'll finish it for you. And you won't like how I tie up the loose ends."

The line goes dead before I can respond. My hand shakes as I lower the phone, my breath coming in shallow gasps. The room feels stifling, the walls pressing in, his threats looping in my head like a nightmare I can't escape. He's not just watching me; he's closing in. I need to do something. Anything. Sitting here and letting the fear take hold isn't an option.

I open my phone again and tap on Luis's name. He answers on the second ring.

"It's Peter," I blurt out instantly, my voice pitched with panic. "He contacted me."

There's a pause on the other end, but Luis's voice, when it comes, is steady. Calm. "What did he say?"

I take a breath and give him the short version. Luis listens quietly, his breathing measured, before finally speaking.

"He might know I'm working on the files, but he doesn't know where I or my friends are," Luis reassures me, his tone firm. "He's trying to rattle you. I've got my setup locked down tighter than Fort Knox. He's not going to find me."

I exhale shakily, but my anxiety refuses to ease. "But what if—"

"He won't," Luis interrupts me gently, his voice unwavering. "Peter's getting desperate. He's throwing everything at the wall, hoping something sticks."

His confidence steadies me, but only slightly. There's a weight to his words that I can't shake, a reminder of how carefully Luis has built his life to shield himself from people like Peter. He's right. Peter is desperate for whatever reason. But desperation makes him unpredictable, dangerous.

"Listen to me," Luis continues, his tone softening. "You're not in this alone. We're close. I know it feels impossible right now, but we're going to finish this soon. Just stay focused on what we're doing and we'll deal with him after."

His words offer a sliver of reassurance, but it's not enough to shake the unease clinging to me like a second skin. I mutter a quiet thank-you and end the call. The logical part of my brain knows Luis is right, but Peter's voice still lingers, his threats curling around me like a noose.

I'm not sure how long I sit there, my mind spinning, but I'm jolted from my thoughts by the sound of voices in the hallway. One of them is Silas's. My eyes dart to the clock. It's too early for him to be home. Why is he back before six? His voice is brief and curt, exchanging a few words with someone, likely Cillian, before dismissing them. The footsteps grow closer, and then he's there, quietly pushing open the door to the guest room.

Silas stops in the doorway, his gaze sweeping over me. I'm perched on the edge of the bed, phone clenched tightly in my hands. His expression shifts instantly.

"Scar," he says, voice cutting through the thick silence. "What's wrong?"

I shake my head, the denial slipping out too fast. "Nothing. I'm fine."

He doesn't buy it. His eyes narrow slightly, his focus unyielding. Without breaking stride, he steps into the room, shrugging off his jacket and tossing it onto my abandoned chair. "You don't look fine." His tone is calm, but there's an edge to it, sharp and probing. "Tell me."

Panic prickles at the back of my neck. I scramble for something to say, something close enough to the truth to keep him from asking more. "I've been thinking," I start, my voice unsteady. "About the attacker. How he's still out there." I exhale slowly, hands gripping my phone tighter. "It's hard not to feel like he's watching. Waiting."

Silas's jaw tightens. He doesn't speak right away, just exhales through his nose, slow and deliberate. The sound is quiet but unmistakably dangerous, like the low growl of a predator ready to strike.

He crosses the space between us, stopping in front of me. his presence is overwhelming—his anger pressing in from all sides, thick and tangible. This isn't the polished, composed Silas the world sees. This is the man who would set fire to everything when he deems it necessary.

"He won't touch you again." The words aren't a promise. They're a verdict.

His hand lifts, fingers tilting my chin up until I meet his gaze—molten steel, unwavering. "Do you hear me?" His voice drops, quiet but unrelenting. "No one gets to hurt you and walk away. No one."

A lump rises in my throat. "Silas, you don't have to—"

"I do." He doesn't let me finish. His grip is gentle but firm, his touch grounding. "You're mine to protect. No one gets to take that from me."

The conviction in his voice rattles something deep inside me. I struggle to hold his gaze under the weight of it, under the weight of all the things I can't say. He sees the flicker of doubt, the hesitation, and his expression softens just enough. His hand shifts, his thumb brushing lightly across my cheek in slow, soothing circles.

"You're safe here." The words come softer now, quieter but no less certain.

Tears sting at the corners of my eyes. Guilt twists in my chest, sharp and relentless. He has no idea how close Peter really is, how much danger we're both in.

"I—" The words catch in my throat. I force a weak smile, swallowing back everything else. "Thank you." It feels like the wrong thing to say, too small for what he's offering.

Silas studies me for a long moment, searching my face. The fury in his eyes dims slightly, but the tension in his body doesn't fade. Then, without a word, he pulls me up and into his arms.

His heartbeat is steady against mine, and I let my eyes close, resting my head against his chest as his arms tighten around me.

The weight of his trust is unbearable. Because this won't last. It's only a matter of time before the illusion shatters, and when it does, I'll have no one to blame but myself.

CHAPTER 32

I smooth the front of my shirt nervously while sliding into the booth across from Natalie. The familiar hum of the Italian restaurant, the clinking of glasses, and the warm, inviting scent of garlic and fresh bread hit me all at once. It feels surreal to be here again. After weeks of being cooped up, the world outside Silas's house feels strange, foreign almost, like stepping into a forgotten dream.

Natalie leans back against her seat, her amber eyes sparkling with mischief as she says, "I can't believe you actually got Silas to agree to this *and* he managed to convince Davey. That's a miracle in and of itself."

I laugh, though the sound feels a little shaky. "Trust me, I'm as surprised as you are."

My eyes dart to the corner of the restaurant, where Silas and Davey sit at their own table. Silas's gaze is locked on me: sharp, focused, and unrelenting. It's the same way he looks at everything he considers important. Davey, on the other hand, is doing his best to act casual, but even from this distance, it's clear he's on high alert, his attention never straying far from Natalie. I force myself to look away, turning my focus back to her instead.

Three days ago, Silas noticed something was off. I'd been quiet, my usual sharp remarks replaced by silence, lost in my own head. When he finally cornered me in the kitchen about it, I admitted the truth—I felt trapped. My days blurred together, confined to the gym and the house, and it was starting to wear on me.

He didn't dismiss my feelings or try to argue. He just listened. Then, with quiet certainty, he told me we'd figure something out, but I wouldn't be going out alone.

The compromise was simple: I could have my Thursday dinners with Natalie, but someone would always be nearby, watching from a distance. It wasn't perfect, but it was better than feeling like a prisoner. For this first outing, Silas and Davey insisted on taking the job themselves.

"Well," I say now, shaking off the memory, "we're here, so let's make the most of it."

Natalie's lips curling into an amused grin. "Agreed. Let's pretend the bodyguards aren't grading us while we enjoy this pasta."

I snort, sneaking another glance toward the corner. Silas hasn't taken his eyes off me, his jaw set like he's daring anyone to even look at me the wrong way. "I swear, I can feel Silas burning holes into the side of my head."

Natalie leans forward, her voice dropping to a conspiratorial whisper. "Oh, absolutely. Davey's probably calculating the exact probability of Silas storming over here in the next five minutes."

That makes me burst out laughing, the sound bubbling out of me like champagne. For the first time in weeks, I feel something I hadn't realized I was missing: lightness. I feel lighter. Freer.

We order drinks and quickly fall into our usual rhythm, swapping stories and trading playful barbs like nothing has changed. Natalie tells me about her disastrous attempt at wallpapering the guest bathroom, complete with an impression of Davey's horrified reaction to her "creative" alignment of the pattern. I counter with a confession about binge-watching an entire season of *The Great British Bake Off* in one sitting, complete with a dramatic reenactment of my emotional breakdown over a poorly made sponge cake.

I'm wiping tears of laughter from my eyes, my cheeks sore from smiling as I take a sip of my cocktail. The cool, crisp flavors wash over my tongue. It's a simple pleasure, but at this moment, it feels like everything.

319

"Excuse me, ladies," a male voice interrupts, catching us both off guard. I look up to see a man standing awkwardly by our table, holding a drink in one hand. He's in his mid-thirties, with a nervous smile and a hint of stubble. "Can I just say you both look absolutely stunning tonight?"

Natalie raises her left hand slightly, her wedding bands catching the light in a deliberate gesture. The man's eyes flick to her fingers, and his face flushes as he shifts his attention fully to me instead.

"And you..." He clears his throat, visibly trying to gather his courage. "I hope this isn't too forward, but can I buy you a drink?"

I blink, caught off guard, but I recover quickly, offering him a kind smile. "That's really sweet of you, but no, thank you. I'm all set."

He hesitates, looking a little disappointed but nodding politely. "Of course," he says, dipping his head. "Well, have a great night."

As he walks away, Natalie lets out a low whistle, leaning her chin into her palm. "You handled that way better than I would have. I would've scared him off with my resting Davey glare."

I chuckle, taking a sip of my drink. "He was respectful. No need to scar him for simply asking."

But the lightness in my laugh fades when I glance across the restaurant. Silas is still watching me, his dark eyes blaze with a heat that makes my stomach flip. The tension in his posture pulses in waves.

My phone buzzes on the table. I glance down to see a text from him.

Silas: The next guy who tries that won't be so lucky.

My cheeks flush, and I bite my lip to suppress the smile threatening to creep across my face. Natalie catches the change in my expression, her brow arching with curiosity. "What did he say?" she asks, her tone laced with amusement. "Something brutish, I bet."

Sliding my phone back into my bag, I shrug lightly. "You know Silas," I say breezily. "Always so charming."

Natalie rolls her eyes but laughs. "Charming. Sure. That's definitely how I'd describe my brother."

We order dinner, and I find myself relaxing more with each passing minute. Natalie's humor is infectious, and for a while, it's easy to forget the tension lingering just across the room. We giggle until my face hurts and I'm halfway through the best chicken carbonara in the city. This all feels almost normal.

As the waitress clears our plates and leaves to retrieve the check, Natalie leans back in her seat, glancing towards her husband and brother, grinning. "You know," she teases, "I should've realized the moment you weren't impressed by Silas that you'd be the one to bring him to his knees. I'd say I'm shocked, but honestly, I think we all saw it coming. Except maybe you."

I roll my eyes, but before I can respond, a shadow looms over the table. I glance up to see Silas standing there, Davey just a step behind him. Silas's expression is composed, though the faint tightness in his jaw betrays his mood.

"The check's handled," Silas says, his tone clipped. "We should get going."

Natalie raises her brows. "Well, isn't that convenient," she says, throwing me a knowing look. "Thanks, Si."

I grab my bag and slide out of the booth, my heart skipping as Silas steps aside to let me out. He doesn't say much, just places a hand lightly on my lower back as he guides me toward the restaurant doors. Davey mimics the movement with Natalie, though his usual dry humor is replaced by mild exasperation.

Once we reach the entrance, the cool evening air greets us, crisp and refreshing. Davey crosses his arms, scanning the street out of habit, while Natalie beams at me, pulling me into a quick hug. "This was fun," she says, giving her brother with a playful look. "Maybe the wardens will let us out again soon."

Silas doesn't rise to the bait. "Goodnight," he says simply, his tone cool and even, though his hand hasn't left my back.

321

Davey wraps an arm around Natalie's shoulders, steering her toward their SUV. "You really can't help yourself, love. Let's go. Goodnight," he calls over his shoulder.

"Goodnight," I echo, looking up at Silas as he guides me toward the idling town car a few feet away. Cillian sits in the driver's seat, waiting. The air between us is charged, though Silas hasn't said much.

Silas opens the car door for me, his hand brushing mine briefly as I slide inside. He follows, closing the door with a quiet finality and the silence between us is the kind that hums. I risk a glance at him, but his gaze is fixed straight ahead, jaw locked, hands flexing against his thighs as if restraining something volatile.

I can't tell if he's angry, frustrated, or something else entirely.

"Take a walk," Silas commands suddenly, his voice sharp enough to cut. I blink, startled, before realizing he's not speaking to me.

Cillian doesn't hesitate. He simply opens the driver's door, steps out, and shuts it behind him. The sound echoes in the confined space, impossibly loud.

And just like that, it's only us.

Silas leans back against the seat, his posture deceptively relaxed, but I see the way his fingers twitch before curling into loose fists. His breathing is controlled but his eyes betray him—molten, smoldering. Irritated.

"So," he starts, those brown irises burning like embers. "You were awfully polite to that guy back there."

I cross my arms, my frustration flaring as I hold his stare. "Was I supposed to cuss him out? He didn't do anything wrong."

A slow smirk spreads across his face, dark amusement flickering in his gaze. "Didn't do anything wrong," he echoes mockingly. "That's cute."

Heat creeps up my spine, pooling low in my stomach. "I was just being polite. I said I wasn't interested and he took it in stride. He was harmless."

Silas tilts his head, his gaze raking over me. "Harmless?" His tongue drags over his bottom lip before he fixes me with a look that makes my pulse stutter. "Tell me, Scar—would you have let him buy you that drink if I wasn't sitting across the room?"

I lift my chin, meeting his challenge head-on. "Does it matter?"

The air shifts.

Without warning, he moves.

His hands clamp around my waist, and before I can protest, he hauls me onto his lap, forcing a gasp from my lips. My knees press into the seat on either side of his thighs, the heat of him burning through my jeans like a brand. My hands fly to his shoulders for balance.

"Silas—"

"Enough," he interrupts, a quiet yet biting command that severs any argument before it starts. His fingers flex against my hips, dragging me closer, forcing me to feel every hard inch of him. His breath ghosts over my lips, his eyes burning into mine. "You've said enough. Now shut up and let me show you who gets to have your attention."

His hands crawl up my sides, slow and deliberate, before finding the button of my jeans. I press against his chest, meaning to push him back, but the moment I feel the steady, powerful thrum of his heartbeat beneath my fingertips, they curl to the fabric beneath them instead.

"Silas," I try again, but my voice betrays me—soft, uncertain.

His smirk sharpens. "Cat got your tongue?"

Those capable fingers slip beneath my waistband, finding me already soaked. My breath catches a fraction, just enough for triumph to flicker in his gaze before it turns into something more depraved.

"You've been like this all night?" he murmurs, dragging his fingers through my slick heat.

I shake my head too quickly. "No."

His lips brush my ear, his voice a sinful whisper. "Liar."

A strangled gasp escapes me as his fingers stroke my clit. Circling, teasing, punishing. My hips jerk forward, chasing the sensation before I can stop myself.

Silas hums, his hand on my back pressing me flush against him, holding me in place. "You like this," he murmurs, dragging his lips along my jaw. "Knowing anyone could be outside this car. That someone could walk by at any second."

His fingers move with perfect, ruthless intent. Stroking, building, dismantling me. My body clenches, trembling with a heat so unbearable it feels like I'm being consumed from the inside out.

Silas watches me struggle, soaking in every shallow breath, every desperate shift of my hips, before he presses his fingers deeper, forcing another whimper from my throat. "Where's that smart mouth now?" He asks.

My thighs tensing around him, nails digging into his shoulders. I have nothing to say—no clever retort, no defiance. Just need.

His smirk curves like the devil himself. "That's what I thought."

The pressure mounts, slow and insidious, like a fuse burning down to its final spark. Every touch, every calculated stroke pushes me closer until the need becomes torturous. Silas feels it and his movements shifting from languid to devastating, pushing me over the edge with a final, savage stroke.

"Say it," he growls. "Say it's only me."

"It's only you," I pant, the words spilling out, breaking on a moan.

My orgasm rips through me, violent and blinding, but Silas let up. He forces me to ride it out until I'm shaking in his arms, my face pressed into the side of his neck as I melt into him. And even then, he leaves his hand against me, palming the apex of my thighs like a claim.

When I finally find the strength to lift my head, he's watching me with a look of pure, unfiltered satisfaction. His fingers tilt my chin up, and he takes my mouth with a slow, bruising kiss. "Good girl," he murmurs against my lips, his tone filled with pride and dominance.

As I try to gather myself, still reeling, Silas zips my jeans with infuriating calm, like he didn't just destroy me in the backseat of a car. Then, with a surprising gentleness, he shifts me back into the middle seat, buckling my seatbelt.

But his own restraint is evident, unmistakable. The hard length of him still presses against his pants, a silent promise of everything he's held back. But he makes no other move than to settle his hand on my thigh, keeping me close.

"Ready to go home?" he asks, his voice impossibly casual.

I nod silently, my cheeks still flushed, and he taps on the window. A moment later, Cillian returns, slipping into the driver's seat without a word.

As the car pulls away from the curb, I lean back in my seat, my heart still racing, my mind spinning. Silas doesn't say anything else, but the faint smirk on his lips speaks volumes. He knows exactly what he's done to me. And as I steal one last glance at his profile, sharp and commanding in the dim light, I know one thing for certain.

Silas Wells is ruining me in the best, most devastating way possible. And when this ends—because it will end—I don't know if I'll survive it.

CHAPTER 33

Chapter 34

"This is... intimidating," I admit, my voice lighter than I feel. "Are you sure this is a good idea? He didn't even invite me."

Silas's grip on the steering wheel tightens briefly as he turns into the massive circular driveway in the suburbs, gravel crunching under the tires. His expression is calm but resolute. "Where I go, you go. My father will learn that soon enough."

I nod, but the unease swirling in my stomach doesn't dissipate. William Wells had summoned his children to dinner under the guise of discussing "family business," a vague and heavy phrase that immediately made me feel like an outsider. Now, standing on the edge of this world—his world—I feel like a ripple in an endless ocean.

After parking, Silas walks quickly around to my side and opens the door. His hand is warm and steady as I take it, the only grounding presence in an environment designed to intimidate. The towering mansion looms ahead, its perfectly manicured hedges and glowing marble facade casting long shadows over us. Each step toward the grand double doors makes my heart thud harder in my chest.

The doors swing open before we reach them, revealing a man in a tailored black suit who radiates the sort of practiced deference that comes with serving the Wells family. "Mr. Silas. Miss," he greets with a slight bow, his gaze flicking to me briefly before returning to Silas. "Everyone is waiting for you in the living room."

Everyone.

The word feels pointed, like a reminder that I'm not supposed to be here. I squeeze Silas's hand slightly, my unease bubbling up, but he doesn't flinch. If anything, he holds on tighter, his grip a silent reassurance as he leads me through the entrance hall.

The interior is grand and cold, every detail carefully curated to exude power and wealth. High ceilings, intricate molding, and marble floors gleam under the soft glow of antique chandeliers make feel impossibly small. Silas doesn't slow as he leads me toward the formal living room.

When we step inside, it's exactly as I imagined it would be: impossibly elegant, designed to intimidate, and devoid of true warmth. A grand fireplace crackles in the corner, its golden light casting flickering shadows over the mahogany furniture, pristine rugs, and shelves lined with leather-bound books. It's beautiful, but it's a beauty that feels sharp.

My gaze is drawn to the far wall, where a large portrait hangs above an ornate sideboard. The woman in the painting stops me in my tracks. Her angular face is framed by dark brown hair, faint streaks of gray blending into the strands. Freckles dust her nose, softening the angles of her features, and her hazel eyes, warm and crinkled on the corners, seem to hold a depth that makes me feel like she's looking right at me.

The resemblance is striking, even with the age difference in the painting. It's in the high cheekbones, the subtle downturn of the lips, the quiet intensity in her stare that feels as though it could pierce right through you. This is Silas's mother, Caroline.

Though I'd seen photos of her online, it's different to see her here, in this room where it feels out of place. A space so carefully curated by William's cold, calculating hand. Yet, it's also the only thing in here that feels truly human.

I glance at Silas, but his expression doesn't shift. He spares the portrait a fleeting glance, his jaw tightening ever so slightly, before he looks away. It's as if the sight of her is too much, or perhaps he's simply too practiced at masking whatever it stirs in him. I wonder if he feels her absence here as much as I can sense it.

The rest of the Wells family is already seated, scattered across the room in their own corners. Natalie and Davey sit together on a sofa, her hand resting lightly on his knee as they chat quietly. Jeremy lounges in an armchair near William, a drink in hand, his posture casual yet alert. And then there's William, seated in a high-backed armchair that might as well be a throne. His presence dominates the room, the sharpness in his gaze slicing through the quiet hum of conversation.

As we step further inside, the low murmur of voices fades, replaced by the faint crackle of the fire and the weight of everyone's attention shifting toward us.

William's eyes are locked on me, his gaze narrowing ever so slightly before he lets a tense smile lift his lips. "Silas. Scarlett," he begins, his voice polite but dripping with veiled disapproval. "I didn't realize you'd be joining us tonight."

The words hang in the air, every syllable carefully chosen to remind me that I'm not welcome. Natalie's head snaps toward her father, her eyebrows furrowing in a flash of irritation.

"She's not just a guest, Dad," Silas says, his voice steady but defiant. "Scarlett will be a part of this family eventually, so you might as well get used to it."

My breath catches, my chest tightening at the firmness of his words. It's a declaration and it makes my heart ache in equal parts warmth and despair. I glance at him, but his gaze remains locked on his father, unflinching and unyielding.

Out of the corner of my eye, I see Natalie's lips curve into a faint smile, her expression softening as she looks at her brother. Beside her, Davey's features remain neutral, though a flicker of confusion crosses his eyes as he shifts uncomfortably in his seat. Jeremy, lounging casually in his chair, raises an eyebrow but says nothing, his attention fixed on William.

William's jaw tightens ever so slightly, the tension rippling through him barely masked as he forces a wider smile. "I see," he says smoothly, though his tone betrays his displeasure. "Well, I suppose we'll adjust."

He gestures toward an empty couch with a stiff motion, but the undercurrent of his disapproval is impossible to miss.

Silas's hand remains firm on mine as he leads me to the couch, his presence a silent shield against the weight of William's judgment. The conversation resumes, polite and practiced, as staff circulate with trays of pre-dinner cocktails. I sit quietly, letting the discussion drift around me like distant static. But William's sharp gaze finds me too often, lingering just long enough to make my skin prickle. Every time, I force myself to sit a little straighter, meeting his gaze head-on, even though every instinct screams at me to look away.

Eventually, William raises his glass, the subtle motion commanding silence in the room. The murmur of conversation fades instantly as everyone turns their attention to him. "To family," he begins, his voice smooth and authoritative, each word weighted with purpose. "Our biggest strength and our greatest responsibility."

Beside me, I feel Silas tense, his hand tightening slightly on his glass. The frustration radiates off him in waves, barely contained beneath his composed exterior. Whatever William's real reason for this dinner is, it's clear that Silas is already bracing himself for a battle.

"Wells Corp is at a critical juncture," William continues, his tone carrying an air of self-importance. "It's essential that we all understand our roles in preserving what I've built. Especially as of late."

The insinuation lands heavily, the words hanging like a blade poised over the room. Silas doesn't let him finish.

"Why not just tell us why we're here, Dad?" Silas's voice cuts through the air. "What's with all the theatrics?"

The room goes still. Even the faint clink of glasses ceases. William turns his attention to Silas, his expression unreadable, though the tightening at the corners of his mouth betrays his annoyance.

"Everything I do is for this family," William responds without answering his question, tone icy but measured. "You've all benefited greatly from the decisions I've made."

"And I'm grateful for that," Silas retorts, leaning forward slightly, his elbows resting on his knees. "But that doesn't mean I can't ask questions. I'm trying to understand you."

Jeremy shifts in his seat, rolling his eyes. "You always do this, Silas," he mutters, irritated. "Just let Dad say what he has to say."

Natalie holds up a hand, her voice calm but firm. "Let's not do this tonight," she says, her gaze darting between her brother and father. "Can we just have one evening without a fight?"

Davey remains silent, his sharp eyes flicking between them, as though he's analyzing the dynamics like a puzzle to be solved.

I sit frozen, my chest tightening as I watch Silas square off against his father. Every line of his body is drawn tight, his need to be heard and respected written into his very posture. Instinctively, I reach out, placing a hand on his thigh. He glances at me, his expression softening briefly before he turns back to William.

"Things are going to change soon," Silas says, his voice calmer now but no less firm. "I know the two of us have had some... growing pains recently. There's going to be an adjustment period for all of us as we get closer to the end of the year. But, Dad, I'm not here to fight you."

William raises an eyebrow, his tone unreadable as he asks, "Is that so?"

"Yes," Silas says, leaning back slightly, his shoulders relaxing. "I know how much you've sacrificed to make Wells what it is, but I also have my own ideas and visions for the future. We need to trust one another. I want to work with you, not against you."

For a moment, William doesn't respond. He takes a slow sip of his drink, his gaze fixed on Silas, weighing him, testing him. When he finally speaks, his voice is calm, but each word is deliberate and cutting. "Trust, Silas, is earned. And if you want to lead, you'll have to prove that your vision won't jeopardize everything I've worked for." He sets his glass down with a measured precision, his eyes never leaving Silas. "I've already been questioning your judgment these past few months. And I don't think I need to spell out why."

Silas exhales sharply, leaning back further into the couch. The tension in the room is suffocating. For a moment, it feels as though everyone else in the room has disappeared, leaving only Silas and William locked in this silent battle of wills.

And then William looks at me. Pointed. Intentional.

I don't care about his approval. I never have. Men like him, powerful and calculating, have never dictated my worth. And yet, the rejection hits in a way I can't shake, sharp and familiar, settling deep in the hollow space left behind by years of being dismissed, overlooked. Just like with my own parents.

Forcing my shoulders back, I keep my expression blank. William turns back to Silas without a second glance, like I'm not even worth that.

"I won't be continuing this discussion with *guests* present," William says, his tone clipped and final. The edges of his words are razor-sharp. "This is a matter for family, Silas. Perhaps we can resume the conversation when the setting is more... appropriate. Until then, you're free to go."

The dismissal lands like a slap across the face, and I feel the sting of it. Silas's jaw clenches, the muscle ticking as he stares at his father, his frustration barely concealed. But he doesn't argue. Instead, he rises slowly and offers me his hand.

"Come on, Scarlett," he says, not holding his father's stare. "We're done here."

This isn't a fight he can win, not right now, not without making things worse. And still, the silence cuts. A quiet confirmation that I don't belong here. It's a dull ache, settling low in my chest. Like pressing on an old bruise I thought had faded, only to find it still tender.

As I reach for Silas, I can't even bring myself to look at his siblings or Davey. The embarrassment flushing up the back of my neck to my cheeks is enough. The silence as we leave is deafening. William doesn't stop us. He doesn't say another word. He doesn't need to. The message is clear: I'm not part of this family, and Silas's position here is as tenuous as his willingness to follow William's rules.

Silas's body thrums as we make our way to his car. He opens my door for me, and I slip inside without a word. When he slides into the driver's seat and starts the engine, the low hum fills the quiet space between us. I can't find the words. I don't even know where to start.

"He doesn't respect me," Silas finally says, his voice low but vibrating with fury. His hands grip the steering wheel so tightly his knuckles turn white. "No matter what I do, it's never enough."

My chest aches for him. Though I despise William, it doesn't stop me from wishing he could be better for Silas. Wishing he could give him even a fraction of the validation he so clearly deserves.

"I'm sorry," I whisper. The words feel inadequate, like they barely scratch the surface of what I want to say. But what else can I offer? He's right, and I can't bring myself to lie to him.

Silas exhales sharply, his frustration bleeding into his words. "I've stopped expecting it. Respect, I mean. Not from him. Since announcing I'm stepping into his role, he doesn't see me as anything more than an extension of himself to keep his legacy alive." His voice grows harder, sharper. "I don't think he ever intends to let go. He'll never fully trust me to run Wells without his hand on the wheel."

He's not wrong, and I hate that he's not. The depth of William's control is suffocating, a force that Silas has been living under for far too long. I reach out, brushing my hand lightly against his arm.

"That's not fair," I say quietly, meaning it with every fiber of my being. "You deserve more than that."

He glances at me, the corner of his mouth twitching into something that's not quite a smile but isn't fully bitter either. "Yeah," he murmurs, his tone resigned. "But wanting something doesn't make it real, does it?"

The exhaustion in his voice grows heavier with each word. I want to comfort him, to tell him he's stronger than his father's shadow, but the truth sits heavy in my chest. He deserves someone who can fight this battle with him, not someone who's already plotting an exit.

The shame is overwhelming. It presses into my ribs, into my heart, until the words tumble out before I can stop them. "Maybe..." I hesitate, forcing myself to keep going. "Maybe you should go back inside. Without me there. If you stay, maybe he'll talk to you and he'll finally explain himself. You deserve that clarity, Silas."

The air between us thins as Silas turns to look at me, confusion flashing in his eyes before anger takes hold. "Is that what you think?" he asks, his voice low and sharp. "That I should just leave you here and go crawling back to him?"

Unable to meet his gaze, I look out the window toward the mansion we just walked out of. "It's not about me, Silas," I murmur. "This is your family. If there's even a chance he'll be honest with you, you should take it."

The silence that follows is suffocating. For a moment, I think he's going to unbuckle his seatbelt and march back up those steps without a second glance. The thought feels like a knife to the chest, but I'd endure it. I'd have to.

Instead, Silas lets out a short, incredulous laugh, shaking his head as if he's finally piecing together some great puzzle. "You *want* me to go back in there without you," he says with a mix of disbelief and hurt. "Don't you?"

I whip my head around to meet his gaze, panic flaring in my chest. "That's not true," I say quickly, too quickly. "I just... I don't want to make things harder for you."

His jaw tightens, the muscle fluttering as he stares at me. "Harder for me?" he repeats, his voice rising slightly before reining it in and exhaling sharply. "Scarlett, do you think I give a shit what my father thinks of you?" His tone is biting. "If he never comes around, if he spends the rest of his life pretending you don't exist, I don't care. As long as you want to be here, as long as you'll have me, I have no intention of letting you go. None."

The conviction in his voice steals the breath from my lungs. Tears sting at the corners of my eyes, slipping free before I can stop them. I quickly swipe them away, hoping he doesn't notice, but I know he does. "Si..." I trail off, my voice trembling as I search for something to say, something that won't betray the storm raging inside me. There's nothing I can say. Not when I can't promise him more than another few weeks, at most.

Finally, I manage a weak, "Okay."

For anyone else, Silas might have taken the quick agreeance as true compliance. But my lack of resistance only unsettles him. Something flickers in his eyes—panic, frustration. He's watching me too closely now, searching for the words I won't say. The sharp edge of his anger dulls, replaced by something that borders on fear.

"Don't do this," he murmurs, his voice quieter now. "Don't pull away from me." His hand lifts to my cheek, the back of his fingers brushing against my skin. The gesture is so gentle that it nearly undoes me. "What he says or thinks means nothing to me, Scar. *Nothing*."

I nod faintly, trying to reassure him, to pacify him, but the sadness is overwhelming. As if sensing the fragile threads of my resolve, Silas doesn't push me further. Instead, he reluctantly turns forward, his hand shifting to rest just above my knee. His fingers press gently into my leg.

The car rolls into motion as he pulls out of the driveway, the low hum of the engine filling the thick silence between us. His thumb begins tracing slow, deliberate circles over the fabric of my pants, the warmth of his touch seeping through to my skin. The lights of the city blur together as we approach the familiar skyline, their glow reflecting faintly on the glass. Every few minutes, Silas gives my leg a reassuring squeeze as a quiet reminder of his presence, both physically and mentally.

I can feel his glances. Brief but searching, like he's trying to gauge where I am. But I don't look back at him. I can't. The remorse bubbling inside me is too close to spilling over, and I don't trust myself to meet his gaze without breaking completely.

My phone buzzes in my bag. I jump slightly, the sound too sharp, too intrusive. I pull it out, grateful for the distraction, but as my eyes scan the message from Luis, my stomach twists painfully.

Luis: We've found important information about the satellite office's security. I'll call tomorrow so we can discuss next steps.

My lungs feel like they're in a vice, each molecule of air being crushed out of them. The text is straightforward, unassuming. But to me, it's a grenade, its pin already pulled.

"Everything okay?" Silas's voice breaks through the haze, low and full of concern. I glance at him briefly, his profile outlined against the glow of the passing streetlights. His knuckles tighten around the steering wheel, and I hate that I'm giving him yet another reason to worry.

I force a quick nod, sliding the phone back into my bag. "Yeah," I say, the lie catching in my throat. "Just a message from a friend I used to work with. Nothing important."

He bows his head slightly in acknowledgment, but his jaw tenses. I know he's not convinced. Silas isn't one to let things slide, but he relents.

The rest of the ride home is silent, the tension in the car thick enough to choke on. When we pull into the garage and the engine shuts off, neither of us moves. The car feels like purgatory, suspended between the chaos of the evening and whatever comes next. I stare at my hands, my fingers twisting together in my lap as I wait for him to say something. Anything.

Finally, Silas sighs, the sound heavy and resigned. "We're home," he says softly, his voice lacking the edge it carried earlier.

I force a small, tired smile and nod, letting him lead me inside. There's nothing left to say. At least, nothing either of us is ready to say yet.

In the privacy of his bedroom, the walls around Silas begin to peel away. He sheds them one by one until it's just us. He doesn't ask questions, doesn't demand explanations. Instead, he shows me in every touch, every lingering kiss, that he's here, that he's *all in*. His hands move over me like a promise, like he's trying to brand me with the certainty that what we have is worth holding on to. That it's enough.

And for a while, I let myself believe it. I lose myself in him—in the way his lips move against mine, the way our bodies mold as though we were always meant to fit together. His warmth seeps into me, chasing away the chill of doubt and fear, and I cling to it like a lifeline.

But no matter how much I try to drown in him, the message from Luis burns at the edges of my mind, refusing to be ignored. It's a constant reminder of the reality waiting for me, of the inevitable choice I'll have to make. This was never supposed to last. It was never meant to become *this*.

CHAPTER 35

William's cold, scrutinizing gaze plays on a loop in my mind in the darkness. His subtle disdain was worn proudly, a weapon he wielded with precision. I can still feel the burn of it, the way it sliced through my composure, even days later.

I glance to my side where Silas sleeps fitfully. The tension is etched into his features. His body shifts under the covers, as if his subconscious is wrestling with the same demons keeping me awake. He's become quieter since that night. Maybe he's regretting it. Perhaps, deep down, he's questioning if I'm worth the fight.

The thought twists painfully in my chest, a knot tightening with every second that passes. At least it would make things easier for him in the end.

I turn onto my side, reaching for my phone on the nightstand. Natalie's text stares back at me from several days ago, and for the third time tonight, I open it, rereading her words I've still yet to answer.

Natalie: I'm so sorry about the way my father treated you. I don't know what's come over him. He can be paranoid, but that was completely out of line. I'm going to talk to him about it. None of us agree with him, I promise you. Just let me know you're okay.

Her kindness only deepens the guilt that's been eating at me for weeks. She doesn't owe me an apology. If she knew who I really am, she wouldn't be sending reassuring texts. She wouldn't be defending me. She'd hate me. Just like her father does. And she'd be right.

I clutch the phone to my chest, squeezing my eyes shut, trying to will away the obsessive thoughts. My skin itches, my thoughts swirl too fast. I need to move. I need to burn this feeling out of me before it consumes me whole.

Carefully, I slip out of bed, my movements quiet so as not to disturb Silas. Crossing the hallway, I grab leggings, a sports bra, and sneakers from the guest room dresser and change quickly. My hair is tied up in a hasty ponytail by the time I reach the back staircase. I descend quickly, my feet silent against the steps, until I reach the basement.

The gym is dark, the air cool and sharp with the faint smell of cleaning solution. I flip on the lights, and the fluorescent glow bounces off the polished machines and mirrored walls. The space feels impersonal, almost clinical, but right now, it's undoubtedly what I need. A place where I don't have to think.

I step onto the treadmill, my fingers brushing over the controls. Cardio has never been my favorite, but tonight, it feels right. The machine hums to life, and I start at a slow jog, letting the rhythmic thud of my steps drown out the chaos in my head.

The built-in tablet lights up, offering distractions I don't care about. I pull up a random show, not because I want to watch it, but because the motion on the screen gives me something else to focus on. But as I pick up the pace, my gaze drifts away from the screen and lands on the wall of mirrors in front of me.

I don't recognize this person. The dark circles under her eyes, the tension etched into every line of her face. She looks like someone who's running on borrowed time. Someone who's already lost the race and is too stubborn to stop moving.

I hate what I see. I hate *who* I see.

My feet pound harder against the treadmill as I increase the speed, my breath coming faster. I'm just hoping that if I push hard enough, fast enough, I might leave this version of myself behind.

The voice in my head doesn't stop, relentless and cruel, whispering every failure, every regret. The treadmill belt whirring beneath me as though I can somehow outrun it. But no matter how hard I push, how fast I go, the thoughts close in, louder, sharper, cutting deeper.

I think of Drew; of her laugh, her friendship, everything about her that was so pure and kind. And I destroyed it. I think of Peter and the web of lies I've woven, the jobs I've done, the people I've betrayed. All for money and survival. I could have stopped before Drew. I could've walked away. But I didn't, even after Peter showed me his true colors because I was too scared and selfish.

Now, Silas and Natalie. Two people who trust a version of me that doesn't exist. Tears blur my vision, but I don't stop. The guilt claws at me, eating me alive. But I can't get away from it. It's always there, a shadow lurking in every kind word, every gentle gesture. Always reminding me that I don't deserve any of it.

I don't belong here. I never did. I'm a liar. A manipulator. A thief. A parasite. Every word feels like a nail driven deeper into my chest. I hate myself for Drew. I hate myself for the lies I'm telling now. I hate myself because I can't stop. Because every time I think about walking away, I see the faces of the people Peter has destroyed. I know what happens when someone tries to escape him. It's only a matter of time before I fall too.

My lungs burn, my legs scream, but I don't slow down. My reflection stares back at me, blurred through tears, but I can still see her. She's a stranger. A fraud. A monster.

You ruin everything you touch, the voice sneers. *You'll ruin this too. You'll ruin them. They're going to hate you, and they'll be right to.*

The voice is so loud now that it's almost deafening.

If they decide to kill you, the world would be better.

A sob catches in my throat, threatening to choke me. My feet falter, the treadmill jerking beneath me as I slam the emergency brake button, stumbling to a stop. I clutch the arms of the machine, leaning forward, my body trembling. The walls I've built crack, crumble, and the weight of it all crushes me. I let it. I sit in it. I deserve to drown in it.

It's only when I feel a warm hand on my back that I realize I'm not alone. I flinch, startled.

"Scarlett," Silas says softly, his voice rough with sleep.

I don't look up. I can't. Shame crawls up my spine, making me want to curl into myself and disappear. His hand doesn't move, steady against my back. Then, slowly, he steps closer, his arms wrapping around my waist. He pulls me upright, his hold firm but gentle. I blink through my tears and see him in the mirror behind me. His hair is mussed from sleep, his expression unreadable, and he's wearing nothing but pajama bottoms. His chest is bare, cool against my damp back.

I'd never thought about how we looked together, but now, seeing us like this, it's everything I've feared. He's beautiful, strong, good. And I'm just... *not*.

"Scar," he murmurs, his voice a low rumble as he buries his head in the curve of my neck as his hold tightens. "What's wrong?"

I open my mouth to answer, but the words won't come. My throat tightens, and all I can do is shake my head. I want to pull away, to hide, but his presence is too comforting.

"Talk to me," Silas says as though he's afraid I'll break. "Let me help."

His words unravel me. My chest aches with everything I can't say. I want to tell him the truth. I want to let him see all of me, even the ugly parts. But I can't. I can't do that to him. Instead, I do the one thing I know I shouldn't.

I turn in his arms and kiss him.

It's a desperate plea he doesn't know I'm making. His lips part in surprise, but he doesn't pull away. His hands tighten on my waist, pulling me closer as he kisses me back, deep and consuming. For a moment, the world disappears, the guilt, the fear, the lies. There's only Silas. Warm and solid and real.

But even as I lose myself in him, the voice in my head whispers, relentless.

People like you don't deserve to keep something this good.

341

When we finally break apart, I'm breathless, my forehead resting against his. My fingers tremble slightly against the tops of his shoulders. "Shower with me," I whisper.

Silas doesn't question it. He doesn't ask me to explain. Instead, his thumb brushes gently against my cheek, wiping away the lingering tears with a tenderness that almost undoes me all over again.

Without a word, he takes my hand, leading me back to his bathroom. As we ascend the stairs, the house feels impossibly quiet. The faint creak of the wooden steps echoes softly, the only sound between us. He doesn't speak, and I'm grateful for it. The air feels heavy with unspoken questions I'm not ready to answer. Still, he holds onto me, his thumb brushing over my knuckles.

When we reach his room, he pauses at the doorway, turning to face me. His eyes meet mine, and for a moment, I can see everything he's holding back. Concern. Patience. The quiet but unwavering promise that he's here, no matter what.

He doesn't need to say it; I feel it in every breath, every look: *take what you need.*

Without a word, he opens the door, stepping aside to let me enter first. It's such a small gesture, but it speaks volumes. He's letting me lead and that quiet act of surrender loosens something in my chest. He's giving me everything and I can't offer him anything except the part of me that still needs to feel something other than pain.

And even knowing how selfish it is, I can't seem to stop myself from taking it.

CHAPTER 36

"Did everything come in alright?" Luis asks during our early evening phone call. There's an undercurrent of concern that I've come to expect from him.

I'm sitting cross-legged on the bathroom floor of the guest room, staring at the spread of discreet packages he sent. They're neatly arranged in front of me, like pieces of a puzzle I'm desperate not to solve. I had made sure to be the one to answer the door earlier, retrieving the packages from a delivery person dressed as a typical courier, their uniform meant to blend in seamlessly with the countless others that pass through this neighborhood daily.

The contents of the packages are painfully utilitarian: a new laptop preloaded with data extraction programs, spoofing software, and every tool Luis and I agreed I'd need to breach the servers. There's a portable Ethernet adapter, a high-capacity storage drive, a fingerprint mold, a spoofed keycard for the warehouse, a multi-tool, wireless earbuds, a backup power bank, and a backpack to carry it all. Everything is efficient, precise, ready to execute its role with cold indifference.

"We've run through the blueprints a million times," Luis continues when my silence stretches. "We've pinpointed the weakest points of entry. Based on the company's manufacturing floor plans, we're confident we know where the servers are housed. With William maintaining a low security profile to avoid drawing attention, this could go smoother than we anticipated." He says it like a reassurance, but to me, it sounds like a reminder of the inevitable.

"Yeah, it all looks good," I reply flatly, the words scraping out of me without emotion. My fingers absently trace the edge of the backpack strap.

I've been a shell of myself since William's dinner. Silas has been patient, his concern evident in every lingering look, every quiet question he doesn't push when I deflect. Even Natalie's sudden radio silence feels intentional, as if Silas has asked her to give me space. I go through the motions, smiling when I have to, pretending I'm okay long enough to ease his worry. But I can feel him watching me, trying to understand the walls I've been putting up, trying to find a way through.

And it's killing me. He doesn't deserve this.

"Are you okay?" Luis's voice cuts through the haze of my thoughts. He doesn't know everything, but he knows enough. He knows I've let Silas get too close. That I've let *myself* get too close.

I clear my throat, forcing out a weak, brittle laugh. "As good as I can be," I say lightly, but the false note in my voice makes me wince.

Luis hesitates. "Were you able to get your things to the rendezvous spot?"

"Yeah," I reply quietly. "That part wasn't an issue."

"Good," he says, his tone firm again, anchoring us both back to the plan. "Then we're ready."

The words hang heavy between us. I close my eyes, willing myself to believe them. "We're ready," I echo.

There's a brief pause before Luis's voice softens, just enough to let some of his worry bleed through. "Try to get some sleep, alright? It's going to be a long night."

I nod, even though he can't see me. My throat tightens as tears prick at the corners of my eyes. "Yeah. Thanks, Lu. I'll see you soon."

When the call ends, the silence in the bathroom presses down on me. My eyes drift to the gear, each piece meticulously chosen, designed to ensure my success. And yet, it all feels like a betrayal.

I take a shaky breath and start packing the items into the backpack, one by one. Each piece feels heavier than the last, the weight of what they represent settling deep in my bones. When everything is inside, I zip the bag closed, the sound loud and jarring in the stillness.

I sling the backpack over my shoulder and stand, unlocking the bathroom door. In the guest room closet, I open the deep drawer where my emergency bag has been hidden these past weeks. A constant reminder that this day was always coming. Now, the bag is gone, already stashed at the rendezvous point, waiting for the moment I disappear.

I place the new bag in its place, shut the drawer, and close the closet door behind me. The action feels final, like locking away a part of myself I'll never get back.

Knowing it's nearly dinner time, I decide to make my way downstairs for my final performance. As I descend the back staircase, my fingers trail along the polished banister. The memories of the first time I came down these stairs resurface. Back then, I didn't know what to expect from Silas or this house. Now, I know too much. And yet, I still feel like I'm trespassing.

The kitchen is aglow with the fading light of the setting sun, the amber hues spilling through the windows. I pause in the doorway, surprised to see Silas leaning against the counter, a glass of whiskey in hand. He isn't cooking, and Kendall is nowhere in sight. His tie is loosened, his shirt unbuttoned at the collar, and his sleeves are rolled up to his elbows. The sight of him like this makes my chest tighten.

"You're home early," I say softly, stepping into the room. My voice feels too loud in the quiet. I lean against the island opposite him, crossing my arms in front of me.

Silas lifts his glass slightly, taking a slow sip before responding. "Kendall's out tonight," he says, his tone cool and detached. "I didn't feel like staying at the office."

I nod, unsure of what to say. I fidget with the hem of my shirt, trying to fill the silence. "How was work?"

"Fine," he replies curtly. His answer is dismissive, and it only adds to the tension crackling between us.

Minutes stretch into an eternity as the silence grows thicker. Finally, Silas sets his glass down with a deliberate *clink* against the counter, the sound sharp in the stillness. Then, he takes a step toward me.

"Scarlett," he says, his voice steady but edged with something undeniable, unrelenting. "What's going on?"

I blink, caught off guard. "What do you mean?" His expression darkens, his grip tightening around the edge of the counter.

"*Don't.*"

The single word is razor-edged, cutting clean through the space between us and I flinch before I can stop myself. His eyes flicker at the reaction, hurt flashing across his face. Then, he exhales harshly, dragging a hand through his hair. "Don't lie to me." His gaze pins me in place. "You've been pulling away, shutting me out. Is this about what my father said? Did he get in your head?"

I shake my head too fast, my throat tightening so hard I can barely get the word out. "No."

His jaw clenches. "Then what?" His frustration breaks through, shattering any remaining patience. "You barely look at me. Do you think I don't notice?" He steps closer, his presence pressing against me like a physical weight. "Tell me."

The command sends a pulse through me—equal parts fear and guilt. I try to swallow, try to force out something convincing, something safe. "I'm just..." My voice wavers, and for a brief moment, I panic. "I've been tired. That's all."

Silas goes still. Too still.

Then, slowly, he tilts his head, his lips parting around a sound that's almost a laugh, but there's no humor in it. "Tired." The word is flat, empty, laced with pure disbelief. Then his expression hardens, his teeth clenching. "Bullshit."

Silas closes the remaining distance between us, eliminating any space I might have used to escape. He grips my arms, not rough, but firm.

"Whatever this is, whatever I did, help me understand." His voice is a quiet demand, but his eyes betray him—burning, desperate, searching. "Let me fix it."

My throat constricts so tight that it feels like I might choke everything I can't say. I shake my head, forcing the words out, trying to reassure him when I know I can't. "It's not you, Silas. You've been... everything I needed you to be."

"Then what is it?" His voice fractures.

I suck in a breath, but it shudders on the way out. I wasn't expecting this. Not for him to poke holes in the dam I've worked so hard to keep intact. And tonight, of all nights. But he does. And once the first crack splits, the rest follows too fast for me to stop it.

Tears blur my vision before I even realize they've escaped, spilling hot and unrelenting down my cheeks. I press my lips together, but the weight in my chest is unbearable, a pressure that has nowhere to go but out. My body trembling from the sheer effort of holding it all in, but I can't.

Another strangled breath slips free. My hands shake at my sides as I whisper the only words that feel appropriate for everything I've done.

"I'm so sorry."

For a fleeting moment, his eyes flicker with confusion—like he hadn't expected an apology, like it doesn't fit with whatever he thought I'd say. Then, just as quickly, worry creeps in. His grip shifts, less forceful now, as his hands slide down to my elbows, thumbs brushing slow, deliberate strokes against my skin.

He leans in, so close our breaths mix. "What are you sorry for, Scar?"

The moment collapses around me. And the words finally slip free, raw and broken. The craziest and most honest thing I've said in four months.

"I think I love you."

Silas goes completely rigid. A single moment of silence stretches between us before his hands tighten again, hard enough to make me gasp, his voice dropping into something low and almost furious.

"You don't get to say those words like that."

He doesn't have to finish his thought for me to know what he means. *Like a death sentence. Like a goodbye.*

My chest heaves as I meet his gaze, as I let him see it—all of it. My hands tremble as I reach up, cupping his face, thumbing trace over the rough stubble on his jaw, memorizing him. Even in all his fury, Silas is the most beautiful man I've ever known.

"I knew you'd ruin me," I whisper, almost to myself. "But it was worth it."

Something in him breaks the moment he hears the resignation in my words. It's visible, the exact second his resolve shatters. His eyes darken, blazing with something desperate, uncontainable.

And then he's on me.

The kiss is frantic, brutal. There's nothing careful about it. No hesitation, no space between us, just heat, need, devastation. His hands grip my waist, pressing into me like he's trying to pull me inside of him. The edge of the kitchen island digs into my back, but I don't care. I don't care about anything but him. His touch, his presence, the way he consumes me so completely that I don't know where I end and he begins.

I don't want to forget this.

His hands find the hem of my shirt, yanking it up and over my head before tossing it aside. My fingers fumble at his shirt buttons but Silas doesn't wait. He grabs the fabric and rips it open, buttons flying, bouncing against the floor like scattered glass. I barely have time to react before his lips are back on mine, rough, punishing, claiming.

His hands slide to my leggings, fingers hooking into the waistband, and with a single, urgent pull, he drags them down, his movements borderline reckless. My heart lurches, aches, pounds.

"Scarlett." His face hovers centimeters from mine as he peels the leggings the rest of the way off, leaving me exposed and bare beneath him. His gaze brands me; dark and fathomless, nearly black. "I love you. Do you hear me?" The words are harsh and guttural. "No one else. Nothing else. Only you."

My soul cracks. Because I see it—a reflection of everything I'm feeling, everything I'm suffering through. Deep and undeniable. Reckless. Nonsensical. He *knows* it's insane to feel this way, but it's unshakeable.

I wasn't expecting him to say it back. I hadn't even let myself imagine it was possible. Scarlett was never supposed to exist, never supposed to matter. But she does. This moment is hers. Silas loves her the way I love him, and I'm the one left breaking for it.

I open my mouth to respond, but he doesn't let me. His hand slides up, wrapping gently around my throat—cradling it, owning it.

"I know I said this would only last as long as you wanted to be here," he rasps with quiet fury. "But I lied. You're not allowed to leave." His thumb strokes over my pulse point, feeling it race. "I won't let you."

The anger, panic, and sheer force of his words are a tsunami, crashing over me in violent waves. It drenches me. Drowns me.

"Tell me you'll stay," he pleads when I don't answer, his voice fraying at the edges. "Tell me you'll give me more time. I'll fix whatever's broken, Scarlett. I'll make this right."

The fear in his voice tears me apart.

I wasn't supposed to do this. I was supposed to slip away unnoticed, vanish like a ghost in the night. But I fucked everything up like I always do. Instead, I broke and pulled him into this. Now, he's sinking in the wreckage too.

I reach for his neck, fingers threading into his hair, pulling him closer. Our foreheads touch, his breath a battle between hope and disbelief. "I'll stay," I whisper, and the words splinter something inside me.

It's a lie I don't deserve to tell, but it's one he needs to hear. So, I say it again, stronger this time, steady enough to hold him together. "I'll stay. I swear."

His eyes search mine warily, and for a moment, I think he sees through me. That he knows. But slowly, he exhales, his breath trembling as the smallest sliver of relief washes over him.

Then he kisses me savagely, like he can imprint this moment onto my skin and bind me to him forever. With his body flush against mine, he lifts me onto the counter, keeping me here. Keeping me his.

His hands move too fast. Too frantic. The familiar sound of his belt sliding free from the loops sends a shiver racing through me and then his slacks hit the floor. A heartbeat later, he's pressing forward, his hips slotting between my thighs, his grip on me unrelenting. Hands tightening just enough to remind me that I am *here*, this moment is *real*.

Lips drag over mine, his voice a solemn promise and a plea all at once. "I'm going to make this better." He tilts my chin up, forcing me to hold his gaze.

He takes me like a man fighting a losing battle. Like he knows, deep down, that something is slipping through his fingers and he can't stop it. His hands map my body. Each touch, each thrust, each broken gasp between us carries unspoken words.

I love you.

Don't leave.

Please.

His forehead presses against mine, our breaths tangling, colliding. "I love you," he whispers the words again, like repetition alone will be enough. His lips brushing over mine, down my jaw. "I'll make you love me so much you'll never want to leave."

Tears streak down my face, mingling with his kisses. Because he's trying to fix something he doesn't even know *I* broke.

Maybe it's poetic—cruelly, mercilessly poetic—that the last time I get to have him is here, in the very place where I first gave into him. As if fate had been waiting to bring us full circle, only to rip it all away.

Too quickly, the moment crashes over us, a violent, shattering wave of everything we are, everything we could have been, everything that can never be.

Silas doesn't let go. He won't.

His arms wrap around me, locking me against him, holding me so fiercely it feels like he's trying to absorb me. I shake against him, body trembling, my tears soaking into his skin.

His fingers dig into my back, mouth pressing against the crown of my head as he whispers into my hair. "I've got you." His voice is thick, uneven, so painfully sincere it splits me open. "We're going to figure this out."

And for one fleeting, fragile moment, I let myself believe that somehow, this will be enough to save me. From my lies. From my betrayal. From the inevitable.

Deep down, I know the truth. I'm lying. To him. To myself. He deserves better. More. And I am the last person on earth who should be the one to give it to him.

One day, he'll realize what I've done. He'll be grateful that I let him go so violently. Hopefully, he'll hate me because only one of us needs to suffer, and it sure as hell shouldn't be him.

But for now, for these last few stolen moments, I'm too selfish to let go. So I let myself be loved by Silas Wells while I still can—because it's reckless, doomed, and the best thing I've ever done.

CHAPTER 37

The warehouse district is silent, cloaked in a night so deep it feels like it could swallow me whole. The air is thick with the harsh scent of gasoline and metal, the remnants of industry lingering even in the stillness. Each step I take echoes against the cracked pavement. Streetlights are sparse here, only the occasional flickering glow from a security lamp breaking the darkness.

The weight of my backpack drags at my shoulders, but it carries more than just supplies—it holds regret, guilt, inevitability. My mind replays the way I left Silas, the memory stretching unbearably thin, like a wound I keep tearing open. His arm had been draped over me, his warmth an anchor I'd clung to for hours as he drifted in and out of sleep, as though he could sense what I was about to do. It had taken forever for his breathing to steady, to fall fully into unconsciousness. Even then, I had waited, frozen in place, tears soaking the pillow beneath me. When I finally moved, slipping out from under him, it felt like I was splitting myself in half.

And now I'm here, betraying him in more ways than I can count. But this was the only move left.

I spent too long afraid to reach a conclusion about what Silas knew—whether he was protecting his father or complicit in whatever was buried in those servers. But now, I feel with certainty that he doesn't know. Silas isn't shielding William; he's fighting for a place in a world his father refuses to let him belong to. And that makes this all the more unbearable. But I can't risk Natalie.

Luis was right. Peter won't stop. Not after everything I've done to defy him. He knows exactly how to break me—just as he did with Drew five years ago. And if I don't act now, he'll do it again. Because he saw the way I protected her in that alley, saw what she means to me. To him, she's a weakness, a vulnerability to be exploited.

This won't end unless I get to the information first. I have to find out what Peter is after before he does. Only then can I decide what to do with it—how to leverage it and keep Natalie safe.

It has to be enough.

My legs feel like they might give out before I even reach the warehouse. I haven't slept, haven't eaten. My body is running on fumes.

Four blocks from the warehouse, I stop in the shadow of an abandoned building and take a deep, shaky breath. The wind stirs loose gravel, sending a hollow rustling sound through the empty street. My hands tremble as I pull out my earbuds and connect the call.

"Luis," I whisper, barely holding it together.

His voice is soft and calm. Like he's been waiting for this moment as much as I have been dreading it. "I was starting to worry."

I don't respond immediately, wiping at my face as fresh tears threaten to spill. "I'm here," I finally manage, but my voice cracks.

"Are you okay?" he asks, though we both know the answer.

"No," I admit, the word barely audible. "But it doesn't matter."

Luis pauses, and I can feel his hesitation through the line. "You're doing the right thing. Maybe when this is over, there'll be a chance for you and Silas to talk—"

I stop in my tracks, my throat tightening as the mention of Silas sends a fresh wave of pain crashing through me. "Please, Luis. Just don't." I snap, harsher than I mean to. I squeeze my eyes shut, forcing myself to breathe.

He hesitates again, then exhales. "Alright. Let's focus. You're close. Head toward the southeast side, just like we planned."

I start moving again, sticking to the shadows as I follow his voice. My hands are still shaking, and I ball them into fists to steady them. As I near the buildings, adrenaline surges through me, but my mind still drifts back to Silas and the way he'd smiled at me just yesterday morning over coffee, concerned and cautious. He'd asked me about taking a weekend trip, said we could go anywhere I wanted. I nodded and played along like I deserved to plan a future with him. But I didn't. I never did.

I stumble over something in the dark, and Luis's sharp voice cuts through my thoughts. "Stay focused. You're almost there."

The smell of oil and dust clings to the air. A chain-link fence looms ahead, and beyond it, the silhouette of the warehouse cluster takes shape against the night sky. I've memorized this place, studied every angle of the buildings. I know where the cameras are, the blind spots, the movement schedules of the guards.

I nod, even though he can't see me, and take a deep breath. "Alright," I whisper. "Walk me through it."

Luis guides me step by step, his voice calm and steady. I hear the faint tapping of his keyboard as he works to loop the cameras. "Okay, distraction in three... two... one."

An alarm of some kind blares to life in the distance. I picture the guards jolting at the sound, their attention snapping toward the sudden noise. I imagine them muttering to each other, some moving to investigate, leaving the entrance momentarily unguarded.

Once Luis gives me the okay, I crouch lower, moving quickly toward the small gate next to the vacant security booth, using the spoofed key he sent me to slip in while the team here is distracted on the other end of the lot. As soon as I'm through, Luis starts speaking again.

"Clear so far," he murmurs. "Head toward the trucks to your left. You've got about a minute before the guards regroup."

I move quickly but carefully, sticking to the shadows before reaching the cluster of trucks and pressing myself against the cold steel of a flatbed. The closest warehouse looms ahead, its corrugated metal walls slick with condensation under the floodlights. The path is wide open, too exposed, and naturally, I'm headed toward the furthest building on the other end of the lot.

Luis's voice buzzes in my ear again. "Give me a few seconds. I'm working on cutting the floodlights."

I'm about to respond when I hear a crunch of gravel behind me. That's not the wind.

Then a voice stops me cold.

"Well, well, well."

My heart lurches as I whip around. Only a few yards away, Peter steps out from behind a nearby truck, the faint moonlight and floodlights catching the sharp curve of his smirk. Just behind him, Harrison lingers, only a few steps back, his gun ready and a sinister glint in his eye. Two more men flank them, their faces partially obscured by shadows. Peter's hands rest casually in his pockets, as if this is just another game he's already won.

He's hardly changed in the year since I last saw him. His medium build and impeccable grooming lend him an air of understated authority. His salt-and-pepper hair is neatly combed, not a strand out of place, and his clean-shaven face is perfectly polished. To anyone else, he might appear distinguished, even charming. But I know better.

"*Elena*," he says, his tone dripping with false affection. "You look... tired."

Hearing that name—*my* name—sends a shiver down my spine. I swallow the panic threatening to choke me. My pulse pounds in my ears, but I force myself to stay still, to keep my expression neutral.

Luis's voice crackles in my ear, frantic now. "What's happening?"

My focus is locked on Peter. His smirk widens as he takes a slow, deliberate step toward me. "Did you really think I wouldn't be watching?" He looks around the property, nose crinkling. "I should have realized sooner they might be keeping secrets in a warehouse."

I don't understand. There's no way they could have beaten me here. Even with all the precautions and planning, they were still ahead of me. How? How did they know exactly where I was going?

I scoff, forcing out a dry laugh. "So, what, you've been stalking me now? Did you miss me that much?"

Harrison snorts, his gun still at the ready. "We were watching your little boyfriend's place for weeks, waiting for you to bolt. And once you got close enough to this area of the district, well... you're not as unpredictable as you think. There's only one real place you could be headed."

I clench my jaw, resisting the urge to snap back. Harrison's smug tone grates against my nerves, but before he can say more, Peter shoots him a sharp look. The irritation is plain in his eyes, the twitch of his jaw giving away his frustration. "That's enough," Peter cuts in, his tone low, controlled. Harrison falls silent, though his smirk doesn't waver.

Luis's voice crackles in my ear, his tone tense. "Someone else is in the network. I'm locking them out, but you need to get the hell out of there. Now."

I grit my teeth, keeping my expression unreadable as Peter regroups from his frustration with Harrison. His head tilts as he studies me like a chess piece he's already decided to sacrifice. "You've been busy, haven't you?" he muses. "You and Luis and whatever band of idiots you've roped into this. I have to admit, you've been more resourceful than I gave you credit for."

My fists tighten at my sides, but I manage an indifferent shrug. "Well, you're here. Go do it yourself."

His smirk falters, replaced by something darker. "But you've done so much of the heavy lifting already. It would be a shame to waste all that effort." He pauses, his tone turning icy. "In fact, once we're finished here, I think I'll pay Luis a visit. We need to have a little chat about loyalty."

I shake my head. "After everything you've done, you think I'm still going to help you? Why the hell would I go through with this now?"

Peter's expression barely shifts, but there's an edge to his gaze, a slight narrowing of his eyes that tells me I've struck a nerve. "Because you don't have much of a choice. Hasn't it occurred to you yet? The guards haven't returned to their post."

Luis swears in my ear, his voice sharp. "He's right. I'm not seeing any movement from the guards. They're either down or staying out of sight. Do not engage. I'm working on an escape plan."

I barely hear him. My mind is already spinning, running through possibilities. But there aren't many. No, there aren't *any*. Not with this many unknowns.

Going into this, I knew that I'd be caught on camera somewhere—I was counting on being gone before it mattered, with Luis scrubbing my trail clean. And Peter knows that. That's why he still wants *me* to go in. Because if I do, I'm the one left complicit. My face. My name. Meanwhile, he stays in the shadows, untouched.

But even if I refuse, he'll find someone else. That much is inevitable. And the idea of him gaining access to that information, whatever it is, is unthinkable.

I can't let it happen.

My eyes dart around the lot, searching for anything I can use. Trucks, pallets, loose metal, machinery—all potential obstacles but none of them enough. Then my gaze lands on a tanker truck nearby, closer to me than to Peter, and the hazardous materials warning gleaming faintly under the floodlights. A desperate idea forms, reckless and dangerous but my only shot.

If I can give Silas more time, maybe he'll figure out what his father has been hiding, what Peter is so desperate to steal. He can put an end to whatever William has done, but not if Peter beats him to it.

"Lu," I whisper, keeping my lips barely moving. "Can you create another distraction? Something loud?"

Luis hesitates. "I can trigger the fire alarm in the adjacent building and cut the floodlights. Thirty seconds max."

I need more time. "Why this? Why me?" I press, eyes locked on Peter. "There are people way better at cryptography than I am. So why was I the only one allowed to work on it? What's the point of making me do all of this?"

Peter exhales sharply, his patience thinning. "You were always going to be my scapegoat," he says, his tone devoid of remorse. "I never realized how much of a nuisance you would be. I assumed you were smart enough to stay in your lane, but I've learned my lesson. It'll never happen again."

The insinuation is so obvious it's insulting. It'll never happen again because he'll make sure I don't leave here alive.

Luis's voice cuts in again, sharp with concern. "What's your plan here?"

I barely whisper back, "Don't worry about it."

Harrison's head tilts, eyes narrowing as he watches me. His gaze zeroes in on my ear. "She's wearing an earpiece," he says, his voice triumphant.

Peter's expression darkens instantly. "What's your game, Elena? Stalling? It won't work."

I smirk, tilting my head. "Afraid I might outsmart you? I thought you liked a challenge."

Before he can respond, a piercing fire alarm blares from the warehouse next door, and the floodlights cut out, plunging us all into near-total darkness. I dart to the side, sprinting toward the tanker truck, purposefully moving in an erratic pattern, praying to whatever god is out there that I don't trip on anything along my path.

Peter shouts behind me, his voice laced with fury. "Stop her!"

Someone fires off a warning shot, but it's at least a dozen feet to my left. Whether it's because their eyes haven't adjusted fast enough or they're too apprehensive to shoot toward the tanker, it doesn't matter. It's the exact leverage I need.

Still running at full speed with my backpack bouncing off my shoulders, I lean down to scoop a loose metal rod I'd noted just a few feet away and use the momentum to swing it with all my strength at the valve near the end closest to me. The metal screeches as it bends, and a spray of liquid begins gushing out; a volatile chemical, by the smell of it. The pounding footsteps behind me come to a halt, boots sliding across the gravel as they realize what's happened.

I quickly pivot, moving myself farther away from the belly of the truck but still using it as a shield. One misfire and we all go up in flames. I know it. They know it. And the outrage on Peter's face is downright haunting.

"What the hell are you doing?" Peter shouts both at me and his team, motioning for the men to move in. They hesitate before carefully creeping closer, expertly positioning to flank me from all angles, but I don't give them the time to recuperate.

Without hesitation, I reach into my pocket, pulling out the lighter I always keep on me after learning more than once that even the smallest tools can save your life. "Ending this," I say, more to myself than him, as I flick the flame to life.

The lighter arcs through the air as I throw it toward the edge of the pooling chemical and take off toward a tall stack of pallets several yards from the trucks. For a brief second, time seems to freeze.

Then, the world erupts.

The explosion is deafening, sending shockwaves rippling outward. The force lifts me off my feet, hurling me through the air before I crash back down, my body slamming into the ground. The impact knocks the breath from my lungs, leaving me gasping as heat sears across my back like an open flame licking at my skin.

My vision wavers, the edges darkening, shrinking into a tunnel of flickering orange and black. Each breath is agony, the thick smoke clawing its way down my throat, burning from the inside out. I try to move, but my limbs refuse to obey, every nerve in my body screaming in protest.

Flames surge hungrily across the lot, but I can't focus on where it's going. Through the rolling waves of heat, I hear Peter shouting, his voice a distorted echo as if I'm hearing it from underwater.

The fire rises higher, its roar a deafening chorus that drowns out everything else. Through the haze, I catch glimpses of movement—shadows weaving through the chaos. Another explosion rips through the night as the flames reach one of the trucks in the opposite direction, rattling the earth beneath me. Shrapnel clatters against metal, followed by agonized screams that cut off too quickly.

The heat is unbearable, blistering against my exposed skin, the acrid scent of burning oil and scorched earth flooding my senses. My ears ring, a relentless shrill that drowns out any other sound. My cheek is pressed against the gravel, and in the sliver of space beneath the trucks, I see them—figures scrambling away, retreating, arms shielding their heads as they run.

It shouldn't feel like a small victory, but it does. Silas will figure this out. If I've bought him even a fraction of the time he needs, it's enough.

Tears sting my eyes, hot and unrelenting.

But I still failed.

The fire's roar dulls, its heat pressing down on me like a weight, pinning me in place. My mind fractures, slipping between awareness and oblivion, the pain numbing into something distant, almost insignificant.

Silas's face flickers behind my eyelids, vivid and unshaken by the haze of smoke and pain. I cling to the memories like a lifeline, desperate for something to hold on to—the warmth of his touch, the quiet rasp of his voice in the morning, the intensity in his gaze, as if I were the only thing in the world that mattered. The way he had watched me last night, eyes tracing every detail, committing me to memory like a man bracing for loss, even when I told him I'd stay.

Regret crushes me, heavier than the wreckage, more suffocating than the fire. I tried—*really* tried—to fix this. To make this right. But it was never going to be enough.

The world shrinks with my vision. At first, it's smoke and embers, but when I blink the last time, it's just flames.

Chapter 38

Three Days After the Explosion

Silas

The only proof that time hasn't frozen completely as I stand in the doorway of the guest room is the slow crawl of sunlight across the hardwood floor, inching up the wall near the fireplace. Everything else feels suspended in some cruel, endless loop. This room is a perfect snapshot of Scarlett's presence: her life here, her imprint on this house, on me. On every goddamn part of my existence.

The bed is pristine, untouched for weeks because she spent every night across the hall with me. But her clothes are still scattered, as if she might walk in at any moment to grab them. The boots Natalie bought her sit haphazardly in the corner, kicked off like she was rushing to get comfortable. And there, draped over the back of the chair by the fireplace, is one of her sweaters. Still slightly misshapen, as though she might reach for it any second.

It all feels so alive. But it isn't.

I think of the time I suggested moving her things into my closet. It was a passing comment that had earned me a laugh and a bemused look. "Hold your horses," she'd said, shaking her head like I was ridiculous, as if she wasn't already fully part of this home and my routine. *Hold your horses.* I hadn't heard those words in decades, but now they're seared into my memory. Another scar she's left behind.

A sharp pain rises in my chest, flaring so intensely it forces me to suck in a shaky breath. My ribs feel like they're caving in as I hold the inhale, as though breathing might rip me apart. Part of me wishes it would. The ache goes so deep it feels like it's hollowing me out. The thought of never hearing her voice again—her low, sultry tone that made my name sound like something precious—slices through me. It already feels like her voice is fading, just a faint echo in the back of my mind. I don't know how I'll survive when it's gone completely.

I take a step into the room, and it feels like trespassing on sacred ground. Each detail screams her name; each corner whispers of her presence. But it's all wrong. It's too quiet, too still. My knees nearly buckle, and I catch myself against the dresser, my fingers pressing into the polished wood as though it might hold me together. It doesn't.

My hand drifts to my pocket subconsciously, the crinkling sound of paper confirming it's still there. The letter. It had been hastily written and waiting for me when I woke up, left on the pillow next to me. The only piece of her I have left.

Before I can stop myself, I'm back there.

The faint imprint of her body is still visible on the sheets, and the moment I see it, I know. I don't need to read a word to understand what it means. But I read it anyway.

Si,
You hate me now and I don't blame you.
I'm sorry I lied. I had to do this to protect Natalie, and you. Hopefully, you'll understand one day.
Don't let your guard down. Keep pushing for the truth and demand transparency from William, whether he gives it willingly or you have to take it. You can fix this.
Please take care of yourself and thank you for everything. Loving you will always be the most honest thing I've ever done.
Scar

The words haven't even fully sunk in before I'm moving. I call Cillian immediately, waking Davey and Natalie, and we start tracking her. Sur-

veillance footage shows her climbing into a ride-share downtown, heading toward the South Side. And then nothing. The trail goes cold, like someone scrubbed it clean.

I'm ready to tear through South Side myself, convinced she couldn't have gone far. Then Cillian calls again.

"There's been an explosion," he says, voice rushed. "In the South Side warehouse district. It's... bad. There are casualties."

His words don't register at first. The district. The servers. My thoughts spiral, caught between finding Scarlett and managing this new disaster.

Then he clarifies, "Luckily, the fire department contained it before it spread to the warehouse we've been using, but a few others... they're gone. Fires gutted them. Whatever happened, it came dangerously close to spilling into our operation."

Relief should come, knowing the warehouse is safe. But it doesn't. People died. And all I can think about is Scarlett's last known location—too damn close to where it happened.

I never make it to my car to find her.

The hours that follow are chaos. Damage reports. Calls. Offers of support to the business that housed our servers. But the relief I should feel is drowned out by something else. An ache. A knowing.

And then Davey calls, already in his car and headed to my home.

"You need to see something," he says, his voice tight. "I've been reviewing the security footage from the warehouse and... you just need to see it."

I don't ask questions. I can't. When I join him in my study, he shows me the manipulated footage. A flicker in the camera feeds just before the explosion. And then there she is. Standing among the trucks, surrounded by armed men, their backs turned to the camera. Their guns are trained on her, but she's not backing down. She's arguing, her body tense, her face pale but fierce. Then the footage shifts to night vision mode. She moves. A loose metal rod. A flick of a lighter.

The screen flares with fire as the truck ignites—and Scarlett disappears in the flames.

My knees weaken as I grip the back of a chair, the weight of it crashing into me like a physical blow. She's gone. Scarlett is dead. The woman I've loved so quickly and fiercely it feels like it might tear me apart... gone.

A ragged breath tears from my throat, but it's not enough. My chest constricts, vision blurs. I force myself to keep watching, to find some flaw in the footage, some sign that it's a trick, but all I see is fire. All I see is her disappearing into the inferno, swallowed whole by the explosion before the video cuts out completely.

A deep, unbearable void yawns open inside me, swallowing me whole. This is the obliteration of my soul. A slow, agonizing unraveling from the inside out.

My hands curl into fists, but the pain is distant, inconsequential. I want to lash out, to destroy something, to tear apart the room, but what would it change? What can I do except sit here and drown in it? Scarlett is gone, and I don't know how to exist in a world where she isn't.

But I force down the suffocating weight in my chest, locking it away with the same ruthless efficiency I use for everything else. Emotion won't help me. Answers will.

My voice is barely audible. "Who the hell are they?" I rasp, staring at the screen like it might offer answers.

Davey shakes his head. "I don't know. But whoever they are, they weren't there accidentally. Scarlett was involved in something, Silas. It's no co-incidence she was there." He hesitates, then adds carefully, "This is the only footage from the warehouses. We need to bury it. At least for now. If William finds out about her involvement..."

He doesn't need to finish. If William finds out, no matter the reason Scarlett was there, he'll blame me for letting her in and everything that happened. It will destroy everything I've been working toward. But even that pales in comparison to the rest of it.

I exhale sharply and shake my head, forcing the memories back into the dark corners of my mind where they belong. It's a cruel, agonizing contradiction, this unbearable love tangled with seething anger. And now, I'll never get the chance to look her in the eye and demand answers.

To ask her why she lied. Why she was at that warehouse and who those men were. If any of it was real.

I can barely think beyond the roaring in my ears. She's gone, and I hate her for it. I hate her for leaving me like this, for breaking me and then dying before I could put the pieces back together. But worse than the hate is the love that still holds me hostage, no matter how much logic fights it.

A knock at the door pulls me from my thoughts. I look up to see Davey in the hallway. "Do you have a minute?" he asks, his voice measured but heavy with something unsaid.

"Yeah," I mutter, turning to face him fully.

I follow him into the study, where he shuts the door behind us and locks it with the biometric scanner. The soft click of the lock twists something deep in my gut.

We both take our seats—me behind the desk, Davey in the cigar chair opposite. He leans forward slightly, his elbows resting on his knees, and for a moment, neither of us speaks.

"We've had our team on-site overseeing the cleanup," he begins, his tone measured but careful.

I nod, bracing myself for what's coming.

"They found two bodies near the trucks," he says slowly. "Both men. By the size and build, probably two of the guys from the footage since the three on-site security officers were found knocked out on the other end of the lot."

I wait for the rush of emotion. Something, anything. But there's only numbness. Davey's watching me, gauging my reaction. When I don't respond, he continues.

"They found something else," he says, his voice dropping slightly. "Near the outskirts of the warehouse fence where there was a gap. A backpack stuck to the wire."

The bottom drops out of my stomach. I don't say anything, but my body stiffens, and Davey doesn't miss it.

"It's filled with equipment," he explains. "And… it looks like the one she had on in the footage."

My throat tightens, but I force myself to ask, "What type of equipment?" My voice sounds hollow, even to my own ears.

Davey hesitates, his jaw tightening before he answers. "The melted contents suggest she was trying to break into our servers. Based on where we found it, and the lack of a body…" He pauses, choosing his next words carefully. "We think she got out."

The debilitating wave of relief that crashes over me is short-lived, hitting so hard it nearly knocks the breath from my lungs. She's alive. Scarlett is *alive*. The suffocating grief that had wrapped itself around my throat loosens just enough for me to pull in a full breath, but it's tainted. Sharp and acidic, burning all the way down because the next realization slams into me, just as vicious and undeniable.

Everything clicks into place. The guilt. The strange behavior. The lies.

My father was right about her. Goddamn him. He was right.

She used me. Manipulated me. And worse, she risked everything I've been building, everything I've sacrificed for.

The relief curdles into something dark and twisted. A brutal war erupts inside me—one part of me grasping onto the fact that she's still breathing, and the other part recoiling at the truth of what she's done.

I loved her. I *trusted* her.

My stomach churns, my pulse hammering in my skull. I had begun to mourn her and it nearly pulled me under. And now, in the same breath that brings her back to life, I have to face the fact that she was never mine to begin with.

Rage rises in my chest, hot and consuming, leaving no room for rational thought. My fingers curl tightly around the edge of the desk as I fight to keep myself in control, but the silence in the room stretches, suffocating. Davey doesn't say anything, doesn't push. He simply waits, his sharp eyes tracking every flicker of emotion that passes across my face.

He'd warned me about her, just like my father had. But I'd ignored them both. Blinded myself to the obvious because I didn't want to see it.

Because I couldn't fathom that Scarlett could do something like this to me. To us.

But she did.

"She can't get away with this," I finally say, my voice low and cold. The words taste bitter, but they're the only anchor I have left.

Davey accepts my words without judgment. "What do you want to do?"

I lean back slightly, forcing my hands to unclench as I drag in a shaky breath. My mind races through every terrible thing I want to do, every piece of vengeance I want to rain down on her, but I push it aside. I need clarity. I need control.

And most of all, I need the *whole truth*.

"We don't tell my father," I say firmly, meeting Davey's gaze. "Just like with the surveillance footage. Not until we have a clearer picture."

Davey's expression tightens slightly, but he nods.

"Figure out what's on those servers," I continue, my tone sharpening. "Every file, every trace. If you don't already know, find out. I don't care how deep you have to dig."

Davey hesitates, his brow furrowing. "There's a lot on those servers I've never touched. Some of it predates my time at Wells. Some of it..." He trails off, his face hardening. "Let's just say there are things William keeps compartmentalized for a reason. I can get us access, but it's not going to be clean."

"Then make it clean," I snap, my patience fraying. "We need to know what she was after. She thought my father was involved in something, and I want to know what it is."

Davey studies me carefully, his expression unreadable. "You don't think she was working alone, do you?"

I let out a sharp exhale, shaking my head. "I don't know," I admit. "But what I do know is that she lied. And I'm going to find out why."

The room feels stifling, every emotion crashing into me at once: betrayal, fury, grief. Scarlett's deception isn't just personal. It's monumental. It's uprooted the very foundation I've been building my future on.

And the worst part? I can't even decide what hurts more: that she lied, or that I still want to believe there was a reason behind it. A *good* reason.

But none of that matters now. Whatever she was after, whatever she wanted from those servers, or from me, it wasn't hers to take. And I'll make damn sure she knows it.

I pull my scattered thoughts together into something sharp and actionable. "This stays between us," I say. It's not a suggestion. It's a command. "No one else can know. As far as anyone else is concerned, Scarlett skipped town. That story holds until we have answers."

Davey's eyes scanning my face. "And Natalie?" he asks carefully. "You don't think she should know?"

I shake my head. "No. Not yet. Natalie was too close to her. If she finds out, she'll try to justify it and make excuses for her. We can't afford that kind of distraction right now. The fewer people who know the truth, the better."

Davey's face reflects his unease, but he nods, accepting my logic, even if it doesn't sit well with him. "Just us, and only the people we absolutely trust."

"Exactly," I say, leaning back slightly in my chair, though the tension in my body refuses to ease. My muscles are coiled, ready to snap at the slightest provocation. "Bring in whoever you need, but be selective. No one outside the circle hears a word of this until we know exactly what we're dealing with."

The weight of the decision sinks in, heavy and suffocating. I've spent years keeping myself out of the darker corners of my teams' dealings, trusting them to handle the cleanup when things got messy. But this isn't business. This is personal. The familiar pull of that darker part of me—the part I've spent years suppressing—starts to rise. It's not rage; it's something colder, something precise. And it's already beginning to claw its way free.

"Davey," I say, the edge in my voice undeniable now. The anger and betrayal coiling tighter, feeding off the realization of how deeply she played me. "I need to find her. Whoever the hell she really is. Wherever she's gone. She almost destroyed everything."

Davey's expression hardens, mirroring my resolve. "Understood," he says simply.

"She lied to me," I continue, more to myself now, my voice heavy with a mix of disbelief and rage. I thought I came to terms with this when I saw the video of her at the warehouses, but I was stupidly holding out hope that there was an explanation I wasn't seeing. Everything about her was a lie. Scarlett Page doesn't exist.

And even though she's alive, she's dead to me.

I stand abruptly, the need to move overwhelming as the flood of emotions threatens to drown me. Pacing the room, I rake a hand through my hair, trying to piece together everything I thought I knew about her. Every memory, every word, every touch... it's all tainted now, twisted into something I can't reconcile. She slipped into my life so perfectly, like she was made for it. Made for me. And I fell for it.

"This stays between us," I repeat, demanding absolute loyalty. "We protect this until we know exactly what we're dealing with. No one else gets involved."

Davey nods one final time, his eyes steady on mine. "I'll keep looking and get the team ready."

"Good," I reply, my jaw clenched so tight it aches.

As Davey turns to leave, I drop back into the chair, letting my head fall into my hands. The fragments of Scarlett spin in my mind like shards of glass, sharp and unrelenting. I would have given nearly anything up for her, and she's broken me in ways I don't think I'll ever recover from.

Whoever she is, wherever she's gone, I'll find her. And this time, there won't be room for pretty lies. No masks. No games.

This time, she'll tell me everything.

What's Next?

BOOK TWO – COMING SUMMER 2025

Want a **sneak peak of the first chapter** and to receive updates on book two's release date?

Sign up for my newsletter!

authorbrianasullivan.com

Special Thanks

To Danny: There are no words to describe how much you and your love mean to me. At the start of 2024, you encouraged me to start writing again. When I was laid off and navigating the chaos of job applications, you told me it was the perfect time to finish this novel. When I decided to pursue publishing, you stepped up to edit the entire manuscript without hesitation. I am endlessly grateful to walk through life with you. Thank you for always choosing me. I love you so, so much.

To Kristopher: I like to think I found the right partner in life because of the way you've always shown me love and respect, especially in adulthood. Thank you for always telling me you were "just waiting" for me to write the next NYT bestseller like it was no big deal. We're not quite there, but I don't know if I'd have had the courage to do this without your unwavering support.

To Nikki and Boufy: My forever rOoMmAtEs and two of my very best friends. The moment I told you I was close to finishing this novel, you were asking for advanced copies. Instead, I handed you homework. Thank you for your enthusiasm, honesty, and support. It means more than you know.

To the rest of my family: I am so fortunate to have the love and encouragement of not just my biological family, but also the family I was lucky enough to marry into. I can't imagine life without all of you in my corner.

To anyone who has been too scared to write that book: I was you. I am you. For me, there's nothing scarier than putting myself out there.

But I'd be lying if I said it wasn't worth it, no matter how many people actually read these pages. Do it for yourself and no one else. Now, get to work!

www.ingramcontent.com/pod-product-compliance
Lightning Source LLC
Chambersburg PA
CBHW030226120726
47903CB00005B/1385